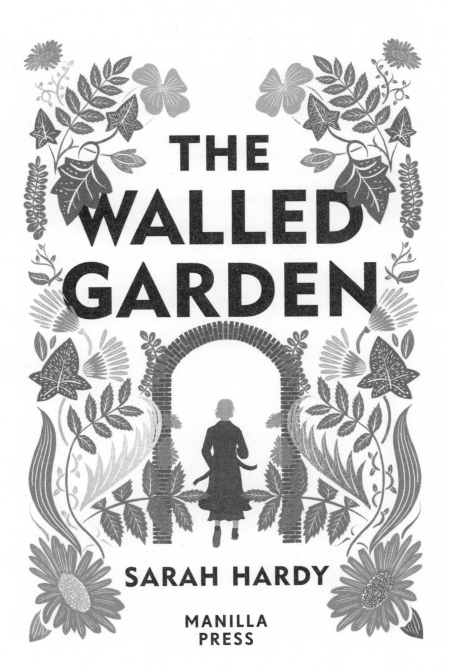

THE WALLED GARDEN

SARAH HARDY

MANILLA
PRESS

First published in Great Britain in 2023 by
MANILLA PRESS
An imprint of Bonnier Books UK
4th Floor, Victoria House, Bloomsbury Square, London, WC1B 4DA
Owned by Bonnier Books
Sveavägen 56, Stockholm, Sweden

A CIP catalogue record for this book is
available from the British Library.

Hardback ISBN: 978–1–83877–925–2
Export ISBN: 978–1–83877–926–9

Also available as an ebook and an audiobook

1 3 5 7 9 10 8 6 4 2

Typeset by IDSUK (Data Connection) Ltd
Printed and bound in Great Britain by Clays Ltd, Elcograf S.p.A.

Manilla Press is an imprint of Bonnier Books UK
www.bonnierbooks.co.uk

Secrets, silent, stony sit in the dark palaces of
    both our hearts:
secrets weary of their tyranny . . .
History . . . is a nightmare from which I am trying
    to awake.

Ulysses
James Joyce

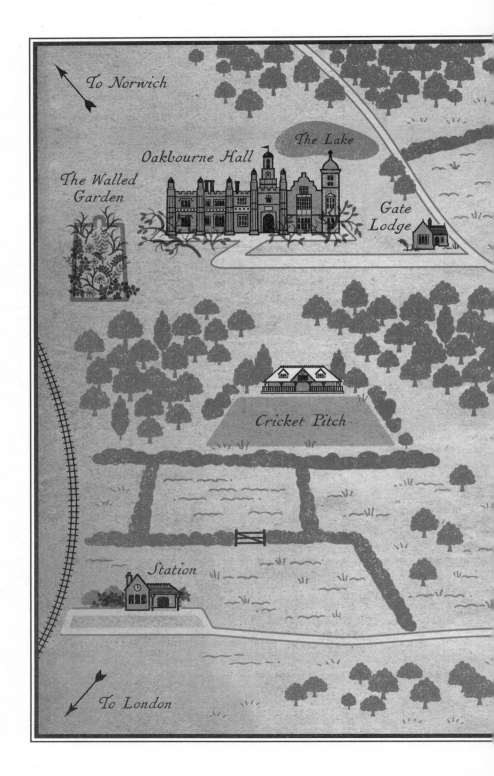

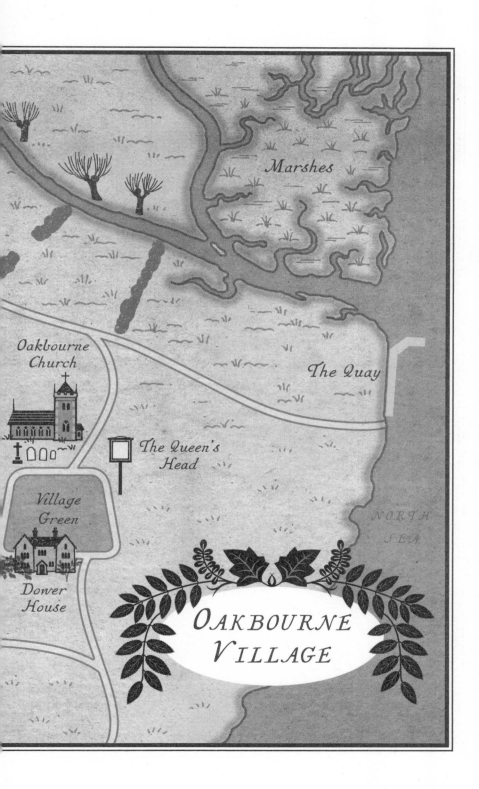

Marshes

Oakbourne
Church

The Quay

The Queen's
Head

Village
Green

NORTH
SEA

Dower
House

OAKBOURNE
VILLAGE

Prologue

SOME SECRETS ARE TOO *terrible to tell. And in 1946 Britain is a country where most keep silent. What you witnessed during the war, what you sanctioned, what you are still afraid of, is left unsaid. For those bitter years of conflict and separation you buoyed yourselves up on sentiment, crooning 'We'll meet again'. And we did meet again, thinks Alice Rayne, only to discover we have nothing to say to one another.*

The wind whipping in off the North Sea slaps her face and, pushing her hair from her eyes, she glances back over the marshes. Arcs of crimson cut through the darkening sky, dazzling and brilliant. Then the sun dips below the flat horizon.

She turns and draws nearer the waves glinting in the raw twilight. Just that afternoon, the army finished clearing the mines, rolling away rusting tangles of barbed wire, tearing down warnings of DANGER. No one will see, she thinks. No one will know. It's been so long since she's felt the sea's closeness, tasted salt on her lips. Before she can doubt herself, she strips off her old tweed coat, woollen dress, the lot, and, naked, runs for the freezing grey waters.

Shock makes her cry out and she almost loses her nerve. Gasping for air, she forces herself in up to her waist then, closing her eyes, she lets herself fall forwards and under.

She knows only cold. But as her temperature drops her body stops fighting. Pain eases, breathing calms. All she has to do is merge into the waves, ice into ice. She's no longer frozen but indomitable. She can stay in forever. She can swim on and on. Away from it all.

A break appears in the clouds and a pale moonlight spreads towards her. It's as if the shimmering train of a wedding dress is lying over the sea. And into her mind flashes the spectre of a bride without a groom.

1

PLEASE GOD, NO ONE is watching, thought Alice, as she scrambled over the shingle, her legs numb. She grabbed her clothes, attempted to dry off, then stumbled up to the dyked path that took her to the short cut through the marshes and out across the fields of winter beet.

In the hedgerows, the first of the blossom held fast to bare, spiked branches. And despite feeling desperate for warmth, she was tempted to linger. Anything rather than go home.

But she'd been gone for more than three hours. She couldn't delay any longer so she continued on to the lane that took her back to Oakbourne Hall. 'Just having a quick walk,' she'd said to her husband as she'd left. 'Will you join me?' He hadn't answered. She hadn't expected him to.

Her pace slowed and she looked up. She could hear the geese before she saw them. Then hundreds upon hundreds of steely grey birds were filling the sky, flying in their V-formations for the migration north – the clearest sign that winter was over. And briefly her senses lifted: it would be the first spring in peacetime for seven years.

All week there'd been hints of sweetness: golden aconites round the abandoned Nissen huts, narcissi piercing the uncut grass, a wren nesting in the ivy engulfing her bedroom window. An enormous bedroom, she reminded herself sternly as she marched on, whereas millions have nothing. When she read the papers, it seemed as if the entire land mass of Europe was still on the move, mile upon mile of exhausted men and women, clutching their children, pushing prams and laden farm carts, fleeing who knew what blood and horror.

But she was privileged to live in what was known locally as 'the Big House'. No matter that the War Office had commandeered it for a battalion of Canadian soldiers and the place was wrecked. 'Some people have all the luck,' she'd overheard the butcher's wife mutter in church when Stephen, her husband, came home from the war 'all in one piece'. He had been the very last in the village to return. From where, he refused to say. Let alone what he'd done. But he was alive.

And you're alive, Alice insisted, straightening her back as she walked on past stumps of centuries-old chestnut trees felled early in the war to make . . . What? Weapons? Coffins? But such thinking was pointless.

Now they could plant new trees.

The world was at peace.

We won.

We actually won.

But a chill, even more brutal than the sea, kept churning through her as if there had been no victory and all the warbling about 'love and laughter and peace ever after' was as elusive as the end of the rainbow. When she thought back to VE Day, almost a year ago, and the nation dancing deliriously in the streets, it seemed as if they'd been caged creatures allowed their one day of freedom who, the moment their euphoria was exhausted, sank straight back down into all-consuming drabness.

But now it was time for rebirth.

In the fields around her, lambs bashed savagely at their mothers for milk, sharp new needles of wheat shot through the hard earth, and overhead crows clawed at each other in a brutal battle for territory. She forced herself on round the concrete pillbox, overrun by rampant rhododendrons.

Her chilblains were stinging now. She'd be thirty soon and already her feet were ugly, crooked things, her hands even worse. Veins stood up in her reddened, roughened skin and her engagement ring – a band of stony diamonds that had been in Stephen's family for two centuries – twisted loosely on her finger.

Again she paused. All too often she was conscious of unease – not of the terror they'd just been fighting, but a new danger she could not quite see. Or was too scared to contemplate.

She thrust her hands in her pockets and kept her head down as the local doctor's blue Rover pulled up outside the cottage where Mrs Martin was expecting her third child. A victory baby, thought Alice. There were two more due in the village.

She heard the doctor groaning and cursing as he heaved himself out of the car. He'd lost his leg after being taken prisoner at Dunkirk and a stab of self-reproach – don't whinge about chilblains – spurred her on to the Gate Lodge where Oakbourne Hall, occupying the one sheltered spot for acres around, lay before her.

At dusk, the fine outlines of the original Tudor manor and its Jacobean, Georgian and Victorian extensions were silhouetted across the lake: the clock tower, the vast bay windows, the marble colonnades, the west wing topped with battlements, the east wing with a dome. And, for these few fleeting moments, she could almost persuade herself there had been no war. The gathering darkness hid the empty oil drums dumped in the shrubbery; the sandbags, split and soggy, spilling out over the terraces; the broken glass.

A light came on in her husband's study.

During all those nights of blackout and appalling anxiety she had longed for this, to come home to her husband, safe at his desk, waiting for her. Yet still she delayed, shivering beside the crumbling gate pillar, a casualty of the army trucks that for five years had rolled in and out of the requisitioned estate.

Lights too were on in the Gate Lodge and she could see into the kitchen where Mrs Harris was standing at the sink, her husband by her side helping with drying up. Their only son had returned after three years on the Arctic convoys. But he was 'in bits', Alice's housekeeper had told her. 'Just sits by the fire, saying he can't get warm.'

Three years, thought Alice. Three years of desperation and worry for his parents, missing the youth growing into a man, aching for his loving presence and now . . . She stopped herself.

Just that morning she had seen pictures in *The Times* of scores of lost children, orphans with dazed and hungry eyes in a monastery in France, and the moment she began to imagine how it must feel to lose your husband or your child or your home she found herself in such a blinding waste of misery it was intolerable. I must go to my husband, she urged herself. I must hurry.

Then, through the window, she saw Mrs Harris lift her arm to her eyes as if to brush away a tear. And at the sight of the woman's sorrow, Alice waited. She could see Mr Harris put down his tea towel, reach over and take his wife's hands out of the sink. Holding each in turn, very slowly, he dried them. Alice stood perfectly still, mesmerised as he lifted his wife's bowed head and brought her lips to his.

Abruptly, Alice stepped away. She did not want to dwell on the tenderness in those gestures. A twig cracked under her foot. A deer barked. The bushes stirred. A storm was getting up. They'd lose even more tiles off the roof tonight.

'Mark my words,' her father had said when she'd married, 'out on that Suffolk coast you'll freeze. There's nothing between you and the Urals.'

She turned to embrace the wind, filling her lungs with mile upon mile of space, beyond the fields and dykes, the rough grey sea, over vast lakes and forests, all the way to Siberia, when a shriek, like the sob of a desperate child, rang out from down by the house.

That cry was a hare and she knew exactly what drama was being enacted. Last night, when she couldn't sleep, she'd watched three fox cubs tumbling over the lawn with their mother. All needing to eat and feed on some living creature. She shoved aside the image of a young leveret – easy prey – in the jaws of a vixen. The nature of things, she lectured herself, beautiful and monstrous. Then, to her astonishment, she saw the window to her husband's study open and Stephen climbing over the sill, leaping down and sprinting across the gravel.

Since his return he'd just dragged himself from hour to hour, barely finding the energy to speak, let alone go vaulting out of windows. Now he was storming into the untended flowerbeds, searching through overgrown thistles and nettles. Then he stopped, bent down, sprang upright and, without any hesitation, smashed his foot into the ground, dealing, she presumed, a quick, merciful death blow.

He must, she realised, have heard the hare cry and found it horribly injured. When she came across rabbits rubbing blind, pus-filled eyes as the paralysis of myxomatosis set in, she too would steel herself to spare the gasping bundles a slow, painful death.

Except that Stephen didn't stop.

Again and again, harder and harder, he was stamping and stamping. She wanted to yell at him that the poor creature had to be dead, but she only shrank further into the shadows as he kicked out and she saw, flying six feet high, the silhouette of a hare – the magnificent hind legs, the long spine extended, reaching for the sky . . . Mid-air, the hare split in two, its head and decapitated body falling into the bushes.

She clasped her hand to her face to silence her breathing. Until that moment, she'd not witnessed the violence her husband was capable of. Whenever she asked him about the war he'd shut her up with a cold glance or storm away as if she was trying to prise open Pandora's Box and he couldn't stand the stupidity of her questioning. So, who he'd killed – or how – she didn't know.

No one survived war untarnished. Not even the sweet, gentle soul she'd married. And she wanted to take him in her arms, to promise she'd make it all better, that her love would soothe whatever demons war had unleashed. Then, overriding her compassion ran fear. What if he turned on her?

There was no denying the power in his body, how he could deal death in an instant. He was stronger than her. Faster. Practised. And she imagined the weight of his boot, her windpipe choking, her neck being crushed.

2

ALICE STOOD AT THE tap in the empty stable block, washing her hands in the icy water. Since last night, she'd avoided Stephen. She'd gone straight to her room, leaving the light on until four in the morning because it was too disturbing to replay in darkness the frenzied actions of the man she loved. But under the brutal glare of the overhead bulb she began to see things differently. The hare, she reasoned, hadn't died immediately. Because she'd been a good fifty yards away, because it was nightfall, she hadn't seen clearly. Of course Stephen *appeared* vicious. Who in their right mind wouldn't rage if given the responsibility of killing such a beautiful young animal?

She rubbed carbolic soap into the scratches on her palm from hacking back brambles. War had done this to her: conditioned her to fear the worst and that incessant sense of dread was lingering on. Even now, the beauty of a full moon could resurrect the terror of the Luftwaffe taking over the skies.

She dried her hands on her skirt then, glancing up as the first of the bats flitted from under the eaves, she saw a plane heading south-west towards London. Nothing to be wary of, now.

Stephen was not the enemy.

Though who he was, she was no longer sure. He refused to talk so she could only guess at what memories he hid. She'd tried to reach him with words, with silence . . . her body. He wanted none of it. From the night he'd come home he'd slept alone in a room up in the attic. The message could not have been clearer.

She scraped the mud off her shoes. After last night's storm the ground was wet and her shoes leaked. She'd neither money nor coupons for new ones. Too bad. The rain had been good for the garden. And for me, she thought, breathing in air that tasted washed and sweet, grounding her with the common sense she'd let career away last night.

She'd already lost six years of her marriage to Hitler. She wasn't going to lose any more because of her own morbid imagination and she hurried inside and found Stephen at his desk, a notepad before him, a pen in his hand. Normally he just slumped by the fire. Please God, she begged. Let him be writing again!

When they first met and she discovered he wrote poetry her twenty-year-old self had been over-awed: Stephen Rayne, the brilliant young diplomat, the civil servant with the artist's soul.

He wrote in French – thanks to his Parisian mother, he was bilingual. Alice's French was limited but she could translate the reviews and his first collection, published shortly after they were married, had been described as 'Wordsworthian, beautiful, bold, generous . . .'

Years ago, they would lie in bed reading Baudelaire and Rimbaud and he would correct her accent, taking her lips between his fingers, saying, 'Hold your mouth like this', and the warmth of his touch was like sunlight pouring through her. She'd thought even if war comes and bombs fall on me this very minute it will be all right, because I have known this.

'What is it?' he asked, not looking up.

Trying to take the eagerness out of her voice, she said, 'Are you—?'

'Am I what?' he interrupted, scrunching up a sheet of paper and hurling it into the fire.

'Writing?'

'Hardly.' He screwed up more paper. She watched that go up in flames. Then a third ball.

'Oh, stop!' she said, intercepting the fourth and smoothing it out. 'Let me read . . .'

'Leave it!' he yelled. 'I said . . . !' At once she dropped the paper as he sprang forwards and grabbed the poker. But he just bashed the paper into the fire, then turned to her, despair written on his face. And she felt a reciprocal pain beat in her. This desperate man was no danger to her. Only to himself.

'It's good to see you . . .'

'What?'

Doing something, she thought. Anything but sit for hours on end, as if nothing matters anymore.

'Don't destroy it just yet,' she said. 'Perhaps it's better than you think. And you're so good.'

'You've no idea whether it's good or not.' He threw the rest of the papers on to the fire.

'When you got it right in the past,' she ventured, 'it brought you . . .' He sneered but she carried on. 'It brought you joy.'

As did I, she thought. She'd unleashed something truly good in him – ideas, confidence, words. Or so he'd told her.

'Did your walk, my dear Alice, bring you *joy*?'

She'd learned to ignore his awful, warped irony. It would pass. 'I was working in the garden actually,' she said. 'But it was lovely out.'

He stared into the roaring blaze, the sudden light emphasising the lattice of lines and hollowness around his eyes. He looked far more than seven years older than her, but it wasn't simply because of the ageing in his face. It was the resignation in all his movements, every expression, his voice.

'I didn't mean to shout earlier,' he muttered. 'I'm sorry.'

She leapt on his apology, almost giddy with relief. 'That's all right.'

'Meet anyone on your walk?' he asked.

She'd just told him she'd been gardening. But she was used to him not listening.

'No,' she said simply. When she did go for walks she deliberately kept to herself as she hated fielding the questions: 'How is Sir Stephen?' Or the enquiring lilt with which people commented, 'We've not seen him for such a long while . . . ?'

'Though,' she continued, trying to engage him, 'yesterday I did see Dr Downes's car outside the Martins'. Their baby's imminent.'

In response he lit a cigarette.

She pressed on: 'There was a taste of spring. You know, blackthorn, odd daffodils, snowdrops on the wane . . .' She heard her clichés prancing about like tired circus clowns trying to grab his attention. 'Perhaps you might come with me tomorrow?'

'What's that?'

'We could go for a walk together.'

13

'No . . . And tomorrow? Is that when we've got this new vicar coming round?'

'Yes, but you don't need to be there—' The last thing she wanted was for anyone to think that this caustic, cynical man was the real Stephen. 'I'll make some excuse for you. I'll tell him you've got a bad cold and you don't want him to catch it.' The new vicar – his predecessor had been at pains to let everyone know – had a heart condition.

'Thank you.' And he gave her a straightforward smile, not his usual twisted turn of the lips. Then, to her surprise, before collapsing into his chair, he laid a hand on her shoulder with what seemed like affection.

Cautiously, she sat on the stool by his feet, so close now, she could reach out to him. You used, she thought, to let me lift your hand to my face, feel your warmth against my cheek and, one by one, I'd slowly take your fingers in my mouth. I would devour that potent mix of strength and tenderness and you loved it.

'You'll catch cold in those wet shoes,' he said.

She didn't move. Her stockings too were sodden. She ought to remove them as well.

The last time she'd undressed in front of him – she could remember exactly – was 18th November, 1943. She'd received a telegram – from whom, she'd no idea – telling her he would be at a hotel in Hastings. They'd have almost forty-eight hours together before he returned – to France, she presumed, doing undercover work, though she'd followed the rules and never asked.

Somehow or other – typically he would not explain – he had brought with him a gold guipure lace shawl. At one point they'd gone for a walk along the seafront and rain had thundered down from nowhere, soaking them through. So they'd hurried back and run a steaming bath. When she emerged he'd presented her with the shawl, wrapping it around her hot, flushed body and she'd danced for him, turning and twisting in the faded, shabby room, naked except for golden lace, until he caught her in impatient arms and told her, over and over, how much he loved her.

She was conscious he was looking at her. Most evenings, if he hadn't disappeared off to his attic, he just sat with his eyes closed, seeing God knew what ghosts. She searched his face but couldn't read anything there beyond exhaustion.

Slowly, she rolled down her stockings. She pointed her foot at the fire and turned her ankle, the sort of ankles, he'd once said, that made him imagine them entwined behind his neck. Still, he was watching her. She slipped off the stool. Easing back, she stretched her bare leg towards him and smiled the smile she used to give him when they were in a crowded room, at a party or dinner together.

Then, letting her skirt fall further up her legs, she rested her foot on his thigh.

'Poor old thing,' he sighed. 'You've got chilblains.' And he walked out of the room.

She felt ridiculous, sprawled on the floor. But he'd actually touched her – put his hand on her shoulder. That was a first. Besides, it was early days. He hadn't even been home six months as he'd not returned till October 1945.

October?

Once more, the questions began needling away. The war in Europe officially ended in May so what the hell had he been up to after that? She'd heard nothing from him. The first she'd known he was still alive was when she received a telegram saying he would be on the next train home. And again her imagination seized her and to stop its claws digging in she leapt up. She'd lose herself in an old botany journal of her father's. Pollen production in foxgloves, the micro-biology of acid soil, effects of temperature on viability of cotton seeds. In the incongruities and intricacies of nature she could forget this world where peace had been bought at such a price, where men and women could still be so cruel, even in their own homes.

She headed off down the damp corridors to make her habitual three hot water bottles. You won't be the only one, she told herself, lying under the covers reading in a cold bed. Men and women had become strangers to one another all over the world.

All over the village. Her housekeeper, Mrs Green, had told her Mrs Downes, the doctor's wife, had to be a saint to put up with the raging temper her husband had come home with after five years in a German POW camp.

In the kitchen she found four empty tea chests had been delivered. They were for transporting a collection of Venetian glass – built up by the Rayne family over generations – to a millionaire steel manufacturer in Chicago. At the end of the week a delivery van would take the glass to Liverpool to be loaded onto the *Queen Mary*. Just this morning men had also finished work in the hall dismantling the Jacobean oak panelling as that too was heading across the Atlantic, along with marble fireplaces from two of the bedrooms – the best ones had already been sold to a Wall Street banker – and the stained-glass window of irises which had somehow remained intact when a truckload of Canadian soldiers

16

coming back from a dance had reversed into a wall, missing the window by inches.

Alice felt disappointment pressing upon her. It wasn't so much for the loss of the dazzling glassware. She'd become ruthless in selling off porcelain, paintings, the better pieces of furniture, whatever could make money. It was a malaise that, she feared, was increasingly like Stephen's.

For almost a year now, since the Canadian army's departure, she'd sorted through dusty rooms, trying to make them habitable again. For her and Stephen. For the children they'd once talked about having. But whenever she mentioned the state of the house to Stephen he'd just mutter: 'I couldn't care less – and nor should you.'

So she'd taken charge, trying to bring Oakbourne Hall into the second half of the twentieth century which, they were forever being told, was going to be so very much better than the first.

She was tempted to leave the packing till morning. The electrics in this part of the house were shot to bits so she'd be working in the dark. But something triumphed over her tiredness and made her drag the chests round to the cupboard in the scullery. She lit half a dozen candles. Lovely fluted goblets, whisky tumblers, brandy balloons, all in such brilliant colours, glittered before her like jewels, destined now for someone else's party.

3

A FIERCE DRAUGHT BELTED under the drawing-room door at Oakbourne Hall as Stephen pulled up a chair for the Reverend Mr George Ivens.

'Thank you,' said Stephen, 'for braving the elements to come and see us.'

'Not at all, Sir Stephen,' murmured the tall young vicar, stooping a little as if he might make himself take up less room.

'One advantage of this wind,' continued Stephen, banking up the fire, 'is that with trees coming down we've plenty of wood to burn.'

The vicar laughed nervously: 'It's certainly been a hard winter.'

Alice smiled at her husband. He had horrified her that morning by saying he'd changed his mind and actually wanted to meet their new vicar. But now he was being his old gentle self, the perfect host to their awkward guest.

Passing Stephen his tea, Alice let her hand linger on his as he held forth about the bitter cold. She'd thought he'd lost all ability to talk about the weather. Since he'd been home they'd not once had anything resembling a social call. Not that they'd had many invitations. His closest friend, Robert, through whom they'd met, had been killed at Arnhem. The few neighbours Stephen had known from childhood were all scattered, one emigrating to Australia, another selling up his huge estate to buy a farm in Devon.

'I'm sorry,' Stephen was saying, 'to inflict this room on you. It's an empty shell these days.'

'No, no,' said the vicar, easing out his long legs in the ancient armchair, 'it's beautiful.'

'It was once. But damp's got to it. See!' said Stephen, as flakes of pale blue paint began descending from the ceiling. He gestured at the dark patches on the walls where family portraits used to hang. 'Though I can't say I miss some of my ancestors looking down on us.'

'A gentlemen's club in Washington bought them,' said Alice. 'Men in scarlet uniforms, all very military. Two generals who'd fought at Waterloo – against each other. Stephen's mother was French, you see. Great-great-uncles, is that right, Stephen?' He nodded. 'And another one who'd been with the Duke of Marlborough at Blenheim and . . . er . . .'

'Malplaquet,' said Stephen.

The first time she went to Oakbourne Hall, Stephen had circled his arms round her waist and insisted, 'You'll never find me up there with that lot. *Never.*'

It was 1936 and he'd just been accepted at the Foreign Office. He wasn't going to follow the family tradition, unlike his elder brother who'd gone to Sandhurst before joining the Guards as their father had done and grandfather and countless great-grandfathers before him. Instead, Stephen went to Cambridge. My brilliant husband, she'd thought, who with his first in modern languages trusted diplomacy was the way to keep peace.

'They were only fit for firewood,' continued Stephen. 'Speaking of which I'm not sure how you're placed lodging at Mrs Turner's, but please make sure you're not short of wood there.'

Alice couldn't quite believe it. He was being kind. Perhaps, patience really was all that was needed for her husband to return to her. He began chatting away about the huts the Canadians had left in the east corner of the park and how one of the farmers had taken them over and was using them to seed potatoes in a new way. 'Though growing things,' he said, 'is Alice's area, not mine.'

'My father was a botanist,' she explained. 'Roses were his speciality. With all the new housing estates being built, he was trying to create varieties suitable for small gardens.'

For the first time, the vicar smiled with more than politeness: 'Creating roses! What a wonderful thing to do!'

'Yes, but much of his work's been lost. You see, he lived in Kent and, like here, the army took the place over. Salvaging roses wasn't a priority with invasion imminent. All the gardens, the greenhouses, were destroyed . . .

'Anyway,' she went on brightly, handing the vicar a plate, 'this is a sort of apple cake. We have bees so we've honey. We're lucky.'

'Bloody lucky,' Stephen said under his breath.

She glanced at him, uncertain what he meant.

But the vicar was speaking. 'The roses? Could you grow them here?'

'It's too windy.'

'What I mean is, do you actually know how to create a new rose?'

20

She smiled. 'I do.' Before the war, she and her father would talk about her taking over the business once it became too much for him.

'You know,' Stephen said, 'we're terribly honoured to have my wife's company. She's actually foregone her beloved garden and walks to have tea with us.'

She caught the surprise on the vicar's face at the abrupt change of tone. 'I'm terribly sorry,' he said, manoeuvring himself forwards in the rickety chair, 'I'd have come at a better time.'

'Stephen's only joking! Aren't you?'

'If they were handing out medals for walking,' replied Stephen, 'my wife would certainly get one.'

Alice's smile widened as if with the warmth of her expression she could dispel the sudden chill. 'Mr Ivens, have you had a chance to meet many people yet?'

'I've just come,' he said, 'from meeting Mrs Downes, though not her husband as he was called away – another baby.'

'How wonderful! You know Mrs Downes is a nurse and covered for the old GP we had during the war. Everyone loved her because she was funny. Even when they were ill she made people laugh.'

'Reverend?' Stephen interrupted. 'Do you enjoy walking?'

This was no innocent question. Members of the clergy were not conscripted, and, according to Mrs Green, the young vicar had already been described in the village as one hell of a lucky bugger. But clearly he was not a well man. When he'd arrived, cycling just the mile from the village, he was white-faced and exhausted.

Alice said hurriedly, 'You're probably too busy for walking.' Though she doubted it. Anyone under thirty

21

was rushing away from the country to the city as fast as they could.

'I've just been getting to know the ropes,' said the vicar. 'But what I've seen is very lovely. The wildness, the flowers.'

'Flowers,' Alice rushed on, 'my sister says, sprang up all round the bomb sites in London last summer, and that at St Giles there were great forests of ferns and foxgloves and brambles and bracken.'

'Ah . . . flowers,' drawled Stephen in the voice she hated. 'Alice is quite the expert.'

'As is Stephen!' she persevered. 'His poetry's been described as "Wordsworthian" and . . .'

'Wordsworth,' Stephen broke in, 'would have been a lot more use if he'd told us how to respond to human evil. Not beauties of nature.'

She made herself laugh. 'You should hear Stephen describe the snowdrops in the woods here. We'd barely met and he was telling me how there are thousands upon thousands of them, glimmering in the darkest—'

'Alice! That was a hell of a long time ago.'

'But the miracle,' she said, trying to take the edge out of her voice, 'is that although snowdrops look fragile, however how hard the earth, they endure, seducing us with their beauty, bringing hope.' She took a breath. 'But Mr Ivens, you'll find Oakbourne a world away from an East End parish. The problems here . . .'

What was she going to say? We've not been bombed. We've not seen our children evacuated.

But I long for the man I married.

She resorted to a platitude. 'At least we can start making plans for the future, now we're at peace.'

'Peace?' scoffed Stephen. 'Tell her, Reverend. Human beings' ability to make their fellows suffer is infinite.'

'Please, Stephen! Don't go all sinister on us.'

'Have you, Alice, even the slightest idea of what's going on in France right now? Why can't you *read* the papers instead of just glancing at them and escaping into your nature books?'

You used to love, she thought, hearing how snowdrops hang their heads to protect their pollen from rain and sleet, that it's the absence of a green calyx that makes them look like drops of snow.

'We've had,' Stephen went on, 'one lot of evil monsters in charge. Now we've another. Communists stringing up collaborators. Gaullists just as bad. Every bit as full of hate as those bastards before them. Christ! Even during the war it was all anyone could do to stop the French turning their weapons on each other. And now it's another bloody slaughterhouse. We've all acted like barbarians there. Not just the Nazis,' he continued, looking fiercely at both Alice and the vicar, 'Spaniards, Catalans, Franks, Visigoths. Did you do no history at any of those schools of yours?'

She forced another laugh: 'I hated school, as you well know.'

'If people weren't so damned ignorant they'd realise. My wife is an expert in where aconites grow, where to watch young stoats play, where you find the first wood anemones. Yet she does not think that here – just *here*, in her own gardens and fields which she enjoys so much she comes home full of the colour of the moon and the brightness of the stars, waxing so very lyrical – is where the Romans pillaged and raped, where Viking mobs arrived, all raging hot with unimaginable cruelties – actually, all too imaginable these days. Even in *this house*, down in the scullery, we've got our very own priest hole – another reminder, if we needed one, of how people love to torture and destroy one another. It's the same everywhere, always has been, always will be. History just repeats itself because people always find reasons to hate one another.'

So this was why he had agreed to appear at tea. So he could lecture the vicar on evil. He was not always like this, she wanted to apologise. He used to find loveliness in the world. In me.

'Just wait,' persisted Stephen, 'soon enough we'll hate the Russians again and want to kill *them*. Or we'll just tolerate everything, ignoring all sorts of horror because we're too lethargic to work out what's worth standing up for. Reverend? Do you agree?'

The vicar put down his cup and saucer. 'I . . . I don't know what the next few years will hold. I desperately hope you're wrong.'

'Of course you *hope* so.'

Alice looked at her husband with fury. Humiliate me all you want, she thought, but not our guest who is new to the village, to us.

She grabbed at something to divert him: 'Stephen used to speak quite differently of the way I like the countryside. Once, during the war, he'd been away for almost six months and he returned with the most beautiful poem about how I love to be out in all weathers, that even when he was hundreds of miles away I would come to him on the wind, whether it was some wild storm bringing down the leaves or a balmy breeze . . .'

24

'Do shut up, Alice. It was romantic tosh.'

'Oh no!' said the vicar. 'How wonderful, to be able to write about your wife with such love.'

'Yes, it was,' said Alice, 'it *is*.'

Stephen wasn't listening. He was pulling down a small volume of his own work from the bookshelves. Please don't, thought Alice. The odds on the vicar knowing much French were zero. 'Here,' said Stephen. 'It makes great kindling.'

Slowly, the vicar began flicking through the book. 'Thank you so much, but my French is pretty dreadful.'

'Just like me!' she cried, desperate not to embarrass him.

But the vicar did not look embarrassed. Instead his face was full of pity as he turned to Stephen and said: 'I do worry about another war. How easy it is to hate one another, to lose sense of what we're here for. And when, when . . .'

For a ghastly moment he looked lost for words. In the silence, Alice heard what she hoped was only a large mouse running under the floorboards, echoes from the chimney – jackdaws must be nesting up there.

Finally the vicar spoke: 'When I was at theological college we had a tutorial. There were twelve of us and we were told we couldn't leave the room until every single one of us had admitted we were capable of killing. And we did, ultimately – not just because we wanted our tea. But because I fear you're all too right.'

'So what do we do about it?' asked Stephen, leaning back in his chair and pressing his fingertips together in a steeple, making Alice think of an arrogant don lauding it over a student.

'I pray.'

'For what exactly?'

'That I might change.'

'Indeed? And you think that might help?'

Dear God, prayed Alice. Make him stop.

The vicar spoke softly: 'I think all of us have this force within us and if we come in contact with something that ignites that force, then all that dreadful power can break free and we can find ourselves more than capable of killing and torture. All of us. Some of us get through our lives without ever being tested in that way. So, if ever I am, I pray that I will know the right thing to do.'

'So,' persisted Stephen, 'when the bomb drops—'

'*If* the bomb drops,' interrupted Alice. 'Stephen is convinced we'll have an atomic war. That what happened in Japan will happen again.'

'I was right about the last war,' said Stephen. 'But no one listened.'

With that, Alice was defeated.

He had been right. By early 1937 he'd been desperate. Why couldn't his Foreign Office colleagues see what was staring them in the face? That evil was stalking Europe and appeasement was just playing into Hitler's plans? He would lie awake, talking far into the early hours. And she would take his face in her hands and caress him and comfort him, telling herself whatever happened nothing could change their love.

She watched her husband staring hard at the vicar as if the strength of his gaze could force the words out of him. Was this what he had done in the war? *Made* people talk?

Her fears were interrupted as her prayer that Stephen might stop was answered. Mrs Green came in to say there was a telephone call for Stephen. They all rose to their feet, and Alice walked the vicar to the front door, appalled by the afternoon he'd been put through.

'Let me drive you home,' she offered, anxious to make amends.

'No thank you. Please don't worry about me.'

She watched him cycle off. He'd spoken with such firmness, she had a fleeting impression he was the one worrying about *her*.

4

IN THE OLD DOWER House, facing Oakbourne village green, Jane Downes heard her husband, the doctor, unlocking the front door.

'Dinner not ready?' Jonathan asked, limping into the kitchen.

It was so obvious dinner wasn't ready Jane was tempted to throw the iron at him. But, thumping it over one of his shirts, she smiled. 'Not yet, darling.'

'For pity's sake!' Jonathan went on as Juliet, their youngest child, began pounding out 'Good King Wenceslas', 'it's almost Easter. Surely she's learned it by now.'

'I'll have a word with her,' said Jane, wondering whether she could get away with not ironing her woollen dress and deciding she couldn't.

Jonathan hurled some coal onto the dying fire. 'It's freezing in here!' He tried to ignite the embers, sending clouds of sooty dust into the room and dropping the poker.

'I'll get it,' she said, as he struggled to bend.

'Stop fussing. Honestly, Jane, you can't build a decent fire on yesterday's ashes. You have to clear the grate.'

Before the war – she had to stop thinking like that. But before the war the grates were always swept. Before the war, two maids in neat black dresses occupied the kitchen. The washing up was done, the table laid, beds changed, floors swept, dinner cooked. The smell of burning wool brought her back to the present.

She looked down at her ruined dress. This had been her parents' home. She had grown up here but moved back in the autumn of 1940 because her own home in Battersea, where for almost fifteen years she and Jonathan had been happily married and had their children, was bombed in the early hours of 2nd November – at exactly three minutes past one. She'd found their carriage clock stopped for good in the rubble.

'Juliet!' yelled Jonathan as their daughter struck up again with her foot on the loud pedal. 'Please! Give us some peace!'

But the maids had long gone, off to factories to make bombs with their friends, and there was no way they would return to work for her, even if she could afford it.

'Mum!' Christopher, their middle child, put his French homework on the ironing board. 'Can you test me?'

'Of course but . . .' There was still no sign of dinner, the sink full of dishes, the chickens to lock up, the dog to walk. 'Why don't you ask Dad? His French is better than mine. Jonathan!' she said to her husband, with his head now stuck in the paper. 'Jonathan!'

'Hmm,' he muttered, shifting his prosthetic leg with a groan so loud Jane suspected they'd heard it in the next village.

'Would you help Christopher with his French?'

'No, don't bother,' said Christopher. 'I don't . . .'

'Don't what?' frowned his father.

Don't want your help, thought Jane. Don't want you here, don't want you home.

29

'Darling,' said Jane addressing her son, 'what is it you're trying to do?'

Christopher glared at her.

'Christopher!' barked Jonathan. 'Your mother's talking to you!'

Don't, Jane pleaded silently, yell at him like a sergeant major.

'It was future imperfect the other night,' she said. 'Is it future imperfect again?'

Christopher rolled his eyes. 'Why would I need to do it again?'

'Enough of that sarcastic tone with your mother!'

'Why not go in the sitting room where it's quiet?' she suggested. 'And I'll make some tea, Jonathan, to warm you up. And here,' she said to Christopher, going to the cupboard where she'd hoarded a bag of sherbet lemons. 'Have one of these.'

Christopher's shrug said, I know you're trying to buy me off. He was almost sixteen, taller than her now, yet so thin, like a coiled spring. All that potential for pleasure and pain, she thought, resisting the temptation to hug him as he tried to reject her sticky offering and punish her for packing him off with his father.

He took the sweet.

'Say thank you to your mother,' said Jonathan.

'He did,' she lied, wanting to bring her hand to his pale, freckled cheek.

'We'll leave you in peace,' Christopher muttered, slamming the door behind him.

Her eldest child, eighteen-year-old Eleanor, walked into the kitchen with her biology textbook. 'What's that awful smell?' she asked. 'Have you burnt something again?' Jane

30

pointed to her woollen dress. 'Oh, good. It's ruined. You look so frumpy in that. Where's Dad?'

Jane nodded to the sitting room and her daughter stuck her head around the door.

'Dad, please can you help me?'

'Give me five minutes,' he called out.

Eleanor was sitting her Higher Certificate this summer and hoped to get into medical school. To Jonathan's delight, she wanted to follow in his footsteps and, thank God, had embraced the return of her stranger of a father she'd not seen for five years.

'What's the problem?' asked Jane, putting away the ironing board.

'Enzymes.'

Before having Eleanor, Jane had been a sister in a London teaching hospital. And, in Oakbourne during the war, she'd often stood in for the GP, Dr Hughes, who'd come out of retirement to look after this remote rural community, but had spent more time being ill himself.

'I can probably help you,' she said.

'Thanks, but I'll ask Dad. What's for dinner?'

'Scrambled eggs.'

'Again?'

The rest of the country was making do with powdered eggs, but thanks to a patient paying Jonathan in kind they were gorging themselves on creamy richness.

'Don't look at me like that, Mum. You know I've always hated eggs. Anyway, there are only nine,' said Eleanor, going to the pantry.

Jane lied again: 'I'm not hungry.' Before the war, this kitchen had seen the creation of feasts of chicken pies, lemon puddings, roast beef, chocolate mousse . . . She clenched her stomach. 'Darling,' she said, 'do you have time to take Rusty for a short walk?'

'Mum! I've got a test tomorrow!'

Her elder daughter always had to be top of the class, to get everything right. And she invariably did. But it didn't come easily.

Jonathan stuck his head round the door. 'How can I help, Eleanor?'

'I don't get this stuff on enzymes.'

'What about Christopher's French?' asked Jane.

'He says he doesn't need me,' he said, joining Eleanor at the kitchen table. Jane handed him a cup of tea, trying not to notice how his hands were shaking. When he'd returned he'd had a slight tremor and she'd hoped it would ease back home, having food and care, doing a relatively non-demanding job. Before the war he was a consultant thoracic surgeon, with what was assumed to be a brilliant career ahead of him. But, if anything, the tremor was getting worse.

'What's for dinner?' he asked.

'Scrambled eggs.'

'Again?'

'*Again*.' She beat the eggs extra hard, listening to her husband talk about substrate molecules and competitive inhibitors and watching Eleanor's face grow more and more anxious. Slow down, she wanted to say. She's not grasping this. She's not as clever or as quick as you. Few are.

'What's wrong with me?' said Eleanor, close to tears. 'I just don't understand.'

Without thinking, Jane said, 'It's only a school test.'

Eleanor turned on her: 'For God's sake, Mum! It's just sixty-two days till the first exam.'

Then Juliet ran into the kitchen and flung herself into Jane's arms. 'Oh, please tell me we're having scrambled eggs again!'

Juliet was her miracle child. Perfectly happy in the middle of the class. Perfectly happy to have her father home – a man she could barely remember. Overjoyed by scrambled eggs. Jane held tight her placid little body then let go as the phone rang out in the hall.

With a stupendous racket Jonathan levered himself up to answer it.

'It's Mr Martin,' he explained on his return. 'The baby's coming quicker than we thought.'

'Give her my love,' said Jane, thinking Mrs Martin would probably prefer to have me with her, a woman she knows and who delivered her first two children. Yet, as she watched her husband checking the contents of his bag, she knew he would do a good job. With his professional coat on, he would find a patience and tenderness that eluded him at home now.

She went to the front door and gave him a light kiss on the cheek.

Watching him drive off, she thought, during the war *I* was the one going out to work.

5

ARRIVING HOME FROM OAKBOURNE Hall, George Ivens removed his muddy boots and placed them carefully on the newspaper Mrs Turner always left by the front door. His meeting with the Raynes had exhausted him and he wished he could sit peacefully a moment, put on the gramophone his parishioners had given him when he left Whitechapel, listen to Mozart and make some sense of his visit.

But Mrs Turner called out: 'Your tea's ready.' And he caught the fumes of bloater.

Keeping his coat on he padded across the highly polished floor to the immaculate dining room. He sat at the place laid for him, directly facing the mantelpiece with a photograph of Mrs Turner's only son smiling confidently in his RAF uniform, shortly before he was shot down in the tail-end of a Lancaster bomber.

The grandfather clock that dwarfed the room chimed. It was only five o'clock and he didn't want to eat yet. But Mrs Turner was preparing his evening meal earlier and earlier. He half-expected her to announce she was giving him his lunch and dinner at breakfast so she might get the day over and done with.

He huddled into his thin coat and tried to make sense of his visit. He'd never before met people like the Raynes – titled, landed and rich. Stephen Rayne, *Sir* Stephen, he corrected himself, was a baronet, the title going back centuries.

In London, he had socialist friends and colleagues who stood for the exact opposite of the Raynes. 'Please don't get sucked into the old feudal system!' they'd said when he'd told them he was moving to the countryside, and he'd laughed and assured them he wouldn't.

Quite the opposite.

He'd known that moving to Oakbourne from the East End would test his own prejudices fostered growing up seeing children going to school with no shoes and no breakfast, their parents ground down in the relentless struggle against poverty. As he'd walked up to the Big House, wondering how you found the moral justification for living in a place with two towers and, so he'd been told, 365 windows, he'd had to keep reminding himself that, be we a child of a tenement or a mansion, we are all part of the mystical body of Christ.

But the truth was, as he'd sat sipping weak tea – in the one cup, he'd noticed, without a chip – and fidgeting in an armchair with a broken spring digging into his thigh, instead of having to manage any indignation at injustice he'd been shocked at the appalling state of the place. At one point when he was talking he'd lost his concentration as he was convinced he saw a rat looking out at him from inside the bald head of an old tiger skin.

He had seen people's homes obliterated in the Blitz, but the defeat in that enormous house was every bit as palpable. Possibly more so, because the slums were better gone. But Oakbourne Hall still had the remnants of beauty. He'd noticed what had once been a minstrels' gallery, a stained-glass window of swallows flying amongst reeds, a magnificent staircase. Now the neglect and ruin of what had once been so very lovely made him forlorn and, to his surprise, he felt sorry for the Raynes.

He glanced out at the overgrown hedge, obstructing what little light there was, then back to the window sill with a selection of works representing different phases of Mrs Turner's son's short life: a clay ashtray inscribed with 'Mummy', the 'y' squashed up in the corner; what Ivens thought was a cat; and then progressing to an exquisite carving of a heron, all dusted by Mrs Turner to within an inch of their life.

'How lovely,' he said, calling upon his resources of optimism as she entered with the bony fish and a slice of bread smeared with margarine.

'My pleasure.'

'Are you sure you don't want me to cut back that hedge?' he offered for the second time that week.

'No thank you,' she replied, pulling the curtains.

'It's no trouble.'

'You've got work to do.'

Work? What work of his might possibly help the Raynes, that pretty, sad woman in a dress that hung shapelessly from her thin shoulders, and her husband with his bitterness and despair? In their huge, loveless drawing room, wondering what torment lay behind her contrived smiles and his cruelties, he'd felt as powerless to bring the peace of God as to stop rain falling.

'Men go mad after a war,' a chaplain who'd served in the trenches said to him once. We all do, he thought, watching Mrs Turner brush up a speck of soot in the fireplace that must have fallen down in the fifteen minutes since she'd last cleaned it.

'This looks delicious,' he said, trying not to feel nauseous at the prospect of the oily lump before him. 'Oh, Mrs Turner, when I was up at the Big House, Sir Stephen said we're very welcome to some wood.'

'I think we've enough, thank you.'

But it's like Siberia, he wanted to cry. There's ice on the windows, and I lie awake shivering. Surely you feel the cold too? Possibly not. He feared the haggard soul before him, her hair scraped back into a net, had trained herself to feel nothing.

'Perhaps I could put a fire in my room?' he suggested.

She hesitated, clearly against the idea.

'Don't worry about the extra work,' he said. 'I'll carry the wood in. Pay for the chimney to be swept. Clear the grate. And I could lay the fire in the sitting room for you.'

'Oh no, I never sit in there!'

You might, he thought, if it was warm. But he was fighting a losing battle. In the month he'd been here, not once had she had a visitor. He'd heard her turning people away at the door and the only time she'd deviated from her automated existence and rigid cleaning routine was when he'd begun coughing in front of her and she'd made him a cup of hot water and honey.

'But if you need a fire,' she went on, 'of course, go ahead.'

Her defeat was infectious. Why bother? he thought. I can make do.

But a howl of wind down the chimney prompted him to say, 'Thank you. I'll see to it.'

Then he turned his energies to the bloater. As he swallowed it stuck in his throat.

'Mrs Turner, please forgive me. I hate to waste this, but I really can't manage it. I should have said.'

'Are you not well? Then this is the last thing you want.' She whisked the plate from under him. 'But what can I get you?'

She gave him a concerned smile. He was supposed to be the one coming to her aid, to be helping this war-weary community, but the only thing that sparked her to life was his neediness.

'Nothing, really,' he insisted, cursing his humiliating, ailing body.

Rheumatic fever at fifteen had left him with a weak heart – and since then he had tried to ignore his frailties. He tired more easily than other men. He could not work as hard. It was not his fault, but he could not rid himself of the shame. He saw how people looked at him. Just today, Stephen Rayne had made some pointed comment. But he could accept that.

What was worse was pity. He wanted to be the strong one, looking after others. But he'd seen pity in Alice Rayne's eyes when he'd arrived labouring for breath at her door.

'Are you sure I can't get you a cup of tea?' Mrs Turner was saying.

'Actually, yes please.'

As she went to the kitchen he felt utterly redundant. All he could do was drink tea.

The saviour, whom he believed in – most of the time – and the saints he had studied had existed in every bit as brutal a world as this one. But, although they had been tortured and crucified – just as men and women had been in this latest war and, like Stephen Rayne, he feared always would be – the life in them had not been extinguished. It wasn't just their certainty that they were going to be resur- rected in the next world, they'd retained an energising spirit in this one. And as Mrs Turner returned with his tea he wished he might say we all know how much evil there is around us but if we shut down our senses, as you have, Mrs Turner, then the evil has won – and your son died in vain.

But he simply clasped Mrs Turner's cold fingers and said, 'Thank you. This is just what I needed.'

6

IVY HAD BROKEN THROUGH the leaded windows in
what had once been the nursery at Oakbourne Hall. Rain
pelted inside.

'I suppose we ought to board it up for now,' said Alice.
'There's no point getting new glass cut.'

'No,' agreed Mrs Green. They both avoided stating
the obvious: all the windows had such rotten frames that
every one needed replacing. 'I'll make sure the ivy's cut
at the base.'

'I've done that,' said Alice. She had gone round with a
saw, hacking at the thick, fibrous stems to stop the ivy eating
further into the brickwork, blocking the gutters and dragging
the house down.

Mrs Green sighed: 'This was such a beautiful nursery.'

Now, thought Alice, it feels even more dead than the rest
of the house. The room was bare except for a broken rocking
horse and she wondered whether she should just let the rain
continue pouring in, rotting the carpet, the floorboards, the
plaster in the ceiling. Limesdale Hall, an even larger pile
twenty miles away, had 'accidentally' caught fire last year
and been razed to the ground. Another on the Cambridgeshire
border had just been sold in fifty lots, the estate split up
into farms, smallholdings, the pub, cricket pitch, woodlands.

Maybe the time had come for Oakbourne Hall to go the same way.

'A perfect place for children,' continued Mrs Green.

And Alice caught the glance at her flat stomach.

She flinched. She knew she was gossiped about in the village. When – or if – she and Stephen were having children provided plenty of delicious fodder: married ten years you'd have thought by now, especially as she's getting on, and he's been back a while, but she's as stick-thin as ever, just walks and gardens. What he needs . . .

But how much did people know? Mrs. Green could be relied upon to be discreet, but not the few part-time maids they'd managed to keep. Flushing at the thought of spies under the stairs discussing her sleeping arrangements, she turned to Mrs Green. 'I'll see to that window later.' And she strode out of the nursery.

It wasn't simply that she and her husband had separate rooms but Stephen chose to be as far away as possible. From her enormous room overlooking the park to his took almost five minutes: along the main corridor with the crumbling cornices, crossing the landing of the great Gothic staircase and on past further bedrooms to the double doors – full of holes as they'd been used by the soldiers as a dart board – opening onto one of the back staircases, then up two further flights of stairs to the top storey, which had been the servants' quarters. These days the entire floor was deserted, except for the one locked narrow room where Stephen had slept since his return.

'I'm afraid,' Mrs Green pointed out as they headed down a back corridor, 'there's more dry rot above that window.'

Alice looked at the decaying wood. There was nothing to say. There was no money to fix anything. She rubbed the unwashed glass to see a skein of swans bending their flight in the wind and wished she was outside with them. But she'd set aside the morning to sort through another of the unused bedrooms.

It seemed to Alice that nothing in Stephen's family had been thrown out for generations. The house was crammed with sentimental knick-knacks, coils of baby hair, flowers pressed between old letters, endless diaries. She heaved open the bottom drawer of a mahogany tallboy and pulled out a pile of red-bound books – accounts to do with pheasants from 1901 to 1914. She threw them in the basket for burning and was then confronted with a photo of a young man, uncannily like Stephen, slim and fair, and laughing. On the back, written in a graceful copperplate hand, was: *Sir James, May 1914*. Stephen's father.

Alice studied the unlined face, unrecognisable in its happiness, as he stood in his whites on the steps of the Oakbourne Hall cricket pavilion, blissfully unaware of what life held. On the few occasions Alice had met him, she'd found him cold and condescending. Stephen certainly had never spoken of him fondly, describing a man forever shouting orders at his wife, his children, his servants.

'Don't let me end up like him,' Stephen had said when he first went away. It was September '39. And, arrogant fool that I was, she thought, I believed we were so charmed and so special we could survive whatever war threw at us.

'This needs to go,' said Mrs Green, showing her a scarlet mess jacket disintegrating with moths. 'And this.' She held up a paisley-patterned cashmere shawl green with mildew. 'But this,' went on Mrs Green, presenting her with a damask tablecloth, 'is still in good condition, somehow or other.'

Alice stroked the heavy silk. In the corner were the initials D and R, Deborah Rayne, Stephen's great-grandmother who had once presided over enormous Victorian banquets at the end of a table seating forty, now scratched and marked with rings where the Canadian soldiers had placed their mugs of scalding coffee.

These days, who could hold the sort of dinner party that demanded such a colossal tablecloth? Who would launder it? Iron it to such geometric perfection? Once, a battalion of staff had ironed and cooked and cleaned, but now there was only Mrs Green and temporary help who always made it perfectly clear they were only here till something better came along.

'Such exquisite embroidery,' sighed Mrs Green, tracing the elaborate monogram.

Alice nodded in agreement. All these lives she knew little of, their treasured possessions and photos boxed up in dusty drawers. What was she supposed to do with them all? Part of her wished the house would fall down, yet it also exerted a claim on her. I was loved and cherished once, it seemed to say. Save me!

Perhaps a child – her child – might love these photos. But, right now, the odds on her and Stephen having children were non-existent. Days could pass without them even seeing each other.

Before Stephen went away to fight. Before his father was blown to pieces in the Blitz. Before his elder brother was killed – how or where, only God and, she assumed, the Gestapo knew, something else that was never spoken of. Before Stephen inherited Oakbourne Hall, five and a half years ago and before so much else, they would lie side by side imagining themselves after the war. They'd live in a warm cottage – they couldn't have got that more wrong. He'd leave the Foreign Office and write, she would grow roses, and they would have children and he'd say he wanted eleven for his own cricket team. Stupid, newly-wed fantasies, she thought, flicking through pictures of Stephen's father as a child in endless Edwardian summer afternoons, elms shedding gentle shade over the gilded little boy.

Then a loose photo fell out of him in khaki: *Marne, September 1914*. There was no mistaking that sternness, the lips set hard, innocence and joy shot to bits, one month of war obliterating forever that cheery soul at the cricket pavilion.

But, unlike his father, thought Alice, war didn't change Stephen at first. When she'd kissed him goodbye in Hastings in November 1943, he was the man she'd always loved. Yes, he was exhausted and had aged far too fast. But he was still himself.

Now it seemed as if their marriage fell in two distinct parts: before Hastings, and after.

On his return last autumn, her first thought was that there was another woman, that in the two years they'd been apart he'd met someone else.

She'd believed the pain irredeemable. But, six months on, she'd almost welcome another woman because then she would know what she was dealing with. Now her suspicions were too terrible to contemplate.

Yet the war was over. Whatever he had been made to do he could put behind him. Move on: that was the message. Politicians, journalists, everyone said so. But their glibness enraged her. And in what she knew was a pointless gesture she dumped another pile of old photos in the bin, as if anyone could ever destroy the past so easily.

7

'THAT'S ANOTHER ROOM DONE,' said Alice a few hours later. 'I'll finish up. You get ready.' It was Mrs Green's afternoon off and she was going to see *Brief Encounter* for the second time.

'I just need to fetch Sir Stephen's bed linen,' said Mrs Green. 'The laundry van will be here shortly.'

'I'll get it! You don't want to miss the bus.'

Not once had Alice set foot inside Stephen's room in the attic. A few times after his return she had knocked on the door but he'd always told her to go away. Once she'd gone up there and he'd been out and the door locked. She could easily have gone in. She had her own set of keys. Yet to intrude where she was so clearly not wanted felt as if she was breaking some moral code.

But there was nothing underhand about helping Mrs Green. Surely?

And she was away, racing up the stairs, to the top-floor landing.

She swung open the door to the wing where the menservants had slept. Before her extended a windowless corridor running half the length of the house, on either side a dozen empty small rooms. She noticed mouse droppings, bat droppings . . .

She stomped noisily across the bare boards, breathing in centuries of sweat and boot polish.

'Stephen!' she called and banged fiercely on his door to make it clear to anyone who might be listening that she was merely up here on some mundane errand. Not spying.

There was no one to hear her and she went to slip the key in the lock but in the darkness she dropped it. She knelt down, fumbling in the dust with her hands. The old oak floor, warped and uneven, creaked. She glanced over her shoulder into the shadows. For a wild moment, alone at the top of the house . . .

Her fingers clasped the key. Fool! she admonished herself. Bluebeard – with Mrs Danvers in tow – was hardly going to burst from one of the locked doors fresh from killing yet another curious wife.

She leapt up and unlocked the door. The room was clean and tidy with the window open, the makeshift curtains – heavy grey army blankets – pulled back. Along one wall was a single bed with a black metal frame. In a corner stood a table, with a bowl, his shaving things, a candle. On the back of a wooden chair hung a shirt. That was it. No books, as he would once have stacked by his bed, no pens, no paper.

But also no secrets.

Nothing, she thought, despising her earlier fears, to be scared of.

Instead, there was something so pitiful about this tiny room. She could see Stephen, the little boy, motherless far too young, growing up lonely in this colossal house with his bellowing general of a father, packed off to school to be bullied by dull-witted prefects; then Stephen, her imaginative, maverick man, sent away to war with yet more morons making him execute God knows what dreadful and impossible orders.

She picked up the bed linen and smoothed her hand over his pillow. It was sodden with sweat. She imagined him lying here, tossing and turning, a man still at war in his sleep, flailing and wrestling with enemies who came to him in the night. And it was her job to help him. Who else could? But she was no nearer to knowing how than on the day he came home.

She hurried downstairs. She heard a van pull up and ran out into the back yard and gave the driver the laundry.

Mrs Green appeared in her tweed coat with fox collar and Alice made herself smile into Mrs Green's soft, lined face.

'Enjoy *Brief Encounter*,' she said.

'Thank you. Oh, those lettuce seeds you ordered have just arrived.'

'Wonderful. I'll plant them now. It'll be good to have some salad in the summer.'

'Won't it? Everything you grow is so delicious,' said Mrs Green, and Alice had the sense Mrs Green was regarding her with an anxious pity.

Mrs Green had nursed her own husband until his death, three years after he'd been poisoned by gas in the Somme.

Since time began, women had found themselves in this role and she had a vague recollection of reading Roman myths, and Ulysses, after he'd been off fighting the Trojans, eventually coming back to Penelope. Though Penelope also had no idea how to soothe her troubled husband. Ulysses had barely crossed the hearth before he'd taken up his bow and arrow and started killing all over again.

47

Alice made her way into the garden – at least bringing plants to life was something she could do – where, to her surprise, sitting on a bench by the stump of a felled oak was Stephen.

'Darling!' He didn't respond. She tapped his shoulder and he started. He was just in his shirt sleeves and the seat was damp. 'You'll catch cold,' she said. So much for epic Penelope and Ulysses.

She tried again: 'Mrs Green told me Mr Ivens has the most wonderful voice so I thought I might go to Evensong one Sunday.'

'Why?'

'To hear some beautiful singing.' And also, she thought, to show him some support, particularly after the way you spoke to him the other day.

'Did you put all those old school reports of mine on my desk?' he asked as she perched beside him.

'I was sorting out a cupboard and wasn't sure what to do with them.'

'Burn them.'

'I thought . . .' That once we'd have had fun looking at them. 'You don't want them?'

'No.'

'They were so good. Especially the languages – what "a natural" you are.'

'"A natural"? God help us!'

'They all went on about your ability to focus. That's a wonderful quality,' she said, the habitual lines of comfort springing to her lips.

His eyes focused on the tree stump.

And she remembered how on the night they met he'd touched the faint scar at the corner of her mouth. It was so tiny no one had ever noticed it before. But Stephen noticed and she'd thought, this man *sees* me. And she'd wondered what it would be like to lie naked with a man who paid her body such attention. Now he wouldn't even look at her.

I return to the past, she thought, to hide my disappointment in the present while he exists in another world altogether. And it's up to me to coax him out of it. But what happens the day I lose the will?

'I'm going in,' he said.

She watched his retreating back.

8

'HERE,' SAID DR DOWNES, taking a pot of damson jam from his case. 'Jim Thompson's wife gave me this. I couldn't charge him, given the appalling state of the place they're forced to live in.'

'All those estate cottages need work,' said Jane, at the sink battling a burnt saucepan.

'Does that justify the Raynes not spending a single penny on them? Thompson's given more than fifty years' hard labour to that family.'

But there's no money left, thought Jane. As a child she could remember estate farms being sold off, the Oakbourne stud closing, the polo field being ploughed up, a local brewery buying the pub. As the assets were stripped her mother, in pained tones, would recall the lost grandeur and beauty of Oakbourne Hall. Now, local talk was of whether the house would even last into the next decade.

She said, 'During the war Alice Rayne lived in one of those cottages looking after her father. He'd had polio.'

'I bet her cottage was in better nick than the Thompsons'.'

'Yes,' she said. 'But from what I hear something's seriously wrong up at the Big House. Sir Stephen's come back a changed man.'

'Who hasn't?'

'I suspect this is something more.'

'What? He's a danger? To himself? To others?'

'Maybe. I don't know. Word has it, he spends all his time in his room doing nothing.'

'Isn't that what the aristocracy always do?'

'Jonathan. You never used to be so simplistic. You go on and on about the damage this war has done. Just because he's rich – or was – you stop caring!'

'That's bloody unfair! Half the world's lost their mind. If there's a problem he needs to come to me. Though God knows there's little enough help. If you ask me, he's damned lucky he's not returned home to discover all the thanks he gets for risking his life and sanity is no job, some hideous tenement and under-nourished children.'

Then he picked up the *Lancet* and Jane went to lock up the chickens.

She took her time, hoping Jonathan would divert himself with his medical research and spare her another lecture on health care and houses and education for this new land fit for heroes. Yet my husband, she thought, chasing a squawking hen, is one of those heroes too.

'No heroics!' she'd pleaded the day Jonathan left for France in 1940. On the station platform, with those hundreds of men, terrified, eager, numb and every single one so very vulnerable, she knew exactly what Jonathan was thinking and she'd said: 'You can't save them all. But if you come home, you can still be a father to our children. A husband – to me.'

He'd promised – no heroics. But what that had meant in the reality of war, she'd no idea. Whenever she asked about Dunkirk or the prison camps, he'd just talk about leaving the past behind so they could create his wonderful new socialist world. But she was already sick of waiting for this better life that felt more and more like a fantasy for casualties of war.

Many of her friends were casualties of the Great War too. Well, that is how she'd seen her unmarried friends as she'd walked down the aisle on her wedding day, holding a bouquet of lily of the valley picked from this garden, those wonderful women smiling at her so generously; strong, vigorous women who yearned for a loving body to lie against theirs but, with so few men around after 1918, had been forced to soldier on alone.

And yet, she told herself, shooing the chickens into their house, good could come out of evil. Her dearest friend from school was now a head teacher at a grammar school, another from her nursing days was a matron in a large London teaching hospital, and the brightest of them all was at Cambridge, working in research on burns.

But on her wedding day she'd felt extraordinarily blessed. She'd got up at dawn to pick her bouquet – 'I want something simple,' she'd told her mother, who'd had different expectations for her daughter's wedding, especially the choice of groom. And on their first wedding anniversary she and Jonathan had gone together to Floris in Jermyn Street and he'd bought her a tiny bottle of lily of the valley *eau de toilette* – long finished, but she'd kept the empty bottle with its lingering perfume evoking love and joy.

She wandered down to the end of the garden where the other day she'd seen new lily of the valley shoots coming through.

They'd gone.

The soil was turned over, bare and empty. Instead of slim, vibrant leaves there was nothing but mud, and for a moment she felt she was going to burst into tears.

Instead she went storming into the kitchen.

'Ross Harris! His mother was desperate to get him out of the house so I said he could help in the garden and he's dug up all the lily of the valley.'

'Jesus!' Jonathan flung down the *Lancet*. 'I thought something serious had happened.'

'But I specifically told him not to. I explained those long leaves . . .'

'Do you have any idea how spoilt you sound? A man who lost his youth in the bloody Arctic and you're having a go at him about flowers . . .'

'You're right, I know, I know. It's just those flowers meant . . .'

Then she caught sight of muddy paw prints all over the kitchen floor she had washed an hour earlier and let out an exasperated, 'Oh, Rusty!' In response to his name Rusty leapt up and wagged his enormous tail, which knocked over the broom and sent a half-full milk bottle flying across the table. She watched the bottle shatter, milk spilling.

'Basket!' she yelled. 'Basket!'

'Why don't you get rid of the dog?' demanded Jonathan. 'You make it quite clear you can't stand him.'

'Mum, no!'

She turned. She hadn't realised Christopher was here.

'Dad doesn't mean it!' she said, getting down on her hands and knees to pick up the glass. 'Really. You know how I love Rusty. We all do,' she added, as the phone rang.

'You go,' she said, desperate to get her husband out of the kitchen.

'Christopher, I'm so sorry,' she said as Jonathan left. 'I was wrong to get in such a state about lilies of the valley.'

Her son's eyes narrowed: 'Then why,' he asked, lowering his voice, 'when Dad was away, did you get in such a state about them on your wedding anniversary? Going on about your bouquet and how he'd be thinking of us because we had such a wonderful father. Bloody wonderful!'

'Christopher, please! Dad doesn't know what those flowers mean to me.'

'Because he doesn't think about anyone other than himself.'

'I've got to go,' called Jonathan from the hall.

Thank God, she thought. 'What a pity,' she said, forcing herself to kiss him goodbye.

She returned to the kitchen, where Christopher stood staring intently at her. 'Mum? Why did you marry him? For Christ's sake, he's a monster. And you keep trying to pretend he isn't.'

'No! And don't swear!'

'He does and you don't stop him.'

'Listen,' she said, 'I can remember the exact moment I decided your father was the man I wanted to marry.'

For a moment, ten years seemed to fall away from Christopher's adolescent face. Of her three children he'd always been the one who loved stories, who would say, 'Just one more page . . .'

'At the hospital,' she said, 'where I was a nurse, I'd heard of your father – everyone had – because he was so brilliant.'

He'd also stood out because of his accent – despite his best efforts he would still drop an 'h'. But Christopher didn't need to hear that. Nor that she was already engaged to the son of close friends of her parents when she fell for his father.

'On this particular day,' she continued, 'the consultant was doing his rounds and he'd a dozen or so junior doctors with him. They were all standing round the bed of this old lady and suddenly she was vomiting and the consultant yelled "Nurse", leaping back as if she was something revolting, as did all the young doctors.

'Except for your father.

'He grabbed a bowl and he held it for this poor woman, soothing her and saying, "it's all right", while the other doctors acted as if she was just a repulsive old lady.' She felt her eyes pricking. 'I'd never seen such tenderness in a man before.'

Christopher was observing her carefully, his face changed again, older than his years. Soon he'd be sixteen. If the war had still been going on, in two years he'd have been conscripted. If he'd been born three years earlier he'd have been sent to the Far East. If . . .

'Mum, I know he cares for sick people and injustice and so on. But what about us?'

'Of course he cares about us. It may not feel like it, but he's doing his best and maybe his best isn't that great right now but he's been through so much. Think of the irony of him enduring a botched job by some vile Nazi when he was such a brilliant surgeon.'

'*Was*,' echoed Christopher. 'I wish he *was* off working in an operating theatre and not here, shouting at us. But his hands are never going to get better, are they?'

'Hopefully they will – with time.'

'But they might not? So we could be stuck here?'

'Would that be so bad?'

He turned away. When he spoke again his voice was quieter. 'Tom Mayhew says it was a real cushy number being taken prisoner, that Dad had it easy.'

'What?'

'He says POWs got fed and looked after, and some got captured deliberately to stay safe.'

'That's terrible!' she cried. 'Christopher! Use that imagination of yours. Remember how thin Dad was when he got back.' She'd thought she'd seen plenty of under-nourished bodies but nothing had prepared her for the shock of seeing her naked husband weighing seven stone. 'Dad went through absolute hell!'

'What about those letters he sent us?' muttered Christopher.

Jonathan's "letters" were five flimsy postcards – the sum total of her communication from her husband in as many years. It was true that he had, in a way, written about life in the camp as if it was a "cushy number": he'd made some great friends – so great he'd avoided all contact with them since coming home – really improved his chess, thanks to a couple of brilliant players in his hut, was learning Greek, and on sunny days the men played cricket with a bat they'd fashioned from a ripped-up floorboard.

Christopher frowned. 'He was lying to stop us worrying, wasn't he? Treating us like little children, as if we can't take reality.'

Maybe we can't, she thought. To Christopher, she said, 'Remember everything he wrote would have been censored.'

'No one's censoring him now. Yet when I asked him what it was like he just bored away again about his beloved

56

Aneurin Bevan and his precious welfare state and said to forget the war.'

'I've no idea what *my* father did in the Great War either,' she said. 'Once I asked him if he'd ever killed anyone and the look he gave me – I was terrified.'

'Are you frightened of Dad?'

'No, of course not. But soldiers rarely talk. Often they simply can't.'

Christopher thought for a moment. 'In Dad's *Lancet* there was an article about how talking can be a cure.'

She sighed. 'We're a long way off from persuading people of that. But Christopher, these boys at school. Do any of the others believe POWs had an easy time? Because if they do—'

'Mum! It doesn't matter.'

'It does! I'm appalled they're talking like this. I realise Tom's lashing out because his father was killed. But what about Jack Ledbury? Was he involved?' Jack's father had not returned from D-Day.

'Stop fussing! I'm all right.'

'You would tell me, wouldn't you? If the other boys . . .'

'There's nothing to tell! Why do you have to turn everything into a disaster?'

She could never give him an honest answer to that. Instead she stretched out to put her arms around him. But he pulled away and hugged the dog.

9

IF HE HURRIED, George Ivens hoped he might still catch the bus back to the village. He'd just given communion to Jim Thompson, who was too sick to make it to church, and he'd ended up staying all afternoon talking. Now it was late and Ivens tried to run down the isolated track. But within minutes he could barely breathe, his heart thumping with its odd, jerky beat, and when he turned the corner onto the main road the bus was lumbering away.

It was two hours until the next one and he cast an inexperienced eye up at the sky, dark with clouds, deciding there was just enough daylight left for him to walk home cross-country – quicker than sticking to the roads. So he headed off along the edge of a recently ploughed field.

It had been raining and the ground was slippery, the turned sods black and wet. His shoes were too thin for this sort of walk and in no time he could feel the damp seeping through and a feverish sweat on his forehead.

He should, his doctors would say, have cut short his chat in the Thompsons' over-heated, airless bedroom, a draught excluder at the door made from scraps of velvet in the form of a giant sausage dog. But sitting at a bedside was where he felt most a minister of Christ. This was his job, to be present with people, open to all their distress and sorrow, to take their pain upon himself, as Christ had done. Well, that was the theory, but this afternoon he felt he had actually put it into practice.

'Please come back soon,' Mrs Thompson had said, pressing upon him a pot of damson jam now clunking against his leg in his coat pocket. And he'd promised to return, but he wouldn't miss the bus again, he told himself, the night drawing in fast with the path getting worse.

Skirting two more fields, he reached the edge of the marshes, and carried on past narrow dykes, running high with the recent rain. Then he came across a glassy patch of water he thought he'd passed before, but was now on his left, rather than his right.

Ivens could find his way blindfold around the streets of the East End – during the blackouts, he'd virtually done so – and in this new territory it hadn't occurred to him that the way would be so difficult, or that he'd lose his sense of direction so quickly. He looked across to the pall of mist hanging over the reed beds, with no idea where he was.

I ought to be worried, he thought, but it was strangely peaceful being lost in this wide-open emptiness. Also, it was wonderful not being stuck in Mrs Turner's cold house. He was in no rush to get back to yet another evening slipping by in a solitude that all too often felt like stagnation. Out here in the bleakness was such a shimmering of shifting greys it was as if the raw miracle – the infinity of creation beyond the conception of any human mind – was being handed to him on a plate. For the first time since leaving London he felt he hadn't just been exiled to the edge of the North Sea, because he was a sick man. Water, land and sky seemed to be melting into one another, in a constant state of flux and metamorphosis, as if to assure him of the solace of his faith: things are not always what they seem. We are always, always, given the promise of change, healing, resurrection.

He reminded himself of the text of the funeral service he would soon be saying for Jim Thompson. 'O teach us to number our days that we may apply our hearts unto wisdom,' he murmured as he slithered through head-high reeds to a tiny clearing with no obvious way forwards. Unsure if he'd completely lost the footpath and had just been following deer tracks he made for a fallen birch tree and sat a moment.

For a while, all was silent. The moon appeared from behind a bank of clouds and lit up the vast, unhurried wings of a heron heading towards the river. Then a pair of swans suddenly took flight and he heard footsteps splashing through puddles. He expected to see one of the farmhands making his way home, but it was Lady Rayne who emerged from the reeds.

She didn't see him at first. Her eyes were following the swans, white and ghostly in the failing light, and he was tempted to stay hidden. But his cough betrayed him.

She looked appalled to find him here. Clearly he was not the only one wanting to be out alone this evening. But no sooner did he note the dismay on her face than she smiled as if she'd encountered him at a picnic.

'Mr Ivens! How lovely to bump into you.' He could only reply with a wave of his hand, as his cough took hold of him. 'Are you all right?'

'Yes! Thank you!' he said, catching his breath and struggling to his feet. 'I was taking a short cut across the fields. But I think I've missed the path back down to the road.'

'You have. The sign's long gone and it's easy to end up going round in circles. So let me show you.'

'No, no!'

'You mustn't get lost on a night like this when it'll rain any minute.'

As if at her command, a light drizzle began to fall. He wished she'd walk on as if she'd not noticed him. It was clear both of them would have preferred that. But he was being churlish. And foolish. He'd been sent to Suffolk for his health and that didn't mean being out in clothes now clinging like wet flannels.

'I don't want to take you out of your way,' he said.

'I'm always looking for an excuse to walk,' she laughed, a bit too brightly.

'But the rain.'

'I love the rain. Truly.' And she glanced up to catch the drops on her face, revealing a string of pearls round her throat. 'How it blurs the edges. And you've given me a good reason for being out in it.'

And it occurred to him that there was an appeal in her eyes. But he dismissed the idea the moment it appeared. Her fingers flew to her pearls as she said, 'With me, you'll be home in no time. It's quickest if we go directly through the marshes. I promise we won't get lost.' She stepped into a puddle and water shot up round her feet. 'Or drowned! I have the most amazing night vision. My husband told me once that it develops the more you go out at night. It's not just eating carrots.'

Unsure what to do with this information, he felt he'd stumbled into a dinner party and he was the awkward guest she needed to put at ease. 'So it's quite normal to find me walking around in the pitch-black,' she continued, 'developing my night vision. Oh dear, it's so wet, like walking on a sponge. I'm worried for your shoes.'

'It's perfectly all right.'

'Really? My sister refuses to come here in winter because of the mud. She doesn't stop moaning about it. Londoners don't understand this place in winter. They think it's nothing *but* mud. Which suits me, because then I have it to myself. During the war of course there were soldiers and airmen everywhere. But this winter I've barely seen a soul.'

Do you really like that? Being so isolated? He wanted to ask, wondering when she'd last talked to anyone, because now she seemed incapable of stopping. As they waded through the marshland, her conversation moved seamlessly on from visiting Londoners to managing otters to protect the fish, then the best beach for catching mackerel. Finally, she interrupted herself: 'We're not far now,' she cried. 'See those alders – those trees.' A small spinney, like a hazy island emerging from a grey sea, lay not far ahead. 'We pick up the path down to the Queen's Head there.'

'Thank you, I can make it on my own now.'

'No, I'll come with you.'

There was no refusing her as she continued to lead the way, in full flow about geese that recently headed back to Iceland, where in the marshes he might find curlews' nests, the turn in the river where trout congregate, how she had found a barn owl that at first she thought was dead, then discovered had only fainted.

'Fainted?' he repeated, his surprise enabling him to get a word in.

'It's a self-defence mechanism. Just to shut down, stop the adrenaline running so it can re-group and, hopefully, heal. Lots of animals do it. They play possum – pretend to be dead or just pass out when life gets too much. How very wise of them. I think . . .'

At last she paused and he wanted somehow to make her realise she could talk to him, not like this, lecturing him on fainting barn owls and migrating geese, but about what on earth she was doing out here. Escaping her husband with his barbed humiliations?

In London, he'd have known how to reach out to her. But he was not used to women whose headscarves were silk and wore pearls with their Wellington boots and who, despite their shabby clothes and bedraggled hair, held themselves so very aloof, shielding themselves with a barrage of words.

The rain was heavy now, but she seemed oblivious and while he hesitated it was she who spoke. 'Forgive me if I'm speaking out of turn, but have you come here, to this bleak coast, in that spirit? I mean, so many people have endured such awful horror these last six years and I thought perhaps you . . .'

'Needed to faint like a barn owl?'

Her expression turned serious. 'In a way, yes. That you needed to retreat. People have come here for centuries to do just that with all those abbeys and priories up and down the coast.'

'I'm afraid it's much more mundane,' he said, as at last they reached Mrs Turner's front gate. 'The Bishop thought fresh air, fresh food – something everyone in London's been short of – might help my health.'

And, as if to prove the point, his cough began again.

63

'What am I thinking of, keeping you chatting?' she cried. 'You must get warm.'

'And you must come on in and phone for your car.'

'No, really! I'll walk back in no time. But I'm worried about you.'

'I'll be perfectly all right,' he said, but he had to get out of these sodden clothes or he'd pay for it tomorrow. 'But I'm worried about you too.'

'Me?' He picked up on the haughtiness in her response.

'Just about you being out in this rain,' he lied.

'Let's both stop worrying.'

'But Lady Rayne, please let us speak again.'

He sensed her hesitation, as if she thought that after their tea the other day a visit to Oakbourne Hall was an experience he'd never want to repeat. 'Perhaps,' she said, 'I could show you the garden.'

'I'd like that very much.' And he slipped off his wet glove to shake her hand. 'You're freezing!' he exclaimed.

'I'm used to it,' she said. Then, with a wave, she stepped smartly away.

10

D<small>R</small> D<small>OWNES</small> <small>PARKED</small> <small>HIS</small> old Rover outside the vicar's lodgings and sat surveying the scene before him. In the village store they sold a postcard of this very view: red-brick eighteenth-century cottages glowing rosy and crimson; fluffy hens clucking under apple trees ebullient with pink and white blossom; and the church, a legacy of fortunes made from wool in the fourteenth century, soaring up into the pale spring sky. Only last summer, a writer from *The Times* had described Oakbourne as one of the most idyllic villages he'd ever seen.

Downes saw the very opposite. I could be back in the Middle Ages, he thought angrily, clambering out of his car. Crammed into these charming cottages with little windows and smoking chimneys were rickety, bowed-leg children; mothers prematurely aged by squalor and sickness; men worked till the life was bled out of them.

As if to prove his point, two labourers were unloading chopped wood from a cart outside Mrs Turner's house and piling it up in the shed. The men had to be getting on for seventy and, as they bent and heaved, Downes pictured old muscles being pulled, tired tendons torn.

'Careful,' he said, half under his breath. But they heard him and he was greeted with two blank looks. 'Your backs.'

'We can manage, thank you, sir.'

It was too late for this generation, he thought. But for the next one, now the war was over, there was going to be a new world order. There had to be. Change was everywhere and he would be in the vanguard. Already he was chairing committees, writing reports, firing off letters, discussing the best way forwards for the new health service that was on its way.

As a child, Downes, a docker's son, had watched his sister die, failed by a system which he believed helped only those with money, failed by doctors whom he now realised had been downright incompetent. Now he felt he must stop others suffering as his mother and father had, as his sister had. As he had suffered, a young boy, helpless to do anything but stand by and watch, until determination, the power of his brain and the skill in his hands took him away from desperate poverty to a scholarship at the grammar school, and then a place to read medicine at Guy's Hospital, where he had been one of the three highest-graduating students in his final year.

He noticed one of the labourers wince with pain and rub his knee. You should be putting your feet up by the fire, thought Downes, not lugging logs around for someone else. And if he had anything to do with it, these men would be. Certainly he'd do his damnedest to make sure their sons were treated with dignity, with enlightenment.

He opened the gate as a Daimler pulled up behind his Rover and Alice Rayne climbed out. Downes noticed the men touch their caps to her as she said, 'Oh, Grahame, Watson. Thank you so much. Is there enough wood till next winter?'

'Plenty, madam.'

'Wonderful!' Then she turned. 'Dr Downes?'

'Yes.'

'I don't think we've ever met,' she said, 'though of course I know who you are.' She extended her hand and introduced herself. 'Your wife was wonderful when my father was ill. I was so grateful. But are you here to see Mr Ivens?' For the last couple of days Ivens had been confined to bed with a fever he couldn't shake. 'How is he?'

'I'm just on my way in,' he said, thinking he wouldn't discuss his patients with the lady of the manor. He knew her type. Wealthy, entitled, thinking the bestowal of a beautiful smile and firewood made up for terrible inequality.

'Please,' she said, reaching into the car, 'give him this. For – you know – medicinal purposes.' She handed him a bottle of brandy. 'I didn't think we'd any left but I found some stashed away so the Canadians didn't find it – in the priest hole!'

Noblesse oblige, he thought irritably. Before long there'd be an end to that. Everyone went on about how the Big House was falling apart. The sooner the better. The place could be put to good use for the whole community: a cottage hospital so people didn't have to travel miles for decent medical care; a home for the mentally sick – what they had at the moment was a disgrace. Forget the Middle Ages, they were in the Dark Ages with some of the institutions round here. He would look into it. So many of the big landowners were on the verge of selling up. His planning mind was already at work when she handed him a brown paper bag, saying, 'I thought he might enjoy this too. Look!'

He had the annoying feeling she was ordering him about. But he opened the bag. Inside was a large flower pot with a small green plant.

'It's a new sort of tomato,' she explained. 'A beefsteak. I'd never heard of them. One of the Canadians brought some seeds over and grew a few in the greenhouses and when he left I restrained myself from eating them all so I'd have seeds for this year. They're so different from what we're used to – beefier, I suppose. As big as four inches in diameter. And a lovely pale pink with green stripes.'

Despite himself, Downes was intrigued. When he was studying at Guy's, every summer, after finishing his exams, he would treat himself to the cheapest seat at Lord's and he would bring a bag of tomatoes and a tiny salt cellar. There was something about watching the perfect curve of the ball, hearing the single note as it hit the bat, and munching tomatoes sprinkled with salt under a warm sun that gave him the feeling that all was well with the world. A feeling he'd not had for years. Nor had he eaten decent tomatoes in ages. Jane had attempted to grow a few last summer but they'd caught blight and died.

Anyway, he wasn't going to stand around discussing tomatoes. Unlike Lady Muck, some people had work to do.

 11

AN HOUR LATER, DR Downes was still talking to the vicar.
The intricacies of the human heart had been his speciality
and he felt a rush of frustration. So much was happening in
this field, new surgical techniques, extraordinary drugs, all
on the horizon, out of reach now, but not for long. And if
it hadn't been for the war, he would have been involved,
helping men like Ivens.

'I appreciate you taking so much time,' said Ivens, putting
his shirt back on. 'Not everyone . . .'

Downes knew what Ivens meant – some doctors went
rushing through the notes, thinking they knew it all, missing
the vital clue. But, if he had anything to do with it, that would
all change. Doctors would be held accountable in the new
health service.

'It's my job. And,' Downes smiled, 'interesting. I'm sorry,'
he said as Ivens gave a hollow laugh, '"interesting" is the
last thing a patient wants to be. You want to be as boring
as possible.'

'Boredom is what I've been prescribed,' said Ivens. '"Live
like a vegetable", the consultant told me.'

That was Downes's own fear: that soon enough, with the
state of his hands, his leg, he too would end up cultivating
nothing but hopelessness.

Ivens reached for the brandy. 'Stay and have a drop of this with me, would you?'

Downes hesitated. Dinner would be waiting, but even if he was home on time it was sure to be burnt.

'I'd love one!' Then, taking a sip, he said, 'Trust the Raynes to have top-notch brandy!'

'It was kind of her to give me some,' said Ivens. 'But have you met *him*?' Downes shook his head. 'Because I wondered,' continued Ivens, 'what happened to him in the war. If there's some common knowledge I've missed.'

'There's gossip – obviously – that he was probably up to something hush-hush. He's bilingual – a French mother. And apparently he's a different man from what he was. But who isn't?'

Downes caught Ivens glance at his leg.

'I'd still have it,' muttered Downes, 'if it hadn't been for a bloody blithering idiot of a Kraut doctor . . . Sorry, Reverend,' he said as Ivens began coughing again. 'Compared to some, I'm lucky.' And Downes hauled himself to his feet, puffed up the pillows and rearranged them. 'There,' he said, 'stay upright if you can. And get up, once the fever abates. Doing nothing works for some people. But others, well, it destroys the soul – your territory, I know. But it does mine. The key . . . The key to life . . .'

'Oh, yes?' smiled Ivens, pouring more brandy. 'Please, do tell me the key to life.'

Downes laughed. He couldn't remember when he'd last talked over a drink. Jane was always in such a rush. No sooner had she put the dinner down on the table than she was clearing it away.

'As I see it,' he said, savouring the warmth of the cognac, 'the key to it now is putting all that's happened behind us. We've a chance to rebuild the very nature of our society. To actually have a Labour government with a majority. The possibilities are extraordinary . . .'

And, forgetting the pain of his missing leg, Downes climbed nimbly onto his hobby horse, outlining his plans for justice, for equality.

'Did you,' he asked, as Ivens refreshed their glasses again, 'if you don't mind my asking, vote Labour last year?' Ivens nodded. 'So you agree with me.'

'With your vision for a classless commonwealth of equals?'

Downes had the sense the vicar was teasing him. But then Ivens said, 'I don't believe utopias are possible on this earth and I'm nervous when people do. We should all hate poverty, whatever party or religion we belong to. But what frightens me is . . .' He began coughing again.

'Sorry,' said Downes, fetching him some water. 'I shouldn't have kept you talking like this.'

'Don't go! Thanks to you I've not had an afternoon of living like a cabbage. But please,' said Ivens, grasping the older man's hand, 'hear me. In London I knew so many people who thought they could create this wonderfully fair and just society. But I worry that in giving power to the state we're giving away our own power, finding an excuse to ignore our own morality. We've just seen the consequences of that in Germany, the monstrosities that were committed. God only knows – and I mean that – what's happening in Russia right now.'

'Russia's different! And Germany! There's no comparison whatsoever with us.'

71

Ivens hesitated, as if he was about to disagree, but then he said, 'Look at Stephen Rayne. I'm just guessing, after meeting him once, but who knows what he did because he was following orders. Perhaps he did something that went against every ounce of his humanity and conscience. And from all accounts it's almost destroyed him.'

'That was war!' cried Downes. 'Are you saying we should just have rolled over?'

'Not at all! But in this brave new world, something might get lost. However many checks and balances you create, believe me, you can't legislate for human kindness. The way you've been kind to me today.'

'And you me,' said Downes. 'You've made me feel a damned sight better too. I do enjoy an argument,' he went on wistfully. 'Well, this sort of argument.'

At home the rows were so draining and pointless. Eleanor was always pleased to see him, and Juliet too, though he suspected she was just as happy to see the dog. But Christopher certainly didn't want him back. And as for his wife, she was always harassed and distracted.

But he couldn't stay any longer.

'Please,' said Mrs Turner, fetching his hat and coat, 'do give your wife my regards. Once, when old Dr Hughes was ill, she came to see me instead. And she was terribly good to me.'

'She's an excellent nurse.'

'She's much more than that. She made me laugh.'

Downes heard the reproach and, he acknowledged, it was deserved. His wife used to have a lovely sense of humour, but that amongst so much else had been lost.

He shook Mrs Turner's hand warmly, saying he would make a point of passing on her good wishes. And I will not, he told himself, get annoyed with yet another charred meal. Jane was doing her best. This evening he'd actually enjoyed himself and he could do so again. They all could. Then, with as much of a spring as his leg would allow, he stepped out into the clear April evening and drove home.

12

ALICE FLICKED THROUGH A weighty history of the Crimean War, gilt-edged and leather-bound, and put it in the 'To Sell' box. A manual of seamanship fell apart and she slung that into the rubbish, along with a mildewy book about muskets. When the Canadians took over, the brigadier had chosen the library as his private quarters and, under his eye, the hundreds of books, the watercolours from Nepal, the collection of Chinese hand-painted ginger pots – an obsession of Stephen's grandfather – had all survived pretty much unscathed. But even though this room had been regularly cleaned, years of dust had seeped into the papers and the stale smell gave her a sinking feeling . . .

Enough! She pulled the curtains to stop the faded paintings fading yet more, killed two clothes moths, then shut the door behind her. Wondering whether she could be bothered to heat up some water to wash the dust out of her hair, she spotted something glittering down where the skirting board had split and picked up a military brass button, embossed with a maple leaf.

It was oddly pretty, but no one needed it now. The Canadians had long gone home, their job done – something to be immensely grateful for. And she was, but the irony was that when the Canadians were here, she'd never known the house more alive.

The memory made her pause and in the empty hall she began moving to a tune in her head. The soldiers would hold dances in the old servants' hall and one of the colonels had been a wonderful dancer. He'd singled her out and taught her the rumba and she'd imagined teaching Stephen because it was so soothing swaying your hips to those rhythms, as if by dancing you could forget how short life is and glimpse a harmony amongst the madness of men. And it was fun.

Fun? That was a word she'd long forgotten. No, she thought, heading up the main staircase to her bedroom to change, the problem isn't the house dying around us. It's the people in it. Me. Stephen.

Mrs Green would bemoan the Canadians' heavy boots ruining the parquet floor, the thumping of the grand piano amidst rowdy singing and laughter. But they made her smile when they called out, 'Great legs, babe! What you doin' tonight?' as she raced past on her bicycle. These were men going off to war, but their cheeky cheeriness was a reminder that, whatever hell you were in, you had to believe in better times ahead. Always life after death. Some basic drives and calls to living that could never be extinguished.

She hesitated, looking out from her bedroom window at the lake shuddering in the breeze, her mind straying to that colonel. He'd liked her. He was lonely. And so was she.

I could have . . . she mused.

He could have.

She'd known nothing of the colonel's mind. They barely spoke except about where she should place her feet, but with his arm around her waist, her face close to his chest, her body, with perfect instinct, anticipated exactly how he would move. And I followed, she thought, turning, dipping, folding into him.

She groaned inwardly. That desperation for a man, when desire claws away at your insides: she knew it. But I also know, she thought, what it is to have that longing met, what an extraordinary gift men and women have been given with their bodies. Whereas some, she reminded herself, pulling on her old gardening slacks, never know. For all their years they lie alone, unable to stretch out their hand to hold another's, never knowing such power over a man, such defencelessness in his arms.

But now she had seeds to sow, plants to water and, despite the wind, conditions were perfect: a fine drizzle falling, the earth lying soft and open, hungry with the penetrating light of spring. But if she could just be near Stephen. If she could just . . .

And, suddenly, instead of heading outside, she was racing down to his study.

'Stephen!'

There was no response and she flung open the door. The draught hit her immediately. His study was in the Georgian part of the house, with the original enormous sash windows and he'd left all five open. She walked in to shut them. The first closed easily, but the second wouldn't budge. She bashed at the warped frame, trying to ease it, when suddenly it shot down like a guillotine and she had to leap back as a loose pane fell out.

Damn! Damn! She grabbed a couple of old newspapers stacked by the fire to wrap up the shattered glass, but then her attention was caught. In the grate, amongst the remains of a fire, were some charred scraps of paper on which she recognised her husband's neat, slanted script.

Instinctively, she checked behind her – there was no one about – then, with the big iron tongs, she tried to salvage the burnt fragments. But the paper disintegrated. She licked her fingers, put her hand into the hot ashes and rescued what was definitely a draft of a poem. The heat had scorched the ink so it was too faded to read properly. Besides, it was in French. Cursing her ignorance, she could only make out the odd word: *tempête* – storm; *vent* – wind; *l'arbre* – tree.

Again she reached into the smouldering cinders and extracted another scrap of paper.

There were frequent uses of *elle*. But she couldn't understand the context. Who was this *elle*? This *she*? Me? wondered Alice. Another woman? Then three words leapt out: *Elle doit mourir*. Even with her French she could translate *Elle doit mourir*: she has to die.

'What the hell are you doing?'

Alice spun round. Stephen was looming above her and for a moment she was too shocked to speak.

'I . . . I . . .' she stammered, staggering to her feet. 'I only came in to close the windows. There's such a draught. Then I saw this and I . . .'

He was already at the door.

'Get out,' he said, holding it wide open.

She crossed the room to him, then clasped one hand round the door frame to hold herself steady. She felt he was warning her not to speak. But if she lost her nerve, there'd be no forgetting: *Elle doit mourir*.

'Who . . . ?' she began, conscious of his body tensing as if he was steeling himself for a blow. Or to land one. 'You'd written *Elle doit mourir* . . . who . . . ?'

The door slammed shut on her fingers. She was so stunned by the pain she wasn't sure how it had happened but it was open again immediately and Stephen was holding her hand, turning it over, telling her to stretch out her fingers, wiping the blood with his handkerchief.

And all the while she felt a lurching sickness as her stomach contracted at the horror of what he had done. To her. His wife. And she was about to retch with pain when his foot swung out.

This time her instincts were quicker. She leapt back to protect herself.

Then she realised: his kick wasn't directed at her. He had put his foot in the door to stop it from slamming again.

'It was the draught,' he was saying, as if reading her thoughts.

'Oh, Stephen!' she gasped, appalled at the violence she'd suspected him of. And so too, it seemed, was he.

'Run your hand under the cold tap,' he muttered, slumping into his armchair. 'It'll reduce the swelling.' Then he assumed his usual attitude, eyes closed, head resting back, jaw tight, unapproachable.

13

THE CLOCK IN THE estate office said two minutes to nine which meant, Stephen Rayne calculated, it was exactly seven months, four days, twenty-one hours and fifty-eight minutes since he'd last killed anyone. He leant over in the leather chair his great-grandfather had brought back from India and tried to slow down his breathing. He would feel sick like this before jumping out of a plane and he ordered himself to get a grip. It was madness to feel such terror in his own home.

As a boy he would find his father in this same chair, behind this walnut desk, furiously shoring up defences to protect the failing estate, fighting to raise money as best he could so Stephen's elder brother, James, could inherit Oakbourne Hall in its entirety. But in February 1941 James was reported missing, presumed dead. Exactly what he was doing, or where, no one knew. Much the same as me, Stephen always assumed.

He glanced up at the large brown patch above the picture rail in the corner. Somehow his father had kept the damp at bay but God knows how even he could have fought off the damp and rot after paying out two lots of death duties.

The night his father was killed, Stephen had been with him. They were in the townhouse in Maida Vale and, with the heavy bombing, Stephen had been trying to persuade him to go back to Suffolk. But his father had shouted: 'I survived four years of them trying to kill me in the first bloody fiasco. I'm not letting them win now.'

Stephen had accused him of having a death-wish and his last words before slamming the front door and heading for the shelter of the Underground station were that his father's actions were, 'Bloody madness.'

Half an hour later a bomb dropped on the house.

At least, Stephen had told himself a hundred times, his father would have been killed outright, because God only knew how long it took for James to die. If Stephen had had to bet on which brother would survive the war, he'd have put his money on James, who looked more French, taking after their mother, dark-haired and olive-skinned. Whereas Stephen, with his father's fairness and blue eyes, struggled to pass unnoticed.

'Bloody madness,' Stephen repeated to himself. He needed to keep focused and not think about who had betrayed James and what those Gestapo bastards must have done to extract what they wanted to know.

He began pacing his father's office. Or rather, thought Stephen, *my* office now. Since his return he'd barely been in here. He straightened a picture of a hunting scene on the nicotine-stained walls, noticed the scratches on the door from his father's dogs.

Dogs.

Dogs were what had prompted this meeting. And, dead on time, at nine o'clock, there was a knock and Stephen opened the door to Bill Reynolds, the Oakbourne kennel man.

For generations, Oakbourne Hall had been a hunting estate. As a boy, Stephen had watched his father on his black heavyweight of a horse, his mother on a graceful chestnut mare, heading off with the hounds on crisp December mornings. But Stephen had decided to put an end to the hunting and this meant Bill Reynolds, who had worked for Stephen's family his entire life, except for two years from 1914 when he fought in France, would be out of a job.

Stephen extended his hand. 'Reynolds, please do come on in. It's good to see you.'

'And you too, sir.'

Stephen gave a thin smile, fully aware of how little he had actually seen of the men who worked on the estate. He'd done as little of the visiting and overseeing as he could get away with. His father and brother would have been appalled. His wife certainly was. Just that morning she'd angrily reminded him of his dereliction of duty in not visiting Jim Thompson, the farmhand who only had weeks to live.

Stephen gestured to Reynolds to sit down and, with the help of a knotted birch stick, Reynolds manoeuvred his maimed body across the room. He's still in pain, thought Stephen. A hip injury, he recalled, at Ypres, and which probably saved his life because he was sent home to recuperate and never returned to the front line.

Stephen's throat constricted, his mouth dry. He was about to fire this good, kindly man. As a boy, he would visit the kennels, play with the latest litter of puppies. Mrs Reynolds would always make a fuss of him, giving him milk from the goats they kept, cake, fruit. They were decent people, courageous and honest.

Get a grip, he insisted, yet again. Reynolds would survive this. This was far from the worst news of Reynolds's life.

Not prevaricating with pleasantries, Stephen launched in: 'As you know, the estate is far from what it was. And never will be. So I'm sorry, and I know this will be a blow as no one could have done a better job than you, but I'm closing down the kennels. I'm putting an end to the hunting here.'

Stephen made himself hold the gaze of the man's weary, bloodshot eyes. 'Rest assured,' he continued, 'your wages, rent, none of that will change. You will continue to be paid just as before.'

'I can't take money for not working.'

'You're not,' said Stephen. 'This is a thank you for all you've done here. Besides, you'll need to find good homes for all the dogs. I know I can leave that with you.'

'But, sir, there are ways of making the kennels pay. If it's about money?'

No, thought Stephen. It isn't about money. It's the dogs themselves. He knew all too vividly that with those blood-hounds on your heels, you were almost certainly done for. If you had to outrun a man, you stood a chance. But a dog on a scent could crash through thorny thickets, leap across chasms without twisting its ankles and tiring. So he'd not have them hungry for a kill on his land, baying and howling, hunting down their quarry until their teeth sank in.

'My mind is made up,' he said. 'The hounds have to go.' Stephen heard himself, the officer issuing a command. And Reynolds, not arguing, replied in kind.

'Yes, sir.' And with that he left.

Typical, thought Stephen. Typical of the cannon fodder of the last generation: just do as you're told and go to your death.

He lit a cigarette.

In this latest war he was responsible for deaths in Egypt, Libya, then Sicily and mainland Italy, and finally in France. He hadn't felt guilty, he hadn't felt proud. For a long while he had managed simply to accept the fact as the horror of war. If he'd sunk into morbidity he would not have been able to do his job. And if people like him hadn't done their jobs, God knows how much longer the killing would have gone on.

But now they were at peace. He stretched out his hands. You need never kill again, he told himself. But where was the consolation in that when he'd already killed so much?

He stubbed out his cigarette. He would also have to speak to the gamekeeper. He couldn't endure men beating the land to force out the pheasants, those stupid birds squawking in a flamboyant flurry of bronzed and golden feathers. Women and children too, bashing their sticks and yelling at the tops of their voices, driving the birds onto the guns in yet more orgies of slaughter.

He looked out over the un-pruned rose garden which his mother had planted – canary-yellow roses with purple tulips at their feet. During the war the squirrels had dug up the bulbs. His father had always tried to keep the squirrels out, shooting them from his bedroom window, his shotgun stashed behind the chintz curtains.

He wandered into the unlit corridor. Speaking to Mr Reynolds had forced his strained, exhausted nerves to engage and there was still a whole day and God knows how many more to get through. He slipped out through a side door, down the crumbling steps and over the uncut lawn. He glanced back at the house. The huge expanse of red brick seemed to loom up into the sky like a ship about to keel over and crush him as he hurried away to what was left of the woods. An old ash tree lay across the path and climbing over it he looked round once more at the boarded-up windows, the ivy flowering in triumph as it snaked round the drainpipes, grass sprouting in the uncleared gutters. The house has also given up, he thought, walking fast to still himself into detachment and, before long, he could see the sea gleaming beyond the marshes.

He'd played here as a boy and knew all the paths through the slippery mud and treacherous ditches. There's a *maquis* here too, he thought, amongst the reeds, places to plot and to hide. You didn't have to travel far to find yourself on the edge of civilisation. Only the other day his wife had wittered on to the vicar about wild flowers growing up amongst the ruins where London had been blitzed. As if that was something to marvel at. Because there wouldn't just be flowers. There'd be looting and stealing, the woman thrown on her back, the knife slipped between the ribs. It didn't take much for everyone to descend into barbarity.

He made his way down to the river, to the spot where he used to catch minnows. In school holidays, after his mother died, he'd retreat here, soothed by the slow passage of water and the smell of the earth mingling with the salty tang coming off the sea. Again and again in the war, and at the strangest times – even when he'd been in Egypt, parched and scorched in a desert landscape that could not have been more different, or holed up in a medieval prison outside Paris, reeking of centuries of torture – his mind would return to this rain-rinsed greenness. These schoolboy memories had come to represent the very idea of peace. Though now he wondered whether, as a child, he'd actually known it was peace and that he was only able to recognise it in recollection.

Whatever, peace now was impossible for him, even here. And almost as if a malign fate was proving a point, he suddenly sensed hidden eyes following his every move and that one face that was forever inescapable, hovering always on the edge of his vision. He glanced round, seeking out what was lurking in the undergrowth. Nothing? But then his keen eyesight picked out a movement in a clump of birch trees.

Alice.

Would there be no end to her questions? She was a good quarter of a mile away so he could walk on, pretending he hadn't seen her.

But it was too late. She was running towards him, her slim legs moving with that quicksilver grace of hers. He recalled how his father had dismissed her as 'a bit of a blue-stocking' and he'd smiled, thinking of how she danced.

'Stephen! Stop! Please! I've just seen Mr Reynolds. What's going on?'

He looked at her as a stranger might. Slight with curling blonde hair and unusually green eyes, tired and angry, but with all her fierce passion and intelligence. The sort of woman any man would want. As he once had.

'I'm ending the hunting here,' he said, once she'd caught up with him.

'But why?'

'You're not the slightest bit interested.'

'It's not got anything to do with me!'

'It's the way of the future.'

He saw the flash of hope in her eyes, that he might, at last, be thinking ahead. She'd retained an optimism that all their dreams might still come true, that they'd make a go of the house, have children. Children? Dear God! He'd have to have it out with her soon. Tell her no way was he bringing children into this world. 'And I'm stopping the shooting.'

'But Stephen!'

'You hate shooting.'

With that, she turned on him: 'Don't you dare pretend this is about me.' He'd never known her so angry – her eyes blazing, her voice raised.

'I'll pay Reynolds as usual.'

'What with? There's no money. And even if there was, it's not about money. Reynolds lost more than his good leg in France. He needs a reason to get up in the mornings. And to take that from him is downright cruel!' She was almost choking with fury and he watched her, oddly indifferent. 'You should know that!' she cried. 'In the past, you'd have realised how much he needs his work.'

In the past he wouldn't lose his mind over baying dogs.

He said: 'Reynolds has got his home, his wages. His wife.'

'His wife?' she echoed and with that her shoulders slumped, and she rubbed her gloved hand, as if easing away pain.

'How are the bruises?' he asked. 'From the door – the other day?'

'Perfectly all right.' That was a lie, he was in no doubt. 'Stephen,' she sighed, *you* have your wife too. I'm sorry I shouted, but sometimes I don't recognise you and how can I help if you don't tell me anything? In the war, I know, you couldn't. But now?' She was at it again with her damned questions. 'I just wish you'd tell me.'

Tell me.

He'd heard those same words before.

86

Dites moi – in the clipped coarse French of the occupying enemy.

Sag es mir – once they realised who he was and knew he spoke German.

He hadn't told then. What a hero. Pain had hammered in, sending him into darkness and the release of oblivion. They had gone that bit too far and this was his good fortune. Who knows what he'd have given away once he came round. But Benoit had come to his rescue, lifting him over his shoulders and carrying him out of that underground hell into the waiting car.

No, there was nothing he'd tell his wife. Because he certainly wasn't going to tell her pretty-pretty fibs. That he'd only killed because he had no choice. That he'd never taken a life unnecessarily.

He ground the heel of his boot into the earth then turned his back on her. Those fairy tales hit the dust long, long ago.

14

DR DOWNES BRUSHED ASIDE the thanks of the old fisherman's wife as she twisted her wedding ring embedded into swollen rheumatic joints. Her husband had had a stroke last year, leaving him paralysed down his right side and a second stroke that morning. Now he lay picking at loose threads on the patchwork bedspread. There was nothing Downes could do for him but, ducking his head under the cottage's low lintel, he promised to call in again first thing tomorrow.

He stood on the quay looking across the estuary to the North Sea where the dying man had spent his life. A group of young lads, about his son's age, full of life, were kicking a football. Yet death lay just yards away. Tonight it bided its time in that wooden bed. But tomorrow? Under the thin ice of routine and familiarity which could crack at any second, there was always, always the descent into darkness.

Normally, Downes had the discipline to suppress such musings. But his Saturday-morning rounds had gone on long into the afternoon and he was tired and his stump hurt like hell.

He glanced back at the boys. He wished his son was out playing football on a spring weekend. Some exercise would do you good, he'd said to Christopher at breakfast, go out with lads your own age. The wrong thing to say, of course. Jane had dropped a ton of bricks on him, telling him to let Christopher be and reminding him that he'd never had many friends as a child.

But Downes hoped Christopher wouldn't be like him but one of those sociable chaps, at ease with others. Saddened by his son's loneliness, he drove on to his next appointment, a baby with croup whose family lived in a derelict boat a mile up the coast.

Fifteen minutes later he was stooping in a cramped cabin, the wind rattling the tin chimney.

'Keep giving him plenty of fluids,' he said to the baby's mother, speaking as gently as possible given the noise of two other tiny children fighting at her feet.

In this enclosed space they would probably catch croup too. Good hygiene stopped its spread, like so much, he sighed, taking in the dirty bowl, the dirty dishcloth, the dirty clothes, the dirty hands. Then, conscious the exhausted woman was fully aware he was assessing her home, he said, 'If his cough gets any worse you really must send for me.'

The child wasn't sick enough to go to hospital. But a baby this young in such damp squalor could quickly deteriorate.

'It doesn't matter what time it is,' he pressed again as he left. 'Even if it's four in the morning.'

He knew some GPs viewed infections as a normal part of life. They led to an end that was inescapable for everyone. But Downes couldn't and wouldn't adopt that placid, genial acceptance.

He thrust the car into gear, jolting forwards, his head aching from that oppressive cabin and the pity and rage that poverty always evoked in him.

At least, he thought, driving past the field earmarked for the new council estate, the next generation would escape such appalling insanitary conditions. And he cursed all those who, from the luxury of their clean, warm houses, were being so snooty about the 'cardboard boxes' – as they were unkindly dubbed – springing up on the edge of their pretty village.

He drove down the sandy estate track to Jim Thompson's cottage, now cursing Stephen Rayne for not mending the pot holes ruining the suspension of his car and cursing anyone else he could think of as Jim was another patient for whom – apart from pain relief – he could do nothing.

Pulling up outside, he saw Mrs Thompson walking down the path to the privy at the end of the garden. He waited discreetly in his car. In the new houses the lavatories, thank God, should be inside.

It turned out Mrs Thompson already had a visitor – Mrs Reynolds, the kennel man's wife. And she was in tears. Sir Stephen, she informed Downes, had put a stop to the hunting on the estate so her husband would be out of a job and forced into retirement.

'He loves those dogs,' Mrs Reynolds was saying. 'Taking them from him is like taking his life.'

Downes made sympathetic noises. But he was torn. He found hunting utterly repellent – a brutal legacy of a feudal hierarchy that should have long been abolished – but the cavalier fashion in which the squire had deprived a man of his work represented everything he hated about a world where the select few exercised such power over their fellow man. And Stephen Rayne should have realised a man like Reynolds, who'd endured the horror of the trenches, needed to keep occupied so he might stop remembering. Unless of course, whatever the gossip, Stephen Rayne's knowledge of war was actually confined to sitting behind a desk at Whitehall.

'Sir Stephen's not a patch on his father,' continued Mrs Reynolds. 'His father would have kept the kennels going, come hell or high water.'

'And his father,' said Mrs Thompson, pouring Downes a cup of tea from the big brown pot, 'would have been to visit Jim. Shown some respect after all those years of service.'

The last thing Downes would want on his death bed was a visit from some lord of the manor, but he nodded his head in shared anger, drinking his tepid treacly tea. Then there was a knock at the door.

'Come in!' called Mrs Thompson.

Speak of the devil, thought Downes as the door opened and Mrs Thompson was leaping up, crying: 'Sir Stephen! Oh do, do come in!'

Mrs Reynolds was also on her feet, her hand flying to her hair, then smoothing her skirt and smiling as Stephen was saying how very lovely it was to see her too.

'Do please let me take your coat,' said Mrs Thompson, her voice suddenly mimicking her landlord's educated vowels. For one appalled moment, Downes thought the women were going to drop into curtseys. 'I don't know if you've met but, Sir Stephen, this is Dr Downes.'

Downes grunted a greeting.

'I fear I've come at a bad time,' said Stephen. 'I'd hoped to see your husband, but if the doctor's here—'

'Please stay!' insisted Mrs Thompson, giving him her chair nearest the fire. 'Have some tea!'

91

The presence of the man whom they'd just been maligning had transformed the two old women. Mrs Thompson was fussing about making fresh tea and Mrs Reynolds was enquiring after Lady Rayne – 'very well, thank you' – while on Stephen's face was the gracious smile Downes had seen on certain officers. They were popular with the privates, full of bonhomie and fake concern. Yet they ran at the first hint of danger, making sure of their places on the boats at Dunkirk and leaving young working-class boys to die or waste away in POW camps.

'I haven't done any baking lately,' Mrs Thompson was saying. 'But if I'd known you were coming . . .'

'I'd have hated you to have gone to any trouble,' said Stephen, as Mrs Thompson whisked the brown teapot off the table, then bent down and stretched into the back of a cupboard to retrieve another, ornately patterned in gold and blue.

Jesus wept! Downes groaned to himself as the best china appeared. He muttered that he was off to see his patient.

Upstairs, Jim Thompson also seemed to have acquired a new lease of life.

'I knew the squire would visit,' he said. 'I knew it. After working here all these years for his father and his father before that . . .'

And he launched into a story about how during the Great War he, along with other young men in the neighbourhood, was given leave to return home to help with the harvest and Sir Stephen's grandfather laid on an enormous dinner and dance on the day the crops had all been brought in.

And, next morning, after your slap-up supper, thought Downes, you were shipped back to the front to be slaughtered.

Downes had such respect for how hard the men and women in his care worked. Yet they depressed him. Why couldn't they see how they were being patronised? That their desperation to impress these selfish snobs colluded in a system that oppressed them? And, looking out of the window, all he could see were muddy fields keeping everyone stuck in their place, and he felt homesick for London. You wouldn't find such deference around the docks.

'Sir Stephen was always known for being a lovely boy – bookish and quiet, not like his father,' Jim Thompson was saying. 'But I won't say a word against the old squire. He was a true gentleman.'

Downes couldn't stomach any more. He returned downstairs, where Stephen was still being fawned over by the two women basking in his easy charm. Charm, thought Downes, costs nothing. No sacrifice, no effort, no risk.

Stephen smiled at Downes and put down his cup of fresh tea – not the over-brewed tar I had, thought Downes, furious now for caring about the bloody tea. But he'd come here to comfort and reassure and it was this suave toff who was making the people he leeched off feel better.

'Here you are, Doctor,' said Stephen, drawing up a chair for him.

'I can't sit and chat. I've got patients to look after.'

Limping across the kitchen, Downes caught Stephen glancing at his leg. Then Stephen sprang up and opened the door for him, and the indignity of pity from this man was too much.

'May I,' said Downes, 'have a quick word.' He couldn't bring himself to say *Sir* Stephen. 'In private?'

There was a flicker of surprise on Stephen's face, but he followed Downes outside. They stood on the path beside the newly dug potato patch and into Stephen's slight smile Downes read boredom, disdain. He hates being here, thought Downes. He hates pretending he gives a damn. He can't wait to get back to his bloody great mansion.

Downes launched in: 'Before you turned up, Mrs Reynolds was crying because you've done her husband out of a job. Did you not think that a man like Bill Reynolds, in constant pain – not just physical, I'm sure, given what he's seen – might need to work for his peace of mind? But no! You make decisions without thinking through the consequences, with no discussion, no effort to understand. You've not got a bloody clue. And if you have, that makes you even worse, not giving a damn about the suffering you cause.'

Downes had wiped the smile off Stephen's face. He just stared ahead as if he couldn't be bothered to listen.

'Thank God,' railed Downes, 'we're going to see the back of people like you. You got the shock of your life when Churchill was thrown out and now, at last, we've got a Labour government and Attlee and Bevan will tax you lot to the hilt – and not before time.'

Downes saw the slight shrug of Stephen's shoulders.

'Tell me,' he continued, 'what gives you the right to play God?'

The patrician detachment disappeared in a flash and Stephen was stepping towards him as if he was going to strike back with his fists.

I've touched a raw nerve there, thought a startled Downes. What did I say?

But, with a savage delight that he'd really hit home, Downes jutted out his jaw. Go on, he thought, hit me. I know you want to.

But instead Stephen spoke so quietly Downes strained to hear: 'My relations with the people on my estate are between them and me. I'm certainly not discussing them with you. Good day, Doctor.'

And in a dozen strides, dodging the puddles with a sprightliness Downes could only yearn for, Stephen was back inside the cottage and Downes was left lumbering to his car, hatred pumping through him like poison.

15

As he wished his small Evensong congregation good-night, George Ivens was aware of Alice Rayne waiting in the watery spring twilight. Not until everyone had departed did she step forwards, exclaiming: 'Your voice! It's so beautiful I half-expected angels to start clapping and take flight.'

Blood rose to his face at the compliment and he felt an unfamiliar desire to show off, to tell her he'd sung solos in the St Matthew Passion, Faure's Requiem, Messiah. But he just mumbled, 'A lot of it's practice.'

'If only! You should hear me sing. People leave the house. Were you a choirboy and all that?'

'All that,' he smiled.

'Well, it was truly wonderful,' she smiled back. 'Normally, as you know, we don't come to this service.'

'How is Sir Stephen?' he asked, wondering what had brought her here. The lovely spring evening? Possibly. A spiritual longing for Evensong? He doubted it.

'Very well. But I'm so glad you're better. But are you? Really better?'

'Absolutely!' He wasn't going into the state of his health.

'Then we must rearrange you coming to see the garden,' she said. 'How about Thursday at three?'

'Perfect.'

He didn't want her to rush off but how did men like him talk to women like her? Her earrings, green stones that accentuated the colour of her eyes, probably cost the sort of money that could feed a family for a month.

'I'll see you then,' she said, but instead of turning and leaving, she leant back against the stone wall, holding him in silent appraisal.

Suddenly she shivered, and he said, 'The other night you told me you'd got used to the cold.'

'I have.' Then she met his eyes, saying, 'Churches have this chilling effect on me, just making me aware of time passing, of death, with all those memorials, hammering it home that things are lost forever. I know your faith makes you see death differently. And I hope you're right.' With that she smiled at him kindly, like a child, he thought, someone she's trying to protect. 'Sorry,' she said, 'you think I'm being condescending.'

'No!' She raised her eyebrows in disbelief. 'Well, yes,' he conceded, smiling. 'But no matter, I can take it.'

And she laughed. 'It's just I sit in that pew where Stephen's brother and father once sat, along with generations before them and, although I'm not dead, all I can think of is the loss, the lovely times that have gone for me too. Like – I don't know – watching my father pour himself a Scotch then just sit and chat. Never to return, like all those other dead people remembered on the walls and that ghastly Victorian thing.' She grimaced at a statue of a couple with ruffs round their necks like Elizabethans, stretched out on a tomb. 'Lying together, but dead to each other, dead to the world.'

'But death is only one side of the story.'

'Thanks to a sacrifice,' she retorted, her eyes flying to Christ on the cross. 'How many have to die for God to be

97

bought off? Hasn't there been enough killing this century? Or does He want even more from us? I know you'd say I'll meet people I love again.'

'I would, but . . .' He was wary of appearing the gauche young clergyman, parroting a fairy tale of happy endings, turning what for him were the profoundest truths into platitudes.

'But?' she echoed. An imperiousness in her voice made him bridle, as if he was a wayward gamekeeper having to explain to the lady of the manor why there was a shortage of pheasants. But then her fingers went nervously to her throat. And the awkward gesture served as a reminder from an all-seeing God. This woman is sad and scared. She needs your help.

'When I look at Christ on the cross I don't just see His sacrifice,' he said. 'I see Him actively choosing suffering – what we all do our best to avoid – to show that, despite enduring some of the very worst of human experience, we will be all right. More than all right. Because God is always with us.'

He stopped and waited for her to speak. Eventually she said, 'I wish I believed you.'

He gestured towards the dusk, a medley of gentle greens. 'But you can be certain, whatever happens next, when we die, it won't be like this. Look at that.' He pointed up at a large bird wheeling and wailing overhead, hunting for its next meal. 'Some creature will die pretty soon – either one will be eaten or one will starve. Aren't you every bit as aware of death out here as in church? And how death is transformed into life?'

'It's a buzzard,' she said. 'Did you know, buzzards don't usually get up till about nine o'clock? It's because they need to wait until the air heats up to ride the warm currents, soaring and circling for miles.'

He pressed on, refusing to be distracted. 'You said the other day you liked winter. But winter's about death, whereas this . . .' For him, primroses and violets were starring the graves, glowing brighter than enamel after the afternoon rain. 'I've never known a spring in the country and I don't think I've ever seen anything more wonderful.'

'But I look at all this virginal "youngness" and all I can see is the incredible effort required to keep going in a battle for survival.'

'A battle that's won!'

'By some, I suppose.'

'Yes,' he insisted.

Her hand went to her throat again. But then she changed tack and said with such calculated brightness he wondered if he was about to hear a speech she'd delivered before: 'Here, in summer, we've so many holiday-makers and people with their "country retreats", when I watch them deserting the place in winter because it's cold and bare, it makes me think of a lover giving up on his mistress once she's starting to lose her charms – her obvious ones.'

'Is that what you tell your visitors?'

'You think I'm being deliberately perverse?'

'Maybe a tad.'

With that she laughed again, throwing back her head, and he felt a pathetic glow of triumph.

'But seriously,' she went on, 'anyone can love summer. I used to. I'd count the days till it started getting light and warm again. And in summer sometimes I'd think I'd found perfection. But now – oh, I don't know.'

'To rise to all that perfection feels impossible?' he suggested.

She gave him another of those appraising looks. 'Exactly,' she said.

'So winter's easier?'

'Much easier,' she replied after a while.

'But that means in winter we only half-live. I know that can feel safe. And, dear God, do we need some safety. But to live as fully as we can, that's what we're here for. Otherwise we can end up in Purgatory, too scared to do anything about it. So we just accept it and sink into lethargy.'

He paused, worried he was preaching too much. But no, there was an interrogative spark in her eyes.

'We compromise,' he continued, 'make excuses for ourselves and for others, and sometimes that's all we can do, endure and shut down like those fainting barn owls you told me about.' He smiled. But the seriousness of her expression made him say: 'The tragedy, I think, is to give up, to shrivel away instead of daring to discover something better. And bigger. Something that breaks you out of your limitations.'

She was looking up at him for more. He'd wanted her attention but now he had it he felt oddly unsure of his ground. Was this why she'd come to Evensong? To find her way out of some private hell?

'But the problems people face . . .' He trailed off.

The hells people found themselves in were infinite, and so often once he got down to the specifics of people's lives he felt all the impossibility of being what he was supposed to be – a minister of Christ. Because how on earth could he say death was only one side of the story when these last few years there had been so many agonising deaths? Would Christ have done as He commanded and turned the other cheek to the Nazis? Christ preached forgiveness but every day, he'd look at Mrs Turner, his landlady paralysed in grief, and wonder how she could possibly forgive the Messerschmitt pilot who'd inflicted such an agonising death on her only begotten son, burning him alive somewhere over Germany. The words were easy but their practice felt the province of angels, not a mediocre human being like himself. Sometimes he believed all he had ever achieved in his work was to keep sorrow company.

He was aware of a gentle pressure on his arm, as if she'd realised he was struggling.

'Mr Ivens?' He looked at her hand in its shabby suede glove. 'I know,' she said, 'what you mean about winter lasting forever. It's all too tempting to bury yourself away when things are too difficult. A living death can be all right, people find. We get by. And however much you might want to help people, you can't a lot of the time, particularly when it comes to the private hells people find themselves in, that no one talks about.

'But,' she hastened on, 'I've not told you what I love most about winter. The point is, it's not all death. Even before Christmas, in the woods, if I pull back the beech leaves I can find the tiny green shoots of snowdrops. Sometimes as early as November. It's all stirring away and alive, you just can't see it. Isn't that what your faith tells you?'

He nodded, ashamed of himself. A moment ago he'd been taking umbrage at the amiable arrogance of the English upper classes. But, right now, Lady Rayne was the one helping him.

'Next winter – if you've not given up on us all by then – I'll show you. And this is not some line I spin to city-dwellers.

101

I appreciate you see through me.' She grinned. 'And your church. You know what I love about it?'

She pointed inside to a small creamy-white statue of Noah, beseeching the returning dove.

'That's so incredibly beautiful, so hopeful.'

From the church door, Ivens could see in the shadows the stranded man, desperate and awestruck.

'I think,' he said tentatively, 'Noah's like us, in 1946. Surviving the deluge, with no idea what's next, only that there's a new world ahead. But he can't see it.'

'Oh!' She grasped his hand, her grip surprisingly strong, he noticed, for someone so slight. 'I'd never thought of Noah like that! Thank you! I love him all the more now!'

Then, letting go, she said, 'In your kind note, you wrote you liked the tomato plant I sent you. When you come to tea – if you're interested – I can show you some seedlings I'm sort of experimenting with – nothing serious.'

'Experimenting?'

'Hybridising the tomatoes. Seeing what I can come up with. If you're walking home now I could explain on the way.' And her hand went to her neck again as she added quickly, 'If you'd like. I don't want to bore you.'

'You wouldn't! This—' This, he thought, is the most interesting conversation I've had in so long. 'This evening,' he said, 'I'm afraid I'm going in the other direction. To the Downes's. They've invited me to dinner.'

At once she resumed her brave brightness. 'How lovely!'

Then she looked up as a flock of starlings rose up from a clump of trees, swirling higher and higher, an enormous ribbon blowing and turning in the wind, then settling back down, out of sight amongst some farm buildings.

'Who knows why they do this,' she said. 'One breaks free and then the others follow. Do you ever wonder how that feels?'

And next thing she was heading out of the graveyard, wishing him a delightful time.

 16

JANE DOWNES STOOD AT the back door about to lock up
for the night. George Ivens had stayed late after a dinner of
disgusting meat loaf which somehow hadn't tasted as disgusting
as usual, and they'd learned he'd spent most of his life just
half a mile from where Jonathan had also grown up and they'd
laughed and chatted and played chess and she'd felt like an
anxious mother – again – hoping her husband might have
found a friend. With someone to talk to and play chess
with – please God, as she hated the game – he might not feel
so out of place in what he kept calling 'this feudal backwater'.

Yet the vicar was not a well man and she knew just how
much damage rheumatic fever could do. Even a mild infection could kill him.

But enjoy tonight, she told herself, gazing up at the stars
which somehow seemed unusually close, as if beckoning her
to reach out, proclaiming that deep really could call unto
deep. Before the child cries and the door slams shut, drink
in the peace, the inky blackness, the glorious galaxies urging
you to live wildly and passionately . . .

'Jane!' Shouting like that, Jonathan would wake Juliet
and Christopher. 'Would you bring me up a glass of water?'

She hurried in and upstairs. Light was coming from under
Eleanor's door.

Of late, she'd become nervous of her elder daughter, her son too. When Jonathan was away, she'd mucked in with the children, let them share her bed. They'd had picnics by the fire rather than dinner at the table, avoiding as much argument as possible because their blacked-out, rationed childhoods were already torn with too much conflict.

Jane knocked softly and found Eleanor in bed, reading her chemistry textbook, her knees pulled up, as if making herself as small as possible. Jane's heart lurched. During the Blitz in London, they would shelter in the basement, Juliet and Christopher in her arms, but Eleanor, twelve at the time, would crouch in the corner, just like this, burying herself in a book, often chanting the words out loud as if reciting a rosary that might keep her safe.

'Eleanor darling, it's almost midnight.'

Eleanor actually smiled. 'I've just finished, though I'll have to get up early tomorrow to go over it again.'

'I'm sure you'll be good enough.'

'How can you possibly be sure of that?'

'Because, my darling, you're clever.'

'No amount of cleverness will pass an exam on catalysts if I've not actually learned the stuff.'

But Eleanor closed her book and Jane braced herself as her daughter began positioning the book exactly parallel with the edges of her bedside table, shifting it a quarter of an inch one way, then another. Since the bombing, for Eleanor everything had to be in perfect order – as if there could be such a thing – and looking round at her child's pathetic attempt to control the uncontrollable, the precisely-folded clothes, the bed made to nursing standards, Jane could have wept.

Instead she sat on the bed, saying, 'Would you like me to brush your hair for you?'

'Please, it gets so knotted in the wind.'

She began brushing, starting at the ends, gently working her way up. 'I always wanted hair like yours,' said Jane.

'You always say that.'

'It's true. You've your father's lovely thick fair hair.'

'Not that he's blond anymore.'

'No.' We've all gone grey, thought Jane. 'Grandma always used to say I should dye mine.'

'Back to red?'

'Well, the colour it was. There's some of the original left. Somewhere.'

'Mum, you look great for your age.'

Jane produced a smile, and smoothed her daughter's hair back from her long oval face. 'My beautiful girl.'

'Hardly. Not with these spots.'

'They'll go.'

'You always say that too,' muttered Eleanor. 'But they don't.'

'You can borrow my makeup if you like, what's left of it.'

Eleanor pulled away. 'Why? Are you saying I need it?'

'No!' cried Jane. 'Just that you might like to experiment. That's all.' To play around, she thought, have fun.

She'd see girls from Eleanor's school, faces made up to a template, gaggles of second- and third-rate Veronica Lakes. But her daughter never even put on lipstick. She kept to her room, studying, her face bare. Sitting here in worn-out Viyella pyjamas, she again looked twelve.

Once, thought Jane, I might have said there's plenty of time for makeup, for going out, for boys. But war has changed that. When what little time there is could be snatched from you so cruelly there seemed no time at all. Of course she wanted Eleanor to become a doctor. To be a pioneer in this new generation of women medics. To find fulfilment in using her considerable intellect. Of course!

But to find love too.

Possibly love more than anything.

Go out and live wildly and passionately, the night cried. But how? She pictured Eleanor's contemporaries, freezing with their bare legs and flimsy coats as they waited for the bus to ferry them to an evening out. Were they living wildly and passionately? She doubted it. In no time they'd be stuck in the domestic dungeon with floors crying out to be swept, children crying out for comfort, the husband too.

In her own room Jonathan was sitting on the bed, unstrapping his leg.

'Thanks,' he said, as she gave him the glass of water. She watched the way his hand shook as he took it. 'Don't look so worried.'

'Why won't you see a specialist?'

'How would that help?'

'You might learn what the problem is.'

'Whatever it is, you know as well as I do it's hopeless.'

He was right. The trauma of the last six years could explain his trembling hand and the best cure for that was as peaceful a life as possible. Or, as her medical mind knew all too well, it could be any number of monstrous neurological conditions and nothing could help him there.

'Isn't the vicar an interesting chap?' she said, to change the subject.

'Yes!'

'How was the chess?'

He sighed. 'I beat him.' She wasn't surprised.

'Easily?'

'Well, actually,' he said, perking up, 'no. In fact, he could be rather good. With time . . .'

But time was what the vicar did not have.

'Can anything be done for him?' she asked.

'I doubt it. But I'm going to look into it. There's so much new research I've missed out on. But what about you? I can tell you're fretting. It's not Christopher again, is it?'

Christopher was saying less and less, but if she ever tried to ask him how he was, she was met with more stony silence.

She said, 'Eleanor's only just finished her homework.'

'So? I used to work all night.'

'I worry she's too sensitive to be a doctor, too much of a perfectionist. How's she going to cope when she can't save people? Or makes a mistake and the consequences are fatal?'

'She'll cope the way we all do.'

'But some people manage failure better than others.'

'You used,' he said, 'to complain half the idiots we worked with should be geologists because they'd got the empathy of rocks. And now your daughter, with immense feeling for others, is going to be a doctor, and if she's an ounce of your ability she'll be a great one.'

Hot tears began pricking the backs of her eyes because if it hadn't, she thought, been for my so-called 'ability', Eleanor might still be that easy-going girl she'd been before the war.

'Let's face it,' he was going on, 'you were the best nurse in that hospital – every bit as good as the doctors – better usually.'

Stop! she wanted to yell. Hearing his compliments hurt as if he was ripping bandages off raw wounds.

'Weren't you?' said Jonathan.

She snapped, 'This is about Eleanor, and I'm worried she's not tough enough – emotionally.'

'Your worrying only makes it worse.'

'Have you actually noticed the state of her room?'

'Yes! And imagine all the mothers who'd envy you with a daughter they don't have to clear up after, who works so incredibly hard. Honestly, Jane!'

You don't understand, she wanted to protest. Eleanor's tidiness is almost pathological. And it's my fault, she cried inwardly, as he gave a great groan, then rubbed the stump of his leg. And now, she thought, watching him fall back on to the bed, you're avoiding talking about Eleanor and we're back on the subject of your damned leg.

She tried to sound sympathetic: 'Are you in a lot of pain?'

'I'm always in pain. Now just stop worrying!'

Stop worrying?

She could kick him as he yawned loudly, rolled onto his side and promptly fell asleep.

She couldn't stop worrying, because the time it had really mattered, in September 1940, she had not worried enough.

She should have left London before the Blitz even started. She should have listened to the warnings – from everyone from the government to her mother – to evacuate to the countryside. She should . . .

Jane put her head under the pillow to shut out the noise of her husband snoring. But nothing could shut out the knowledge of how she had risked her children's lives. If she'd come to live in Oakbourne sooner they wouldn't have

109

been bombed. Her son might not scream in terror in his sleep and Eleanor might not think the roof was about to cave in – again – if her textbooks weren't in parallel lines, if she didn't get one hundred per cent in every damned test.

She heard Christopher cry out. She wanted to go to him, but, at fifteen, the last thing he would want was his mother rushing to his bedside.

Now she was wide awake. She got up and stood by the window, stroking one hand over the other. Her husband began grinding his teeth. She'd never told him her secret – the selfish reason she'd stayed in London. If she couldn't forgive herself, how could he?

 17

STEPHEN SQUINTED AS HE stepped out into the glittering spring afternoon. His head was aching but he'd shaved, then forced himself out of the gloom of the attic. Heading for the shade of the woods, he walked quickly round the south face of the house, over the lawn and past brick walls straddled with old fruit trees, when suddenly he was aware of his wife laughing from within the walled garden.

It had been so long since he'd heard her laugh, a smile instinctively came to his lips and his memory flew back to the night they met.

It was Easter, 1936, he'd been staying with his old friend Robert from Cambridge and they'd gone along to a dance in the village hall. Earlier, he'd overheard Robert's mother warning her young daughter: 'You don't want to end up like Alice.' And he'd been intrigued to meet this woman who had, he was told, run away from five different schools and had had to be educated at home. Normally he only met women of the head girl variety – certainly not ones who'd been expelled, let alone five times. Quite what he'd expected he wasn't sure. But not such a reserved beauty, observing quietly from the shadows.

Then she'd danced and he'd watched her turning in some man's arms, her skirt lifting. He'd glimpsed the taut, slim lines of her ankles, her timing faultless. A clichéd, Cinderella fantasy but he was suddenly determined she dance with him – not that clot – and he was so nervous he'd trodden on her toes. Instead of being annoyed though she'd just said, 'You need to dance more. A lot more.' And the lovely candour in her smile made him never want to let her go. The miracle was she'd felt the same and now, standing in the clear sunlight, a flicker of joy leapt to his throat.

The moment fled as swiftly as it came. The door to the past, to his life before 1st August, 1944, slammed shut. His head renewed its throbbing as if his body was mocking him: if you think you can evade your guilt, you're an even greater fool than you realise.

From within the walled garden she was still laughing. Who the deuce was she talking to? Not that he cared, he just knew he couldn't bear to listen to all her happy-happy optimism. Silently, he moved away. In a couple of minutes he'd be unreachable amongst the trees and if anyone was capable of covering ground without being spotted it was him.

But then he heard an almighty crash of glass and a cry. He couldn't bring himself to ignore it and ran to the walled garden. His wife and the vicar – what the devil was he doing here again? – were standing outside one of the greenhouses.

'Everything all right?' he called.

'One of the panes fell out of its casing,' said Alice. She looked furious rather than shaken.

'But no one hurt? Reverend?'

'Not at all,' said Ivens. 'It was one of the side panels from the greenhouse over there.'

'That's all right then,' said Stephen. 'Half of the glass was already missing.'

'It's not all right,' said Alice, her anger barely concealed. 'Someone could have been walking by.'

'Well, they weren't,' said Stephen. 'And these greenhouses haven't been used for so long no one comes in here.'

'I do,' said Alice.

'Why? What are you up to?'

He watched her compose herself. 'I'm growing tomatoes – new ones.'

'It's extraordinary!' said Ivens. He gave Stephen a shy smile. 'How anyone can invent new fruit.'

'It's not quite that simple,' said Alice.

'Sorry!' laughed the vicar. 'I didn't mean it like that.'

Alice also laughed and she touched, Stephen noticed, the vicar's arm in reassurance.

'It's just,' continued Ivens, 'I hadn't thought about it. I know so little about plants.'

Stephen had been every bit as fascinated when Alice showed him the work she and her father were doing. He'd loved visiting her home in Kent. He'd felt more himself amongst her family than he'd ever done at Oakbourne Hall. There was her father, a Professor of Botany who, if he wasn't in his gardens, was writing academic papers; a much older sister, Catherine, a doctor; a library devoted to wildlife and flowers; greenhouses with roses in different stages of development. And the more he'd fallen in love with Alice, the more he felt sure of his own ground and he'd poured his love into his writing and somehow the words had flowed too. All that acclaim his poems had received in Paris – he doubted he'd have managed it without her ardour and belief in him.

'Didn't you ever want to follow in your father's footsteps?' Ivens was asking Alice. 'Perhaps go to university?'

Years ago, Stephen had asked Alice just that. She gave Ivens the same answer: 'I was hopeless at school. I can't spell, you see.'

'Spelling,' said Ivens, 'is hardly a measure of intelligence.'

'To get even basic Science Leaving Certificate you still need to be able to spell "cellulose", "molecule", whatever.'

Always being bottom of the class explained – in part – why she'd hated school. But her reputation as a wild child was, Stephen thought, grossly unfair. Like him, she'd been twelve when her mother died, and she'd kept running away from school because she'd terrified herself into believing that if she wasn't at home to look after her father, he too would die.

When he pictured this grieving adolescent with her misplaced sense of responsibility, he'd been full of pity. And also admiration. Even if he'd hated school – which he hadn't as it had been a relief to get away from his father – he knew he would have just accepted that he had to be there. Certainly, at twelve, he would never have found her courage and initiative.

'Don't look so sad for me,' she was saying to Ivens. 'I've had one-on-one tuition with some brilliant scientists as my father was always having people to stay. I'd be there at dinner, staying up late listening to all these amazing minds talking and arguing. It was a privilege really.

'Anyway,' she continued, still addressing him, 'to follow in my father's footsteps and actually hybridise plants success-fully requires real commitment and these days . . .' She gestured up at Oakbourne Hall. 'There's so much other stuff to do. And I'm not sure I've got the patience any more?'

'But you had it,' persisted Ivens.

'Not like my father. His patience was phenomenal. Having polio, he'd had to develop it. He'd say that polio saved his life, because unlike his brother he wasn't called up in 1914.'

So, thought Stephen, instead of digging trenches in the Somme Alice's father dug beds for roses. But before him appeared the memory of Alice's father, contorted into his wheelchair, his right leg paralysed, clearly in constant pain. And not once did Stephen hear the man complain. His stomach turned with shame.

'Stephen?' said Alice, her hand now on his arm. 'What is it?'

'Sorry, yes, sorry, I . . .' His injustice towards her father spurred him to make an effort. 'I was trying to remember the name of your gardener who thought you should start growing grapes and create an English wine.'

'Edward Withers. He was killed. In Bordeaux. Ironic,' she said, her voice suddenly bitter and she brushed her hand to her eye. Surely that wasn't a tear. Not once in ten years had Stephen seen his wife cry.

'Hard for you,' Ivens was saying, 'giving up all those roses, all your plans.'

'When you think of what some people have lost, I got off lightly.'

'That's no argument,' protested Ivens. 'It's your loss.'

'That's rich coming from you! You told me you'd had an easy war. And I've no idea what you mean by that.'

'Just,' said Ivens, 'that not once did I leave the East End.'

'Hardly,' she said, 'to continue the theme of the afternoon, a bed of roses.'

'Nor was your war,' Ivens said gently.

'Oh, why do we talk like this? People either say nothing or . . .' She paused and Stephen wondered whether she was going to start up her questions again. But she just looked at the earth as she said, 'Or they mumble that they got off lightly. It's not a competition.'

It's bloody obvious, thought Stephen, why people don't talk about the war.

'So many people now carry secrets,' Ivens was saying. 'Things they'd rather forget.'

Stephen studied him. 'What's your secret, Reverend?' he asked, then caught the sudden appeal in Alice's eyes: are you mocking this man? He looked into Ivens's young face and for a moment saw such sadness it appeared as though the vicar was going to be overwhelmed with emotions so contradictory he could not answer.

'I . . .' began Ivens. Then, in a rush, he said, 'I think we live in an age where so many of us have secrets. But they can be so terrible we keep them to ourselves because we're frightened of burdening other people. Or we simply don't have the words, because how can you expect someone to understand what it's like to put a bayonet through another human being if you've never . . . never . . . Oh, you know what I mean. But the gulfs between us all just widen.'

'So, your secret, Reverend?' persisted Stephen.

Ivens simply ignored him and, retrieving his bicycle clips from his pocket, said: 'I must hurry. Dr Downes is expecting me. I've challenged him to a game of chess. He beat me last time so I want my revenge. But I think it'll be a while coming. All that practice while he was a prisoner of war.'

Stephen glanced at Alice, wondering if she would say anything. She was brilliant at chess. She could play three games at once. He'd been amazed when he first learned of this talent of hers – hidden, he'd thought, like so much that had seemed extraordinary about this woman he'd once fallen in love with.

But she was just smiling as Ivens continued: 'Would you believe, Dr Downes learned Ancient Greek while stuck in some dreadful camp? The Red Cross sent textbooks. Extraordinary! Or insane! Or . . . Or . . .' He threw up his hands in exaggerated confusion. 'I'll see you Saturday.'

Saturday? thought Stephen, appalled. Please don't say my wife's found religion. He'd had his fill of Christianity and its message of turning the other cheek. He'd seen more than enough of that cosy creed manipulated into collaboration. All very convenient. And he was about to say as much but Alice forestalled him: 'Don't worry, Stephen! You only have to keep out of the way. I've just heard about this tradition that on Easter Saturday the women in the village pick flowers from Oakbourne Hall to decorate the church. They've not been able to do it for years.'

Then Ivens was shaking his hand and saying, 'I'll leave you to this gorgeous spring day. Amazing. Bumble bees, butterflies. It's as if everything's drunk on sudden warmth.'

And he was gone.

Stephen felt Alice assessing him as if he was dangerous terrain. 'You know,' she said, 'there's more to Mr Ivens than meets the eye. He's not some Mr Collins caricature. He's surprising. God knows what he meant about secrets. But his singing's no secret. Honestly, Stephen, he has the most glorious tenor voice. Come to Evensong with me. Not for God, I know, but the music.'

He shook his head.

She sighed. 'As you wish, but please put in an appearance this Sunday. It'll just seem so odd if I'm there on Easter Sunday without you.'

He couldn't be bothered to have the argument. 'All right, all right. But what was he talking about when he said your war wasn't a bed of roses?'

'Nothing.'

'You must have said something for him to think that.'

'He asked whether I'd been here during the war and I said yes. But . . .' She hesitated.

'What?'

She looked him in the eye. 'Sometimes, Stephen, I envied you—'

'Jesus!'

'I realise,' she said quickly, 'to you this might sound roman-ticised nonsense. But being stuck here, looking after my father. By the end he was so disabled I had to feed him . . .'

Her face creased and his initial instinct to say 'Be careful what you wish for' suddenly seemed shabby.

'Once,' she went on, 'I timed how long it took to get him from his chair in the garden to his chair in the sitting room. And this was in a tiny cottage, remember. But it took thirty minutes. And, as I was helping him put one foot in front of the other, I had the wireless on with all the news of the Normandy landings coming in and I sort of wished I was there too, doing something, rather than just waiting and moving unbelievably slowly because my father kept insisting if he gave in completely to his wheelchair all his muscles would waste away.

'Oh, I don't want to think about it. I only told the vicar because he asked and I thought given how he wasn't called up he was in the same boat. But that was naive of me. Downright stupid actually. Being in Whitechapel during the Blitz I suspect he saw more than he's letting on. Though he's really cagey about it all. What a surprise!' she added bitterly. Then she gestured to the broken glass. 'Whatever you say, these greenhouses are dangerous.'

'Greenhouses are the least of our worries.'

'But I'm trying to put some life back into the walled garden. And I've got Ross to help me.'

'Who's Ross?'

Annoyance, sadness, defeat, all three appeared on her face.

'Ross Harris from the Gate Lodge. His mother asked if we'd give him some work. Not that he knows much. Or cares. He's made it quite clear he wants to escape Oakbourne as soon as possible.' She walked away and prodded cautiously at a glass pane. 'This place is a death trap. Not just the greenhouses. The house itself . . . the roof.'

'The roof is not going to fall in,' he said. 'At least not this minute. Stop turning something so unimportant into a catastrophe.'

'I'm not going to find it unimportant if I wake up with the ceiling on top of me. You can't keep avoiding this. I read the other day Milton Manor is going to be sold and turned into a girls' school.' He looked at her blankly. 'That Georgian house with its own cricket pitch. You got a hat-trick there.'

'Did I?'

'Before the war. And it rained just after tea and you had to call it a draw.'

'Doesn't ring a bell.'

119

'Well, Oakbourne Hall could be a school. A nursing home. Lots of things. You've got to address this, Stephen. No one will buy the place if we let it deteriorate anymore.'

'So what if it deteriorates? There's more than enough room for us. Really, Alice,' he said, heading out of the garden, 'there are things a damned sight more important than the state of this house.'

'Yes, but I . . .'

He strode away.

But what is important? he asked himself as he glanced up through the canopy of trees. Then, as if in answer to his question, he saw a plane fly over, grey and military, from the nearby airbase. There are young men in that plane, he thought grimly.

That's what's important.

Because one day they'll be told to carry out their orders and they'll have no choice but to drop God knows what lethal weapons of mass destruction. And to escape his wife and the drone of the plane above him, he headed for the marshes.

 18

AT MIDDAY ON EASTER Saturday, Jane Downes and her two daughters arrived at the church where a crowd of women were helping Lady Rayne unload flowers from the back of her Daimler, while their children charged round the graveyard.

'I told you so,' Eleanor moaned to her mother. 'Everyone's falling over themselves to help the lady of the manor with her fancy foliage and I've got so much revision. Why can't I go home?'

'Eleanor, please. Just put in an appearance.'

'But I don't even believe in God.'

'This isn't about God,' said Jane, gesturing to the women carrying vases, watering cans and the last of the daffodils into the church. 'It's about a community trying to make a statement that we're at peace. I used to help with the Easter flowers as a child. Grandma too. It was something everyone did.'

'Not everyone,' muttered Eleanor. 'Just women, poor fools. And now we have to fawn over Lady Rayne.'

'No one's asking you to fawn. Can't you see? This is a symbol of life returning to normal.'

'If you think things are going to return to what they were, you're wrong.'

'You sound like your father,' said Jane, heading into the church, aware of dust in the air and the smell of perspiration – what they would all give for some decent soap. There was also a hint of something she couldn't identify. She looked round at the women. Most were simply exhausted, their clothes thin, their faces thin, their children thin. It was almost, thought Jane, a smell of defeat. Yet we're supposed to be the victors.

'Dad's right,' Eleanor was going on. 'Even you voted in a Labour government. The Raynes of this world, all those old Tories, are on the way out.'

But, thought Jane, will it really be any different if we just replace one lot of entitled, privileged people with another? And her eyes were drawn to two women believed to have done very well for themselves out of the war: Mrs Grainger, a local councillor whose genius for bureaucracy and interfering in people's lives had come into its own with all the wartime regulations; and Mrs Lubbock, in yet another new frock – what on earth did that cost and how did she get the coupons? – whose family owned the largest farm in the area.

'Today's certainly about putting the past behind us,' she said to Eleanor. 'It's years since we were allowed to set foot in the Hall grounds with the Canadians there.'

'Thank God! Imagine what they'd have thought of all the local women descending upon the place, prancing around with secateurs.'

'Eleanor! Enough! I've spared you picking the flowers, just do half an hour helping arrange them.'

'But I'm even worse than you at that sort of thing. And I bet we'll only be let loose on filling vases with water with Mrs Grainger in command.'

'She's certainly efficient,' said Jane, watching Mrs Grainger issuing orders about how to manoeuvre a ladder around the altar.

'Hitler's Handmaiden more like.'

'Keep your voice down!'

'That's what you called her when you were on that sewing committee and she made you re-do those pyjamas. And when she took the Harrises to task about hiding that pig. Everyone knew, but no one said a word, except for her because she's so bossy. And all the while her husband didn't half coin it. Very convenient owning cement works just when we're building bunkers and pillboxes everywhere. And did you know it's her husband who's wangled the contract to build all those council houses?'

Jane did.

'They certainly didn't do well out of the previous war,' she said, thinking of Mr Grainger whose face, even with all her nursing experience, made her flinch. 'Imagine! Newly married to a handsome young man and then he's gassed and comes home so blistered and burnt he's unrecognisable.' And no children, thought Jane. God knows what other damage was done. 'It's understandable Mrs Grainger wants to control things.'

'Don't start being nice, Mum! I know you loathe her.'

'What I loathe,' whispered Jane, 'is the idea of being under the thumb of interfering busybodies like her forever.' During the war, she'd accepted the interminable restrictions, but it seemed as if they'd never be lifted. 'And I worry that this new world your dad wants is not going to be the paradise he keeps painting.'

'It'll be better than having to be grateful to Lady Rayne – Lady Muck, as Dad calls her – just because she permits plebs into her garden.'

'I didn't think she looked at all well when she got here,' said Jane, wondering whether there might soon be a new heir to Oakbourne Hall.

'None of us look well. Except for the Lubbocks. They're not making do on rancid margarine and ersatz jam and disgusting spam.'

That's her father talking again, thought Jane. Jonathan was forever going on about the obscene profits farmers had made from the war and the Lubbocks had acres of land and a prize-winning herd of cattle. But Jonathan's right, thought Jane, surveying the magnificence of Mrs Lubbock and her three daughters, plumped up with luscious, golden milk, roast beef dripping with rich juices, hunks of strong, crumbly Cheddar and – oh, stop thinking about food, she told herself. Instantly though she remembered a birthday party for the Lubbocks' youngest daughter. Juliet had been invited and Jane had been asked to stay for tea and she'd not restrained herself in front of piles of fluffy whipped cream. Later, both she and Juliet, their stomachs in shock after all that richness, had spent the night being sick.

Mrs Lubbock came sashaying down the aisle in her new pale pink and gold-spotted dress with yards of material in the full skirt.

'You look lovely!' said Jane, as the thought at least I'm slim, flashed through her mind. And pathetic to compete about weight. But she looks so glamorous, acknowledged Jane, glancing down at her own neat brown shirt-waister, that had been bought 'to last' and, dear God, had it.

124

'Thank you,' smiled Mrs Lubbock. 'Isn't it a relief to be doing this again! And to be allowed back into Oakbourne Hall grounds! Though if my father could see the state of them now it would break his heart.' She lowered her voice: 'I know there's talk of Lady Rayne trying to get the walled garden up and running again. And good luck to her. But when you think of my father with twenty men working for him, what hope does one woman have?'

Mrs Lubbock's father had been head gardener at Oakbourne Hall – her grandfather too – and she never let anyone forget it. But Jane spoke genuinely when she said, 'The grounds were truly beautiful. And the walled garden! I still think of it as an enchanted place.'

She had once, as a child, almost forty years ago now, climbed in. It had been a glorious June evening and, miraculously, no one ever found out. Once the gardeners had all gone home, she'd scaled a peach tree, up onto the wall where, to her astonished eyes, the garden had seemed to stretch on for ever and ever, all its beauty rushing to meet her. She'd clambered down and simply run and run under arches of cascading roses and ancient wisteria; round beds of strawberries, raspberries, gooseberries; up and down through row upon row of lettuces, radishes, onions. One minute she was in a forest of runner beans twisting up bamboo pergolas; the next in the midst of what felt like millions of tomatoes, the plants sown in perfectly perpendicular lines, staked to bear the weight of so much fruit.

But amongst all the delicious-tasting beauty was beauty grown purely for its own profligate glory. She'd discovered borders of sweet peas, larkspur, peonies, great towering pink puffs and scarlet mantles of flowers she couldn't identify, her cheeks brushing against feathery green leaves, orange powdery pollen mingling in her hair. At the end of a corridor of delphiniums she'd come to a vast orchard with the beginnings of pears, apples, plums, and cherry trees already ablaze with red, ripened fruit.

At eight years old she'd had no idea of the word 'fecundity'. But that, thought Jane, breathing the church's musty air, is what she'd experienced in the profusion of perfumes, the surfeit of colours, the explosion of sweetness.

'With my father – and grandfather – working there,' Mrs Lubbock was saying, 'even in winter the place was a "cornucopia". They'd bring home leeks, cabbages, spinach, you name it.'

Jane gave a vague nod, remembering discovering the monumental greenhouses, the hot and heady air – unlike anything she'd breathed before – drawing her in to find trees with oranges! Lemons! Apricots!

With a jolt she was brought back to 1946 as Mrs Lubbock said, 'One thing you can be absolutely sure of – that garden will never be what it was. However hard she works.'

Mrs Lubbock gave a pointed glance at Alice Rayne, now up a ladder and lifting a large urn onto a window sill set high into the wall – clearly not pregnant. 'I hear she's forever digging away, night and day, come rain or shine. And, always on her own, so I'm told.' Mrs Lubbock raised her eyebrows, the implication quite clear: God only knew what Sir Stephen was doing with himself as the Big House fell into 'rack and ruin'. 'Since no one sees *him* these days,' she continued, 'Mrs Grainger is going to have a word with *her* about holding the Oakbourne Hall cricket match again.'

126

Jane smiled, sincerely again. Every year Oakbourne had hosted a cricket match against the neighbouring village on Whitsun Saturday, and she'd always loved the way it marked the start of summer.

'It'll take a lot of work to get the pitch in shape again,' said Mrs Lubbock. 'But my husband says he'll get volunteers to help – he adores his cricket.'

'Jonathan too! He loves . . .' Jane began. He *used* to love cricket. But now? With an artificial leg? Perhaps he could still bat – thank God he wasn't a bowler – and Christopher could run for him. But Christopher loathed all sport so that would precipitate yet another row.

Jane changed the subject. 'How can we help today?'

'Ask Mrs Grainger. She always has everything under control.'

Jane ignored the snort from Eleanor and turned to find Mrs Grainger holding an enormous clipboard.

'Congratulations to your husband!' said Mrs Lubbock, giving Mrs Grainger a kiss on the cheek. 'Have you heard?' she asked Jane. 'Mr Grainger's the new chairman of the governors at the General Hospital.'

'How . . .' How did he manage that? she wanted to ask, thinking Mr Grainger knows nothing about looking after the sick. Instead she said, 'How very exciting.'

'Isn't it? Such extraordinary times we live in.'

'I've heard they're really expanding the hospital,' said Jane, wondering whether Mr Grainger had the contract for this too.

'Absolutely,' said Mrs Grainger, fervour in her faded blue eyes. 'Because the change in provision of care is, well, revolutionary, and it all needs to be *planned*.' So that's where people like you and your husband come in, thought Jane, as Mrs Grainger tapped her clipboard, saying, 'Would you and your daughters be so kind as to start filling vases with water?'

'Told you,' muttered Eleanor as they headed for the vestry to collect watering cans. There, the eldest Lubbock girl, with painted-on lips and eyes in an impressive imitation of Betty Grable, was applying fine, scented powder over her pretty little nose.

'Mrs Downes, Eleanor, hello,' she smiled and then disappeared in a waft of perfume.

Jane caught the pained expression on her daughter's face. Does Eleanor want to look like that too? she wondered. Am I missing something? And the contrast between a practically perfect pin-up girl and her own unmade-up daughter, her skinny, rationed body in shapeless shirt and slacks, suddenly cut her to the quick.

'Sweetheart,' she said, 'go home now. You've been here long enough.'

'Oh, Mum! Thank you!'

'Don't work too hard. You know,' Jane went on, desperate to say something loving to her serious, studious daughter, 'you look like a Modigliani.'

'A what?'

'That painter. He did these extraordinary pictures of beautiful women, with long pale and interesting faces like yours. And you're like that. Naturally so. Not an imitation of some over-polished film star. You're yourself.'

'What are you going on about?'

'I'm . . . Oh, never mind.'

Go back to your desk, if that's what you want, she thought, watching Eleanor slip from the church as the Lubbock beauty's joyful laughter rang out. Jane glanced up at a stained-glass window of Eve with that beguiling snake. It's my job, she thought, to help my daughter navigate this world everyone is so intent on rebuilding. But who, asked Jane, standing at the vestry sink, is actually doing all the reforming and renewing? Embittered men like my husband creating a new society out of rage and pain? Women cut from the same cloth as Mrs Grainger, who'll know all there is about procedure and whom I've not once heard say anything interesting or original?

She lugged the watering can back into the church, where Mrs Harris sat in the front pew trimming branches of apple blossom. What new world would *her* son want as he seethed with resentment from spending his youth tossed about in a cramped ship at the mercy of U-boats on the icy waters of the Arctic? Or Sir Stephen who, by all accounts, spent most of his time up in his attic and seemed to have turned his back on this new Jerusalem they were being promised.

And what of his wife? she thought, as Alice Rayne headed towards her, holding one arm out in front of her.

'Are you all right?' asked Jane, seeing blood on her hands.

Jane received a glittering smile in response. 'Yes! I'm such an idiot! I cut myself on the hawthorn – it's such lethal stuff.' And she disappeared into the cloakroom.

There were also, Jane noticed, ugly, yellowing bruises on her hand. How had she got them? Gardening?

I have, Jane told herself, to stop imagining the worst, but the hottest topic of village gossip now was Sir Stephen: What had happened to him – or what had he done – to make him hide away? Most of the talk was charitable. But not always.

She'd been queuing at the butcher's for a gristly bit of oxtail and overheard the snide suggestion that perhaps he returned home long after everyone else because he'd been in a military prison. And that gave rise to mutterings about desertion, cowardice, cruelty . . .

Jane shuddered.

'Please do be careful,' said Mrs Grainger's voice behind her, 'you've spilled the water and someone could slip.'

Jane returned to the vestry to hunt for a mop.

'Mrs Downes?' It was Lucy Clarke with her new baby. 'I thought I'd feed Sophie in here.'

'How are you?' asked Jane. 'And your husband?'

He and Lucy had married eighteen months ago, as soon as he returned from Arnhem. He'd been amongst the one in three who made it home. The rest lay forever in Holland or had been forced to march east to incarceration behind barbed wire.

She watched Lucy smile at the beloved baby in her arms. So war hadn't destroyed everything. Lucy could also think back on 1944 with joy, because she'd been young and beautiful and in love.

'He's got a job working for the council,' Lucy was saying. 'In the Finance Department. And we're down for one of the houses on that new estate.'

'Oh!' said Jane, trying to dismiss the worry of how a man who'd leapt out of planes and seen his friends die in the disaster that was Arnhem – what appalling planning had happened there? – would cope with working nine to five, catching the bus back and forth to the new 'cardboard boxes' that Mrs Grainger's husband and his friends were building as fast as possible.

To Lucy she simply said, 'I'm so pleased for you.'

She went to mop up over the cold flagstones and polished brasses. Under one was buried 'Arthur Renault, a beloved son', who'd died aged twenty-three in 1646. Exactly three hundred years ago, during the Civil War, she thought, suddenly remembering her school history textbook with battles listed down the left-hand page: 1642 – Edgehill; 1643 – Adwalton Moor; 1644 – Marston Moor ... Her pretty history teacher had said this was the war when England suffered her worst losses, in that the greatest percentage of the population was killed.

So much pain, the awful living reality of it, now reduced to a page of dates livened up with line drawings of men with flowing locks or round tin hats aiming pikes and muskets at each other, while meanwhile on Easter Saturday it was turning into a glorious spring afternoon. She looked through the arched doorway into the sunlight. Three hundred years ago, men and women had no doubt stood in this very place, staring across this same countryside in all its Easter beauty, grappling with the horrors they had seen. How does mankind do it? she wondered. Face the consequences of our vicious, senseless cruelty, generation after generation? How have we developed such extraordinary endurance? Such carelessness?

'Mrs Downes.' It was the vicar, in his coat, clearly hurrying away. 'Thank you for all your help.'

'Not at all. Are you rushing off?' she asked.

'I'm not needed here,' he grinned. 'And I've been invited to hear a friend sing in a concert. So yes, I'm rushing.'

Her sharp eyes assessed his smiling face. '*Look* at a patient,' her nursing supervisor used to say. 'Trust your instincts – all your knowledge and experience.' Some impulse made her grab his arm. 'Enjoy! Do, please, have a marvellous time!'

'I will! I'm really looking forward to it.' And he walked away, head held high.

Is this what a belief in God does? she asked herself as she heard him singing, his lovely tenor carried on the breeze as he went through the lychgate and on towards his concert and ultimately who knew what fate. Her mind leapt ahead to a hospital bed. Does God cut through all the pain and fear? Can the sight of spring blossom promise you that despite the wars and the sickness in your young heart, there is always, always hope?

'Mum!' Juliet was by her side, repressing giggles. 'I've just heard Mrs Grainger talk to Lady Rayne about the cricket match and I could tell the last thing she wanted was a cricket match but Mrs Grainger got her way. And I think Her Nibs was upset so I told her about the Lubbocks' amazing teas so if she hated cricket at least there'd be something nice to eat. Mum!' Suddenly, Juliet was crestfallen. 'I feel so ashamed. All I can think about is food.'

'Oh, darling! I know just what you mean.'

'Do you remember those custard tarts we had?'

'Of course!' smiled Jane as life contracted from love and eternity to custard tarts.

'And I said that if I kept cutting it in half over and over again we'd always have a piece left and the pleasure would never end. But it did.' Juliet slipped her hand into mother's. 'Even though you gave me most of yours.'

132

19

THE FLOWERS WERE ARRANGED to Mrs Grainger's satis-
faction and Alice drove slowly away from the church. In
her rear-view mirror she saw the women delighting
in the warm weather, calling to children, laughing together.
Surely she couldn't be the only one reluctant to go
home. But how could she know? She was 'Lady of the
Manor'. No one would think of confiding in her. Nor she
in them.

The truth is, she thought, speeding up past fields with
new-born lambs, I'm alone here. Alone with my husband
locked away in his attic so sometimes I feel I've got Mrs
Rochester prowling about up there. Though he'd certainly
have plenty to say when he learned she'd been talked into
hosting a cricket match.

She braked to avoid a partridge with her chicks. The
church had felt packed with beautiful children flying
around like blossom in the breeze. And babies. She'd
watched Lucy Clarke sitting in quiet servitude feeding her
tiny little girl and Mrs Martin, not quite so Madonna-like
with her other two racing up and down the aisles, but with
her babe-in-arms. What I would give . . .

She pulled up at the junction to turn right for Oakbourne
Hall. Pause, she told herself. Just look.

Nature can cure, she reminded herself, glorious scenery does heal: new green leaves with the softness of velvet, the sky so clear it's as if blue silk has been stretched across the heavens, so incredibly lovely and painful and overpowering. And suddenly she felt she might scream, the living creature within her demanding excitement, energy, contact. Life is short, fragile, lost in an instant and gone forever. Hasn't the war at least taught you that? It's Easter Saturday, the day before the Resurrection, with all its extraordinary promises. For how many more years are you going to accept this dreary deal you've made with life?

A hoot from a car behind snapped her out of herself and instinctively she signalled right, towards home. But reality imprisons us, she thought. The reality of a war-damaged husband. So I have to extinguish this longing. Or I will lose my mind. And, to the blasting of more horns, she swung left, taking the road towards the sea. I'll walk, she told herself. Further up the coast to the sand dunes where there's no danger of meeting anyone. Perhaps rip off all my clothes and swim.

She sped away but had barely gone half a mile when she came across the Norwich bus broken down by the side of the road, its passengers spilled out on the kerbside, the bonnet up, smoke coming from the engine. As she pulled round she noticed, lying on his back, chewing on a blade of grass, the vicar. He'd mentioned he was going to a concert. Now, she thought, he'll miss it. This bus was clearly going nowhere and the next one would be ages.

Ivens, she was sure, hadn't seen her. I could go straight on, she thought, have my walk, and no one would be any the wiser. But Ivens had been terribly excited about this concert.

His friend was a soloist and how often, she wondered, did he actually get to go anywhere? Or see an old friend? About as little as her, she suspected.

She parked on the verge.

'Mr Ivens!' she called. 'Would you like a lift to your concert?'

He scrambled to his feet. He was transformed, beaming at her. 'Really?'

'Really!' And she found herself thinking, it's actually rather an attractive smile, the widening of brown, long-lashed eyes, the hint of mischief about the lips.

'Thank you! I've been so looking forward to this. And I don't want to let my friend down. Though, I confess, my reasons for going are also utterly selfish. I've read about this new work. And I'm dying to hear it. But are you sure? Haven't you other plans? And the petrol? It's a hundred miles, there and back.'

'There's plenty – we've not used the car for ages – and I was only going to have a walk. So let's go.'

He climbed in and, resting his head back on the navy upholstery trimmed with yellow, sighed, 'What a car!'

'I'm very lucky,' she said, trying to sound it.

'A work of art,' he said, reaching out and running his fingers over the walnut dashboard. 'Beautiful!'

'It was Stephen's father's.'

'That engine purr! Music!' he laughed as she drove away. 'Thank you so much. I can't tell you how grateful I am. Look, why don't you come? To the concert? It'll be really special. It's by Michael Tippett,' he said questioningly, as if to ask if she'd heard of him. She hadn't. 'I don't know his music,' continued Ivens, 'but this, my friend tells me, is wonderful.'

135

'So it's very modern?'

'Indeed it is.' She caught amusement in his voice.

'Do I sound a complete philistine?'

'I'd never say that.'

'But you'd think it.'

He laughed once more. 'Seriously though,' he said, 'you might enjoy it. I'm sure there'll be tickets. A cathedral's a big place to fill.'

'Stephen and I heard *The Messiah* there, years ago.'

'Wonderful.'

'Yes.'

'And this is the story of . . . well . . .' He sighed. 'Another persecuted Jew – Herschel Grynszpan.'

'What?' Stephen had been in Paris when Grynszpan, a seventeen-year-old Jewish refugee, killed a German diplomat there and the Nazis used this as a justification for Kristallnacht, systematically destroying Jewish property two days later. 'That's been put into music?'

'It's intended to be a message of hope.'

'Try telling that to the poor boy's family. If there are any left alive.'

He sighed. 'It's called *A Child of Our Time* and is about reconciling different parts of ourselves, the good and evil that's in all of us, winter and summer, how if you know your shadow and your light you can be made whole . . . . But I'm not persuading you, am I?'

She steered carefully round a narrow bend. 'It's just,' she began. 'It's just . . .' He waited in silence. 'Sorry, it's just so much modern music . . .' Again he waited for her to speak. Is patience part of the clergy's training? she wondered, manoeuvring past a tractor. You never finish someone's sentence?

'It's so discordant,' she said at last, 'and we've had so much discordance – to put it mildly. Art's the same. I see modern paintings and they're so tortured and I accept they're great in as far as they arouse all these strong feelings. But they're feelings of grief and fear and for that I don't need Picasso. I can just look at my bedroom wallpaper—'

A car suddenly swung out in front of her and, braking unexpectedly, she collected herself. She did not want such a personal conversation. She said, 'Perhaps we want discordant art because life now is more terrifying than it has ever been.' He was rubbing his chin. 'Don't you think? Mr Ivens?'

'I was thinking perhaps you should change your bedroom wallpaper if it brings on such turmoil.' She glanced at him uncomprehendingly. 'Lady Rayne, I'm not serious.' Then suddenly he was apologising. 'I'm so sorry, that was glib of me.'

'No! No.' Had she spent so long on her own she couldn't tell if someone was joking? 'But you're going to think I just want prettiness as my wallpaper has lovely pink roses – well, I think they're lovely,' she said, conscious she was gabbling. 'It's just – I don't think evil can be transformed into something beautiful. And after all the evil we've seen . . . I want . . . I want . . .'

Here I go, she thought, the bleating child again. 'Oh, never mind,' she said with sudden briskness.

'Please,' he said, 'talk to me. I've not had a conversation like this in ages.'

She glanced at him, wondering whether however much he believed his God was by his side, he was lonely, in a part of the world he didn't know, with strangers.

'I suppose I want art to be healing,' she said, thinking she'd given him the cue to launch into some homily. But, to her astonishment, he began to sing:

'Deep river,

My home is over Jordan.

Deep river, Lord,

I want to cross over into campground.'

The voice that emerged from this tall, thin man filled the car as effortlessly as birdsong. She felt that she'd stumbled into a musical and, as if reading her thoughts, he said, 'I promise not to start dancing.'

She had a ridiculous vision of stopping the car and him breaking into a jitterbug. With his musical abilities she imagined he'd be rather good. Certainly he'd have a great sense of rhythm.

'Tippett,' he was saying, 'uses spirituals like "Deep River", instead of traditional big choral numbers. The idea is that spirituals speak to anyone who has felt an outcast. So it's not just a Christian piece, but talks to everyone – Jews, atheists, agnostics, us all. And that melody's beautiful, isn't it?'

'Very. And you sing it . . .'

She was about to compliment him, but he didn't give her the chance.

'You want something healing,' he said. 'And that can be a burst of music, an evening out of the usual routine, something spontaneous and lovely and different. I'm not making all those promises for this concert. But what I can promise you is that my soloist friend has a truly magnificent voice so that, certainly, will be worth hearing.'

Why not? she thought. Why shouldn't I have what he calls a burst of music? I can phone Mrs Green when I'm in

Norwich and let her know where I am. Stephen won't even notice. And not letting any more hesitation creep in, she said, 'I'd love to.'

'Excellent! And I won't trouble you for a lift back. My friend is driving me home and staying the night.'

'How good for you to have a friend visit,' she said, oddly relieved that he wasn't as lonely as she'd feared. 'To see where you've moved. And your church. Is Mrs Turner putting him up?'

'Actually, my friend's a "her". Stella.'

'Oh!' At once she reddened with embarrassment, conscious she'd sounded like a shocked matron. Of course he'd have friends who were girls. Or girlfriends.

'She's a soprano,' he was saying, 'and is going to sing at our Easter service tomorrow, from St Matthew's Passion.'

'How lovely!' She felt ridiculous, as if she only wanted her vicar to be the confidante of unhappy women over plates of cucumber sandwiches. She wasn't sure what else to say. Nor, clearly, was he, because for the next few miles they drove in silence.

Only once she had to stop at a level crossing did she turn to him again.

He'd fallen asleep.

It was so long since a man had slept beside her, she'd forgotten how it felt. She'd not noticed before how very curly his hair was and into her mind flew Samson and Delilah. How little it would take to do him harm. Her eyes wandered over his face, free now from all strain, his lips slightly parted. The skin on his chin was reddened, as if, she thought, he'd spent all day kissing. Which of course he'd not as he'd been in church with her and all the flower arrangers and their children. He couldn't have got up to much kissing in there.

But what, she began wondering, would he be like? Perhaps he'd sing? And at the idea of him serenading her in bed she was aware of a smile spreading over her face.

20

FOR THE SECOND TIME that day, George Ivens was conscious of sitting beside a beautiful woman as Stella, in her golden evening gown, drove out through the unlit Norwich streets.

'George, we do miss you,' she was saying over the rattle of her old Austin 7. 'That landlord was all for locking us in.' After the concert they'd gone to a pub with her orchestra friends and sat around a piano, performing Cole Porter songs. 'I doubt he'd ever heard a vicar sing "Night and Day". Truly, it was brilliant.'

'Thank you,' he said, grateful not just for the compliment but for being reminded what it was to have a night out.

'Haven't you got any sort of choir where you are now?' she asked.

'There's a chap who plays the organ, but he's in his eighties.'

Stella groaned. 'But no one who can sing?'

'Not really. There's not much music about.'

'Please don't tell me you sit in some dreary lodgings every night with nothing but your gramophone for company.'

'Not every night,' he said.

'But most nights?' He didn't answer. 'George, I'm being serious now, is it really helping your health being stuck out here? I know there's fresh air. And I'm guessing you're not short of scenery. But compared with friends, scenery is vastly overrated.'

'You should say that to Lady Rayne. She'd make a good case for scenery.'

'Lady Rayne!' she mimicked. 'I hope you're not doing too much forelock-tugging, though you've obviously a talent for it if the lady of the manor's chauffeuring you around. In a Daimler! Mark will be so jealous.'

'Is he all right?' he asked of Mark, his old school friend and now engaged to Stella. 'In his last letter he didn't really say, just made me laugh about his boss.'

'He's the boss from hell. It's not fair that those who were called up are all entitled to get their jobs back, but people like Mark who *volunteered* have the right to nothing.'

In 1939, Mark was working as a journalist in Fleet Street, but joined the RAF when war broke out. Now the only job he could find was as a lowly sub-editor on a local newspaper in Croydon.

'When you think,' she railed on, 'that Mark, without being asked, willingly offered to risk life and limb, and now he's the one shoved back down the ladder. While some little creep, who never put himself at risk the way Mark did – just reported on the war – is doing his old job.'

'Didn't you tell me during the war they had a woman running the Features Desk?' asked Ivens. 'Hasn't she been given the push now?'

'All right, all right. It's not fair on women either. But don't you dare start giving me a lecture on women's rights. It's just so, so . . .'

142

So, so difficult, thought Ivens, suddenly weary, when so often giving to one means taking from another.

'But knowing Mark,' he said, 'he'll work his way out of that job in no time.'

'That's what I keep saying.'

'And he has you,' said Ivens.

'Yes, he does.' He saw her smile in the darkness. 'There's something I need to ask you. We'd like to bring the wedding forwards.' Ivens was due to officiate at their wedding in October. 'Much more forwards. In fact . . . As soon as possible.'

Then she gave him an uncharacteristically shy glance and he realised what she was saying. 'Oh, my!' he cried.

'I know – professionally – you should disapprove. A baby out of wedlock and all that. But please say you're happy!'

'Of course I'm happy. But you?'

'Yes! It's not what we'd planned – obviously. But it's helped Mark. You know how low he's been. So angry. Not sleeping.' The tyres squealed as she took a corner too sharply.

'There isn't any hurry,' he said.

'But I feel there is! That there's so little time we have to pack it all in. Oh, George! Forgive me! That was really tactless.'

'Stella, please. Don't apologise. For now, I'm all right. Just tell me more good news.'

'Well . . . the baby's meant Mark's painting a room for a nursery and putting shelves up instead of just talking about what's the point of it all, which was so awful. I'd think we're having a nice time, having a meal, going for a walk or something, then he'd start up on evil and death and there's no end to all that.

143

'At least he's talking and I know that's unusual – my sister's still no idea what her husband was doing, except that he was in Africa. But at times I just longed for Mark to shut up. Young men dying . . . the way they died . . . I – It's pathetic to say I couldn't bear it.'

'But you did bear it,' said Ivens. 'You listened.'

'I suppose. Anyway, he looks upon this baby as a miracle. God knows why since people are always having them and the fact that the shelves have stayed up is much more of a miracle. And George, we'd love you to be a godfather. We're not brooking any argument.' The argument being, thought Ivens, that I won't be around to watch this new life grow up. 'Please!'

He smiled. 'I'm honoured.'

'Good, but now Mark will be furious because he wanted to ask you himself but you know I can't keep my mouth shut.'

'I'll pretend you haven't asked me.'

'I can't ask a man of the cloth to lie for me and Mark doesn't actually get angry with me. Just the rest of the world. But with me . . .' She gave that shy smile again. 'Never really.'

Ivens looked at Stella, the radiance of her face, the splendid strength of her magnificent singer's body. How lucky Mark was to have a woman like that beside him. By night. And day.

He was aware of his damaged heart knocking angrily. He'd pushed himself today and now his body was protesting.

He pulled his jacket around him, sick of the way physical needs defined his world. But no, he thought, it's not that simple. The physical side of life is what I long for. What I'm sick of is my own wretched body, of my weakness, of the long, lonely hours in a cold single bed when I yearn to live like other men.

144

He had schooled himself in acceptance. But tonight he felt the depth of his loss. In theory, of course, he too could marry. The Anglican Church was quite clear. Celibacy – or not – made no difference to your ability to spread God's word. Clergy could marry 'at their own discretion', whatever best served their 'godliness'. Desire for the body of Christ did not preclude the desire for the body of a woman, and Ivens was in no doubt how his own 'godliness' would be better served. To have the needs of the flesh and the heart met in one person, to experience human tenderness in all its forms . . .

He stared out into the night. He could not indulge such hopes because even if someone did love him, how, in all conscience, could he inflict the care of an invalid – because that's what he would be – upon another vibrant life?

'But what I want to know,' Stella was saying, 'is how someone like you, who's virtually never set foot outside London, is finding country life. And start with Lady Rayne. She's not too much of an old battle-axe, is she?'

An image of Alice Rayne's slender body flashed before him. 'No, no—'

'So what's she like?'

In the darkness, he caught the sparkle of the tiny sapphire in Stella's engagement ring and he found himself thinking that although Alice Rayne wore a band of diamonds as hefty as lumps of coal, her hands were rough and bruised, the nails broken, as if she lived outdoors. 'She's incredibly knowledgeable about plants.'

Stella burst out laughing. 'So she's got a lot in common with a boy from the East End who's never even had a window box!'

'You'd be most impressed. I've discussed roses, snow-drops, even become quite an expert on tomatoes.'

'Oh, poor you! Honestly, George, you're a saint.'

'Actually,' he said, suddenly feeling disloyal, 'she's fascinating.'

21

'THE LORD IS RISEN,' smiled Ivens, holding out his hand to Stephen Rayne after the Easter Sunday service.

'Is He indeed?' muttered Stephen.

Alice quickly piped up by his side: 'How kind of your friend to sing for us! Such a beautiful service. And the concert last night! Wonderful!'

'Did you enjoy it?' Ivens asked. 'I know how sceptical you were.'

'I drove home uplifted.'

'Uplifted?' said Stephen. 'You said it was inspired by Kristallnacht!'

'It was. But there was a message of hope.'

Suddenly Stephen was livid. How dare she see the world with such complacent simplicity? 'When do you say it was written?'

'In 1941.'

'For God's sake. Tippett could be hopeful then! Kristallnacht was a vicar's tea party compared with what came after. Dachau, Auschwitz, Ravensbrück, shall I go on?'

Alice's voice dropped. 'I think we can do that for ourselves. But you're missing the point.'

'And the point, my dear, is what?'

She flicked her eyes towards him, then looked away, biting her lip.

It was Ivens who answered: 'The point, I think, is that humanity has – to use that old Biblical word – fallen. And we're in need of help. But there is still help available.'

'From God? What the devil He's up to in this damned mess of a world I've no idea.'

'Of course there's help from God,' said Ivens. 'But I was thinking of help from men like you, Sir Stephen. In Stella's solo, she sang, "My heart swims in tears", and you do not need to spend long in your company, Sir Stephen, to realise your heart is doing exactly that.'

Stephen drew back. Vicar or not, Ivens had overstepped the mark. Admittedly no one would have heard him, the rest of the congregation keeping a respectful distance. But this was far too private a conversation to be having at the church door with half the village swarming about.

'It's the men and women whose hearts swim in tears whom we need now,' Ivens was carrying on as if oblivious or, suspected Stephen, deliberately impervious to the embarrassment he was causing. 'If we're going to have any chance of resurrection, of rebuilding our broken world, stopping ourselves killing each other.' He held up his hand, as if in anticipation of Stephen's argument. 'Please don't tell me again how high you think the odds of war breaking out in Manchuria, the Balkans, the Middle East. Wherever. Sadly, I agree with you, so that's all the more reason why we need men and women who understand, who know – the way you clearly do – what we're all capable of. History – memory even,' he went on, nodding at the Great War memorial, 'hasn't taught us much. But men like you, I hope – I pray – might help us, possibly, stop it all happening over and over again.'

For one of the few times in his life, Stephen wasn't sure what to say, but he was damned if he'd listen to more pontificating and was tempted to say so.

Ivens beat him to it. 'Sorry,' he said, 'I'm preaching again and you've got lunch to get home to.'

Stephen had – yet another rare experience – the sense this young man was dismissing him. He was aware he was being given a valedictory handshake, that his wife, murmuring a polite 'goodbye', was pulling her coat tightly about her as if trying to make herself invisible. Then Ivens was giving his attention to Mr and Mrs Harris from the Gate Lodge.

Stephen strode off at a smart pace through the graveyard, nodding quick hellos, hurrying to get away.

'What's wrong with him?' he asked Alice once they were alone, heading back to Oakbourne Hall along the path with the crab apple trees coming into bud.

'Nothing whatsoever! He's only telling you what you're too wrapped up in your own tears – as Ivens says – to recognise.'

'Good God! None of you are pulling your punches today. What I meant is what's wrong with him physically? There's some heart problem, isn't there? He might have told you. The pair of you seem to chat enough.'

'Not about his health. I get the impression he doesn't want to.'

'You could have asked.'

'I've asked if he needs anything. I made sure that wood you offered him was sent round to his house.'

'Very gracious,' he drawled, and she winced at his tone, as he knew she would.

149

'People have secrets. Don't they, Stephen?' There was a challenge in her eyes. 'If he doesn't want to confide in me, I have to respect that. What choice do I have?'

Then she turned her back on him and he watched her walk away. No doubt people from the village often saw her walking alone like this, her head bowed, lost in private grief. An unhappy woman.

This was not the marriage they thought they'd have. But war had come. And that was how it was. And would be. He supposed he should feel some compassion for her. But he felt nothing. Except, right now, thanks to the rumble of a huge plane overhead, rage.

Even on Easter Sunday they were at work on the nearby military bases. Who knew what the next few years would bring? Here in one of the most unpopulated parts of the country, stuck out on a limb, looked down upon by London, was the perfect location for developing the weapons of the future. It wouldn't surprise him to see those War Office characters out in the mud flats, or deep in the forest, assessing the possibilities.

To think his wife, now veering off into the undergrowth, wanted to bring children into this world where, even here, he sensed its evil.

'There's a young deer,' she called out, looking back at him. 'It's dying. Something's been at it. A buzzard or – I don't know. It's already covered in flies.'

She broke a branch off an old sycamore and lifted it to smash against the back of the fawn's neck. Then she hesitated. Her face crumpled in misery and she slammed the stick into her own forehead.

'What are you doing?' he cried. She could have taken her eye out.

'For Christ's sake,' he said, running to her. 'You're terrifying it!'

'I can't bear more killing . . .'

He pulled out the pocket-knife he always carried, grabbed the fawn's head and whipped the blade across its throat.

'See?' he muttered. 'Killing's easy. Too easy, once you know how.'

She stood stock-still, staring down at the blood streaming over the young deer's pretty dappled coat, the ugly angle of its neck. And he snatched the stick from her, suddenly raging because she couldn't face what war really demanded. Instead she – and that vicar – sat in a cathedral listening to songs of war then wittered on about how lovely the music was, how there was light in darkness. Jesus! The violence he'd inflicted – beatings, bullets, bombs. All the lives he'd cut short, the mercy he'd denied. The lies he'd told: 'Trust me – I'll keep you safe.'

'Get me to do the killing for you! Find some mug to do your dirty work so you're free to enjoy pretty war requiems and moon on about hope!'

Then he realised that he was standing there with his arm raised, the stick in one hand, the bloodied knife in the other. She was trembling.

He let the stick drop, hurriedly wiped the bloodied knife on the grass, casting about for something to reassure her – and himself – that he was not just a brilliant killing machine.

Though who was he kidding? And standing in the garden where he'd played as a boy he could hear, yet again, the mild tones of his commanding officer: 'You're a natural.'

It was November 1940 and the two of them were chatting on the steps of the baronial estate in the Highlands where he'd just completed his training. He'd never been to Scotland before and although he was fluent in four languages – six if you counted Latin and Ancient Greek – nothing had spoken to his soul with the power of that glorious wildness and he'd promised himself that, if he survived, he would bring Alice here.

But the man he was that day had not survived so how could he say to this terrified woman, standing before him in her Easter Sunday hat with the dead fawn at her feet, I wanted to take you back to where I was trained?

Trained to kill with whatever came to hand – rifles, pistols, bayonets, knives, wires, knees, elbows, fists. And I proved exceptionally good at it.

Not that I ever got a taste for the work. *I didn't*, he insisted, avoiding his wife's frightened face.

Though some did. He saw it in their eyes. They loved the power.

But I was never like that. *I wasn't*. And yet, the truth was, soon enough, he'd stopped recoiling from the killing. Because, as the colonel also said, 'Without men like you, Christ knows when the dying will stop.'

He'd waded through blood on the Dunkirk beaches and when, after that debacle, Churchill called for volunteers for a new special operations force he'd put his name forwards. Anything to bring a quick end to the war.

Recruitment had taken the form of a hellish endurance test, perhaps not hellish enough, Stephen later wondered given that survival rates for undercover work were catastrophic. Men – and women – were kicked off the course or dropped out in droves because they couldn't handle route marches, parachute drops, sleep deprivation, the foretaste of torture.

But he was in his element. He had what it took to live in constant terror, to know whom to trust – no one, virtually – to kill when he had to smell the sour breath from the throat he was slitting.

On that afternoon in Scotland, the colonel, topping up his glass of peaty whisky, had said, 'I'm sorry, you'll have to write to your wife and tell her you won't be going home for Christmas.'

'Yes, sir,' he'd replied, the model soldier. In seventy-two hours he was being sent to North Africa, to lead an expedition behind enemy lines.

Part of him had been devastated. He'd not seen Alice for months. In her ardent letters she'd write that every day he survived was a day nearer him coming home. But another side was exhilarated that all his abilities, his ease with languages – indispensable for working undercover – his quick thinking and, he realised later, his diplomatic skills – critical when he was in France, trying to keep the warring factions in the Resistance all on the same side – made him the right man in the right place at the right time.

He and the colonel finished their drinks then headed back inside to get to work and discuss the attack on an airfield outside Tobruk.

Before closing the door behind him, he'd looked up into the afternoon darkness of a Scottish winter. Pegasus was winging his way across the sky, Orion hunting high amongst all those stars and galaxies. And they're indifferent to me, he'd thought. Indifferent to my wife, indifferent to the slaughter it's my job to stop. Even then he was aware that a part of him might be killed with the very efficiency he'd learned to wield in the field. He was a poet, wasn't he? A diplomat who believed in the power of words? Not a military man, like his father and all his forebears whose portraits used to look down on him.

But here he was, back at Oakbourne Hall, with his wife of nearly ten years scared and bewildered, while all the pitiful shreds of the man whom he'd hoped to be were either irrelevant or dead.

'I'm sorry,' he murmured. 'I don't know what came over me.' Then, trying to speak normally, he said, 'What's for lunch? I don't suppose it's roast lamb.'

She looked at him with such disbelief the deer might have sprung back to life.

'There's just bread and spam.'

'Oh, yes.' That's what he usually had. In his room. For dinner sometimes too.

'Stephen, thank you,' she said with surprising force. 'You did that deer a kindness. It had to die.'

He turned and fled. From the present, from the past, from the memory of *her* blood on his hands, its warmth, its smell. That August morning back in 1944 he'd learned no one had the right to play God.

 22

OVER THE NEXT FEW days, when Stephen put in the odd appearance for meals, Alice only broke their silences by commenting on some anodyne news. He'd mutter a response of sorts, while she remained taut with questions: what was the 'dirty work' he had to do? And she'd find herself reliving the night he'd kicked that young hare to death: what was he trying to stamp out? A memory? A deed of his own? And *Elle doit mourir*? *Who* had to die? And she'd frighten herself into thinking that if she raised the subject she'd reignite all that pent-up aggression and he would turn it on her. But this fear only fed another: she was being hysterical, trapping herself in a vicious circle of her own making.

Yes, he was snide and dismissive. Yes, she had to tread round him as carefully as the men who'd defused unexploded mines on the beaches. But he hadn't used that knife on her. That stick. He'd never do that. Never. She was certain.

So she made herself go about her days as usual – helping Mrs Green in the house, working in the garden. But this morning, when Mr Butley, the grocer, telephoned to say his van had broken down so he couldn't deliver her order, she decided she'd drive into the village and collect it. She could have a perfectly ordinary chat, because even the interminable domestic stuff she discussed with Mrs Green now felt charged with tension. There were too many polite enquiries about how her hand was healing – perfectly, thank you – and surreptitious glances that seemed to be checking whether she'd been caught in any more doors.

Early afternoon she escaped the house and was standing in the high street, discussing tinned peaches with Mr Butley.

'I'm sorry,' he said, loading the boot of her car, 'they haven't come in.'

'What a shame!'

'People have been looking forward to them,' he muttered. 'I know I was.'

'They are lovely,' she agreed. He grunted in response then she said, 'With your van out of action I'm happy to drop anything off for you round the village.'

'I couldn't possibly impose on you, Lady Rayne! And anyway, Mr Grainger's sending over one of his vehicles for me to borrow. Ah! Talk of the devil!' A large red van with 'Grainger's Constructions' on the side headed towards them. 'I wasn't expecting it so soon. I'm sorry! I needn't have put you to all this trouble.'

'It's no trouble.' And she was about to ask after Mr Butley's wife and their children. But he was already gone, waving at the van driver to head round to the back of the shop.

Alice hovered a moment by her car. On the other side of the road she saw Mrs Downes and Mrs Lubbock talking. Then a voice behind her said, 'Lady Rayne.'

Alice turned. 'Mrs Harris! Good afternoon! How are you?'

'Very well. And thank you, again, for giving that work to Ross.'

'Not at all.' Alice was about to comment on what a muggy day it was and how a storm would be nice to clear the air when Mrs Harris said, 'Goodbye,' and was on her way.

From across the road, Mrs Downes, finishing her chat with Mrs Lubbock, caught Alice's eye, then waved and hurried on. And that, thought Alice, as she drove away, is my human contact for the day.

She ought to head home but she was sick to death of Oakbourne Hall. Its emptiness. Its never-ending problems. Her only break had been a trip to Norwich for a concert. With the vicar.

She supposed she could visit him. But she'd never before turned up out of the blue at the vicar's – any vicar's. And she wasn't sure on what pretext she could call in.

She pulled into his street. The children were at school and it was quiet. A cat walked along a fence, a dog sat scratching its chin, a pigeon cooed at the top of a laurel tree. She saw Ivens's front door opening and Mrs Turner emerged and headed off with her shopping basket.

Suddenly music burst from his house, an Italian love song she recognised. It had to be him, playing a gramophone as if, with the landlady out, he could really turn up the volume. And, telling herself she'd come up with something to say when he answered the door, she almost ran up the garden path.

The music stopped abruptly. Then she heard his footsteps. And once more she felt unsure. What was she going to tell him? The truth? My husband's act of mercy unleashed a madness in him and half the time I feel I'm going mad myself?

'Lady Rayne!'

'I heard the singing,' she blurted out. 'I was in the street.'

'I'm sorry, I shouldn't have played it so loud.'

'No! It was wonderful.'

He was watching her, as if waiting for her to explain her unexpected visit, and she was about to concoct some nonsense when he said: 'Stella gave me the record when she came to stay.'

Fool, she berated herself, for intruding upon time he wanted for himself listening to a song his girlfriend had specially chosen.

But then he said, 'Stella's fiancé's an old school friend of mine. And they thought I'd like it. It's Caruso. Come on in!' He swung open the door with a grand flourish. 'And listen properly.'

She followed him into a room over-crowded with large heavy brown furniture. 'That song you were playing, "O sole mio",' she said. 'I've never known what it means. My soul?'

'My sun – and don't we need it!' he said, looking out at the heavy cloud. 'Please, take a seat.' He gestured to a wing chair shoved awkwardly up against the open window to grab as much sun and light as possible. He put the record on once more. 'Now,' he said, 'let's imagine we're by the Mediterranean.'

He sat on the window sill. She was conscious of him glancing at her, and she hoped he wouldn't ask why she'd called. But he just asked if she wanted to hear the song again, which she did. And after that he said he'd another record of Neapolitan songs and he'd play that if she'd time.

She had time.

So they listened to Caruso promising sweetness and love, until Ivens said, 'I've actually already got two records of "O sole mio". You can have this one if you like.'

'That's so kind! But I don't have a gramophone. Well, I do. But it's broken. The Canadians played it to death.'

'Well, if you get a new one . . . Giving me that record's a sort of joke. Caruso leaves out one of the verses – one I used to sing at parties.'

And, to the tune of 'O sole mio', for the second time in their acquaintance he sang for her.

'Lùcene 'e llastre d'a fenesta toia
'Na lavannara canta e se ne vanta
E pe' tramente torce, spanne e canta
Lùcene 'e llastre d'a fenesta toia.'

Then he said, 'Caruso's a pretty hard act to follow!'

'No, no! It was lovely!'

'But do you know what it means?' And he sang once more, in English this time:

'Light shines from your window panes,
The laundress sings and boasts about it
And while she wrings out the clothes and hangs them up to dry, she sings
Light shines from your window panes.'

She burst out laughing: 'That's awful! You realise, I'd be none the wiser if you'd just made that up?'

'I promise, that's a pretty accurate translation.'

'You'd think,' she smiled, 'all that wonderful-sounding Italian would be about passion and yearning. Not laundry.'

'Indeed you would!'

'Do you actually speak Italian?'

'Enough to know what I'm singing. And now,' he said, dragging out from underneath the sideboard a large cardboard box stuffed with records, 'this is Caruso again. *La Bohème – "Che gelida manina".'*

159

He stopped the record after a minute or so.

'You know what he's saying here?' he said,

'How her hand is cold.'

'Yes, but after a couple of lines he sings *Al buio non si trova*. Listen out for it.'

This time he played the song all the way through. Then, resuming his position on the window sill, he said, 'What's happened is that Mimi's lost her key and Rodolfo is helping her find it. *Al buio non si trova* translates as "it's not possible to find it in the dark".'

'I'd always thought he was professing undying love!'

'Afraid not. Stella and I and our friends would sing all these big songs which you were better off not knowing the meaning of. It was fun . . .'

He trailed off.

'You must miss your friends,' she said.

'I do,' he said, but he was smiling at her and she found herself wishing she too might know all this music and laughter, sitting with someone beside her. She heard a clock chiming four. She'd been here more than an hour. She really ought to go. But he leapt up saying, 'But it's always a pleasure to make new friends, and we have this afternoon!' And, returning to his box of records, he asked: 'What are your views on Cole Porter?'

'I love him!'

'Then you're in luck.'

She knelt beside him. '"Begin the Beguine"! Oh, please play this!'

Once she would dance the rumba to this sultry tune, moving her body to a beat that reached along the lowest and surest routes. And she wondered whether at all those

160

parties he seemed to go to, he didn't just sing but danced too. Then, as she found herself imagining reaching up and putting her arms around his neck, he got to his feet and returned to his window sill.

She resumed her place in the wing chair.

'Did you ever want to sing professionally?' she asked.

'I wanted nothing else, for years. But although my voice is good it's not good enough. And even if it was, I don't have the stamina for the life. So I tell myself that makes me a better clergyman. Learning the hard way that we don't choose our way of service in the world.'

Whether he was speaking bitterly, she couldn't tell as he was up again, putting on another record.

'"Night and Day",' he said, 'probably my all-time favourite – of Cole Porter's, that is.'

'What a genius he is,' she said as 'Night and Day' came to an end. 'And all such brilliant songs to dance to.'

'Oh, you should get a new gramophone!' he said. 'You're missing out on so much.'

She had no answer to this. And they fell silent.

'Please,' she said, after a while, 'would you play something else?'

'Of course! Of course! How about "Anything Goes"? Or "I've Got You Under My Skin"?'

But, before she could answer, they both started. The front door was opening.

'That's Mrs Turner,' said Ivens. 'I would ask you to have some tea, but Mr and Mrs Clarke and their baby are coming ...' The doorbell rang. 'That'll be them. The baptism is this Sunday and we're going through the details. But this afternoon – all this music – I've really enjoyed it.'

161

'Me too! Thank you,' she said, getting up so quickly she suddenly felt lightheaded. She'd forgotten her loneliness, her fears for Stephen, for herself – all her reasons for calling in the first place.

Then she was out in the hall saying hello to the Clarkes and wishing Ivens goodbye. And as she drove off she wondered whether to tell Stephen about 'O sole mio' and Mimi losing her keys.

But when she got home, he was up in his attic and she decided that without the music to play there was nothing to tell. She'd keep 'O sole mio' to herself.

 23

EVEN THOUGH ALICE APPEARED to be reading *The Times*, Stephen knew her attention was on him. He'd grown used to her covertly assessing his mood. He gave her a half-smile and clearly she saw that as an invitation to break the silence because, with a nod at the paper, she said, 'Sophie Montagu has had twins. A girl and a boy.'

He shoved the breakfast plate away. She kept doing this: giving him little snippets about babies and once again he regretted not having it out with her on that very first night he came home. Just saying bluntly: 'I know we said we wanted a family, but I don't. Not anymore.' Then all this skirting around, this ghastly tension even as they sat eating toast, could be done with.

He took a swig of tea and glanced over at her. She was wearing a dress she'd had before the war. It hung loosely on her now. She'd longed for a child. For a family.

But so too had he.

He'd always been the one saying, 'Let's not wait till the war's over.' But she'd been so anxious: what if you don't come home? What if our child grows up never knowing its father? What if . . . ?

But when they were last together she'd surprised him. In that grim hotel in Hastings, she'd said, 'Let's take a chance. If it happens, it's meant to be.'

If it happens, it's meant to be? Had they really been so stupid? He gripped the sides of his chair. Was what happened since meant to be?

Thank God, there'd been no baby. That was some mercy. He looked at his watch. Nine twenty. He had an appointment at ten with the gamekeeper to end shooting on the estate. Perhaps now was also the time to end her hopes of a child. Sort two problems in one hour. Kill two birds with one stone. He grimaced at the image. If he could just get through his life without more confrontation.

'Stephen? Are you all right?'

Get it over with, he told himself. Stop messing about.

'There's something we need to discuss,' he said. 'Not discuss because there's no discussion to be had. But you need to know I don't want children. And if you think you'll win me round in some way, you're wrong. I'm not bringing a child into this world. Do you understand?'

She looked utterly astonished, as if them having a family was the last thing on her mind. Then she gave him an unusually shy smile. 'I had,' she said, 'got the message, with you sleeping at the other end of the house.'

Then she went on, speaking so carefully it occurred to him she'd been preparing for this conversation and already had her arguments marshalled.

'Do you remember,' she said, 'how you wanted eleven children? Your own cricket team.'

'I wasn't serious.'

'I did realise you weren't serious about the number,' she continued quietly, beginning to tap the table with her finger. 'Though you were serious about being a father – one who'd be very different from your own.'

'If you're hoping I'm going to change my mind, I'm not.'

'You've changed your mind already, you could change it again. People do.'

'Alice, I'm adamant about this.'

She was holding herself very still, except for that tapping. Perhaps he should goad her so they had a full-scale battle, because he would win. He always won. He wouldn't be here otherwise. There'd been no 'killed in action' escape for him so here he was, back home amongst the remnants of breakfast and his wife going on, now tapping harder, clearly not as calm as she looked.

'Remember Hastings?' she said. 'Thursday 18th November, 1943?' So, he thought, like me, certain dates resonate in her like a curse. 'That was the last time we made love. You – we – we both wanted a child.'

'That was then. The war's changed everything.'

'Not everything.' Her voice was gentle but he knew her well enough to realise how much effort this calm was taking.

'Only someone who hasn't experienced it could say that.'

That was a cheap shot, he knew.

She didn't rise to it. 'What I'm saying,' she continued, 'is that it's not simply the war. You got back from Dunkirk and you weren't like this, even though you'd seen . . . But you turned to me for comfort. And afterwards, I know you couldn't talk about all that top secret stuff you did, but none of that changed the way you were with me. The way we were together.'

'It was different then.'

'But why? God knows what awful things you had to do in North Africa.' He flinched. Not once, after 1940, had he ever said where he was. 'You only get as tanned as that somewhere like Egypt. Or was it Libya?' She steadied her voice. 'But you came back to me even after that. I remember the whiteness and softness of your skin where that fierce sun hadn't touched you. But *I* touched you there. My lips, my fingers, my tongue—'

'For Christ's sake!'

'And you certainly showed no resistance. The war hadn't changed you then either.' Her tapping was getting fiercer, her breathing shallow. Any minute, he thought, she's going to lose control.

'So don't,' she said, 'rewrite history. Nor had it changed you when we had those two days in Hastings. Remember, Stephen?'

She brought her face closer, a sudden edge in her voice. 'Remember how you wanted a baby? Remember all our gorgeous, raunchy, blissful fucking?' She'd never spoken to him like this before. Well, it was better than tears. 'Oh, for God's sake, Stephen! Something happened after Hastings and that was what changed everything. If it's – if it's another woman I understand, I do, I really do.' He gave an ugly laugh. 'What's funny? Lonely, terrified, thinking your life might end at any minute – I bet there are loads of men—'

'Jesus! If only it was that simple: "Sorry, sweetheart",' he snarled, '"I had an affair, but let's pick up where we left off".'

He hadn't even been tempted to. He'd shut himself down so every ounce of his energy was on the job he had to do. And that was why he'd done it so well. Brilliantly, in fact. He could return to Egypt – she was right, he'd been there – to Italy, to France and be hailed as the great hero. 'If people knew what you've done,' his men had said to him, 'they'd be awarding you the Victoria Cross.'

Thank God they didn't know all he'd done. He sank his head in his hands.

'Stephen?' Her voice was gentle again. 'Why can't you trust me anymore?'

But he could trust her. That was the point. If there was one soul to whom he could reveal the dark it was her. He could look into her intelligent green eyes and tell her all of his shame and guilt. And she would listen with tenderness, exacting no dreadful penance.

And then what? Alice would offer him absolution. She would take him in her arms – of course he remembered how heavenly she was in bed – and pour over him the balm of her love. 'It was war,' she'd say, 'lines get blurred, we're all victims, blah, blah.' People everywhere were anaesthetising themselves with just such excuses.

But he didn't deserve to know joy again. And he would never let himself forget it. Figures flashed before him. Then that face. Those eyes. Of course there was no escape. However much he tried to run he was always drawn back to what he fled.

'Stephen! It was war, terrible things were asked of us.' Here she goes, he thought. 'You're the victim – we all are – of the age we were born in.'

'I'm no victim! Look at me. I'm not dead.' He caught the rise of her eyebrows as if to say he might as well be. 'I take full responsibility,' he said, 'for the decisions I made.'

'But whatever you did, however bad it is, you can tell me.'

His eyes hardened. It wasn't Alice's forgiveness he needed. 'This isn't about *you*.'

'It's about *us*.'

'No, it bloody isn't.'

'Of course it is. Whatever happened affects us both.'

'Then let's just end it. Get a divorce.'

He might have shot her. She slumped back into her chair.

'Is that what you want?' she said, her voice hoarse.

The truth was, he didn't care. He didn't know why he'd even mentioned divorce. It was as if he'd fired a bullet without thinking of the consequences. He wanted to be the man he was before 1st August, 1944 but that was impossible.

He sighed: 'I'd make it easy for you.'

'Stephen! Is it me? Do you not want children with *me*?'

'Christ! How many times do I have to say this? It's nothing to do with you. No one in their right minds would bring children into this world.'

'That's no argument. I know, dreadful, dreadful things have happened. If we're capable of the most awful atrocities—'

'There's no "if" about it.'

'But we're also capable of the opposite. Of beauty. That the world's a perilous place is as certain as us all dying one day. But it hasn't stopped people living, thinking they might still know joy. Human beings go to war. And signs are they always will. But you're too intelligent to believe that's justification for giving up.'

'What the hell's intelligence got to do with it? In war, first thing you do is chuck out everything my fine education taught me – subtlety, seeing both sides of an argument. Instead you become as narrow-minded as possible. I'm right, he's wrong. So I too am justified in committing atrocities.'

He saw her recoil: what 'atrocities' were on his conscience? Well, he wouldn't tell her. Or anyone.

'Stephen, whatever you did, you're not to take all the blame. The war wasn't your fault. For God's sake! They started it.'

'They started it,' he mimicked. 'He's a baddie, I'm a goodie. And you know what? The heroes – and in some people's eyes I'm a hero, God help us – are the ones who are able to see the world so simplistically. Otherwise they can't do the job. So no, Alice, I'm not bringing a child into this world just to suffer the way I've made people suffer.'

She'd stopped tapping, her hands clenched together, the knuckles white.

At least it was over now, he told himself. There was no more to be said. If she wanted a divorce, so be it.

He made a point of looking at his watch. 'I've got to go,' he said.

'Wait! You owe me this.' Her face was ashen, but her eyes steely and searching. 'You don't think you're entitled to happiness, do you? That's the real problem.' He said nothing. 'I don't know what you're punishing yourself for, what you did that you think is so unforgivable, but do I have to be punished too? Perhaps I could argue your remorse, regret, guilt is indulgence.'

'You weren't there,' he said, getting up. 'You've no idea. Just for a change, it's justice.'

24

OUT ON THE TERRACE, Alice leant over the balustrade, her cheek on the cold stone.

Divorce.

The word alone horrified her, yet more destruction and loss. She kicked at a bramble shooting up between the flagstones, breaking it off at the roots.

She'd foreseen the argument about children. But she'd held on to the belief that eventually her love would bring him round. Now such confidence mocked her because she'd imagined reasoning with the dear, dear man she had married.

What idiocy and ignorance, she thought, pulling at the dandelions in a cracked urn, to believe you could undo all the damage of six years of war. Face facts, Alice Rayne. They got you in the end. There's no victory for Stephen. Nor you. Nor for the thousands who discover the Nazis have, after all, invaded our hearths, defeating our souls, robbing us forever of peace.

She paced up and down the uneven terrace, buckling and splitting with damned ragwort devouring nutrients and water, destroying everything in its wake. She crushed a shoot between her fingers. She could hear her father telling her only to handle ragwort with gloves on and then burn the stuff. It was poisonous to horses and if it began seeding it would be impossible to stop.

To hell with the ragwort, she thought, chucking it on the ground. But that meant to hell with the horses and is that how it all starts? You become indifferent to one life and before you know it you are turning a blind eye to God knows what atrocities. Because what had Stephen also said? *I too am justified in committing atrocities.*

She brought her hands to her face, thinking of the news reported from the Nuremberg trials, the evil man was capable of. But her husband? Surely not?

'I love him,' she murmured. But she lacked conviction. 'I love him,' she said again, but another voice was asking, 'Really?'

She hit her hand against the stone, harder than she'd intended, but the pain eased the awful possibility that no, she did not love Stephen and her fear she was at the limits of her endurance.

But what should she do?

She certainly wouldn't cry. She'd been schooled in not shedding tears. A few months after her mother's death, she'd asked her father, 'Do you ever cry?' With a look that had petrified her twelve-year-old self he'd snapped, 'What's the point in that?' And he'd grabbed her hand and taken her out to the greenhouses.

Work, work and yet more work! That had been his salvation.

I too have work, she thought, glancing back at the house with its blank windows, the ivy tossing over the walls in flailing branches. She could devote her entire life to stopping that great tomb descending dust into dust.

But she couldn't face another day of dead men's things. She traced her fingers over the intricate patterns of lichen thriving on a headless stone lion and glanced at her pretty marcasite watch – a present from Stephen the day he left for France in September 1939. It was only ten o'clock.

Another whole day to get through. The prospect made her feel as if a rope was tightening round her neck. Breathe, she told herself. Breathe.

'*Solvitur ambulando*,' her father would say. 'It is solved by walking.' Perhaps because the most ground he could cover at one time was a mere quarter of a mile, he'd wanted her to walk for him, to do what he could not.

But she was sick of her father intruding into her thoughts. Because, right now, she could hear him saying: 'Don't get married! If Stephen's right and there's going to be war, you've no idea who he'll be by the end of it.'

Glowing with her certainties, she'd protested.

'Love him,' he'd said. 'Just don't marry him.'

Her sister, Catherine, had said the same, giving her the name of a doctor willing to provide contraception to unmarried women. 'Dad's right,' Catherine had said. 'You wouldn't believe the number of unhappy women I see stuck in awful marriages because they wanted sex.'

And Alice recalled looking at her sister with pity because Catherine did not know what it was to love and be loved as she was. She and Stephen were two halves of the one ring, once joined they would be bound together for life, strengthening and supporting each other, body and soul, till death parted them.

Jesus Christ! She hit her hand again upon the cold stone. You stupid, stupid girl! She pulled herself up off the broken lion and hurried down the moss-covered steps.

There was warmth in the sun and the clouds were clearing. Normally, on a day like this, she would head down to the sea, striding towards the horizon with the larks spiralling above her. Somehow, standing at the water's edge, listening to the slow unchanging rhythm of the tides, brought peace.

Not today.

She headed to the west of the house. Nature was on the rampage here, ground elder colonising the borders, dandelions running riot in the grass, nettles unstoppable. Amongst all this life at work, a thrush at her feet, boldly tugging at the moss for a nest, wood pigeons making a racket in the ruins of the huts the Canadians had left, a kestrel hunting low in the distance, she had to find a way to pass the time, the next hour . . . the rest of her life.

Get a divorce. Is that what her husband really wanted?

She paused by a dilapidated fountain, a big Victorian thing with fat cherubs, and looked into the stagnant water, teeming with mosquito larvae.

But you, Alice Rayne, what do *you* want? Apart from the impossible – the man you married, the man who did not speak of committing atrocities.

Atrocities?

And she broke into a run, as if by moving fast she might slow down her mind.

You're in shock, she told herself, brushing past thickets of pink and white may, on through a dark alley, then into a tangle of rhododendrons. These were questions she did not have to answer today. For now, all she needed to do was take stock. She wondered whether to telephone Catherine for a dose of her sister's relentless common sense. But Catherine, living with a married man whose wife was refusing to give him up, would be the first to advocate divorce.

She doubled over, gasping for breath. Even these days, divorce still meant scandal. But she'd lived with disgrace before, the feral girl who kept running away from school, the dunce who couldn't spell. But I managed, she thought. More than managed. And I found love. I married Stephen.

I don't want to live without love, she cried inwardly. But who was she to have a life so blessed?

'We don't choose our way of service in the world.' That's what the vicar had said. She supposed if she needed to hear a friendly voice she could visit him but since they'd spent that afternoon listening to music together, for unaccountable reasons, she'd found herself avoiding him. If, she thought, I had a faith like his, I might be able to accept whatever life had in store. But Christ had escaped life through death and suddenly it seemed to her that, for all the agonies, He had taken the easy way out. Dying could be a merciful release from this endless soldiering on.

She came out by the south side of the walled garden. A line of peach trees, their branches outstretched, spread and nailed against the old red brick, was slanting dangerously forwards. She stopped to scrape at the mortar, crushing it easily between her fingers. At any moment the edifice of ancient fifteen-foot-high walls and trees could collapse on top of her.

That would be peace of sorts, to be left to sink into the soil, away from broken promises and the torture of other people's suffering. And with that dreadful hope the wall suddenly gave way.

She jumped back and slipped, twisting her ankle and jarring her shoulder as she crashed onto a pile of stones. She lay very still, swallowing the hurt, wondering what damage

174

she'd done. She could smell the damp earth. She heard a blackbird with its glorious song, a wren – amazingly loud given its tiny body – a robin, as wistful as ever. Then she was aware of her finger being bitten, red ants crawling all over her hand and she leapt up as best she could.

She cradled her foot, waiting for the pain to ebb, then tested her ankle. Nothing seemed broken, but she certainly couldn't walk far.

She stood on one leg amidst the bricks and fallen trees. They'd not been pruned for six summers and the extra weight of the overgrown branches had brought everything down. She picked at a bud of white blossom with its exotic perfume. The trees would die if left like this. She was the only one around with any idea of how to save them and what else was she going to do with her day? Lie back in the dirt and let the ants feast on her?

No . . . she thought weakly, I don't want to die. There's work to do. If Stephen could live incarcerated like a monk up in his attic, then she could live like a nun here in the walled garden. She knew the village thought she'd not a hope in hell of restoring it to its former glory, all on her own. Well, they didn't know her. What she was capable of. She could save the walled garden.

Or perhaps it would save her.

Echoing from the woods came the mellow call of a cuckoo, that lovely intimation of an English spring. One early morning during the war she'd stood amongst the bluebells, listening to those same reassuring notes, when a Dornier on its way back home across the North Sea to Germany offloaded its bombs on the village. She could recall the explosion, the way the earth trembled, the dreadful sound of death just

175

down the road. Two whole families killed outright, all of whom had worked here in the Big House, one man a very talented gardener. But dead now, along with all his expertise. She owed it to him, to all those who lost their lives, not to give up.

She limped over to one of the sheds where there was a collection of rusting saws and secateurs. If she set to work now, the trees stood a chance.

25

IT WAS MIDNIGHT WHEN Dr Downes put down the phone. He dreaded to think what the call had cost. But it was worth every penny. For the past hour he hadn't been the provincial GP sitting in his draughty hallway, but the brilliant doctor, using his fine brain to assess a complex case.

He'd been discussing George Ivens with a thoracic surgeon in London, Mr Alec Fraser, who'd been his junior before the war but was now working on new developments in heart surgery. Like I should be, thought Downes, gripping his right hand with his left as if he might still the trembling. For now it was almost imperceptible but he would never again be allowed in an operating theatre. And this was yet another unquantified cost of war. If he'd spent the last six years doing the work he loved what might he be in a position to do for George? In his lifetime he was in no doubt his former colleagues would be operating on the human heart. And that should have been me, he thought, entering the cold kitchen where his wife was darning socks.

Immediately putting down the needle and thread, she asked, 'What did Fraser say?'

'He wants me to persuade George to go and see him. But I'm not sure. Anyway, I'm off to bed. I've had it for now.'

'But Jonathan!' she protested. 'I've stayed up specially to find out.'

'All right,' he said, because it appeared she would actually listen, not nod at him with that abstracted look while she made dinner or whatever. 'But put the kettle on, would you, love?'

And, with an enthusiasm he'd not felt for ages, he explained what Fraser had told him of the advances being made in repairing the damage caused by rheumatic fever to valves in the heart. She gave him her full attention. In another age, he thought, she'd have been a doctor too. At least his clever daughter would have these opportunities.

'But the problem,' he concluded, 'is that none of this can really help George. In a few years' time, yes, they'll probably be in a position to give the surgery a shot. But it's still so basic.'

'But you say Fraser wants to see him. And won't charge, presumably?'

'He's not looking for guinea pigs if that's what you're asking.'

'Some of those surgeons would risk their own mothers if they thought it'd help their career.'

'Fraser's a decent man. And all these experimental things are being monitored so closely. But the odds on them being able to do anything for George right now are virtually nil.' He put his head in his hands. 'I don't think he should see Fraser. To be told there's all this hope, but out of his reach, would be downright cruel.'

'Would you want to know?'

'George seems to have made his peace with what's inevitable. I don't want to destroy that.'

'I asked,' she said, 'if *you'd* want to know.'

'Well yes, I suppose *I* would.' She gave him a searching look. 'You think,' he said, 'I should tell him about Fraser, don't you?'

'I think George should make the decision, not you.'

She was right, he realised, and he felt sorry for her, using her fine intelligence to darn socks. 'I don't know what I'd do without you,' he said. 'You know that, don't you?' She gave him a weak smile. 'You're absolutely right, of course. At least,' he continued, 'packing George off to this God-forsaken place with nothing but fresh air to recommend it means he's less likely to catch an infection. And it'll help if Lady Bountiful keeps supplying him with wood so that miserable house he's in stays warm and dry.'

'Lady Bountiful? Oh, Jonathan! You don't miss an opportunity, do you? You have to turn everything into some class war. It just gets so boring.'

'It gets pretty boring being cold and damp.'

'The Big House is even more cold and damp than here. And I don't think George finds this place God-forsaken. It's you that does – and don't we all know it.'

'What's that supposed to mean?'

'Just that we're *here* – for now at least. We have, somehow, to make the best of it.'

She grabbed his half-finished tea to wash up. 'Our family – God knows how – survived. Compared with George – with millions – we're miraculously lucky!'

Does she really think that? he wondered, as she scrubbed the violets trailing over the teacups with such vigour he thought she'd rub them off. But as he glanced round the cluttered kitchen, at the shoes by the back door, at Juliet's drawings of countless dogs, the photograph on the mantel-piece of the five of them in the spring of 1940, he thought, she's right, again. It is a miracle that, six years on, we're still together under the same roof.

He knew all too many men who'd come home to find their wives had left them for somebody else; or the husbands had fallen out of love with their wives. And it was the fathers who invariably lost the children. But he still had his family and he adored his hard-working, ambitious Eleanor, his eternally happy Juliet. Admittedly Christopher whom, in those interminable years behind the wire, he'd remembered so heartbreakingly as the little boy who loved to play football with his dad, now looked upon him with open hatred. But maybe, he thought, I'd have been the same at fifteen if my father had been around.

He watched his wife, now attacking the crumbs on the kitchen table, her hair scrunched up in an untidy bun. The truth is, he thought, she's exhausted. She pushed straggly strands of grey hair out of her eyes, that beautiful, extraordinary hair of hers.

The first time he spoke to her, almost twenty years ago now, it was her hair that had struck him, rippling loose down her back, a mane of such thick burnished bronze he felt he'd stumbled into Leighton's painting, *Flaming June*, the beautiful woman, the sun made flesh. He'd just discovered the image because every three weeks – the length of time you could borrow books from the public library – he'd choose a non-medical subject in a frantic attempt to educate himself in art, philosophy, economics, literature, politics, you name it. Now, sitting in his kitchen, full of family life, he felt pity for his twenty-two-year-old self, ploughing through

180

a book on nineteenth-century art because he was scared of being written off as a working-class oik.

But Jane had somehow always made him feel he already knew what was important, that the rest was just window-dressing. She didn't give a damn about those doctors with fathers in the string-pulling medical patriarchy, who already knew the rules of the game. Instead, he was the man she wanted to draw her gorgeous hair around so they'd lie enclosed in a world of reddish-gold, making him think of a Viking goddess, of centuries and centuries of beautiful women making love and laughing and bringing peace to men, like him, poor and hungry.

But her hair had faded, along with those feelings. How could such passion disappear, almost as if it had never existed?

'Mum!' Christopher was standing in the doorway.

'What are you doing up?' Downes demanded.

'I couldn't sleep,' said Christopher, looking at him nervously. 'I want Rusty.'

At his name, the dog leapt up.

'Go on,' said Jane hastily. 'The two of you.'

Downes watched her usher Christopher and the dog out of the kitchen. He knew what she was doing. Getting her son out of his father's reach because he thought she mollycoddled him.

What a cliché, he thought, the soft mother, the tough father. The trouble with Jane was that she saw danger every-where. Was this the war? Or simply motherhood?

He stretched out towards what was left of the fire, groaning with the pain, ignoring the annoyance on Jane's face. But the stump of his leg was always cold and these cloudless spring nights were bitter. None of them, he thought, rubbing

181

his butchered thigh, have any idea of what it means to have all those nerve endings severed, the unnecessary agony that was with him every goddamned hour, every minute—

'Jonathan!'

'Were you saying something?'

'Everything's locked up and I'm off to bed.'

Trying to keep his voice measured, he said, 'When's Christopher going to sleep without the dog?'

'When he stops getting nightmares about being bombed.' He could freeze on the iciness of her tone.

'That,' he said, 'was more than five years ago.'

'So?' He was shocked at her vehemence. 'You've no idea what it was like! You go on and on about making the world a better place but in your own home . . . In this village . . . Some of the men, right here, under your nose, have come back half-mad. And our son! Lying in that rubble! The last to be found! And you just have it in for him!'

'I don't! Christopher's only problem is that you're encouraging him to grow up so wet.'

The disgust on her face was like a lash. 'You just don't understand!' Then she walked out as if she never wanted to see him again.

'I do understand,' he muttered to the dying fire.

It was Jane who needed to understand that Christopher had to toughen up because Downes knew just what happened to nervous, sensitive types like his beloved son. Downes rubbed his eyes hard as if that might eradicate the memory of a boy – at nineteen he really was just a boy – who'd ended up in the POW camp with two badly broken legs. Downes had decided against amputation, a bold decision under the circumstances, with virtually no medical supplies, but the bones had knitted extraordinarily well. And, at the time, Downes had prided himself on his excellent work.

Over the months, Downes heard the boy's story of growing up an only child, bookish and musical, with a place to read Classics at Oxford. But he'd wake at night screaming for his mother, unsettling the other men. To distract him, Downes asked for help with his Greek because the way to cope with those camps was to keep busy. Learn Greek, play chess. Whatever. Because if you dwelt on the lunacy and loss you could not survive.

Within a year or so, the lad could just about hobble around.

Sitting in his kitchen, Downes choked down a sob. Because he couldn't forget the boy standing in line on the first morning he was strong enough to make it to roll call: how he suddenly broke away, not so much running but tottering like a new-born colt towards the barbed wire, the goons up in the watch tower levelling their machine guns, yelling, '*Halt! Halt!*'

Downes hunched over in pain. Why couldn't Jane see she was turning Christopher into the sort of man who'd also bottle it and end up with his back full of bullets, his darling child lying dead in the dirt, as Downes cried and cried at him to stop running, carrying on crying when the poor boy was long past hearing?

Whether the boy ran deliberately to his death or in blind panic Downes could never know. What he did know was that if he hadn't healed those broken legs the child would still be alive.

Downes hauled himself up, the chair screeching across the tiles. He could not look back. He had to ignore the damned tears pouring down his face. His job now was to make history, not let history destroy him.

26

Making his way along the path by the Oakbourne estate, George Ivens was in no hurry. If what Dr Downes had just told him was correct, that new medical research could – possibly – help him then – just possibly – he might see more springs as lovely as this.

'To put it bluntly,' Downes had said, 'I don't think we're in a position to help you yet, but it might be worth a trip to London to see Alec Fraser. He's in on some fascinating research. But I don't want to give you unrealistic expectations.'

Ivens put his hand on his heart, aware of the irregular beating. 'Dear Lord,' he murmured, breathing in the air perfumed with newly opened blossom, 'give me strength – strength to deal with this hope.'

He'd assumed he would not grow old. This was a truth, one so many men of his generation – and his father's – had faced. But it was not, Ivens had consoled himself, the *length* of time you lived, but *how*.

This conviction had helped him sit with mothers mourning the deaths of their sons, officiate at the funerals of too many children. In February '45, when one of Hitler's new rockets fell on a school in his Whitechapel parish, he'd buried seventeen: Janet Tompkins, Mark Baker, Katy Morrison . . .

Why weren't those children spared?

Was it simply luck that he was the one so alive on this ravishing day, the late afternoon sun sweet on his shoulders, the bees trembling as they gulped down nectar from flowers in a canopy above him? Never had he seen blossom so consolingly lovely: on a spectrum from rich red to translucent white, and luminous against a sky so blue it made him think of Mary's cloak. And in his heightened state he felt he had tumbled into a corner of paradise.

Was this, he wondered, how men felt before they went into battle? This fierce awareness of life? Because right now he would promise anything to be allowed to live like other men, to fall in love, have children, simply know the sun on his face. Just not to die. But even as he made the promise, he knew the Spirit he did his best to believe in was not one you could bargain with.

He watched a dark pink petal float to the ground. This too, this heavenly spring day, would pass. Yet as he continued out from under the trees to a path lined with hawthorn, for a blissful few moments, he felt a deep trust that there were answers beyond his understanding.

As he drew nearer the Big House, he passed fallen-down outbuildings and potting sheds, the disused game larder, when suddenly he heard a scream from the walled garden. He pictured the greenhouses shattering, a body lying under great shards of glass, and he pushed his way through the thorny hedge, ran across the rough ground until he came to a small door, hanging off its hinges, and into the walled garden.

At first he couldn't see anything amiss. Quite the opposite. The place had been transformed in the few weeks since he'd last been here: beds cleared and raked ready for planting;

185

dead undergrowth piled up for bonfires; paths swept. But then, in the far corner, he saw Alice Rayne kneeling in the midst of a patch of nettles.

'Are you all right?' he cried, rushing over. Drawing closer, he was appalled. All over her arms were great scarlet weals, swollen as if about to break into blisters. 'What's happened?'

'Nothing.'

'But you screamed!'

'There was an adder. I screamed to frighten it away.' She pushed her hair out of her eyes. 'Don't worry. It won't come back.'

'I'm not worried about adders!' Her shirt sleeves were ripped, her cheek scratched and he wanted to cry: it's *you* I'm worried about.

'You *should* worry,' she said. 'This sudden heat's bringing them out. But they're more frightened of us, so if you see one just make a noise.' Then to his horror she gripped a stinging nettle with her bare hands.

'What are you doing?'

'Preparing the ground,' she said, yanking on the thick stem.

'This is madness! You need gloves!'

'I have to get these out,' she said, pulling up a trail of yellow roots.

'Not like this!'

'You don't feel the sting after a while.'

'But look at you!' He grabbed the nettles from her and dropped them immediately. 'They hurt like . . . ! Stop! Please!' And he took her hands in his to stop her doing herself any more harm.

She didn't pull away as his fingers clasped about her wrists. On one hand he could see black and yellowing bruises and across her knuckles was a deep gash. 'You've cut yourself,' he said.

She shrugged, letting her hands lie lifeless in his.

'But what are you doing?' he tried again. She twisted her head at an angle. He put a gentle pressure on her right hand. 'Lady Rayne?'

'I'm restoring the garden,' she said, staring away from him into the distance.

'But look at—' Look at the state of you, he thought. He said, 'You've got a thorn here, right in your palm.'

'As problems go,' she said, 'I don't think a thorn's much to worry about.'

'It will be a problem if you get an infection. Lady Rayne?' Her head bowed. 'Here,' he said, 'let me.' But his nails were too short.

He lifted her wounded hand to his face and, his lips pressing against her skin, he pulled out the thorn with his teeth. Immediately, he let go.

But, instead of dropping her hands to her sides, she kept them outstretched and he found himself thinking of Oliver Twist, begging for more. There was something so pathetic about the gesture that again he grasped her hands tightly between his.

Ivens had been trained for this. Sometimes there was nothing you could do but be still with people and hold their hands. He was aware of the frailty of hers, so cut and torn, the bruises. But he was also conscious of their strength. To have done all this work in the garden required downright brute force. And his mind flew back to the blossom, blown by the slightest breeze yet vigorous enough to break into tremendous, glorious life, like her hands with their power for building and destroying, yet also, he thought, as she held on to him, for love.

His mind ranged. To be loved, and to be loved in return. How he longed . . .

He ignored his training and broke their silence. 'You're transforming this place,' he said. 'I imagine you could grow all sorts of things here now. So what might you plant? I'm hoping,' he persisted, as she scuffed the ground with her shoe, 'to persuade you to give me one of your nature lectures.'

At this she did give him a half-smile. 'Is that how it feels? That I'm lecturing?'

'Not at all.'

She sighed: 'In the past, they grew all sorts of delicious things here. Exotic soft fruits. But for that you need money. Apples would do well but even they're a big investment.' Then she took him completely by surprise by asking, 'Is your mother alive?'

'No, but why—'

'When did she die?'

'Two years ago.'

'How?'

'Pneumonia.' He saw the sympathy in her face, but he was determined not to talk about his losses. 'But why do you ask?'

'I keep thinking about my mother. After she died, I used to like watching the gardeners working for my father. The best ones treated the roses like children, stroking the leaves as if they were caressing a baby's cheek, wondering what do they need? Feeding? Watering? More sun? Less sun?' Suddenly, she looked at him sharply. 'Don't be sorry for me. There are little children who've lost their mothers. At least I can remember mine. But your father?'

'He's dead as well, but—' He didn't want her playing her trick of making the conversation about him but she was already asking when his father had died.

'In 1918,' he answered. His father was just twenty-one when the freezing waters off the West Coast of Scotland had closed over him, only days before the Armistice.

'So you never knew him?' He shook his head. 'The war?'

'Yes.'

And she cried out, 'What did we do? Our generation? To deserve two wars like this? And Stephen's convinced there'll be a third. And he was right about the last one.'

Her face contorted as if she might burst into tears, but instead she cast her eyes around the garden and said, 'Yet right now we have all this.'

Horizontal shafts of the setting sun were accentuating the light so Ivens felt they were standing together in the midst of a glittering green prism.

'Such incredible beauty,' she said.

She was holding her face close to his, almost, it seemed, as if beseeching him. But what could he say? Yes, the beauty is heaven-sent, glorious, incredible. But it is not enough, because it is not the joy of resting your head upon a loved one's shoulder, of bringing your lips to another's, of lying together, your skin touching, naked as Adam and Eve.

Obviously not! He was minister of the parish and a deeply unhappy married woman was turning to him for help yet all he could think of was the feel of his lips on her hand as he'd pulled out the thorn and how much he wanted to take her in his arms, holding her as close as humanly possible. For the second time that day, he prayed: give me strength.

189

He moved away from the nearness of her and asked, 'Does Sir Stephen ever talk to you about the war?' She raised her eyebrows as if that was the most idiotic question. 'A few do talk,' he said in explanation. 'Though they're the exception. Yet we've taken these men away from all they know and we've brutalised them, but then we expect them to take up where they left off. To wipe their feet on the doormat, not to let crumbs fall on the floor, when not long ago, God only knows what they were doing.'

'Or what,' she murmured, 'we've made them capable of.'

He gave her a quick glance up and down, chaste and professional, he assured himself. Too many meek and mild men had returned from war only to pick battles at home with a meanness of spirit and fists no one had ever suspected they possessed. He'd seen the curtness verging on cruelty with which her husband spoke to her, heard the village gossip that he slept alone in the attic.

The waste! Of this beauty! This woman!

He told himself he wanted to let go of her hands, that she was the one holding his so tightly. What was the matter with him? Was it the hope from Dr Downes? The feel of this woman's flesh against his own? He'd held women's hands before, but hers touched the emptiness in his own short life and right now his loss felt unbearable. Over the last couple of weeks he'd thought back with pleasure to the afternoon they'd spent listening to music together. Too much pleasure. Because I want her, he thought. I want her. And with that admission he extricated his hands and folded his arms, forcing himself back into his role as her vicar.

Her hands fell to her sides and, with a bit of her usual combativeness, she said, 'I suppose you think there's love here in the gentleness of the colours, the sweetness of the perfume. But plants are brutal! See that honeysuckle? Look how it's twining itself round what's left of that clematis, cutting it off from life, like putting a noose around someone's neck or hanging them on piano wire. As bad as humans.'

'No, these are plants! Unlike us, they've not got any choice.'

She gave that weary shrug again. 'Do you think we've really much choice in war? I don't. If I was ordered to commit some atrocity otherwise my own child would die, I know I would. I'd do terrible things to protect those I love. And myself no doubt. Human beings are vile. Please don't look like that. It's true. You only have to read the papers, about Nuremberg. What we all do to one another is so unbelievably evil sometimes I just want to dig and dig and lay myself down and be covered by the earth so I don't have to endure the horror anymore.'

What was she saying? That she wanted to die?

'Listen!' he said fiercely. 'To me—'

And an instinct which shocked him as he obeyed it made him take her face between his hands and lift it so she would look at him. 'You are as full of life as the earth here, the blossom, the spring.'

And he had to stop himself soothing that lovely, tortured face but the moment he went to move away she brought her own hand up to his, as if she might cradle her cheek in his palm. Then she closed her eyes. It can only have been for a second but in that time he was so conscious of her he feared he was going to make some dreadful transgression.

He stepped back but she held on to him and said, 'I hope you're right.' Then she clasped his hand between both of hers. 'But even if you're not, that's the most lovely thing I've

191

been told in a long, long time.' And she brought his fingers to her lips and kissed them.

The kiss of peace, he told himself: that ancient practice of wishing your brother and sister in Christ love and charity. Hastily, he trawled his memory for texts he'd read at college, aware of the way her hair fell across his wrist, the glorious earthy, peachy smell of her. St Augustine: 'When your lips draw near to those of your brother, do not let your heart withdraw from his.' *The kiss of peace.*

Could it be more than peace?

The second he asked himself the question she dropped his hand.

'Forgive me,' she said, 'I've been going on. And on!' She looked at her watch. 'Good grief!' She picked up the garden fork, stuck it on top of the wheelbarrow and, trundling it back to the shed, called over her shoulder, 'You must be wanting to get back to your tea. I know I'm hungry.'

He stood there feeling dismissed as he watched her clattering about, putting away garden tools. What had just happened?

Nothing. He'd been as absurd as a Jane Austen vicar, losing his head over the lady of the manor and he was forced back into a humiliating awareness of himself – the awkward, sickly clergyman.

'All done,' she smiled, the ramparts truly back in place.

'Thank you, for listening to me,' she said, when they reached the turn in the path where they parted. 'I know it's a difficult time for everybody. And compared with many I'm so very lucky.'

She avoided his eye, looking straight ahead to the pasture where crows cawed and dived over the grazing sheep.

'A lamb must have died,' she said. 'Or they're in the throes of finishing it off. When you think how we were promised bluebirds over the white cliffs of Dover. All I can see are crows feeding on carrion.'

27

STEPHEN STUMBLED OUT OF bed, sweat pouring off him. Every night was the same. Dynamiting bridges, destroying trains, setting fire to oil refineries, it didn't matter what mission he was on but, always, always, he clasped that dead body in his arms as phantoms with vaguely familiar faces hunted him down. He was never fast enough. Leaping up spiralling stairs ending in thin air, falling into bottomless pits, the dogs, without fail, caught him and he'd wake cowering, the weight of the corpse in his arms.

Steadying his hand, he reached for a glass of water. Now he wasn't terrified of the SS, of the burning paper stuffed down his shirt, of his head being held under the water. And he certainly wasn't frightened of death. What woke him was this hell where there was no escape from what he'd become.

He went to light the candle by his bed, then held back. There was enough light in the room from the moon, a perfect creamy circle in the sky's blackness.

During the war he'd both dread and long for a moon like this. Sometimes he found himself secretly desperate for a cloudy night so the mission would be aborted and he got to live another day in England. But that meant another twenty-four hours of anxiety and most of the time he decided it was best to get it over with.

'Anxiety is the devil's greatest weapon,' his mother used to say whenever he was fearful as a boy. Though now the devil's arsenal seemed infinite.

He shut his eyes tight. But even in the darkness he could sense the moonlight and an evening he thought he'd forgotten returned to him in lurid detail.

It was a sabotage mission, an arms factory near Rouen, and he was leading a unit of eight men. Stephen had worked with them all before, except the youngest, just married to a woman he'd known six weeks. You're too young to marry, Stephen had thought, and too young to be recruited. But he was bilingual so there was no place for niceties about age.

On the flight over they'd run into heavy cloud and Stephen had gone into the cockpit to discuss with the pilot whether to turn back. But just before they reached the French coastline, the cloud had cleared and they'd flown on.

The boy was gunned down as he landed. The other men, more experienced, had lain still as the Germans opened fire. But this young lad had run, making himself an easy target. As Stephen had pressed himself into the cold, wet earth, all he could think of was the boy's young bride, without her groom.

Alone, like his own bride tonight, in her bed at the other end of the house.

He punched the hard, unyielding mattress. The last time he and his wife had shared a bed was in that Hastings hotel when he'd been so in love with the warmth and joy of her neither of them had slept. Even now he could recall her wanton, wonderful body, how she'd danced for him. But that was another time, before that glorious summer's morning of Tuesday 1st August, 1944, when he was an ignorant fool and believed you could segment the world in distinct halves: the one where you made love to your beautiful wife; the other where you snapped the neck of a stranger.

One German lad had been just eighteen. A child in the wrong place at the wrong time. Afterwards, Stephen had gone through the boy's pockets and found a birthday card, along with half a bar of chocolate, which he'd wolfed down.

He believed he'd done the right thing. This was war. The man – or boy or woman or girl – to whom you showed your humanity, could turn round ten minutes later and pull the trigger. And you'd be the one dead.

He hauled himself off the bed and rested his forehead against the window pane. Slowly he hit his head against the glass, again and again. Bloody madness. He'd thought that if he survived the war he could *live* – come home to his wife, grow old with her. But after what he'd done that August morning, that was impossible.

So he'd deliberately courted danger, volunteering for whatever high-risk ops were going, the more dangerous the better: attacking tanks with a grenade, storming an enemy machine-gun nest. And after the war ended, he'd stayed on in Germany, helping track down Nazi war criminals. But however much he put himself in the line of fire, no German bullet put him out of his misery.

It was as if immortality was his punishment.

And here he was, back home.

On the day he eventually returned, Alice was waiting at Oakbourne Station in an emerald coat he'd bought her the Christmas before the war, her hair loose the way he'd loved it, soft and curling over her shoulders.

Fine strategist that he was, he'd thoroughly prepared himself for meeting her. He would immediately make his intentions clear – not even touch her. She had run towards him – as he knew she would – but with the press of her body against his, the feel of her bare fingers on his neck, he'd hesitated, suddenly unsure of himself. As her face had dropped with confusion at his lack of response, he collected himself. It was perfectly simple. All he had to do was walk away from her. So he did. Because that was where he wanted her – as far from him as possible.

His head rocked harder against the window. I could keep on doing this, he thought. Then hurl myself through the glass, no parachute to break the fall, dropping through the air to find a final peace.

He moved himself away from temptation and sat back on the bed.

'Bloody madness,' he muttered, trying to calm himself.

Many of his old colleagues were drinking the past into oblivion. Benoit had started down that route long before the war even ended. Wine, brandy, meths. Benoit would be dead soon, he thought. And I could be too. He caught the glint of his cut-throat razor. One quick slash. He'd done it enough times to others.

But he could not choose that route. This was retribution: a life sentence.

He looked again at the silver blade. Seconds were all it would take.

'Bloody madness,' he repeated in an attempt to control himself. '*Bloody madness.*'

The first time he'd parachuted out of a plane he'd muttered these words over and over. Oddly, they had eased the terror. Instead of fearing he would never again make love to Alice, drink a pint at the Queen's Head, write a poem, play cricket – the list of what he was about to lose on the flight felt infinite – he stopped caring about anything.

'Bloody madness,' he'd say as he fell into the void.

But then, what was extraordinary was that with the jolt on his back as the parachute opened, 'Bloody madness' became 'Bloody marvellous'. Floating down over the moonlit countryside – be it the rolling landscape of France or the Italian hills, it didn't matter where – for a blissful few moments he knew peace. Then his feet would hit the ground. And he would do his job.

He thought of the chaos of summer 1945, SS officers swinging from gallows as partisans meted out justice. He'd turned a blind eye, unmoved by the vengeance executed by men with power back in their own hands.

I should have intervened, he thought, resting back on his bed. Not because there'd been no trial and no jury, not because of all the fine arguments that we're better than this. But because death was too good for those bastards. They should be living and suffering as I do with the full knowledge of what I've done. Because, asleep or awake, the memory was unforgettable, begging him in the creaking of the house, clinging to him like the dust in his hair and crying out on that unforgiving easterly wind.

28

'THAT'S IT,' SAID ALICE, sealing the last of the wooden crates. She and Mrs Green had packed up the family's dinner service, commissioned from Wedgwood by an ancestor of Stephen's for a ball to celebrate victory at Waterloo, every piece hand-painted with trails of honeysuckle and roses suggesting an eternal English summer. Alice had sold it to an oil tycoon in Texas.

'I can't imagine this in the Wild West,' said Mrs Green.

'I don't think it's exactly wild these days, not if they need a ton of antique porcelain.'

'I hope,' Mrs Green sighed, 'Sir Stephen doesn't mind seeing it all go.'

Stephen wouldn't give a damn. She'd not even told him. They'd not exchanged a word since that morning he'd mentioned divorce. He'd kept to his attic and she to her garden.

'It's just,' persisted Mrs Green, 'when you think of all the generations who've enjoyed this beauty, this history, and then it's gone in the blink of an eye. It's such a shame.'

Surely, Alice wanted to say, trying to concentrate on the fact that with the sale of this china she could finally finish paying the death duties incurred after Stephen's father and then his brother died, you didn't expect life to return to how it was before the war? That the boiler would be replaced, the furniture unswaddled from its moth-bitten dust sheets, the silver polished for forty-strong dinner parties?

But, looking at Mrs Green's forlorn face, she simply said, 'This is miserable work. Why don't you call it a day? Have some tea?'

Once Mrs Green would have had an army of staff to make her tea but now, thought Alice, she's helping demolish the world she was born to, packing off its artefacts to the next empire so American millionaires can dine off an English summer where the sun never sets.

Mrs Green filled the kettle. 'Will you have a cup too?'

'No, no,' said Alice. 'I need to get out.'

Over the last couple of weeks, she'd made great progress in the walled garden. Work, work and yet more work! And she ran upstairs to fetch an extra sweater.

Emma and Gladys, the last two of the maids who were both leaving shortly to start secretarial courses, were in her room chatting.

'But how old do you think she is?' Emma was saying.

'Forty? Maybe more.'

Alice's composure faltered. She was thirty. Had she aged so very much beyond her years?

'My grandmother had my father at forty-five, so it's not impossible but . . . ?' Gladys stopped mid-sentence as she caught sight of Alice at the door.

Emma leapt up from the chair at the dressing table and brandished a duster. 'Lady Rayne, we thought you were with Mrs Green.'

Alice went to her wardrobe. 'Everything all right?'

Emma replied: 'We were just saying what lovely news it is about Mrs Harris – that she's expecting.'

'How wonderful!' cried Alice. 'After all they've been through!' She recalled the evening she'd glimpsed Mrs Harris and her husband washing up together as if it was the most tender courtship. 'I'm so pleased!'

She caught the glance between the two girls, the superior sneer of youth: what a sad old thing you are, with your delight at someone else's baby because in your solitary bed you'll no more have children than fly.

I'm pathetic to them, thought Alice. But one day they'll be my age. They'll know what I know. Because it was always the best news – life after death.

'Alice!' She heard her name and, to her shock, it was her husband calling and in a giddy moment she wondered if he actually wanted *her*. That there had been a miracle. That she too might know life after death.

'Alice!'

And there he was, in her bedroom, ghostly white, with blood dripping from his wrist. Gladys screamed and Alice had to stop herself crying out, 'What have you done?' Instead, she ran to him, grabbed his arm and lifted it above his head.

'Sit!' she commanded, pushing him down against the wall. 'Gladys! A towel! To stop the blood! And Emma, phone for Dr Downes. Run!'

'For God's sake, stop panicking,' said Stephen. 'It's only superficial. I'll need stitches, that's all. No one's dying.'

Emma halted, looking between them for instructions.

'Still hurry please, Emma,' said Alice, concentrating on not betraying the extremity of her thoughts. By how much had he missed killing himself? She pressed a towel over the

201

cut. 'Gladys, please go – now – and tell Mrs Green what's happened so she knows where to bring Dr Downes.'

Then she smiled, playing the competent lady of the house dealing with a little domestic accident. But she was sick with alarm. What thoughts led him finally to take this step? If he'd deliberately harmed himself what had made him stop? Would he do it again? 'And tea! Bring a cup of tea.'

'Jesus wept,' muttered Stephen. 'Tea!'

'Gladys, that's all, thank you.'

Alice pushed the door shut. Questions fired inside her like bullets.

'Don't look at me like that,' he said. 'I broke a glass, then forgot it and went to grab for it in the dark.'

'The dark? It's midday!'

'I had the curtains closed. The glass was on the floor. I reached down onto the jagged edge. Like this,' he demonstrated.

She supposed that was possible. He stared at her coldly. 'One thing you can depend upon,' he said, 'I'm here to live out my days, however long it takes.'

'I don't know what you mean by that.'

He grabbed her hand. 'I mean I'm not going to top myself.'

He was crushing her knuckles so hard she wanted to cry out but she steadied her voice and asked: 'Do you want to?'

'If I'd wanted to, believe me, I wouldn't have botched it. Now bring that chair over,' he said, letting her go, 'so I can rest my arm on it.'

She fetched the chair, then sat beside him on the floor, their bodies almost touching, the closest they'd been since his return. And as she watched his blood seep through the towel wrapped round his wrist it occurred to her that just as Mrs Green hoped life would go 'back to normal', she was every bit as pitiful. Packing up the china, she'd been thinking she'd go out later and thin the snowdrops, lift the bulbs from the woods and plant them at the door to the walled garden, so next winter their whiteness would pierce the January gloom.

But no garden was an escape from this man with blood on his hands. She'd persuaded herself that the crimes emerging from the war were *over there*. Not in her own country, her home, her bedroom. She'd yearned for his hands on her, for their power to caress, to bring alive. To love. But now she felt only their power to run a knife into soft flesh, pull the trigger of a heavy black revolver . . .

'Sir Stephen!' The doctor's wife burst in. 'My husband's on his rounds. So I've come instead. How are you?'

'It was an accident,' muttered Stephen, his eyes blank.

'You'll need stitches,' Mrs Downes was saying as she examined his wrist. 'Four at least, maybe six.'

Alice missed nothing as her thoughts acquired a cold clarity. She observed Mrs Downes's hesitation as Stephen told her not to bother with a sedative but just get on with it. She saw Mrs Green's anxious glances. She watched a weak light spread like the incoming tide, drowning the faded roses of the Aubusson rug. She caught the cries of curlews.

In that moment, she knew she had to get away from Oakbourne. And Stephen. Not for good. Perhaps. At least, not yet. She would go to her sister's in London, stay there for a few days to decide her next move.

'Lady Rayne!' Mrs Downes was looking at her in alarm. 'Are you all right? You're terribly white.'

'It's the blood,' she said. 'Simply the sight of so much blood.'

Then Mrs Downes asked for hot water.

'I'll get it,' she said. And Alice closed the door behind her.

 29

IN MR FRASER'S CONSULTING room at St Thomas's
Hospital, George Ivens stared at the outlines of 'X's on the
windows where tape had been stuck to protect the glass
from bomb blasts. 'I'm sorry we can't do more for you,'
Fraser was saying.

Ivens made his voice devoid of emotion: 'Dr Downes made
it clear not to have any expectations.'

'The Americans are ahead of the game on us so the best
I can offer is to send your details to a doctor in New York
who's terribly good.'

How the devil could he afford to go to New York? He'd
never travelled, not even seen the sea until he went to Suffolk.
In fact, thought Ivens, watching the dust floating in the early
evening light, Suffolk was the farthest he'd gone from the
street where he was born, because he'd been left behind
while so many men his age had travelled the world. And
although they'd gone under the menace of death, they'd
watched the sun set over Pacific seas, stood on deck as
contours of exotic islands appeared out of the mists, explored
twisting paths perfumed with hibiscus, bougainvillea . . . Oh,
stop! He wasn't in some *Boy's Own* comic.

'Discuss it with Downes,' Fraser was saying. 'I'll write to
him too. I know he's keen to keep up with all the research.

But it's difficult when he's – well – stuck out in the middle of nowhere. I hope,' continued Fraser questioningly, 'that Downes is all right.'

Fraser left a silence but Ivens didn't fill it. Downes, Ivens was certain, was trying to compensate for the loss of his ambitions, his leg and steady hands by championing the new health service, channelling his strength into fighting resistance from his fellow GPs, the bulk of whom believed putting the state in charge of medical care would be to the detriment of their power and pensions. And their patients.

'He was such a brilliant surgeon,' continued Fraser, getting to his feet. 'What a waste.'

What a waste.

In the stale air, the words hung like circles of smoke. That's what I am, Ivens said to himself, because what might I have done if I hadn't got sick?

He'd been blessed with a musical gift and, even more blessed for a boy from his background, given the opportunities to develop it. His voice had won him a choral scholarship, excellent schooling, but at fifteen he caught the rheumatic fever that damaged his heart.

Since then, he'd persuaded himself he'd served God better by entering the Church. But did Christ, Ivens often wondered, believe His life to be a waste? As He was nailed to His cross was He thinking, I've failed? My ministry finished just three years after it began, dead at thirty-three. Though I'll be lucky to make it that long, thought Ivens, following blue arrows to the hospital exit.

But you find your way through, Ivens lectured himself, tramping past signs to rheumatology, orthopaedics, infectious diseases, oncology, reminders – as if he needed them – of the betrayals and vulnerabilities of the body. You learn to stand apart from your disappointments. You hope to find some sort of acceptance.

Perhaps that's why Downes and I get on, he thought, getting into a lift to take him down to the ground floor. We're both building a life on others' needs because we can't fulfil our own – Downes with his welfare state, me with my church. But waves of disillusionment drained him, because if his desire to love his neighbour as himself was simply a way of nourishing himself on the problems of others, then *what a waste*.

The lift landed with a great clunk and he made his way to the packed forecourt, people surging along in the evening rush hour. Standing in the crowd he didn't know which way to turn. The prospect of returning to Stella and Mark's flat depressed him. He didn't want their kindness nor to have to find the grace to look generously upon their happiness as he lay on his bed made up on the sofa. He supposed he could take a detour via his old parish. He'd be assured of a warm welcome there. But the consultation had tired him. London tired him.

And his future terrified him.

Not so much death itself, but the slow agonising end, his heart failing so he lay an invalid, at the mercy of others, a burden. There was a lot to be said for the bullet in the head, he thought, wondering whether he should walk up to the Thames, but that meant passing what had been the northern wing of the hospital, now a pile of rubble in a crater. He could remember the night the bombs dropped there, the great fireball lighting up the sky. Ever since, the place had been cordoned off to stop children playing amongst all the broken glass and masonry, all the remnants of Victorians, Georgians, Tudors, of the Middle Ages, Dark Ages, Romans and a time long before anyone even knew what it was to build on all this London clay. Three wards had been destroyed. It had taken days to extract the bodies, lives extinguished, now dust to dust.

Dust . . . He cleared his throat. London was covered in the stuff. He hadn't really noticed when he'd lived here but now he saw with fresh eyes. Nothing had been washed for years so even buildings that had escaped the bombs were filthy. In the past he'd kept up a shield against the piles of broken stones fenced off with rusty wire, the tarpaulin roofs over once famous buildings, the unrelenting desolation. But today, his defences were down and he wanted to weep. For these poor people, for this beautiful city that had changed forever.

'Mr Ivens!' He felt a tap on his shoulder and turned round. Before him stood Alice Rayne. 'I thought it was you!'

'My goodness!' he cried. He'd not seen her since that afternoon he'd found her in the walled garden. He feared she'd been avoiding him but on her face, albeit drawn and tired, was what seemed the most welcoming smile he'd ever seen. Then he noticed her suitcase and it occurred to him she was about to be admitted to hospital.

'You're so pale,' he said fearfully. 'You're not ill, are you?'

'Not at all! My sister works here and I've just picked up the key to her flat. I'm staying with her,' she explained. 'But she's suddenly had to be on call so I need to let myself in. But you? I heard you'd gone to London. But that it was to see friends. Is everything—?'

'Everything's all right,' he interrupted, anticipating her question. 'Just a check-up.'

He was unsure what else to say. All he knew was that he could recall exactly the feel of her face between his hands and now he was desperate she didn't rush away to all her London friends and smart restaurants and fashionable nightclubs and whatever else she might be up to. Right then all he would ever again ask of life was that she would speak with him as if he was a healthy man, not this sorry, sick creature whose doctor had just sympathised that nothing could be done.

'So you're visiting your sister,' he said lamely, raising his voice as a bus rolled up, choking out fumes and passengers. She nodded, then replied with something he couldn't catch as she was drowned out by an ambulance siren. 'I'm sorry, I didn't hear.'

'Oh, nothing.'

'No, please, what?'

'It's just . . .' She stopped again and whether it was her hesitation giving him confidence or the awareness that with not long to live he might as well take his chances, he took her arm, drawing her away from the shadow of the hospital, to a bench amongst stumps of plane trees.

'Here,' he said, 'please, talk to me.'

She perched on the edge of the wooden seat, still and upright, but her eyes were agitated, darting about. Then she said, 'I've not been to London since before the war. It's a shock, isn't it? The devastation. I wasn't expecting it to be quite so dreadful. Of course I've seen the photographs . . . but to experience it for real . . . The cab took me round St Paul's. Those ancient buildings! Just gone! And we drove past Christchurch, Greyfriars – well, what's left of it.'

He remembered Greyfriars going up in flames and, that same night, another seven Wren churches.

'I went to a wedding there,' she said, 'before the war, and I thought it was heavenly the way the sun shone through those arched windows. And all the people over centuries who'd found joy or comfort in its beauty. Samuel Coleridge apparently. And Charles Lamb, Charles Wesley. Mendelssohn too.'

Ivens couldn't stop himself. 'I sang there a few times as a boy,' he said. 'And later, the Bach Magnificat – the tenor solo.'

'That's incredible! But you know how very lovely I think your voice is.'

Colour flooded his face.

'And what a privilege,' she said, 'to be part of all that history! But now . . .' She cast her hands before her. 'Your history and mine are blown sky-high. I know if you want to play a numbers game, you can find places with more damage, but what's the difference between ones and thousands if amongst the dead is one whom you love? My mother . . . Oh, nothing!'

'No, please! Your mother?'

'Once, she took my sister and me to the City to see what she called "Tudor London". I kept moaning I wanted to go to the zoo, but I wish I'd paid attention as now it's too late. And I know lots of people think destroying the past is a good thing and are all set on planning us new towns and societies and new everything. But as I sat in the cab I thought we've lost so much! And so fast! Oh, sorry – I'm going on. I'm just tired. I really ought to go.' But she didn't move. 'And let you get on.'

'No, no. The friends I'm staying with are working tonight.' His mind was racing for words of consolation. Then she reached for her suitcase and he thought now she will get up and leave.

But instead she said, 'If you don't have to be anywhere, would you like – perhaps we might—?'

In unison they spoke over each other. 'Have a drink?'

They both gave an awkward laugh.

'You're not in a hurry?' he asked.

'Not at all.'

So she wasn't rushing off into a glamorous social whirl.

'There's a pub just round the corner,' he suggested.

'Lovely! I'm so pleased to see you!'

30

THE PUB WAS BUSY with office workers, doctors chatting up nurses, builders from the bomb site round the corner but, just as Alice and Ivens arrived, a couple staggered up from a booth near the back.

'Why don't you take a seat?' he suggested, speaking loudly over the noise. 'And I'll get the drinks.'

What Alice wanted was a brandy but she was reluctant to make Ivens spend much money.

'Would you like,' he asked, 'a brandy?'

It was so long since someone had realised what she might like she was unnerved. Ten minutes ago, she'd been so distressed at the sight of bombed London, she was relieved to see a friendly face. But there was little Ivens missed and last time they met, when he'd found her pulling up stinging nettles with her bare hands, she was embarrassed at how easily she'd let down her guard. No one could know that she was seriously thinking she might leave her husband, least of all the vicar. No, not 'leave', she corrected herself, taking off her coat in the stuffy heat. The word was 'divorce'.

At home, she'd kept up appearances, not wanting to precipitate a crisis. She'd made sure Stephen's cut was healing; fielded Mrs Downes's and Mrs Green's all too astute concern; kept her appointment with Mrs Lubbock to discuss the tea for next Saturday's cricket match, all the time wondering whether anyone in the village had ever actually had a divorce. She could hardly ask. Most people either put up and shut up. Or simply ran off.

One step at a time, she kept telling herself. But the steps kept leaping all over the place so she lost track of which one came next, let alone where they were heading. She would need to instruct a solicitor. She would need to find somewhere to live. She would need to work out how to support herself. She would need . . . . The steps just went on and on and she was at a loss to know where to start. Not with a drink with another man.

He was fighting for a place at the bar where glasses were being slapped down for a crowd of young men in ill-fitting Demob suits, seemingly getting on with their lives and putting the past behind them. Yet there was an air of desperation about them, their laughter forced, as if to say: I will have a good time! I will! I will!

I'm not, she thought, the only one putting on a front. This time last year, those men were in khaki, God knows where, the Far East probably. Or, if they were still in Europe, they were being told that having fought one war here they had to take their chances all over again against Japan. And once all the killing stopped, what had they come home to? Wives who'd waited for them? Wives they'd fallen out of love with? Wives who'd had babies by other men?

The papers were full of such stories. There'd never been so many divorces – yet more casualties of war. But she herself didn't know anybody who'd gone through with one.

Stephen had said he'd make divorce 'easy' for her. That meant he'd spend a night in a hotel, find a woman to join him, and she'd need to hire a private investigator to report back. And that was the 'easy' option. The alternative was standing up in court and accusing him of cruelty. Or desertion. Or incurable insanity. Certainly he was cruel. Certainly he'd deserted her emotionally. Was he out of his mind? Quite possibly. But if I stay with him, she thought, I too will go mad.

She put a smile on her face as Ivens returned. Persuade him to talk about himself, she told herself. Keep it light. She launched in: 'How long are you in London for?'

'I get the eleven-ten train home tomorrow.'

'Where are you staying?'

'With Stella's fiancé.'

'Stella with the wonderful voice?'

'Yes.'

He took a small sip of his beer.

'Does he live nearby?'

'No.'

'Where?'

'Streatham.'

With that, conversation, such as it was, came to a standstill. It was his turn to ask her something but he just stared into his pint. She didn't understand. He'd been so pleased to see her but now his monosyllabic responses were downright rude. Then she glimpsed what she thought were tears in his eyes.

'Mr Ivens! What's the matter?'

'It's the smoke. Being around so many cigarettes after all your Suffolk fresh air.'

True, the air was thick with tobacco, but then he blinked fiercely and at once her intentions of keeping the conversation anodyne were shot to bits.

214

'I don't believe you,' she said. 'Something's wrong.'

'No, no . . . It's just, like you, I was shocked by all the destruction when I got back to London. But seeing everyone in civilian clothes again, I was thinking at least with buildings you can *see* the destruction. Yet with people the destruction can be completely hidden.' He nodded towards the bar. 'Who knows what they're all concealing.'

But the only secret she was interested in was his. She could sense an ache in him like damp in the air. If there was a time to ask, it was now.

'Your health,' she began, 'all the secrets we carry. I just wondered—'

He interrupted: 'I had rheumatic fever which probably saved my life as it meant I couldn't join up. Compared with most I had an easy war.'

'Living through the Blitz was hardly easy.'

He just shrugged and after a moment said, 'I presume you're going to this Whitsun cricket match?'

'You're like everybody else!' she cried. 'Avoiding saying anything by changing the subject. Pretty clumsily too,' she added in an attempt to make him smile.

But making it quite clear he was not in the mood for confidences, he continued, 'I understand your husband opens the batting.'

Stephen was the last thing she wanted to talk about. 'Someone from his family always does,' she muttered and they fell into silence which, after a while, he filled by asking about her sister. What was her speciality?

Obstetrics.

Did she have a family?

215

Alice was about to say 'no'. But instead she said: 'My sister actually lives with a married man whose wife won't grant him a divorce.'

She felt she was setting him a test, though she was unsure on what. Whether he thought her sister 'immoral', whatever morality meant these days? If he believed that love, by definition, could never be illicit?

'You would hope,' he said, 'that if you really loved someone but knew you made them unhappy you'd give them your blessing and let them go. That would be love. Easy to say, of course. The wife is probably angry, frightened. It's hard being a single woman – especially financially and, whatever women hoped, I don't think the war's changed things.'

He was right. When she'd rung her sister she'd intended mentioning her ideas for reviving their father's business, but Catherine had just gone on about the injustice of some man being made a consultant rather than her.

'My sister,' she said, 'has just been passed over for promotion by a man whom, she says, anyone with a brain would know was a liability.'

'Had he fought?'

'At Dunkirk. Then he was captured.'

'Poor devil. Like Dr Downes.'

'Yes, but—'

'But it's not fair on your sister, nor to all his patients.'

'No.' The complications of life churned about her. Over by the bar someone began playing the piano and she twirled her brandy balloon as a crowd gathered, wailing the chorus of 'We'll Meet Again'. She saw Ivens glance over. Then he winced.

'What is it?' she asked.

He dropped his head, speaking quietly. 'I loathe this song.'

'Me too!' She grabbed his hand.

And, for the first time since they'd arrived in the pub, he met her eye and he gave her the smile that had struck her when she'd driven him to Norwich. The glint in intelligent brown eyes, the suggestion of sympathy, affinity.

'Really?' he asked.

'Really!' She drew nearer as noisy laughter erupting from the booth behind made it almost impossible to hear. 'I've never confessed it before. It seems blasphemy! But all that false hope of blue skies when the reality is so so . . .'

He just clasped her hand tightly, as if he completely understood, and the next moment he was on his feet, urging her up. 'Let's give them a night to remember!'

'What—?'

'Lady Rayne—'

'Alice! Please!'

'Alice, we – you and I – are going to sing!'

She burst out laughing. 'That's preposterous. You sing! I can't!'

'With me, you'll sing.' That smile again. And it had its effect. With his hand now in the small of her back she was letting him guide her through the packed pub to the bellowing of 'Underneath the Arches', and they ended up squeezed together at the piano. Then someone called out for 'Danny Boy'. And there arose a collective cry of 'Oh Danny Boy, the pipes, the pipes . . .'

Ivens joined in. Amongst the hoarse, plaintive voices his pure, unaffected tenor stood out. The other singers paused. The pianist too stopped playing.

Alice saw strained white faces soften, hands brush at eyes. Crushed up beside him, she was conscious of his breathing, the swelling of his chest as he wrought every ounce of yearning from the familiar song.

'. . . . And I shall sleep in peace until you come to me.'

There was a moment's silence, then a huge applause broke out.

'That,' he whispered, under all the cheering and clapping, 'was probably too sentimental for you.'

'No, no,' she protested, but she doubted he heard as he was fending off congratulations and offers of drinks. She saw the pianist catch his eye. And all at once he was shifting the mood with 'Daisy, Daisy', waving his arms to encourage everyone to join in.

'You too,' he said to her.

So she sang.

'See,' he said, after a roaring crescendo, the pianist bashing hard, his foot on the loud pedal, 'I told you, you could sing.'

'You're mocking me now!'

'Never!' And then he was being asked if he knew 'Shenendoah'. He did. And they were off singing again. Followed by 'Greensleeves'.

She noticed Ivens say something she didn't catch to the man at the piano. But the man gave Alice a wink, then got up so Ivens could take over.

'All right?' he smiled, glancing up at her.

She nodded, catching sight of a woman in the grimy mirror by the bar, her colour heightened, her eyes blazing. A stranger, she thought, barely recognising herself. Vibrant. Happy.

She didn't know the melody Ivens was playing. But it was a waltz and, at a table near the back, a couple got up to dance. With their arms around each other, their bodies melded together in perfect time. Others followed and she felt such a longing to join in, it was almost a physical pain. Then Ivens segued into a tune Alice knew well: 'Begin the Beguine'. She'd told him how she liked it that afternoon she'd turned up at his lodgings, and she wondered if he'd remembered or if it was just a coincidence.

'I didn't know you played the piano,' she said, watching how his hands ran effortlessly over the keys. 'Let alone so beautifully.'

'There's no reason you would. But I'm told you're a wonderful dancer.' She looked at him askance. 'You know how people talk,' he said in explanation. But before she could give Oakbourne gossip another thought he was singing 'Night and Day'.

'A voice like that,' said a woman beside her, 'could charm the birds from the trees.'

'He brings tears to my eyes!' said another, her mascara running. 'Lucky you, to have a husband who sings like that . . .'

Alice was about to explain, but in a moment of defiance she stopped herself. She was away from home, from 'talk'.

She simply continued accepting compliments on his behalf and when he beckoned for everyone to join in 'Westering Home' then 'Bye Bye Blackbird' she sang too. God only knew what racket she was making, but she was past judgement. If she couldn't dance she would sing. Just so long as the evening went on because this very indifferent pub now felt like a haven of safety. Of blessed forgetfulness. Of joy.

Before she knew it, the bell was ringing, the landlord calling out for last orders and Ivens was getting up from the piano.

People were congratulating him, then leaving, the pub emptying.

'You were wonderful,' she said. But he was suddenly distant.

'It was nothing.' And next thing he was fetching her coat as if he couldn't get out of the pub fast enough.

She tried again. 'What a gift to do that for people – to cheer them so.'

But he was already picking up her suitcase, his face a white mask. The night was over.

'Shall we go?' he said. And he led the way.

A storm had blown in. Rain sluiced down, bouncing high off the pavements. In the distance, she heard thunder.

'How are you getting to your sister's?' he asked, as they hovered in the pub doorway.

'Taxi – if possible.'

But a man also sheltering said: 'You'll be lucky. In this rain. With no buses or trains.'

Ivens stepped in: 'Not another strike?'

'Afraid so. It's just been called.'

'They keep having these lightning strikes,' said Ivens. 'The best bet is for us to start walking and if a cab passes you, grab it. But the chances of finding one tonight are virtually non-existent, I'm afraid. I'll carry your case for you.'

'But if there's no transport, how will you get to Streatham?'

'I'll walk.'

'But that's miles. And you can't walk in this weather.' As if to prove it, a gust of wind took hold of her hat and he ran to catch it. 'Leave it!' she cried, as it went flying over the road. She caught up with him and gripped his arm. 'There's room at my sister's. I can make you up a bed on the sofa.

Her – her . . .' She was unsure what to call the man Catherine lived with? Her lover? Hardly! Oh, what did it matter?

'The flat's empty,' she said, 'as they're both on call, so you staying the night is no problem.' Though she was fully aware it could be construed as the opposite. But walking in this would be the death of him.

He was still hesitating. But a lorry lumbering past and drenching them both with a spray of dirty water settled the matter.

'If you're sure,' he said.

She was sure.

# 31

THE KEY ALMOST SLIPPED from Alice's wet hands as she unlocked the heavy engraved-glass doors to Catherine's block of flats and hurried into the well-lit lobby. The heat! There was such a rush of hot air from two colossal radiators she felt she'd walked into a greenhouse in mid-summer.

'What a relief!' she said, shoving the doors shut behind her. 'It's like the end of the world out there.'

With the storm battering down, they'd barely said a word, skirting puddles, jumping over gutters. His trousers were sodden and her legs splashed and grimy.

Then she caught him eyeing the shifting patterns of pale polished marble, the curves of the staircase, the lift with its doors of brass twisted into willowy lilies. He whistled softly.

'My sister works very hard,' she said, suddenly on the defensive because in Whitechapel you certainly wouldn't find apartments as warm as this where radiators, moulded with elegant tulips, doubled as works of art.

'I'm sure,' he said, as they got into the lift.

Please, she thought, uncertain if there was an edge to his voice, let's not have a class war. Not tonight.

As they headed up to the top floor, she took in his threadbare jacket, his scuffed shoes. He looked so shabby. But so did she in her pre-war coat. She wanted to say, at home, I'm so cold I go to bed with three hot water bottles. But there was no point in a competition in suffering. She'd lose, obviously. And if someone else was cold, did that mean you could not enjoy being warm? If you sat down to a good dinner, was it robbed of all flavour because others were hungry? Could you never be at peace? Not even for one night?

The lift came to a smooth stop, and they walked in silence along the corridor to Catherine's flat. Alice opened up, then they both halted uncertainly. The hallway had a parquet floor, but beyond that stretched an expensive pale green carpet with a thick velvety nap.

'Walking on that carpet,' said Alice, with forced lightness, 'is a bit like stomping over the wicket on a cricket pitch. I always fear I'm trespassing on hallowed ground. I'd better remove these.'

She slipped off her soggy shoes. He untied his laces and removed his brogues. There were holes, she noticed, in the heels of his socks and her own feet were black, soaked through with dirty rainwater. They'd mark the carpet but she could hardly take off her stockings in front of him. He too was hesitating, looking at the spotless carpet and the state of their feet when there was the clunk of coal falling in the grate.

'Is someone here?' he asked.

'The porter does the fire,' she said, wondering how he'd receive signs of yet more privilege. 'My sister would have asked him to light it – as a treat, because Oakbourne is freezing.'

'It's certainly a treat, but are we going to spend all night marooned on this patch of wooden floor? Or find a way across this beautiful carpet? My feet and, by the looks of things, yours are very wet. But since yours are considerably smaller, they won't leave such large footprints, so perhaps you could leap across and get a towel.'

'I'm so sorry. Yes, yes of course.'

'Alice? Are you all right?'

'Yes!' she said, tiptoeing to the bathroom.

Behind the door she pulled off her stockings and wiped her feet, unsure how she'd ended up alone with him. If the storm had held off half an hour . . . If tonight hadn't been the night for a bus strike . . .

She returned with a snow-white towel, edged with a pattern of emerald shells, as silky and soft as swan's down. It made the towels she had at home feel like wet rags. She suspected Ivens was drawing the same comparison. Oh, so what if he was? She'd be back to dank dampness soon enough.

'Look at my feet,' he said. 'They'll ruin this perfect towel. Have you got another one? Black, ideally.'

'Don't worry, please. Use this. I'm so sorry, it seems such a lot of fuss about a carpet.'

'Not at all. Mrs Turner always puts out a sheet of newspaper by the door for me to leave my shoes on.'

She pictured his welcome in that dark house. No warm embrace. Simply an admonition not to get the floor dirty. Though, it wasn't much different for her. Going home was every bit as bleak.

She stood watching over him, recalling something about vicars washing people's feet at Easter? Or was it the other way round? She'd always accepted the dismissive attitude to religious rituals she'd grown up with – they were irrational, tainted by sentiment and sanctimony. But the humility of a man kneeling to dry his feet touched her. For a fleeting moment she was tempted to reach out to help him.

The instant the idea crossed her mind, he was already straightening himself up, saying, 'I think I can venture forth now.'

'Sorry! Sorry!'

'Alice?' He'd assumed a professional expression of sympathy: I'm your vicar. The hero of the hour entertaining a London pub had gone with last orders. 'What's troubling you?'

'Nothing!'

'But you keep apologising. Look,' he said, 'what would you be doing if I wasn't here?'

'I suppose I'd have a bath.' And she was vindicating herself yet again: 'We don't have hot water at home so I have to run up and down stairs with kettles.'

'Then have your bath. And I'll sit by that fire. Perhaps I can put my jacket somewhere to dry.'

Taking his jacket, she brushed his hand. 'You're freezing!' His lips she now noticed were drained of colour. He was perishing cold. 'Here's what we'll do,' she said. 'I'll get you some dry clothes. My sister's – er – David I'm sure won't mind. But you – we – need to warm up or we'll both end up with pneumonia. I'll run you a bath.'

'I thought you wanted one.'

'I need to unpack first.'

This was a lie, she'd hardly anything with her. But now she was anxious he'd catch cold.

She went to run the bath, gave him an enormous towel that had been left warming on the heated rail and gestured round at the untouched bar of pale blue soap, perfumed with wild hyacinths, jars of green bath salts. (How on earth did Catherine get hold of these? Presents from grateful patients?) 'Help yourself to whatever you need. I'll fetch those clothes for you.'

They almost collided in the narrow doorway.

'Sorry, sorry,' they both said in unison.

He moved into the hall to let her out and into her sister and David's bedroom.

'These should do,' she said after she'd found him a shirt and trousers. 'But I'm afraid they might be on the small side.'

'They'll be perfect,' he said, the bathroom steaming up behind him, his face inscrutable. What on earth was going through his mind? More to the point, what was going through hers? Because bubbling to the surface came the question, when did I last have a bath with a man?

'I'll leave you to it,' she said quickly, retreating to the narrow spare bedroom.

She unpacked her good dress, re-hemmed several times and mended after it ripped, but which, even though she was so thin, still hinted at pliable curves, and, if you were looking, brought out the green of her eyes. She hesitated, wondering whether to wear it this evening. Then she heard the splash of bathwater and, dismissing the image that flickered before her, she hung up the dress and got out her old slacks and shirt, baggy and comfy. Unflattering.

She'd have to offer Ivens something to eat, but in the 'galley kitchen', Catherine had left a note apologising for how little there was: just tins of Spam, half a loaf of bread and a dollop of margarine. As a present for Catherine, she'd brought a bottle of brandy and half a dozen Suffolk eggs. Perhaps we could have them, she thought, suddenly ravenous.

226

'What bliss!' Ivens was standing behind her, rubbing his hair dry. 'Thank you so much.'

'Not at all.' He takes up so much space, she thought, because, for all its luxury, the flat was small, the rooms compact, the ceiling low. She opened the brandy. 'Would you like one?'

'Would I! Is this the delicious stuff you brought me the other week?'

'Yes.'

'Dr Downes and I have been really enjoying it.'

I wanted *you* to enjoy it, she thought, not give it to Dr Downes, who is desperate to see Stephen and me out of Oakbourne Hall. Well, he'd get half his wish soon enough.

'It turns out,' Ivens continued, 'he and I grew up not far from each other so we've that in common. And we play chess. Oh! I've been meaning to say – I was told you can play three games of chess at once.'

'How on earth did you hear that?'

'Mrs Turner mentioned it.'

'Village "talk",' she muttered. Then, in case Ivens decided to challenge her to a game, she said, 'My father insisted I learn to show everyone that just because I couldn't spell, I wasn't stupid. But I hate chess now, having to perform in that way.' And she changed the subject. 'There's not much to eat, I'm afraid.'

'I'd far rather be hungry than cold. And I'm certainly not that. It's so lovely, being here.'

'Really?'

'Yes, of course. Why wouldn't it be? Alice, please! What's worrying you so much?'

That you'll dislike me, she said to herself, the way Dr Downes does – for my big house, title, all that. Not that I really care what Dr Downes thinks. But you?

She came out with it: 'I'm frightened of being hated for having so much.'

He gave her a strange look. 'Do you really have so much?'

'Of course! For starters, look at what we're drinking!' Excellent brandy too, she thought. 'Help yourself,' she said, rather grandly.

'Thank you. But why don't you warm up? You've had a long journey. Please, pretend I'm not here. I'll sit by that fire and leave you to it.'

With that he squeezed past her into the sitting room and she locked herself in the bathroom.

She hurled bath salts under the running water and undressed quickly. Wiping steam from the mirror she saw a slender body. Still desirable? She stretched out her arms. She'd acquired muscles – all that gardening. She'd not noticed. But when had she last stood naked in front of a mirror like this? When had anyone last seen her body? Really looked?

She lowered herself into the hot water. This bath is what she'd been longing for. All week she'd been telling herself that in London she could unwind, then calmly work out the way forwards. But it was impossible to relax with him outside. She couldn't rid herself of the thought of Ivens soaking here a short while ago and she kept flip-flopping about like a newly-landed fish. The flat was too loaded with his presence. It wasn't simply that he took up so much room. It was . . . what?

I want his approval, she thought, for him to like me, but that was no reason to feel so overwhelmed.

228

She hadn't wanted the evening to end. And it hadn't. So what did she want? Now?

His good opinion? His conversation? His company? Yes! Yes! But more.

His body? His love? Is that what it is?

She slapped her hand over her mouth for fear she'd cry the words out loud. Could it really be that she wanted his love?

She assessed the evidence, counting up the times they'd actually met. Not many. But enough. Enough for him to give her something she'd lost.

Hope.

On that evening she'd found him lost on the marshes she'd discovered he was someone she could talk to. She'd told herself he was interested in plants, the garden, but perhaps she'd been the one unconsciously seeking him out. Going to Evensong. Driving him to Norwich. Turning up uninvited at his house and thrilled he'd sung for her – not any old song but what seemed some of the most romantic music she'd ever heard.

How could she not have seen this coming?

She brought her wrist to her lips – she tasted of wild hyacinths – then examined her face in the mirror, bare of makeup. She appeared exactly the same. But she wasn't. What she was feeling now wasn't giddiness or excitement. Instead she felt oddly composed.

But Ivens? George? She'd never spoken his Christian name. What was he thinking about her? He liked her, she was in no doubt. Who knew if it was more. But, these days, who knew what anyone was really thinking?

She began untangling her wet hair and looked again in the mirror. If, she told herself, he views you as a pathetic parishioner, a sad woman seeking excitement in a stunted existence, it's all right. It really is.

She pictured him sitting by the fire. She'd believed she could only ever love Stephen.

But now?

She no longer knew. But what she did know was that she was about to take a step she'd once believed impossible.

32

IVENS HAD FELT ALICE'S bewilderment when he'd suddenly rushed them out of the pub. But the joy of singing for her had become unbearable. The connection he'd desired so deeply only reminded him of all he was about to lose. He'd been in heaven – heaven on earth – and despite the warmth in this extraordinary luxury, he shivered. Before long he'd know exactly what heaven was.

If there was one.

Ye now therefore have sorrow: but I will see you again. Such glorious language, promising life after death. The cadences of the King James Bible touched the very core of his being, but tonight they seemed no more than great literature, the myth man had concocted to assuage disappointment in this world.

When in doubt, a priest he revered would tell him, pray. Let God do His work.

He bowed his head: *Oh Lord, let me live, now and forever, spare me now and forever, before I go hence, and be no more seen.*

Let me live!

'I don't know about you.' He swung round and Alice was there, her skin rosy and flushed, her eyes bright and enquiring. 'But I'm famished! We could treat ourselves to the eggs I brought for my sister. Do you like *real* scrambled eggs?' She laughed and before her vitality he felt himself dimming into insignificance. 'Daft question!'

He attempted a smile. 'That would be lovely,' he murmured.

'Good! Now please talk to me while I make them.'

So he inched into the tiny kitchen, trying not to be in the way as she asked him to slice the bread. But there was so little room they stood almost touching. He watched her find a frying pan, crack eggs, stir them over the stove. He asked if she wanted the bread toasted – she did – so he manoeuvred himself around her to the grill. Then she was saying she needed to get to the cupboard for plates and she was reaching up to him, putting her hands on his shoulders and moving him gently to one side and he could feel the pressure of her hands, her slightness, her strength, almost as if they were about to dance together, a perfect fit.

Is this what marriage is? he wondered. The two of you moving in sympathy, an invisible current holding you in unison?

He placed his hand where she'd briefly held him. He was so rarely touched. In London, some of his parishioners who'd known him for years might give him a hug. Or friends, like Stella, would kiss his cheek. With tenderness, yes, sisterly, maternal.

Not a tenderness that felt so ineffably arousing.

He dropped his eyes to the floor. She was saying they should eat by the fire and he forced himself to act normally, to do as she asked, to carry a tray, to leave the cramped kitchen and return to the sitting room. He didn't know where to put himself. The room felt charged with possib-ilities. She'd already taken the sofa, curling up her bare feet. Beside her, there was space for him. He chose the armchair.

'Enjoy!' she smiled.

What might have been? If circumstances were different – such a pointless, destructive train of thought. But if, if . . . The joy he found in talking to her! They made each other laugh! Or he might sit like this, sharing a meal in companionable silence, knowing that at the end of the day she would be there in his bed, her lovely graceful body lying beside him, the whole night long.

He allowed himself a quick glance at her but she was already watching him from under flickering eyelashes, not coyly or coquettishly, but uncertainly.

She said: 'Earlier, you asked if I really had so much. What did you mean?'

That, he thought, despite your big house and all those trappings, your misery is palpable. But he was nervous now of saying something so intimate and sought safety in generalities.

'Just that I meet lots of people who've survived the war. They've been given this gift of life but they can't grasp it anymore. It's as if the war has taken their right to live.'

He'd once preached a sermon on these lines. He believed it was true of so many. But what of this woman leaning towards him, her chin in her hand, her eyes fixed upon him, as if debating what she might reveal?

She said, 'That's true for Stephen – as far as I can tell. But not me. At least I'm trying not to let it be so. Unlike you, I don't have a faith. I just keep my options open.' She gave him a faint smile. 'But I do believe in tangibles, which is why I work in that garden. So whatever the horrors of the last six years, I believe – or try to – that war doesn't – shouldn't – negate the good things: that snowdrops gleam at night, that a rose can be coaxed back to life . . . you know what I mean – you've had plenty of my "nature lectures". Not that I always practise what I preach. Sometimes the misery still gets the better of me. But, despite all we've been through, the good is still true, isn't it?'

'Yes,' he said, trying to retain an expression of detached sympathy. 'It's all true.'

'And even a heathen like me knows that Christ's first miracle was turning water into wine. Good wine too, wasn't it? At a wedding party?'

He nodded.

'So does that mean,' she continued, 'Christ believed it's our duty to be happy?'

Again he nodded.

'So we don't have to suffer because others have? You'd argue, wouldn't you, that Christ has done that for us? He took on all our suffering on our behalf?'

Once more, all he could do was move his head up and down in agreement.

'George?' She'd never before used his name and she seemed to say it in a way that gave him the grace he always felt he lacked. 'So, George, shouldn't we enjoy all the amazing gifts we have? Be they God-given or the result of some extraordinary accident of colliding planets? And isn't that one thing war should have taught us? That we take from every moment whatever joy and beauty we can? Because it might be our last?'

Yes! Yes! But where does that leave us? he thought desperately. You? Me? Sitting together, just inches apart. In

different circumstances, he would have joined her on the
sofa, taken her hand with professional sympathy. If they were
not here, away from Oakbourne, away from neighbours,
away from her husband. If she was a different woman. If his
feelings were not so devastating.

If, if . . . If I was not in love with you.

'George?' That voice again. He knew he was supposed to
answer her question. Should he enjoy the gifts of God? But
he didn't trust himself to speak. He was aware of her getting
up from the sofa, the faint woodland perfume of her.

Now she was kneeling at his feet.

'Please,' she said, 'look at me.' He kept his eyes fixed on
the fire. 'I didn't mean this to happen but – I think I could
fall in love with you. And I think you might feel the same
about me.'

So was this the miracle? That she felt as he did? That
she'd been brave enough to tell him the truth?

'Lady Rayne . . .' She frowned at his sudden formality –
he owed her more than this. He had to match her honesty.
But where should he begin? Tell her he longed for her in
a way that broke all the rules of his vocation? Confess that
he was dying?

'Alice, you're married. And I'm a clergyman, *your* clergyman.'

'That's true. But it's not the whole truth.'

He heard the fire crackling, her quickened breath. She
did not move. She just sat at his feet looking up at him as
if they had all the time in the world.

Then she brought her fingers to her neck and simply undid
the buttons of her shirt.

She was naked underneath.

Dear God, he prayed, help me now.

'George?'

He knelt, reached forwards and slipped the shirt from her shoulders. Then he folded her into his arms and brought his lips to meet hers.

And, that night, he lived.

 33

ALICE CLIMBED ONTO THE Ipswich train at Liverpool Street. She'd spent the last six days in London, talking and walking and being dragged round shops by her sister. She'd told Catherine about Stephen, but nothing about her night with George. Heaving her suitcase up onto the rack now she felt exhausted, but what weighed her down was the note she'd found on the bedside table the morning after.

'*Thank you, darling Alice. God bless you.*'

Those seven words were the last she'd heard from him. The click of the flat door closing had woken her just as it was getting light, and there it was: his gratitude, his endearment, his blessing, but no idea as to how he felt about what happened between them.

As the train juddered into action, she dropped onto the greasy seat. Last week he would have taken this route home past the very same skeletons of gutted warehouses, streets awaiting demolition. But what, she asked herself for the umpteenth time, had he been thinking?

'*Thank you, darling Alice. God bless you.*'

Was that thank you for your love? Thank you for a fleeting moment of pleasure? Or a polite brush-off?

All week, she'd replayed the events of that night. Think, she'd tell herself. Be logical. You know love. You know love's power to transform. And that night, so did he.

But her logic also brought the conclusion that her behaviour had been so brazen he'd believe she'd thrown herself at him simply because she'd been let off the leash away from home.

Or, worst judgement of all: she'd used him in her desperation to snatch from life a glorious night. She'd taken advantage of his loneliness and caused that dear, dear man pain.

She looked out at the shell of a church, mountains of corpse-grey concrete, tall cranes towering to the heavens. She'd see him at the cricket match tomorrow where they'd have to fake neighbourly politeness in front of the village. She could manage that, as no doubt could he. But I want him, she thought. I want— She couldn't finish the sentence.

Think . . . Be logical.

She wanted him to be fit and well. Obviously. When she'd lain her head on his chest she'd been conscious of the strange racing of his heart, as if a wren was fluttering within his ribcage. She'd ignored the unbidden recollection of the steady beat of Stephen's healthy heart and had wished she might ask what, exactly, is wrong? But when she'd enquired about his health, he'd brushed her aside. So she'd kept quiet in his arms, nervous of anything that might release his hold on her.

Yet, as the week went by, she'd begun to worry he might be seriously sick, so much so that yesterday she'd telephoned Mrs Green on the pretext of confirming the time of her return train and made some convoluted reference to 'Mr Ivens'. But Mrs Green only mentioned she'd heard he'd been at the Queen's Head and sung 'Greensleeves'. 'Quite beautifully, apparently, and even reduced a couple of grown men to tears.' And she was angry over her unnecessary anxiety because if he was off singing down the pub, there wasn't much wrong with him.

She'd considered telephoning his lodgings, but with Mrs Turner hovering in the hallway they would only be able to speak as clergyman and parishioner. Not as lovers.

Lovers?

She had a lover.

It was, it occurred to her as she sat primly, her gloved hands in her lap, a most beautiful word and she smiled, not primly. But then, as the train lumbered round a bend, she caught sight of a house with its entire front blown off, an unmade bed still on the first floor, an upstairs wall flapping in the wind. It was monstrous, like a diabolic bird hovering over death and destruction, and she shut her eyes tightly so she might return to the safe haven of that night and recall the long line of his spine, how her fingers reached under the hollows of his shoulder blades, how the two of them lay in a tangle of limbs without the merest fraction of an inch between them.

But what brought her joy might have mortified him with guilt. He was a clergyman. He'd broken a commandment. What number, she'd no idea. But adultery had been committed. So was he – right now – tearing himself to shreds because of some sin he believed he'd been party to?

She got up to close the window, which was letting in gusts of damp, soot-filled air.

Oh, these men and their damned guilt! She was sick of it because didn't guilt show a lack of faith in the all-forgiving God he professed to believe in? He'd made love to her, yes, a married woman. But so what, when the sight of her gold wedding band made her feel stifled for breath, cursed like

Midas? And the miracle of that night was that she had felt, for the first time since the end of the war, that life was being handed back to her.

And it would be a life without Stephen, a husband who didn't speak to her unless to be cruel, a man capable of the worst sort of violence and which she feared would be unleashed upon her. A husband she no longer loved.

She'd achieved what she'd set out to do when she went to London. She had formed a plan of action. Thinking and logic had been of some service. As soon as she got home she would tell him she wanted a divorce. She would set the ball in motion.

As for George, she'd wait and see. She'd made a conscious decision not to tell him she was considering divorce so that whatever happened could be purely about them, not legalities, with all the constraints of the world intruding and undermining and sullying. It would be clear soon enough whether he wanted to see her again.

I had my beautiful night, she thought as the train pulled into a station – which one, she didn't know, as the name signs still weren't back up – and she squashed into the corner as the compartment filled up with a large party heading out for the day for a picnic. *And whatever happens, whatever people say, whatever you say, no one can take it from me. It's mine.*

She felt the sudden joy on her face and she turned away from the sight of the other passengers settling down with bags and children. She hadn't even told her sister because she didn't want to expose him to the world. If she kept him a secret he could stay a miracle, not a subject for discussion. Or worse. For bawdy laughter, for delighted moralising, for all mankind's unkindnesses.

She turned her attention outside, the train picking up speed now, trundling on past streets with long queues outside the shops, grim-looking hotels, identical terraced houses and then through more leafy avenues with gardens backing onto the railway line and eventually into the open countryside.

During the war and still after Stephen's return she had waited and waited. She'd been so patient. But not anymore. She pressed her strong hands together. Now she would take control.

34

GEORGE IVENS DITHERED OVER whether to play a knight or a bishop but, though his eyes were fixed on the chess board, his mind was on Alice. The grandmother clock in Dr Downes's dining room had just struck three which meant any minute now she'd be arriving at Ipswich Station: getting off the train in her grey coat, walking along the platform, crossing over the wooden bridge to the little branch-line train that would bring her back to Oakbourne. As much as anyone ever knew another's heart, he was pretty certain how she was feeling. She had offered him love and he had received it, yet he'd vanished in her sleep, leaving her to wake in an empty bed to his note. She would be hurt and bewildered. And he felt unworthy of the gift bestowed on him.

He moved his knight and Downes gave him a glance, more professional than friendly.

'Check,' said Downes. 'Your mind's not on this, is it?'

Ivens made a deprecatory gesture.

'I know,' sighed Downes, 'you weren't expecting much from Fraser but that's the trouble with hope. It's a bugger when it's killed off. But – if it's all right with you – he's given me the name of the top man in the States, so I'm writing to him. If that looks promising – and you never know, the research is moving so fast – there might be ways of finding the cash to get you over there.'

The last thing Ivens wanted was more impossible dreams. The cause was surely hopeless.

'I don't want to give up,' Downes was saying. 'And you'd be the first to say that we should never give up on hope, never despair.'

And that we have to accept what we cannot change, thought Ivens, but at that moment Downes dropped the queen he'd just won. As it went rolling under the table Ivens saw the fear flicker over Downes's face – was his tremor getting worse? He *needs* to be my saviour, thought Ivens, watching Downes clutch at his hands.

'You're a kind man,' he said, reaching to pick up the queen.

'Rubbish,' said Downes. 'I just need someone to play chess with.'

'You know,' said Ivens, 'that Lady Rayne plays. Or used to.' I've done it, he thought, brought her into the conversation as though she's just a casual acquaintance. Downes looked as interested as if he'd learned she enjoyed tapestry. 'I imagine,' continued Ivens, 'she's rather good.'

Even now, he could hear her voice: '*I could fall in love with you.*'

The word made flesh, for consolation, for joy, for peace.

Whatever proprieties he'd breached, whatever sins he'd committed, for those few hours he'd been filled with the amazing miracle of being alive, of the uniqueness of this woman who made love, who could bring plants back to life, a woman unlike any there had ever been or would be again. With her in his arms he'd held the absolute conviction that there was a creator whose love explained their existence, that they weren't some accident, spinning round and round on a planet hurling into oblivion.

'I suppose,' Downes was saying, 'we'll see the Raynes at the cricket tomorrow. Did you know he opens the batting? Some feudal thing for the lord of the manor to hit the first ball. Don't worry,' he smiled. 'I'm not expecting you to say anything unkind about your flock.' He got up, patting Ivens's shoulder as he went to the window. 'I just hope this miserable weather clears up.'

Ivens had no intention of going to the cricket. He'd plead some excuse – sickness, a pastoral duty, because he did not want to meet her in full view of the village and her husband. *Her husband.*

He felt no guilt for breaking the seventh commandment – though he was fully aware few, if any, of his Anglican colleagues would be as sanguine about adultery. But he was at fault. He should have told Alice the truth – why he was at the hospital.

I could fall in love with you. He'd been unable to refuse the love. But if she really could fall in love with him, then sooner, rather than later, he'd be someone else she mourned for. She was lonely and he would make her more so. Oh, Alice! My sweet love! I'm sorry. But remorse was pointless now, guilt an indulgence, he believed, a mistaken belief that if you put yourself through enough pain you could somehow undo the wrong you'd done another.

'You'll be there, won't you?' Downes asked.

'Oh, yes,' Ivens lied.

Another sin. How easily they piled up.

But he would be honest with Alice. He'd already sent a note to Oakbourne Hall asking her to meet him at the church

244

after the cricket match. Then, tomorrow evening, he would explain he'd left her the other night because if he'd stayed, in the cold light of day, he'd have had to tell her how sick he was. Just for that night, he'd wanted to be himself, unfettered by illness. Not an object of pity. Or a cause.

All week he'd tried to imagine her response. Might she say – as he was forever preaching – that it was not how long you lived that mattered? Nor for how long you loved. Simply that you loved. Then they might have months together. A year ... maybe two ... three. Miracles happened. To be called beloved. To be held as if you were the most precious creature on earth ...

Downes was back on the subject of Sir Stephen opening the batting. And Ivens tasted all the ugliness of his own envy: Sir Stephen was fit and well, did not know the fear of becoming a useless invalid.

'Instead of all this forelock-tugging,' Downes was saying, 'someone really ought to stand up to that man.'

And I have, thought Ivens, wishing the doctor goodbye. I stood my ground the day we first met when the man lectured me on evil over tea; I argued back on Easter Sunday. And he's no idea how I've restrained myself. How I could hold him to account for his arrogance and cruelty and ...

Ivens stopped, appalled at the hatred in his heart. And, walking home in the grey mugginess, all he could think was how he wanted never to have caught the rheumatic fever that had curtailed his life. He wanted, like so many, the impossible: that what could never be undone had never happened.

35

As Alice swept up the drive to Oakbourne Hall, she had it all planned. The moment she walked through the door she would find Stephen and tell him she agreed to a divorce. But before she'd even parked Mrs Green was flying out, crying: 'Thank God! You're back! There was a telegram – early this morning for Sir Stephen. Then, later, a letter – from the War Office. I saw the address on the envelope. And now he won't stop laughing. But not laughing as though something's funny.'

Alice heard him as she ran into the house: grim, lurching cries, almost as if he had, for the first time since his return, been drinking and was now paralytically drunk. She flung open the drawing-room door and his eyes flickered over her so malevolently she wondered for a moment if this was about George. But how could he know? And whatever had brought on this hysteria ran far deeper than male ego.

'Stephen! What's happened? Mrs Green said there was a telegram?'

He took a long drag on his cigarette, threw the stub into the fireplace and fumbled in his pocket for more cigarettes. His fingers were trembling as he struggled to light the match. 'It was to tell me to expect *that*.' With his foot he pointed to a letter ripped in two.

She picked it up off the floor. Typewritten, it was addressed from La Mairie, Engenville, a French town she'd never heard of and she read, '*Capitaine Lièvre, Aussi insaisissable que jamais . . .*'

'*Lièvre* is hare, isn't it?' she asked. He nodded. 'Captain Hare,' she began, struggling to translate it. 'As *insaisissable* as ever . . . ? What's that mean? I don't understand.'

'Nor me.' She looked at him in confusion. 'I've not forgotten my French,' he said, 'I just don't understand why we've got to go through this charade.'

She ran her eyes down to the signatures, Jacques Paquet, the mayor, Jean Benoit and Claude Leclerc. 'Who are these men?'

'Paquet is a shit of the highest order. Benoit and Leclerc are amongst the best men I've ever known.'

'From the war?'

She jumped as he kicked the table. 'Of course from the bloody war.' So, as she'd assumed, he'd been in France. 'The War Office, in their infinite wisdom, forwarded on the letter.'

'What do they want?'

'Leclerc's coming to London for a few days, for his work apparently, and wants to see me. I'm not having that. But the main thing . . .' Slowly, enunciating every word, he said: 'They want me to go back to France.'

And, as she asked, 'Why?', she felt the sort of jolt that wakes you from sleep, as if you've been plummeting into an unending well then are shocked into consciousness. Was this the moment she learned the truth? What he was required to go back and face?

'You and I,' he said, 'we never went to Engenville, did we? Shame, as it's actually not that far from the Chateau de Rossignol.'

Chateau de Rossignol was where they'd spent their honeymoon. There they had not stopped laughing and talking and loving – all the good things of life compressed into two weeks of glorious beauty. And it struck her that whatever men she might know in the future – be it George Ivens, or another – she would never again know such joy. It wasn't simply a loss of innocence. Something greater had been stolen – a spring of faith that trusted in the future.

'You'd have liked En-gen-ville,' Stephen was saying, a hideous twist to his mouth as he exaggerated the vowels. 'Pretty cobbled streets, Gothic church, café with red-and-white checked tablecloths. And wild irises growing by the roadside. You'd have been tempted to dig up the bulbs. Actually, are they bulbs?'

And to her horror, as he asked the question, he beat his fist against the wall so hard he could have broken his knuckles and he bawled her name: 'Alice?'

'Yes?'

'Are you sure? Because I think you're wrong.'

He was shaking now, clearly terrified. Of what she'd no idea. But the fear itself was real and she felt it too. She stepped backwards quickly, her hand reaching for the door.

'Alice!'

He stormed towards her, thumping his hands on the wall above her shoulders, bringing his unshaven face so close she could smell the smoke on his breath.

'I thought,' he said, breathing hard, 'they were called something else.'

She'd no idea what madness he was asking. 'What are?'

'The *bulbs*.' Had he lost his mind? His eyes were manic. 'The irises! I thought they had another name.'

'Rhizomes?' she said, reeling from the absurdity of what she was saying.

'Ah yes!' He eased himself down on the sofa, his breath slowing. 'That's the word.'

She was conscious of sweat on her palms. He was out of control but this was the most he'd ever spoken of his war and if she left now, whatever dreadful secret he was hiding would slip from her grasp. She remained perfectly still, nervous of doing anything that might provoke him.

Slowly, he finished his cigarette, lit another and said: 'Those irises! I felt I'd stepped into a Van Gogh. Such blues and purples. Even black. And Engenville's town hall! I can see it now. Napoleon built it – there's no escaping these megalomaniac monsters. And as the sun went down it glowed a gorgeous apricot colour, lighting up the whole square and so very beautiful the SS also took a liking to it and one summer's evening they rigged up a gallows from an upstairs window and hanged twenty-one men, and forced the rest of the town to watch them swinging there, dying slowly, one by one.' He rubbed his eyes hard, blinking as if trying to regain his focus. 'Can you imagine how long that took?'

He drew fiercely on his cigarette, then swung his legs up on the sofa and lay back. 'They're building a memorial to those men and all the people who worked in the Resistance. So there you have it – a bloody farce. And before you ask,' he said, moving his hand to his temple and driving his fingers hard into his skull, 'it's a farce because thanks to the last war, we've got more than enough memorials. Yet do they change a damned thing, Alice? Answer me, Alice!'

She said weakly: 'Perhaps this memorial is meant to be a comfort. If you've loved someone who's laid down their life . . . ?'

'Laid down their life!' he repeated, with awful false piety. 'I expected better from you than clichés. You make it sound so noble.'

'Weren't they?'

'Some were. Certainly nobler than me. But others?' He stubbed out his cigarette and dropped the matches trying to light another. She bent to pick them up for him. 'Leave it!' he yelled. 'Many only found nobility because the Nazis did something so unbelievably stupid, I still don't understand why.'

Suddenly his derision disappeared and he looked at her in utter bewilderment. 'In the spring of '43, they began rounding up all Frenchmen, transporting them to Germany to make armaments and do all the hard physical labour their own men couldn't as they were away killing us. Did you realise, Alice? Or were you too busy with your gardening books?'

She steadied her voice. 'No, I didn't realise.'

'Thought not,' he said, coughing over the first long gasp of smoke. 'Anyway, it was a dreadful error for the Nazis because all these bloody noble Frenchmen who'd ignored the vile, vile things going on under their noses so they could get on with their petty lives, when given the choice of being a slave for the Third Reich or fighting to get their country back found it in themselves – at long bloody last – to fight for France. So in the space of a couple of months I went from having twenty men under my command to more than two hundred.'

He put his head in his hands and groaned. 'But some of the best ones were hanged above those irises. And they only got caught because one chap ditched his mistress and in revenge she ditched him to the Gestapo and that led them to rounding up a whole network. Pretty, eh?' He sat up, his eyes vacant. 'You can imagine what the Communists did to her at the end of the war.'

She could. 'But *you*?' she made herself ask, her mouth dry. 'Why do they want *you* back? Are you in . . . trouble?'

'Me? The great Capitaine Lièvre?' He gave her a gruesome smile. 'I'm guest of honour! Invited to give a speech!'

For months she'd tortured herself, fearing the atrocities he might have committed. But *he* hadn't! Oh, thank God!

Relief flooded her but he was shaking his head from side to side. 'But they don't know the truth. I'm no hero, far from it. And I'm not going back to be treated like one. Never. *Never.*'

The phone was ringing in the hall.

'It can wait,' she said, but he leapt up and grabbed the letter from her, tearing it into shreds.

'Lady Rayne?' Mrs Green was at the door. 'Mrs Lubbock is calling about tomorrow's tea.'

Stephen's mirthless laughter resumed at full force.

'Oh, Alice!' he roared, rocking back and forth. 'Please don't tell me you're having a tea party!'

'It's for the Whitsun cricket match. She can wait.'

'Jesus! I suppose I'm expected to open the batting!' He bounded over to the fireplace and grabbed the poker. 'You can forget that idea.' And he swung the poker as if he was belting sixes across the boundary. 'Do you think I give a damn about cricket?'

You used to, she thought. But that was a hopeless argument.

And so what if he was there or not? He hurled a cushion into the air and hit it, splitting the worn silk. It was just a stupid cricket match.

Except it wasn't.

She watched Stephen pause in his mock-batting, tap the poker against his leg, then collapse onto the sofa as if exhausted. And this gave her courage.

'You weren't here,' she said, 'but during the war people talked a lot about those lovely cricket days at the Big House, wondering if they'd ever have them again. For generations they've sat in that pavilion – as children, with their parents and grandparents.'

He was staring at her now.

'For men like Reynolds, who were in the trenches,' she continued, 'fighting a war they were told would end all wars, these last six years must have been the most appalling mockery. Now they need to believe their sacrifice was worthwhile. That's why they're building that memorial in France. That's why this cricket match – and you being there – means a lot to people. For their sake, you must come.'

'Must?' he said. 'Are you ordering me?' He was looking at her, but without seeing, as if addressing a stranger. 'I'm done with being ordered about by damned idiots who've not got a clue. And you've got no bloody idea! I was over here once – on your birthday actually. Yes, Alice, sometimes they called me back and I couldn't tell you. Your birthday was not a priority and there was this jumped-up colonel, safe and snug behind his desk, who insisted I do some particular job. I said it wasn't worth it, that the reprisals would be beyond anything we'd seen so far.' He was laughing again. 'There was an SS officer in the area who could take sadism to new levels. And didn't he just.'

Then he flung down the poker and in two strides was looming over her again, his hands on her shoulders.

'Stephen!' She struggled to stay calm as his fingers pressed deep into her. 'I'm not the enemy!'

But then tears began streaming down his cheeks. 'I didn't want to hurt you! I didn't! I didn't!' And the next moment he was talking in French, as if she wasn't there. What he was saying or to whom he was pleading, she'd no idea. All she understood was that he was in a chaos of fear and guilt as if nothing could ever make sense again.

She glanced back at the shut door. She would not make it in time if he turned on her. Then he brought his mouth to her ear and whispered, 'Alice, listen carefully. I've done terrible things. But I won't hurt you. Or anyone. I've done enough of that. And, to shut you up, I'll play in your ruddy match. But after that, you must let me be.'

36

FOR A BLISSFUL MOMENT, when Stephen awoke, he felt at peace. He'd dreamt he was back in France. Before *that* day. He was in the forest, in a clearing amidst the pine trees, the sun streaming down as he played chess with the most exquisite set he'd ever seen. One of the men had carved it using a pen knife and he'd wished he might show it to Alice: the king, his brow furrowed by fear of failure; the queen, with a lined, grieving face; the bishops, rapt and gazing upwards; the pawns smiling as if wholly confident of love.

It had seemed miraculous to produce such beauty under those circumstances, yet despite the war there would be these moments when Stephen found himself marvelling at his fellow men. Their brilliance, their endurance, their ingenuity. Because there they all were, in the summer of 1944, more than three hundred men, hiding in that forest sixty miles south of Paris, hungry and filthy, in the most primitive conditions, living in constant fear of discovery.

Yet, in this drowsy state in which he'd just woken, it occurred to him that, despite the evil lurking all around, there had been good times. Not just chess. They'd play rudimentary golf and cricket, fashioning clubs and bats themselves. There were tables and chairs hewn out of tree trunks and branches, pots, pans and cooking fires. Food, brought to them by the local Resistance, had been basic, but better than the starvation some men had suffered: ersatz coffee from roasted barley seeds, bread and green apples, beans with a little rabbit. Occasionally fish. They had a doctor too – a veteran from the Great War who'd visit regularly from a nearby village – and every week a barber would come and cut their hair.

A few of the men, teachers in civilian life, gave talks on history, literature, whatever their subject. Another set up a poker school, anything to alleviate the frustration of being holed up behind enemy lines. There'd been a camaraderie and, Stephen recognised, much of that good fellowship was down to him: his leadership, his speed of decision-making, his gloss of glamour and magic that gave men the confidence to follow his orders.

Le lièvre: this was his pseudonym.

The Hare: that magnificent creature, forever on the alert, who instinctively knows when to run, when to fight, when to hide, the man whom the Resistance now wanted to honour.

He looked at his watch. Almost eight. He'd had more than ten hours' sleep. He'd not slept more than two hours at a stretch for years. What on earth had brought this peace?

He reached for his glass of water and then, in the empty teacup by his bed, he noticed granules of powder. Suddenly he tasted the bitterness still in his mouth. Alice had drugged him. He saw it now: after that terrible scene when she got home, he'd left the house and walked till nightfall and when he returned Alice was waiting, acting as if that letter from France had not arrived. She'd had a cup of tea ready for him. He'd thought it tasted odd. But

255

she'd said the milk was off and he'd taken her word. When he'd got back to his room, he'd downed the tea and slept the sleep of the innocent – the last thing he deserved. This was why he wouldn't allow himself the luxury of drugs: there could be no whitewashing, no rose-tinted spectacles or whatever coloured gloss you used to rewrite the past. Because the reality of that Robin Hood fantasy of a boy-scout camp in the woods was fear and violence, even amongst men supposedly on the same side. The poker school had lasted just six days. He'd banned it after too many fights broke out.

But it'll all get retold, he thought, in a way to suit the interests of whoever has an axe to grind.

The whole damned war.

And his mind ranged back to June 1940 when the Nazis arrived in Paris, that beautiful city where his mother was born and he loved so dearly. He'd been in Dunkirk, fighting to get men back across the Channel, but Benoit had been part of the exodus from the capital, the roads packed with people walking in a desperate, futile bid for freedom from the advancing German army. Benoit had headed south with his wife and two young children, all on foot, and he'd told Stephen of having to stop to let Bugattis by and gleaming Talbot Lagos piled high with linen, silver, champagne even. In one car an entire seat had been taken up with a golden cage holding a parakeet, the driver honking his horn to get past children clinging to exhausted mothers, old women bent double with nothing but the clothes on their backs, men pushing their belongings in a wheelbarrow as the parakeet and champagne were rushed to safety.

Stephen hauled himself out of bed. Human beings were disgusting, hateful creatures. And, as the war progressed, their true nature was revealed in all its foulness.

He picked up his razor and looked in the small mirror.

Et tu, Capitaine Lièvre?

37

THE EARLY MORNING RAIN had cleared into the perfect afternoon for cricket. Jane Downes stood on the boundary clapping as Sir Stephen and Ross Harris walked down the grassy slope from the newly whitewashed pavilion.

Breathing in the scent of freshly mown grass, she looked straight ahead, wanting nothing to intrude upon this vision of peace: the men in white flannels, the fields of unripe barley lying in the distance, a vivid gleam of buttercups in the pasture where brown cows lowed gently with their calves.

'Did you believe,' said a voice by her side, 'we'd ever do this again?'

'Mrs Turner!' exclaimed Jane. She'd rarely seen the vicar's landlady at village events. Grief for her only son kept her hidden away but perhaps, in this lovely meeting of spring and summer, friends and family, they really were all beginning to heal.

'I wasn't going to come,' said Mrs Turner, 'but Mr Ivens asked me to sort of represent him as he's not feeling too well.' She patted Jane's arm. 'Don't be alarmed. He says it's nothing a quiet afternoon won't cure. And I get the impression he's not a great fan of cricket.'

Jane laughed. 'I know how he feels. My husband adores the game but he was always so desperate to play well I ended up hating it, I got so anxious.'

'My son loved it too. But I'd feel sick when he went out to bat, especially,' said Mrs Turner, nodding at the bowler, 'if he was facing that boy – well, man now. He was the best bowler for miles and before the war there was even talk of him playing for the county, but then – well – you know.'

You know: there was no reply to this. They'd all been fighting for their lives and lost something of themselves in the process. But the war was over. The only battle that mattered now was a cricket match between two villages where everybody abided by respected rules with Mr Reynolds, the former kennel master, umpiring over a world of fair play.

'Here we go,' she murmured, as the game commenced, the bowler striding purposefully and then accelerating into a run before launching the ball at Sir Stephen. A collective intake of breath seemed to echo round the pitch as the ball landed almost two yards from the stumps. Mr Reynolds, umpiring, stretched out his arms to signal a wide. The next two attempts were even worse.

'Perhaps he's just nervous,' said Mrs Turner, her fingers at her throat.

'Let's hope,' murmured Jane, aware of the tension mounting around them. The fourth ball flew so high above Stephen's shoulder, that it too was a no-ball.

Jane knew enough about cricket to realise she was witnessing a young man suffer horrible humiliation. The fifth ball simply slipped out of his hand and rolled slowly towards the stumps. Stephen patted it gently back.

After the next no-ball Jane couldn't watch. You send a nineteen-year-old to war, then have the stupidity to imagine he'll return the same brilliant, joyful boy he once was. Turning away, she saw her husband limping towards her.

'Poor devil,' she said, nodding at the bowler.

'Yes – this is agony for all of us.'

'Can't someone else step in?' she asked.

'If only. He's supposed to complete the over – six legal balls.'

'So we could be here all afternoon watching him bowl no-ball after no-ball?'

'In theory – every bowler's nightmare. Oh, Jane! Sometimes playing well is all in the mind. He was a real star before the war apparently. But he was in the Far East for two years.'

And that, she thought, explains everything.

Then he bowled in a way that did not seem as wild as before. Sir Stephen stepped forwards and hit the ball – not, as he should have done, a cover drive along the ground, but dollied up in the air, straight back at the bowler, directly into his hands.

The squire was out! Caught and bowled!

Cheers rang out from the opposing village as if to dismiss their poor bowler's distress as loudly as possible.

'What a stroke of luck,' Jane whispered to her husband as Stephen strode back to the pavilion, where he was met by a chorus of sympathetic remarks: 'Don't worry, sir . . . If I'd a guinea for all the ducks I've had . . . it happens to us all.'

'So sorry,' Stephen was saying as Mr Lubbock walked out to take his place.

The match resumed. The over finished with no more no-balls. Ross Harris played a brilliant shot, Mr Lubbock scored a couple of runs and the game began to settle into a pleasing pattern.

Then Jonathan turned to her anxiously. 'I hope I don't make a complete fool of myself out there batting.'

Platitudes plodded through her mind. You were a fine cricketer . . . You've scored centuries in the past . . . Everyone has bad days . . . And you can't do worse than Sir Stephen, whose educated voice was still apologising: 'It was a dreadful, dreadful shot. I got under it. Such a stupid error.'

Suddenly it occurred to Jane what he'd done.

'Did he,' she whispered to Jonathan, 'get himself out on purpose?'

'That's what I'm wondering.'

Standing tall amongst men whom a generation earlier would have been his employees on the estate, Stephen was listening attentively, making jokes, laughing. He has presence, she thought, a natural-born leader of men. But she saw the strain etched on his face, his eyes sunk in hollows, and recognised a man obviously unable to sleep at night, whose mind even now she suspected was elsewhere.

Her husband was watching him too and she hoped he wasn't going to make some point about *noblesse oblige*, lords and ladies thinking a few gracious words righted the wrongs of inequality.

'If,' she said, 'he did get himself out deliberately, it was good of him to put us all out of our misery.'

To her surprise, Jonathan agreed and her mood shifted once again. This is how life should be: men acting selflessly, recognising true kindness, sparing each other pain, not inflicting it. She wondered where Alice Rayne was, whether she'd recognised her husband's good deed. But she wasn't about, probably helping with the tea – as I ought to be, she thought, reluctant to go inside, away from the tender sunshine.

The game rolled on. Runs were scored. Mr Lubbock was bowled out, fooled by a 'crafty leg spinner' as Jonathan

261

pointed out. Ross Harris hit two sixes in a row and was then caught. This is what they had all come for: the soothing, eternally English monosyllable of willow on leather, the ball flying over the boundary, the gentle clapping after a good shot, the sense of connection, the promise of tea.

'I really ought to offer to help in the kitchen,' she said to Jonathan.

'Did you make anything?'

'Cherry biscuits without the cherries and which I left in the oven too long, or maybe not long enough. Oh, I don't know. But they're too soft and fell apart.'

'Just like me,' he said, giving her a gentle smile.

He was making a joke! The first one, she realised, since he had come home from that damned camp and she laughed as she headed for the kitchen, thinking that was the sweetest thing he'd said to her in ages.

Juliet was hovering on the pavilion steps with the dog. 'Mum! I heard Mrs Lubbock saying there aren't enough strawberry puffs. What are strawberry puffs?'

Jane had a recollection of golden pastries splitting at the seams with cream and scarlet fruit.

'You had them when you were very little, before the war,' she said, picturing her parents' dining table arranged as colourfully as a patchwork quilt: snowy-white meringues next to ebony-dark chocolate cake, a tower of ginger biscuits – neither too soft, nor too hard – beside bitter-sweet lemon curd served in a white china bowl looking, her father always commented, 'like a giant daisy' . . .

'Mum! Did I like them?'

'You adored them.'

'What if there really aren't enough?'

'Then you can have mine.'

The look of love that spread across Juliet's face almost took Jane's breath away. But then her precious little girl was gone, skipping out into the sunshine with the dog following.

'Put Rusty on a lead,' she called. 'No one will forgive us if he eats everything. And there are calves in the field at the end so don't let him near them or their mothers will go berserk.'

She headed into the kitchen, where more mothers were making what would have to pass for the cricket tea: two sunken sponge cakes lost in the middle of enormous plates; minuscule splodges of real cream on scones which Mrs Grainger was explaining at length used only one quarter of an ounce of fat per dozen; dried egg custards wobbling in little dishes; sandwiches spread with margarine that always tasted to Jane of an industrial waste product and filled with intestine-coloured Spam – God only knew what was in that; loaves with bits of apple on top which Mrs Lubbock – in yet another new dress – was sawing into thin slices. She caught sight of the strawberry puffs, the stars of the show – so small, she thought, a blackbird could swallow them whole.

But these haggard women were working so hard, trailing nasturtiums around currant-less rock buns, placing dark velvety pansies on some unidentifiable sort of pie. Even her biscuits didn't look too awful, with flowers like deep blue stars on each sorry specimen.

'May I help at all?' she offered.

'Thank you,' smiled Mrs Lubbock, pausing in her sawing. 'But we've more than enough hands on deck.'

'You've done an amazing job!' On the table were jam jars full of blue forget-me-nots and coral-red sorrel, enormous roses like powder-puffs. 'And this tablecloth,' said Jane, feeling the heavy softness of white damask patterned with chrysanthemums. 'Exquisite.'

Mrs Lubbock gave an uncharacteristically embarrassed smile. 'It's the tablecloth my mother used for her wedding breakfast. And I had for mine. So I thought today – well, this is a special occasion.'

Suddenly Jane felt overwhelmed by the pathos of all these efforts to transform this paltry feast into a banquet.

'Very special,' she echoed, looking round at these women, some of whom had husbands, brothers, sons and lovers who were now mud and dust. And she couldn't help herself but next minute she was hunting for her handkerchief because here they all were, trying to show how life can be – not just blood, sweat and tears, but transformed by charm and companionship, lavish and open-handed, working together, sharing tea.

'I'm sorry about my biscuits,' she said.

'Don't worry,' soothed Mrs Lubbock.

'You've made them look nice with those flowers, whatever they are.'

'Borage. Lady Rayne arrived with all sorts of flowers she said you can eat – they taste quite nice actually.'

'I must thank her.'

'I sent her home. She didn't look too well,' added Mrs Lubbock, giving Jane a loaded glance.

Jane knew what that look meant: is she pregnant? Poor Alice Rayne, she thought, being the subject of such village scrutiny. But her spirits lightened. Because wouldn't a baby at the Big House be a happy occasion? Remind us all that life goes on? Perhaps impending fatherhood explained

264

Stephen Rayne's presence, the effort he was making today. Though there was a blankness in his eyes as if he was playing an old part from memory, it was a start.

'Mum!' Eleanor appeared in the kitchen. 'Dad's about to bat!'

She hurried outside to see her husband and her son, who was running for him, head out to the wicket. Please, she prayed to a God she didn't believe in, give him this tiny little victory.

He hit the first ball feebly. At least he wasn't out. But then, to her amazement, with a confidence she'd thought he was no longer capable of, he moved his good leg to the next ball and played a perfect shot, sending it through the fielders to cross the boundary. There was a large round of applause. And then he hit another beautiful four. The clapping from the boundary intensified: their doctor who'd lost his leg to Hitler had not lost his skill on the cricket pitch. Jane's relief was out of all proportion. He was playing well. Christopher was running for him. Father and son working together. Oh, thank God!

The home side's innings ended with Jonathan having scored fifty-two not out, and returning to the pavilion for tea and congratulations. For once there was a big smile on his face.

Sometimes, life was sweet. It really was. She laughed and chatted, gave Juliet her strawberry puff, talked of how delicious borage flowers were. Even Christopher, who was becoming more and more withdrawn at home, seemed to be enjoying himself. Perhaps she was worrying about him unnecessarily. And Eleanor, now her exams had finished, didn't have her head stuck in a biology book. She was talking to Ross Harris, who was clearly flirting with her. Ross, she'd heard, had a job in a car-manufacturing factory, was going away to build a new life near Birmingham.

New lives.

That is what they were all going to have, she told herself after she'd helped with the washing up and was resting back in a deckchair by the tall hawthorn. A group of little girls lay sprawled in the grass, plaiting forget-me-nots and daisies into chains. She looked for Juliet, expecting to see her head of auburn hair. She wasn't there. She'd probably taken Rusty for a walk.

Jane closed her eyes, delivering herself up to the blue and green drowsiness.

A cuckoo called from the woods. A robin sang in the cherry tree by the pavilion. A dog barked. Her mind drifted. And then a scream ripped through the sweetness of the glorious May afternoon.

 38

IN THAT SPLIT SECOND it seemed to Jane the world stopped: the chatting on the boundary, the bowler in his run-up, the boys playing in the nets. No one moved. No one acted.

Then she was aware of Stephen Rayne running, vaulting over the fence to the pasture beyond. And she saw: in the field at the far end of the cricket pitch the herd of cows was charging, heading straight for her darling Juliet, who stood as if paralysed, Rusty in her arms.

Jane forced her legs to move. The dog, she realised, must have frightened the cattle. But as she ran, already she knew it was hopeless. No power on earth could get her there in time. Or anyone. They would all be too late.

But Stephen had not given up. Shouting and waving, he'd manoeuvred himself between Juliet and the stampeding cattle. But the cows were too fuelled with fear for their calves to stop, heading right for him; at any second they would trample him into the ground and crush her child, the hooves breaking her bones, rupturing her young flesh.

Then Stephen stopped his yelling and gesticulating, and turned his back on the frenzied cattle. He's going to run for safety, she thought, save himself. But instead he ran straight for Juliet. Then he flung himself over her, his own body shielding hers.

All Jane could see was a blur of bellowing, snorting animals and she was running so fast, she slipped. When she looked up, men were brandishing cricket bats and whistling, herding the cows and their calves into a corner, a heap of white sprawled in the churned-up grass.

She heard a cry: 'Mummy!' And Juliet crawled out from under Stephen Rayne's body. Still clutching the dog, Juliet leapt up, her long childish limbs moving freely, and fell into her mother's arms.

Juliet was crying, choking over her words: 'Rusty slipped his lead. I had to save him. Don't blame Rusty. Don't let the farmer shoot him. Promise, Mummy. Promise.'

Anything, thought Jane. Anything. She opened her mouth to respond. But she couldn't make a sound. Yet, with the lucidity that comes from adrenaline, she was running professional hands over Juliet. Slowly, incredulously, she realised her daughter was unharmed. No bones were broken, her skin untouched.

'Darling!' Jonathan was levering himself down.

Juliet clutched at her father, who gave Jane a desperate, enquiring look. 'Is she all right?' And she nodded and Jonathan buried his face in his daughter's neck. 'Thank God.'

Then Jane saw the doctor in him return. Struggling back up, he gave her a sharp glance as if to say: we must help.

A crowd had gathered round where the bodies had lain and she ran forwards, bracing herself for what she might find.

'Don't move him!' Jonathan cried, but Stephen was slowly getting to his feet.

Jane saw blood on his cheek, his right shoulder protruding through his shirt – 'dislocated' said a distant part of her brain – the greyness of his face.

'Thank you, thank you!' she heard her husband crying.

'Is she all right?'

'Thanks to you!' Jonathan grabbed Stephen's hand. 'What you did was so – thank you, thank you, I don't have the words.'

From all round questions were being fired. 'But how on earth . . . ? What exactly happened?'

'The front ones swerved,' said Stephen. 'The herd split round us.'

'Your shoulder!' said Jonathan.

'It's nothing. But your wife,' said Stephen, looking at Jane, 'I think she's in shock.'

Jane was aware she was shaking but Stephen's concern for her forced her to focus. In a hoarse whisper, she said, 'You could have been killed.' He muttered something she couldn't hear. 'To save her life,' she continued, 'you'd have given yours . . .'

She had to stop. The possibility of his sacrifice for her child left her unable to speak. Stephen was right, she was in shock because, as she replayed the scene which even then she knew would be with her all her life, this man dressed in pure white, moving with such a speed he might have grown wings, appeared to her like an angel.

She heard Jonathan: 'You put yourself in so much danger . . . sir . . . I'm forever in your debt. How you survived—'

Stephen cut him off: 'I told you. They swerved. Stop making a fuss.'

But all around, people were lauding him as a hero: 'Such incredible courage . . . a miracle they weren't both killed . . . I thought the cattle would plough straight on over them . . .'

'I'm not a hero,' said Stephen. 'I'm not.'

And Jane sensed a real rage in his voice and from nowhere came a fear of a man whom she'd just been likening to an angel.

'Let me help you!' Jonathan was pleading. 'Sir, your shoulder! The pain must be excruciating.'

'Really?' said Stephen, laughing emptily.

Was anyone else, wondered Jane, aware of how strangely he was acting? How the agony on his face looked more mental than physical? But she couldn't worry about Stephen Rayne. And, as her husband, desperate to help, led him away, she gathered her shuddering, sobbing child in her arms, promising over and over the lie that had seen so many mothers through the war: that she would keep her safe from harm.

39

STEPHEN SAT IN A deckchair, his arm in a sling. The match had resumed, but there was a giddy party atmosphere. An innocent saved! A hero in their midst! The goodwill towards him was palpable, all his neglect of the village forgiven.

'Sir,' said Mr Reynolds, limping over. 'Back home, I've a bottle of brandy. You could have it, for the pain.'

With his good arm, Stephen pulled up a chair for Mr Reynolds, a man who had every reason to resent him after he'd put a stop to his job running the kennels. 'That's so kind of you,' said Stephen, 'but the quack's offered me morphine.'

Not that he'd had it. The throbbing in his shoulder took his mind off the weight of that other young body that had once clung to him for safety.

'It's the best brandy, sir. Your father gave it to me when I got back from Ypres – for my hip. It's unopened.'

'But that was thirty years ago!' protested Stephen. '*You* should enjoy the brandy!'

'It's a comfort, just knowing it's there,' continued Mr Reynolds, 'that if it gets really bad, there's always something.'

The old man's kindness, the respect in his voice was too much. Helplessly, Stephen asked: 'Is the pain really bad?'

'My dancing days are over.'

Stephen put the appropriate smile on his face, because that's what many do, he thought, turn disability into a joke. And perhaps humour was the best armament in all the madness of war. But not for his actions.

'They've let me off umpiring duties so I'd be more than happy to get it for you,' Reynolds went on. 'What you did just then – it was magnificent.'

Already the myth was developing, his reputation for bravery and sheer good luck scaling new heights. This is what had happened in the war, why they wanted him back in France. We need our heroes, he thought, men and women who satisfy our desperation for miracles.

'Anyone would have done it,' murmured Stephen.

'No, they wouldn't.' There was force in the old man's tone. 'You know that.'

Of course he did. Most people do their damnedest not to die. But most people hadn't done what he had.

'I just meant,' he began.

He stopped. What he meant was that he'd only risked his life because he didn't care about losing it, and there was nothing heroic about that.

'Never mind,' sighed Stephen and he shook Mr Reynolds's hand to suggest that they, two soldiers together, had shared an experience but there was nothing, in the end, they could actually say about it.

And Mr Reynolds picked up the cue, gesturing to the pitch. 'It's going to be a great finish. They need sixteen off three overs.'

So they sat watching the match as if their minds were free of all but cricket, clapping, taking deep intakes of breath, muttering: 'Lovely shot . . . beautiful ball.' Then Ross Harris took the final wicket and the game was over, Oakbourne the winners by five runs.

Stephen got to his feet, helped Reynolds to his and applauded the cricketers as they headed back to the pavilion.

Flushed and talkative with the day's excitement and a barrel of cider provided by the Lubbocks, everyone hung about, not wanting the day to end. Stephen stood on the pavilion steps as if utterly relaxed and untroubled, the centre of attention.

How was he? people asked. Did he need a lift home? Was Lady Rayne all right? She just had a slight headache. Already his shoulder was easing. The doctor did a great job.

Everything was going to work out, he seemed to be saying as the villagers, just as his men had done, hovered around him like bees circling their hive. And he had the awful sensation that he was back in 1944 in that forest. Because this is what he'd do: keep flagging spirits high, his presence alone giving reassurance as he endlessly made the rounds of the makeshift camp, creating the illusion that he could keep them safe.

Slowly, the shadows lengthened and the crowd began to disperse, the young men arranged to meet at the Queen's Head, families collected tired children, others set off down the dusty track, laughing and chatting amongst the flower-filled hedgerows.

Eventually, Stephen was alone.

He sat on the steps of the pavilion. He'd survived. Yet again. Even lying down before a stampede of cattle could not kill him.

As he'd thrown himself on the girl and the pounding hooves closed in, he'd thought, at last, now it will all end,

273

not in a cowardly way, not by my own hands, but in some sort of atonement. He could give up his life because he was saving another.

But he was still stuck here, a glorious summer's evening stretching before him and God knows how many more summers to get through. Certainly he didn't want to face Alice with her headache or whatever problem she'd rustled up. So he headed off in the opposite direction from home, taking a rarely used path back towards the village.

Last time he'd walked here was 1939, the first Christmas of the war, and he'd been with his brother. They'd argued. James was convinced that France – its people, its army – would stand up to Germany. Stephen had not been so sanguine.

I was right, thought Stephen, pulling himself free of the brambles that had taken over. The speed at which France had caved in to the Nazis had not surprised him and, to his horror, warm tears began falling down his cheeks. He could not remember the last time he'd cried but the pain and the freakish day ate at his self-control and he brushed the tears aside, because the throbbing in his shoulder was nothing compared to the agony James must have endured.

Oh, James. His stupidly fearless elder brother must have walked into a trap. Stephen had seen it again and again – people you thought were on your side turning you in to curry favour with the Gestapo. Horrific images began hammering into him, rocking his whole body, and he feared he might faint.

He sank to the ground and put his head between his knees. Why had he survived? And not James, or all the men, women and children who died too young? Like that one innocent soul whose corpse, even now, hung round his shoulders?

If only he could give up here. Nobody used this path. He could lie down in the dirt and not be found for days.

But this is your punishment, he told himself, to carry on and even if ninety-nine per cent of you is broken, use that remaining one per cent. This was a message he'd hammered home to his men: 'Find the part of you that's still alive and draw on that to survive.' He crunched down a couple of Downes's morphine tablets. Walk on! he ordered himself and hauled his body upright. Walk on!

But the bitterness of the pills made him retch and he was terribly thirsty. His mind returned to a flaming hot afternoon in the war when he'd been almost delirious with dehydration. He'd stopped at a priest's house for water and the man set a dog on him.

That will all be forgotten, he thought, hitting at the nettles with his cricket bat. We'll all be heroes when we come to concoct the history books, our hatefulness wiped clean.

He came out onto the lane that led to the back of the churchyard. The drystone wall had collapsed and he climbed through the gap. No one lives for ever, he told himself, looking at the lichen-covered headstones. The one thing you can guarantee is that fifty years from now you too will be lying amongst the daisies and chamomile, gleaming in the evening sun.

Fifty years. He began doing the sums. Six hundred months. How many days? Fifty times three hundred and sixty-five – his head hurt too much. He needed to sit somewhere cool, to let the drugs take effect. There was the church. He hated its odour of self-righteous hypocrisy, but at least the old building would be quiet.

40

STEPHEN HAD ASSUMED THE church would be empty, but as he walked down the aisle Ivens leapt up from a pew near the altar. There was such tenderness on the vicar's face, it crossed Stephen's mind that this was the actual truth of Christianity – he was in the presence of pure love.

But the next instant, Ivens's smile was replaced with open hostility and he drew himself up to his full height, legs apart, arms crossed. It's the morphine, thought Stephen, distorting my vision and, with a slight wave of his hand, he called out, 'Sorry to disturb you, Reverend.'

'What do you want?'

'Nothing,' said Stephen, bewildered by Ivens's aggression, 'I'll be off.'

But Ivens bellowed: 'Wait!' And in six strides he had closed the gap between them, sweat on his brow, his breathing too fast.

'Mr Ivens,' said Stephen, wondering what on earth had unnerved the man, 'is everything all right?'

'Are you here to give thanks for your life?'

'What?'

'After your great heroic act today – saving Juliet Downes's life and for that I thank God. But was it really heroism?' The words came out in such a garbled rush, Stephen wondered if the vicar had been drinking but, with him standing so close, Stephen could smell mint – not a hint of alcohol – on his breath. 'You see,' the vicar was saying, 'when I heard about you throwing yourself in front of a herd of stampeding cattle, I thought of a man who, during the Blitz, was always the first to run into the burning house to save the child. What a hero, people said, but the truth was this man was sick, and even being burnt alive seemed to him better than a long drawn-out death, enduring all the monstrous degradations of illness of which you, Sir Stephen, know absolutely nothing.'

'Ivens! What the devil's got into you?'

'I want to know why you think you've got the right to make other people's lives a misery?'

Had the vicar lost his mind? 'I don't know what you're talking about.'

'You don't?' Ivens's voice was thick with sarcasm. 'Then let me explain: you ignore all your responsibilities at the Big House, to men and women round here. To your wife, sneering at her the way you do, humiliating her in front of others.'

'My wife! I see. So she's had a good old whinge about me.'

Pure hatred filled Ivens's eyes and Stephen, realising he was still clenching his cricket bat, put it down out of easy reach, and contained himself.

'Not once,' said Ivens, '*not once* has your wife said a single derogatory word about you. You should know better!'

That was true enough. Alice would never go bleating about her problems.

'Ivens, I don't know what's up with you tonight. But with all due respect, you know absolutely nothing of what I've been through.'

'I've a pretty good idea.'

'Like hell you do! Have you ever held a gun? Let alone
killed somebody? You never even caught sight of the enemy,
so you've not the faintest clue. The choices I faced. Day in,
day out. Making life and death decisions and knowing that
if I got it wrong—'

'*If I got it wrong*,' interrupted Ivens. 'I see. So the great
Sir Stephen can't get it wrong. Is that it? The star at school,
the star at Cambridge. Then the Foreign Office – star
posting in Paris. But the great Sir Stephen couldn't just be
a brilliant linguist and diplomat. Oh, no! You're a published
poet too!'

'I don't have to listen to this.'

'But I'm right, aren't I? And you married a beautiful,
beautiful woman! How much more does a man like you
need to have a good opinion of himself? And I'm assuming
you were quite a star in the war as well, according to all the
village gossip. Until whatever it is you did that is so unforgivable. Yes, village gossip again. You used, I'm told, to be
so sociable, so charming. Now you don't leave the house.
You don't have to be a mind reader to work out the problem.'

Stephen assessed the vicar. Even with his right arm in a
sling, with his left he could still shut the man up with a
single blow. He made himself turn away.

'What I'd love to know,' said Ivens, 'is why even your
mistakes have to be greater than everyone else's? Because
you know what I suspect your real sin is?'

'My sin? To hell with you, Ivens.' And Stephen headed
for the door.

'It's your damned arrogance. Not what you did in the war.
We've all suffered but you think you're entitled to suffer
more than the rest of us.'

Ivens was so clearly gunning for a fight Stephen was tempted to rise to it, to hammer into someone with all his unexpressed fury. He'd seen so much of this during the war, the sadistic pleasure of yielding to violence, the release in an orgy of blood-shedding.

'Please,' called out Ivens, 'do tell me.'

Tell me?

'For Christ's sake, Ivens! Enough!'

But the vicar was unstoppable: 'Do you see yourself as some paschal lamb sacrificed on behalf of us all?'

Tell me! Ivens seemed to be yelling.

Tell me!

Dites moi!

Sag mir!

Sag mir!

Ivens's face began to blur. And Stephen could again see that fat, rosy-cheeked colonel issuing lethal orders safely behind his desk in Whitehall; the dapper young priest refusing him a glass of water; the lush, lovely, conniving lips of Benoit's jilted mistress informing the Gestapo exactly where Stephen was hiding; the SS guard's grin as he pushed Stephen's mouth under the running tap. And all the faces began coalescing into a gargoyle of evil and, before he realised what he was about to do, he'd clenched his fist, walked back down the aisle and struck Ivens on the cheek.

The crash, as Ivens fell against the wooden pews and onto the stone floor, reverberated round the empty church.

And Stephen was appalled. Shaking, he dropped to his knees.

Ivens was gasping, his neck at an angle, his skin white as if already starved of oxygen.

'I'm so sorry!'

Ivens could die. Because of him. Because of who he was. A brute. A butcher.

'Your head?' he cried, raising Ivens up so he might breathe more easily. 'Did you hit your head?'

Ivens just lay slumped against his chest without answering and images of brains spilling out of skulls swam before Stephen's vision. But then Ivens seemed to regain his strength, struggling to get away as if he couldn't bear to be touched.

'Did you hit your head?' repeated Stephen.

'No!' Ivens spoke in a hoarse whisper.

'Shall I fetch the doctor?'

'No!' Resting against the side of a pew, Ivens eyed him directly. Stephen had expected to see fear and loathing but instead he saw only sadness and exhaustion.

'I'm so sorry, Reverend. I'm so—'

Ivens held up his hand. 'Stop!' he said with surprising authority and Stephen obeyed. 'I'm the one in the wrong here.'

Stephen could see the red mark where his fist had landed on the vicar's face. 'But I—'

'Please!' Ivens gave him a vicar's smile. 'Accept my apologies. I knew just what I was doing – goading you like that.'

Ivens wasn't making sense. 'The way you fell,' said Stephen. 'I could have killed you.'

Stephen saw another flash of anger, then that smile again. 'A fall is the least of my worries.' Although Ivens spoke slowly, his mind was clearly as alert as ever. 'You asked me once what my secret is. Well, an infection that *you* could shrug off with a hot whisky will probably kill me. That's my secret – how sick I am. I've been lucky this winter. But next winter? Who knows?'

Stephen was at a loss. He'd known that Ivens was not a well man, but not this sick. 'I'm so—'

Ivens cut him short. 'I envy you. Because you did survive. Why you were spared God only knows. But you were. And I long to live in this world, as you can.'

'I'm—'

'I don't want your sympathy, anymore than I expect you want mine. But this afternoon, you'd have happily given up your life, wouldn't you?'

Stephen had the deranging sensation he was the one near death, not the vicar. He suddenly felt very cold and just wanted to get out of here. And he began – ridiculously, he knew, but he couldn't think straight – walking up and down the pews looking for his cricket bat he'd left somewhere.

'Sir Stephen.' Ivens's left eye was half-closed and bloodshot now. 'Please! Sit with me.'

And there was no denying the injury on that face. Stephen sat down in the pew behind Ivens. Then Ivens bent his head in prayer.

There was a quiet in the church as if the stone effigies and carved angels were holding their breath. But no peace. Stephen was nervous. He could have split Ivens's head open and he could be sitting here a murderer. Again.

He couldn't leave him to walk home on his own, but Ivens's praying seemed to be going on forever and he didn't know how to interrupt the silence. Then, in the fading light he made out the creamy-white statue of Noah, his arms outstretched, stranded and yearning.

'Why,' he ventured, 'was Noah the one chosen to survive the flood? What was so special about him?'

Ivens lifted his head. 'Nothing. That's the point. The good die, the bad survive. The opposite too. But to us, there's no justice. It's a beautiful statue, isn't it? Someone told me it was what they love most about this church. And unlike you, Noah was grateful to live. As I would be.'

'You don't know what you're envying. What I live with.'

'But what makes you more unforgivable than the rest of us?'

Stephen wrung his hands. He could see the muscles flexing in his index finger, sinewy and strong from pulling triggers, killing men and women. And children. And although the church was cool and quiet he could almost hear again the sounds of that scorching morning in 1944, the insects humming loudly, his mind and body so alert it had seemed his ears could catch the corn growing, the bursting of seeds opening, before that moment when the guns destroyed his peace forever.

'We need to go,' he said sharply.

In response, Ivens said, 'You could have killed me. I know I provoked you. But if you leave now you will continue to see yourself as a monster.'

'Which is what I am.'

'Talk to me. Let me help you.'

Stephen saw tears in the vicar's eyes and he wanted to turn away but Ivens held his gaze. Then Ivens took charge and, as he gripped Stephen's hands between his own, Stephen realised that something in him was about to be defeated by the defeat mirrored in that bruised face.

'Isn't it time,' said Ivens quietly, 'you told someone what happened?'

41

STEPHEN WAS SO PRACTISED in concealment he responded with glibness. 'I suppose the house of God is as good a place as any to make a confession – a God I no longer believe in, by the way, if I ever did. Anyway, I can't tell you anything. It was all classified, top secret.'

'I am an Anglican priest.'

'So that's all right then – because you priests can always be trusted.'

Ivens ignored the insult and simply said: 'I hear people's secrets all the time.'

'Wartime secrets? Do tell!' He couldn't help himself. Aggressive and threatening, Stephen leant forwards as if he was the one doing the interrogating.

Ivens sat unmoved.

'I wonder . . .' began Stephen, then he stopped.

I wonder, thought Stephen, how long you'd last under torture. A question he would ask himself with new recruits.

'I wonder,' he actually said, 'what the point is of telling you things? I'm not asking for God's forgiveness.'

'I realise that,' said Ivens. 'But sometimes – not always, sadly – talking helps.'

'I'm not looking to absolve myself. I know what I did.'

'And it's still destroying you. And those around you.'

'If you're thinking of Alice, I've told her she can divorce me if she wants.'

Uncertainty flickered across Ivens's face, as if he was suddenly unsure what to say. But his voice was steady: 'Your wife, the people of this village, this country – we're all trying to come to terms with loss and rebuild a better world. We need your brains, your energy.'

'Pretty words, Reverend, and you've lectured me on this before.'

'Because it's true,' Ivens sighed. 'In the Great War we didn't just lose all those young men, we also lost the men they'd have become. They'd be in their fifties and sixties now, doing everything from engineering to teaching, running hospitals, factories. All that experience and knowledge we might have had. Gone! Never to exist. So that's why I'm telling you again, someone with your gifts has a duty to play a part in this world.'

'I've done my bloody duty.'

Compassion returned to the vicar's face. 'I'm sure you have.'

'How can you be so sure?'

'As I said, there's talk in the village about what the squire was doing for the war effort.'

'I bet. And what are they saying? That I was sitting on my arse in some cushy number in Whitehall, sending others off to be butchered?'

'Actually, people thought you were a commando.'

Stephen shrugged. With his languages it was pretty obvious he'd be sent behind the lines.

'And people thought,' continued Ivens, 'you'd be pretty high up. That you had a lot of responsibility – and I'm presuming you liked that.'

'If you're asking,' said Stephen sharply, 'would I prefer responsibility to having other idiots tell me what to do then yes, I'd rather make my own mistakes than have some stupid bugger put me and my team at risk.' He glared at Ivens. He was being unreasonable, he knew, but suddenly he wanted to take it out on this vicar who sat in church taking orders from some make-believe, benevolent deity who promised happy ever after.

Ivens said: 'Having all those men dependent on you—'

'Not just men. Women.' Stephen gritted his teeth. 'Children.'

Now there was pity in Ivens's eyes and he didn't want that.

'What was it like?' Ivens was speaking softly. 'Can you, at least, tell me that?'

'It was hell,' said Stephen, as though that explained everything.

He'd lived constantly on his nerves: was the safe house he was holed up in actually safe? Was this person really who they said they were? At times he thought he'd go out of his mind with the strain of never, for a moment, letting down his guard because that could mean not just his death, but the death – agonising and hideously drawn-out – of hundreds.

'But you managed hell?' said Ivens. 'And, I'm thinking, you managed it exceptionally well?'

He gave a bitter laugh. 'Oh, yes! "You're a natural": that's what people said of me. And I was. Ironic, really. All my efforts not to be like my family and it turns out I'm just like them after all. A bloody brilliant soldier. You know,' he said, suddenly changing tack, 'what was one of the most wonderful things about marrying Alice?'

Ivens's face was a blank, but Stephen continued: 'I thought with her I could be different from what everyone expected me to be. I wrote my best poetry after I met her. It's still sentimental rubbish. But it's better than some of the drivel I was coming out with. But the thing is, my brother and I were expected to follow set lines, play the game. Whereas her family – they were so different. And I thought she would help me forge a completely new path, my children too – those were the days when I wanted them.'

Ivens's face was still completely inscrutable. Well, he preferred inscrutability to pity.

'But Hitler,' continued Stephen, 'decided to invade Poland and I soon discovered I'd been kidding myself. Put me in a war zone, and I'm your man. Few better! And now there's no escape.'

'From who you are? Or what you did?' asked Ivens.

'Both.'

'But they're not the same thing. And presumably you were following orders.'

Stephen looked askance at Ivens. 'Yes, I was following orders,' he said, his lip curling with sarcasm. 'That's what those Nazi monsters are saying in Nuremberg right now too. *I was following orders.*'

'And you followed your orders at a cost? A terrible one?' ventured Ivens. Stephen nodded. 'A cost to you?'

'I don't care about that,' shrugged Stephen. 'It's what I deserve.'

'As a punishment?'

'Yes.'

'For getting it wrong? That's what you said earlier.'

'Yes.'

'And you're going to carry what you got wrong around with you for the rest of your life, letting the war destroy you, never knowing peace. When we first met, you mentioned all the wars fought on this land, right here. Romans, Vikings, Protestants against Catholics, Royalists against Roundheads. Do you imagine you're the only man ever to make the mistake you did?'

'I don't give a damn about other people's mistakes.'

'I appreciate you can't break the Official Secrets Act. But what happened to you is not information that could benefit the enemy. Not now. Not ever again.'

Ivens was right, but the habit of secrecy had become second nature.

'Don't give me actual names,' Ivens was suggesting. 'Don't say, for instance, it was Paris. Tell me it was a city.'

'It wasn't a city.'

'So where was it?'

'A forest,' Stephen said at last. 'Much bigger than the forests round here – sixty thousand or so acres of ancient oak trees and beech and birch and pine, with herds of deer – fallow ones. Wild boar even.'

'And in this forest?' prompted Ivens.

'And in this forest, there was a camp and in this camp there were many men . . .'

He could be telling a fairy tale, with monsters and a tragic ending, where blood had been shed over centuries, the lives lost of as much significance now as lambs led to the slaughter.

'And these men,' Stephen said. But he couldn't go on. He was conscious of the slight rasp of Ivens's breathing, night drawing in. These men, he thought. Nothing he said

287

or did could put a stop to the eternal story of men killing each other.

Then Ivens ventured: 'It sounds a very beautiful wood.'

'Very beautiful,' said Stephen, when suddenly there was a loud click as if the latch to the church door was being lifted. Startled, he leapt up, instinctively scouting the shadows.

'Sir Stephen!' Ivens called out, almost shouting. 'Just sit!' he commanded. 'Let me check who's there. Please!'

Ivens ran down the aisle and disappeared into the porch. Stephen thought he heard whispering. Then, after a while, Ivens returned, and it seemed to Stephen as if the vicar was now dragging his feet.

He lowered himself into the pew beside Stephen. 'It was a parishioner,' he explained. 'I've promised to speak to her another time. So I beg of you, believe me. You're safe here. Nothing you say tonight can harm you. Or anyone else.'

And Stephen heard the truth in Ivens's words and, for the first time, in the hollow silence of the musty church, he talked.

42

'THE OAKBOURNE GOSSIPS WERE right,' Stephen began. 'I was a commando.'

He was also in more secretive Special Operations outfits – but Ivens didn't need to know about that.

'And I was in France, though not to begin with. Where doesn't matter now. But November '43 I was recalled to London. France, they told me, was to be the new – hopefully decisive – battlefield. You know all this now, of course – D-Day, Normandy Landings, Operation Overlord. My orders were to mobilise the *Maquis* – the French Resistance.'

He heard himself: rattling off the facts as if he was at a debriefing. And he remembered thinking that, my luck can't hold much longer. This time I won't return. And he'd suspected that the major who'd instructed him had indulged in a moment's pity because at the last minute he was told he could have forty-eight hours with his wife. A hotel was booked, or rather a grotty boarding house in Hastings in November rain, though to them it had felt like The Ritz on the Riviera.

In those few hours they'd had together, he'd given Alice a gold lace shawl. He'd been in Florence prior to London and the elderly woman who'd sheltered him had insisted he have it: '*Grazie, grazie, dallo a una donna che ami.*'

Thank you, thank you, give this to a woman you love.

He'd wrapped the cobweb-soft silk round his wife's naked body and she'd danced for him and he'd feared he would never see her or anything so lovely ever again.

That too, Ivens didn't need to know.

'The *Maquis*,' he continued briskly, 'needed not just arms but someone who could bring together all the different factions. The Gaullists and Communists hated each other almost as much as they did *les Boches*. My task was to stop them turning their guns on one another. And I did keep everyone on side, at least enough to lead sabotage missions, co-ordinate arms drops.'

He paused for breath. He'd reduced the dangers and deaths to a sentence. All those young men victims of their place in history and geography. But now was not the time to dwell.

'Then, in April '44, I was recalled to London.'

He made getting home sound like catching the bus. It was not. He was passed from one Resistance group to another to reach the Brittany coast, but while he was being rushed across the Channel the young radio operator who'd liaised with the navy, arranging the boat to pick him up, had swallowed her arsenic pill with the Gestapo beating down her door.

He'd known none of this of course as he sat in the back of the staff car racing across the Kent countryside. He'd felt only relief, because for that moment he was safe, in England, and he might see Alice.

'In London,' he said, 'I had three days of meetings.'

He'd been taken straight to Baker Street, where he'd sat in a smoke-filled office of an organisation so secret, most of Military Intelligence didn't know of its existence.

'I was told there were hundreds of our boys stranded in France – mainly airmen shot down on bombing missions who'd evaded capture. They'd had an escape route of sorts, down through France, over the Pyrenees and into Spain. But come '44, that came to a halt because we were bombing the railways lines in the south, trying to stop German reinforcements making it to Normandy. So our boys were stuck, mainly in Paris, but a few in Amsterdam, Brussels, hiding in houses of sympathisers, unable to move.

'By then, the Gestapo and SS were cracking down on the Resistance with every monstrosity they could come up with – and dear God could they – taking out their vengeance on any of our boys they could lay their hands on. And if you were in the Resistance and caught, then God help you. Not that God did.'

At this he glanced at Ivens who was perfectly composed, seemingly oblivious to the taunt.

Stephen sighed: 'The point is, the danger was accelerating crazily and we knew full well once the invasion got underway there'd be no holding the Germans back. So my job was to get these men home. As quickly as possible. Not just because of the fear of all the carnage but because lots were pilots and navigators and we needed them – their skills, their training.'

Suddenly he grasped Ivens's hands. 'The war was still a long way from over. You have to realise that. Because people will forget we didn't know then that we were going to win. We thought the war would just go on and on. And right up until the end, Hitler was working flat out on the atom bomb and imagine if he'd got there first. And he might well have if he hadn't forced all those Jewish scientists out of Germany.'

He dropped Ivens's hands, embarrassed.

'That makes me think there might be a God after all. At least a God of Irony. Future generations, when they judge us – and God knows they will – they'll forget how desperate we were. Instead they'll judge us from the peace and safety which we had to die for. And kill for.'

He clenched and unclenched his hands.

'You know what? Killing can be worse than dying. Because if I could have died, just ended it all, I would have. But no, that God of Irony decided to keep me going. So here I am.'

And suddenly he turned to the stained-glass window, and yelled at the young Christ looking up at St John the Baptist with his lamb: 'Thanks very much!'

Then he stared back at Ivens. In the half-light the vicar's face looked so drawn, as if the life was already draining from him and, to Stephen's surprise, he felt a moment's pity for the young man before him, his dog collar loose about his neck. A man, thought Stephen, who believes he has a truth to speak, but the actions of his fellow men make him absurd. And redundant.

'I'm sorry,' he murmured. 'Much of my reputation was because I was so calm under pressure. But tonight . . .' He spread his hands in a gesture of hopelessness.

'These men,' said Ivens, unperturbed. 'How were you expected to rescue them?'

'My orders were to set up a secret camp – a hideaway – in a forest some sixty-odd miles south of Paris. The Resistance would bring the men to me and protect the area. Then we'd all lie low until the Allies came to liberate us – just wait to be rescued. *Just wait.*' He grimaced. 'Some of these men had been doing nothing for so long they were desperate to get

back at the Nazis. One chap had been looked after by a
family in Amsterdam for more than a year. They'd shared
their food – what there was. They were virtually starving
and he'd carved an extraordinary chess set out of splinters
of firewood. He was going to leave it as a thank you, but
what happened to that poor family . . . Oh, no matter. The
thing is, I knew I'd have as much trouble restraining men
like him as I would hiding them.'

Suddenly Ivens raised his hand and began coughing, the
breath breaking from his heaving body.

'Shall I stop?' Stephen asked, as Ivens fumbled for his
handkerchief.

'No!'

'Are you sure?'

'What do you think? That I'm too sick even to listen?'

Yes, thought Stephen. 'Of course not,' he said.

As Ivens's breathing calmed he said, 'I didn't even get a
chance to see Alice. It was her birthday and I kept thinking
how happy she'd be if they'd let me have one day . . . But
time was of the essence. News came in of a Gestapo raid on
a baker's in Paris. He was sheltering two of our pilots – the
men got away, but his family . . . There were five children.
And people with children talk very, very quickly. A whole
network collapsed in hours.'

He was aware of Ivens studying his face. He could do
with a cigarette, a moment's remission from the story. But
he could hardly light up in church. Then the vicar, as if
sensing his hesitation, said, 'So you went back to France?'

Stephen nodded. The moment the final meeting ended in
London he was driven straight to the aerodrome in Biggin
Hill and for the next two hours he'd sat strapped in the

belly of a Halifax, trying to focus on the job in hand as the bomber droned across the Channel to France.

He'd done these drops into enemy territory so many times. He knew, all too well, the vomit-inducing swooping and swerving as the pilot avoided searchlights and flak; the blast of the slipstream catching you full in the face as the hole in the floor was slid open; the wait for the green light. But he recalled retching with nerves.

Or perhaps he thought, sitting in the dark, calm of the church, this was hindsight talking. Perhaps he was no more terrified than usual and he only remembered the fear because now he knew exactly what dreadful deed was going to be required of him.

To Ivens he just said, 'The journey went like clockwork.'

The flash of the torch from the reception committee, the signal to jump, and he was on the ground with his parachute still billowing out behind him as a man in a black sweater and beret came running towards him. Others had emerged out of the darkness and together they'd searched for the containers that had been dropped with him. For the Resistance – Bren guns, 303 rifles, explosives and grenades; for the camp – tents, tools, basic rations to get things going.

He could see them now: loading everything into a small lorry and then setting off down country lanes, slipping past towns and villages, plunging deep into the forest. His senses had been so sharpened he could recall all those details, and the fierce exhilaration and purpose that few experience in their entire lifetime. The truth is, he thought, looking round at the altar, it was war, certainly not that wooden cross, that gave my life meaning.

He was aware of Ivens still scrutinising him closely. Ivens didn't need to hear him say that, for all its horrors, living under the menace of death he'd never felt more alive. Right now there'd be men and women all over the country feeling just that.

He said: 'Even the weather in France was in our favour as it began to rain really hard, so the roads were emptier than usual. We reached the forest – they'd already earmarked a site – so we lugged everything in and got to work. Two days later the first men arrived. By the end of the week there were already thirty of us.'

He caught the question in Ivens's eyes.

'There was a chain of escorts who'd get them to us,' he explained. 'They'd travel on forged documents – take the train from Paris, then walk or cycle the last bit. Come the D-Day landings, I'd a hundred and fifty or so, straggling in from all over France, often carrying pitchforks, hoes and suchlike so they could slip into a field in an emergency and pretend to be farm labourers. And when they got to the forest they'd have to convince the men on guard they were genuine. By the beginning of August, we were more than three hundred, waiting for the Allies to reach us.'

He hesitated. 'You know what's odd, I had a dream about the camp this morning.'

Ivens gave a half-smile. 'But it was a dream, not a nightmare?'

Stephen shrugged. 'Day-to-day life in the camp wasn't a nightmare – not when you think of what else was going on then. More tents and medicine and clothes got parachuted in, and it was summer so sleeping rough was bearable. And the men who'd been in Holland probably ate better than they had for ages as the *Maquis* organised supplies from local villages.'

He paused again. He felt as though a fist was tightening about his throat, and he had to force out the words: 'There was a young girl.'

He swallowed hard.

'Agnes.'

There, he'd said her name.

Then, as if his story was a train belting onto its destination and he dared not stop, he said, 'Agnes was the daughter of one of the Resistance. She'd bring fresh bread and milk on a horse-drawn cart.

'I thought she was about twelve. Though it turned out she was older – almost fifteen. Not eating properly, I suppose, made her look so childlike. She was a pretty little thing. Always cheerful. And so incredibly brave – because if she'd got caught . . . Children!' he rushed on. 'How they love to be brave. Of course Hitler knew this better than anyone. Give youngsters a cause and you can get them to do pretty much what you want. And she was bright. She'd come looking for me and insist I spoke to her in English. When the war was over she wanted to visit Buckingham Palace, see where the king lived, go to the Tower – see the Crown Jewels.' He smiled. 'A typical French Republican.'

In the deep shadows of the church he could see her enormous gap-toothed smile, hear her heavily accented chatter: Captain Hare! In English! Please! How do you say . . . ?

'She had, I suppose, a bit of a crush on me. You see, to her, I was a hero.' He looked straight at Ivens. 'You know

I got a letter yesterday from the Resistance asking me back to France – to be honoured in some way.'

Ivens, he was relieved, didn't come out with platitudes of praise about his expertise in the face of atrocities, but simply gave a slight raise of his eyebrows.

'The thing was,' continued Stephen, 'I was always pleased to see her. She was a break from the evil of it all. A reminder of innocence. Yet what we were asking that innocent to do was so dangerous. But what choice did I have? The food and medicines she brought were important for morale and some of the men were really very weak.' He paused, conscious he was pathetically trying to vindicate himself. 'And a child – which is what I thought she was – was least likely to attract suspicion.

'But the Germans had got wind of us. One night a unit camped just a few hundred yards from us.' He'd ordered complete silence – douse the fires, don't eat, talk or sleep. 'We got away with it that time. The Germans pulled out next morning. But the more the Allies advanced, the more danger we were in from the retreating Nazis. So I took to going to the edge of the forest myself to keep watch.'

As soon as light broke he'd head off, desperate there would be nothing to see, no unexpected movement, no action.

'Then one morning—'

He could hear the cicadas shrieking in his head, taste the wild lavender in the air, feel the warmth of the dry earth under his body as he lay flat on a grassy bank beyond the pine trees.

'It was the first of August,' he said, 'and I was thinking the odds were the Allies would be here by the middle of the month. That I might actually pull it off – get everyone home. That it was only a matter of days – weeks at most.

'Hubris.' He smiled grimly. 'Sometimes I wonder if the Greeks had it right – there are plenty of deities having a fine old time toying with us for their own amusement. Certainly not your God of love.'

Ivens ignored him. 'It was the first of August, you say.'

'Yes, a Tuesday. It started like any other day.'

 43

'I'D BEEN OUT FOR a couple of hours,' said Stephen, 'just skirting the edge of the forest. I'd seen nothing unusual. And then I spotted Agnes in the distance – again, nothing unusual.' She was on her way to the camp with supplies, leading her horse and cart down a farm track alongside fields of fresh-cut barley.

'Seeing her cheered me up,' he continued. 'And I began thinking of our English lesson later on. She'd told me she wished she could do Latin like her brother and I was thinking that I'd explain how she already knew about a thousand Latin words because they were the same in French – English too of course. "Amor" for instance, in Latin. It's the same in French but spelt with a "u". And in English we have the same root . . .'

With studied slowness Ivens crossed his arms as if, thought Stephen, he's saying he has the patience to listen all night to me distracting myself with linguistics.

From beyond the church came the screech of a barn owl and he felt on the cusp of screeching out too – that he'd reached the end of his ability to relive this memory, that he was at the limits of language because what he'd learned that day in 1944 was that we are all capable of absolutely anything. He clenched his jaw – he would not cry out – and fell into silence.

'You were scanning the horizon?' Ivens said at last. Stephen nodded. 'And?'

About a mile or so behind Agnes he'd spotted a haze of dust rising in the air and he'd grabbed the binoculars and zoomed in on the disturbance. Slowly, it came into focus against the blueness of the sky.

'I saw a line of German soldiers,' he said. 'An armoured car. Two armoured cars. Then four. And they were all coming in our direction. About fifty men. Not fast. Just slow and sure. You know how a cat stalks a bird? Like that, certain of their prey.

'Agnes clearly hadn't spotted them. She was walking along completely oblivious, leading them straight to us, towards the forest, to the break in the trees where you picked up the path that led to the camp.

'The path was virtually impossible to spot unless you knew where to look. Which, of course, she did. I'd taken no chances. Only a fool – a dead one – underestimated the Nazis, so the entrance was really well-camouflaged.' He heard himself, making excuses again. 'Someone must have talked, or the bastards squeezed it out of some poor sod that she was a link to us. I never found out.

'My first thought was to rush back and order the men to make a run for it. But that would destroy all we'd worked for. The camp would be lost and the men almost certainly hunted down. And besides, I'd another fifty or so due to arrive at any moment.'

He'd trained his binoculars on the advancing Germans and as he identified the insignia and shoulder flashes he'd had the sensation of falling into an abyss.

'This lot were SS,' he said to Ivens. 'Of the type who just ten days earlier had wiped out an entire village for helping the Resistance. Men, women, children – almost six hundred in all – doused in petrol and set alight. And now they were on to us.

'I could hardly wander down with the Geneva Convention and explain these were unarmed men who should be treated as POWs. Or ask for mercy for Agnes as she was only a child and please don't shoot us out of hand. Though a quick bullet wouldn't be as bad as what I was in no doubt they'd do – torture every last one of us to discover the Resistance networks that had brought them here.

'I knew I had to steer them away from the camp. So I ran down to Agnes.'

He'd done the dull, trudging work of exploring the terrain countless times, so he reached her without being seen. She'd been startled when he suddenly appeared out of the grass, then delighted it was him. He'd grabbed the horse's bridle, telling her to keep looking straight ahead, to stay close. And then nudged the horse away from the path to the forest, veering off in a different direction, desperate for the Germans to take the bait and follow.

'I promised her we'd be all right. That we'd lead them away, then make a break for it. "You know I won't let you down," I told her. "Trust me."

'And she did.

'I talked to her to try and keep her mind off the danger – in English, about the weather of all things. And she was amazing, not panicking, not once turning round. I remember she asked me what the word for storm was and we talked about the similarity between *tempête* and tempest, while all the time . . .

301

'I was terrified that, with this change of course, the Germans would smell a rat. And I couldn't look back in case they realised I'd clocked them.'

He'd appeared calm to Agnes but his heart had been sprinting. 'We had to walk so slowly, Agnes, the horse and cart. I had to force myself not to change pace and speed up.'

Every step had been a step further from the concealed entrance to the forest and not till they were a mile away and they'd rounded a ridge and he was able to drop behind it, did he check if they were being followed. And they were. The Germans were hard on their heels.

'We fooled them,' he said to Ivens. 'Saved the camp. So now we had to save ourselves.

'I let go of the horse and cart, grabbed Agnes's hand and ran.

'We were in full sight of them by then, but I knew what I was doing. I'd got to know the geography round there really well so I'd a plan.'

He heard his self-justifying whine again, a schoolboy telling the teacher what a good boy he was because he'd done his homework. But the pictures flashing through his mind were the obscene out-takes of his nightmares: racing through that field of sunflowers, their great drooping faces taking on grotesque expressions, up over a hill where the rosemary spread in strong wiry nooses, through gorse bushes with thorns of cut-throat spikes, and all the time the increasing volume of the roar of the armoured cars, the bark of their fearsome dogs as the SS drew closer.

'I knew that half a mile or so ahead of us, the ground dipped into a small wooded valley and once we got there we'd be out of sight long enough for us to get into the trees and they wouldn't know in which direction we'd gone. There was a stream – we could wade through that to lose the dogs. And with any luck we'd be able to duck into the deepest part of the forest and hide until they gave up the search. Then we'd make our way back to the camp.

'Well, that was the idea.

'But Agnes was tiring and I needed her to speed up so I told her the plan – painted out the bare bones – and that we were almost there.

'It's amazing how offering people that bit of confidence suddenly gives them a new lease of life. I found that with my men, if they were flagging. Once, I had to . . .'

He caught Ivens's patient smile.

'Agnes speeded up – as I'd hoped – a textbook soldier. She actually raced on from me, calling, "*Vite! Vite!*" As if I was the one slowing us down.

'It was then that she fell.

'Her foot must have caught in a root or something, because she landed flat on her face. She screamed – for the first time in all of this – and she lay sobbing, gripping her ankle, obviously in excruciating pain. I tried to lift her up, but she collapsed again, her right foot just dangling uselessly. It was clear she couldn't go on. We'd no hope of making it to the woods now.

'She wanted me to leave her and to save myself. Can you believe that selflessness? Even though she was terrified. I still . . .'

I still hear her, he thought, the tremor in her voice as the adrenaline ran riot, her sacrifice, her words inescapable, a dripping tap in his memory.

'She said I knew too much. That *I* had to run. That she'd be all right. Though she can't have believed that. She knew just what the Nazis might do to her. But she said she'd spin some story about taking food to her cousins in another village, and she'd panicked when she saw she was being followed. And now she needed help and would they please ... And no, there hadn't been anyone with her. They must be mistaken.

'Of course they wouldn't swallow that.

'There was a small hut amongst the gorse, a refuge the shepherds used in winter. So I bent down and got her to put her arms round my neck. Then I piggy-backed over a field, across a stream and into the hut.

'I thought if we kept our heads down, stayed absolutely silent, there was a chance the Germans wouldn't see us and those damned dogs not find us. We'd wait till nightfall and then I'd go for help. But she had to stay very still and try not to yell out with the pain. I made her as comfortable as I could and gave her my handkerchief to bite on if the pain got worse. "Trust me," I told her. Again.

'For a while, nothing happened. There was no sign or sound of the Germans. I began to think we'd thrown them off the scent somehow. That we might make it.

'I dared to hope.'

He closed his eyes. He could have been slung through time and space. The flies buzzing, the sheep dung on the floor, a lizard racing up the wall, and Agnes, grey with pain and fear, biting on a blue handkerchief Alice had given him, now seemed more real than sitting here in the church where he'd been baptised. And so he raced on, as if he might alter the truth by rattling off the facts as quickly as possible: 'I peered round the door of the hut and saw helmets in amongst the bushes. Next thing a bullet smashed into the wall beside me.

'I ducked as more gunfire opened up. They were closing in. I fired back. Two rapid shots. A volley came back in response. I sat back beneath the wall and counted my bullets – four left in the chamber, two clips of six in my pocket. That was it. I'd been out on reconnaissance, not expecting a gun fight. The best I could hope for was to take a few of them with me, before . . . before . . .

'Again Agnes told me to run for it. That I'd make it on my own.

'But I'd never have done that. Really. I'd never, never have left her. But just at that moment a line of them came rushing over the open ground, rifles blazing. I fired, one fell, I fired again, and again. And they retreated.

'But it was only a matter of time.'

He felt suddenly dizzy, as if he was about to lose his balance. But in that hut he had never been more clear-headed, his brain operating with all the indispensable, ghastly pragmatism of a soldier: don't let Agnes fall into their hands. Or yourself.

Speaking so quietly that Ivens had to lean forwards to hear him, he continued: 'You know what they'd have done to her if they'd taken her alive? They'd have stripped her, tossed her around from one to the other, ripped her apart like a rag doll. It had happened in Russia. Women, girls – no more than children. Though they'd have beaten and half-drowned her first until they found out everything she knew.'

He faltered. Ivens didn't need to know more. Because what could Ivens or anyone say about the time he'd boarded a train in Florence? He'd walked head down along the carriage, trying to stay as inconspicuous as possible, but passing one of the compartments his eye had been caught by something so surreal – an SS guard playing with two puppets on his hands.

But the puppets were white ankle socks on which someone had drawn two faces. And the socks belonged to a girl lying on the floor in a pink dress ruched up her legs, her blood scarlet against the white of her skin. He'd thought she was dead, hoped to God she was. But suddenly the girl's legs twitched. And he'd had to walk on, past a child lying helpless with what was left of her life marked by rape after rape.

How could he let that happen again?

'Whether Agnes realised what I was planning, I don't know. But she said, "We're going to die, aren't we?" And she had this extraordinary dignity about her, an acceptance of the inevitable.

'Then she told me it was her birthday next week – that she'd be fifteen – and she was going to die having never been kissed.

'And she began to cry – not hysterically, just slow tears, like a weary old woman at the end of her life – a woman who'd seen too much. So I took her in my arms, cradled her – she was like a little bird, so fragile, just nothing of her – and I was holding her close to my chest and she looked up at me in this beseeching way and I put my lips on hers and I kissed away the tears on her cheeks. And I said, "It'll be all right. Trust me."

'*Trust me?*' His voice compressed with pain. 'I told her how beautiful she was and when the war was over men would fall in love with her. And I think she actually believed me. I had such a reputation for courage, you see, for luck, for pulling miracles out of nowhere. There was suddenly hope in her eyes. True hope. As if it was all just a nightmare and I really could be trusted to make it end happily ever after. And she closed her eyes and a half-smile spread over her face and, as gently as I could, I brought my revolver to the nape of her neck and I pulled the trigger.'

44

SHE DIED INSTANTLY, SLUMPING in his arms, blood pouring from her. Now it was his turn. He told himself to be quick as he laid Agnes on the floor and held the gun to his temple.

'This was the ending I'd been trained for. Even at school. I stood there, remembering that damned Kipling poem:

'When you're wounded and left on Afghanistan's plains,
And the women come out to cut up what remains,
Jest roll to your rifle and blow out your brains.
An' go to your Gawd like a soldier.

'God, I hate it. But it makes the point. I knew I'd no choice. They'd caught me before so I was under no illusions that eventually I'd crack under torture. And already the Germans had started up again, making another assault on the hut so I ordered myself, "Do it." And my finger was on the trigger.

'But suddenly, grenades were going off – and part of my brain registered that the Germans shouldn't be chucking grenades. They'd want to capture me in one piece. Then all hell broke loose. Bren guns were rattling like mad – the Resistance's machine guns, not the rifles the Germans had been firing – men shouting *Tuez les bâtards*, and then screaming, terrible screaming.'

He put his head in his hands and whispered: 'The Resistance – my comrades, coming from all sides.'

Ivens gave a sharp intake of breath: 'Oh! I see! Oh, dear God! I see now!'

'Hordes of them,' continued Stephen, 'taking on the SS. Men I'd help train, fighting so bravely. But too late. Too late for Agnes. If I'd stayed my hand by just . . . I try and work out how much longer I should have waited. I go over and over exactly what I did from the moment of – of killing her in cold blood, of murdering her.'

'No! Not murder.'

'Damn you! I don't need you soft-soaping it! At the absolute outside it was ninety seconds. More likely only sixty. But that's what made the difference. If they'd just been seconds earlier. Seconds!'

Years of pent-up French anger had exploded in a fierce, all-out battle. The Germans had tried to dig in but they were outnumbered and outgunned, their armoured cars useless on the terrain, and they'd picked up their wounded and run. All he could do was watch in shock. Shocked he was alive. Shocked at the realisation of what he had done.

'Agnes was everything I was fighting for. But instead I played God! I took a life I had no right to take.

'Or did I?

'That's the thing – I don't know right from wrong anymore and I can't bear the responsibility of having to decide. Yes, in the war, I wanted to be in charge – you're right. But not now. Not ever again.

'All the other killings I can justify, I suppose. But not this. And Reverend, don't preach me a sermon on forgiveness, because then I made things even worse.

'You see, Benoit – he was one of the best men – found me and he didn't see Agnes at first. He was full of how they'd smashed the SS, how one of the look-outs had spotted me, seen I was in trouble, so they'd got everyone together as fast as they could. He kept saying they'd not let *les Boches* get hold of me, that they needed me, and thank God I'd managed to hold them off till they got here.

'Then he saw her. He gave this terrible howl. How she was just a child, and they'd make the Germans pay for it. And then another of the men rushed in and he began shouting about how he'd string them up, gouge out their eyes, cut off their balls.

'That's when I should have butted in and told the truth. That it was not a German bullet in her head but a British bullet, *my* bullet.

'But then her father was there and all I could think as I watched him was that I should have covered her face – taken off my shirt, I don't know – because – well – her head had a bullet – my bullet – through it.

'Then more men came into the hut and they were making all this noise about how they'd kill every stinking Nazi they got their hands on. But her father was almost silent, just making this terrible whimpering sound, cradling her, as I had done, except now her head . . .

'Leclerc – he was the Resistance leader – was taking charge and all around me the men were shouting about what they'd do to those bastards if it was their little girl who'd been killed.

'Then her father turned to me and said, "*Merci, merci, Capitaine.*" He thanked me – her executioner – for being with her and trying to save her. And did she suffer? And to please tell him she didn't suffer.

'I'd still not said a word. Even then I could have explained that I'd done it to protect her, that I was about to kill myself too. But I just said no, she hadn't suffered and told him how incredibly brave she'd been. And he said she'd adored me. Loved her English lessons and would practise at home, wanting to impress me.

'What was wrong with me? No! Don't answer, Reverend. I know damned well. I've had plenty of time to think about it. And the rest of my life too. I watched a father hold his dead daughter in his arms, and was too much of a coward to speak the truth.

'And a hypocrite. After all my fine posturing I suspect I actually wanted to be a hero.'

Then, with mock bravado, he cried: 'The great and fearless Capitaine Lièvre, whose fine example and courage spurred the Resistance to their greatest battle. They'd seen off the SS! Restored their pride. And it was all apparently down to me.

'And now they want to honour me. Jesus Christ!'

45

JESUS CHRIST! THERE SEEMED no end to the horrors this war had put people through, thought Ivens. Not once had he conceived of a dilemma as dreadful as this. Force a man to make a terrible choice and however strong his spirit, you can destroy it. And he was in no doubt about Stephen's strength. There'd been strength in the way he'd told his story, strength in his stricken conscience, strength in his self-criticism, and phenomenal strength in taking that decision to pull the trigger. Yet that decision was destroying him, as it had that poor girl.

But now *he* had to make a choice. Help me, Ivens prayed, because in his heart he knew the compassion he felt was corrupted by his own dilemma.

He glanced round at the altar, a shadow in the gathering darkness.

'Let me put some lights on,' he said, playing for time, and he made for the vestry where he stood trying to collect himself with a prayer for the grace of God to guide him.

He'd pressed, cajoled and manipulated a man in terrible pain to tell him what he had been unable to confess to a soul. And now, Ivens admonished himself, own up: all you wish is to be rid of him. Stephen wasn't alone in being exhausted by responsibility. Tonight, Ivens too wished he might be relieved of his duty of Christian love.

He brought his fingers to his lips. This evening, he'd thought he'd be the one making the confession. To Alice.

It had been her opening the church door, responding to his note asking her to meet him after the cricket match. When he'd caught the click of the latch lifting he'd called out Stephen's name so loudly to stop her coming in.

She was standing in the church porch, holding the door ajar as if ready to run away. But, on seeing the bruising on his face, for a horrified moment he'd thought she was going to storm inside. He'd put his hands on her arms, keeping her still. Stephen was here, he'd whispered, but no, not because of her. He knew nothing and now she had to go and he would speak to her as soon as he could.

If he'd been in any doubt about her feelings, the love in her eyes dispelled them. And then she'd kissed him.

Oh, dear God! he prayed, his thoughts not thoughts at all but a battleground. Stephen might be strong. But tonight Ivens knew he was the man who wielded the power.

I could crush him, he thought.

For my own ends.

I could say God will forgive him, as God forgives us all. By putting his trust in Him he will find the peace that passes all understanding. And I could say that although divorce is desperately sad, it's a blessing men and women can be liberated from such comfortless unions. I wouldn't be perjuring myself so that Alice might be free – free to be my friend, free to be my . . .

'Reverend!' From the church Stephen called out.

Ivens knew he was being tested. In those awful days of the Blitz he hadn't thought twice of risking his life to run into bombed, burning buildings to save the crying child.

313

Like Stephen, he knew what it was to want to die quickly. And a hero. But now he was being asked to sacrifice his chance of happiness.

'I'm going,' he heard Stephen say.

'Wait!' Ivens switched on the lights. 'Please!'

He hurried back into the church but sat in the pew in front of Stephen so he could avoid looking him in the eye.

'Reverend.' There was a new gentleness in Stephen's voice, a sense of all passion spent. 'I know you mean well, that you have my interests at heart, but I don't believe in your wonderful world of love and forgiveness. I wish I did. But it's evil out there. And you can't convince me otherwise. There's no saviour to die for our sins, no one to help us.'

Ivens turned and, for a few silent moments, sat surveying the desolation in Stephen's face.

'I do believe,' Ivens spoke at last, 'that the grace of God can help you. Can help us all. And I'm in no doubt that you – we all – are forgiven. Even Hitler. Yes, Himmler, Goebbels, the lot of them. I know that's enough to put you off heaven. But, to me, the whole point of Christianity is that we all fail. God doesn't draw up balance sheets of who fails more than others. You see,' he went on, 'there's light and shadow in us all.'

He'd said the same to Alice that Easter Saturday she'd driven him to Norwich cathedral. Over the last few days, he'd relived all their meetings and now it seemed life could offer no greater joy than being by her side again, talking, laughing, discussing all that was dear to his heart.

'And I believe,' he said, 'you would find His grace in prayer.'

Then he faced the altar. 'But you will also find His grace – in abundance – if you go home now and find your wife and tell her everything you've told me. That is where you'll find salvation – in your marriage.'

There, he'd made his choice. Ivens looked fiercely at the crucifix as if demanding: is this what You want?

But Stephen was protesting: 'I don't know how to speak to my wife anymore. Or anyone for that matter. I speak another language. And I, supposedly so good at languages, can't understand them either.'

Perhaps he's right, thought Ivens. Perhaps they should just divorce and go their separate ways . . .

He spoke quickly: 'Although I don't think any of us can really understand another human being, in your wife I'm in no doubt, you have someone who'll listen, silence nothing, judge nothing.'

'I realise that,' said Stephen. 'She'll tell me my intention was good and it's the intention that counts, that with hind-sight, etc., etc. Don't you think I know all the arguments for absolving myself? But the gulf between us is unbridgeable now. I mean, she worries about the state of the house and the bloody greenhouses, which can fall down on top of us for all I care.'

Before he could stop himself Ivens cried: 'But *she* cares!'

And she cares about you, about how wild things grow, about living in this broken world. And, he thought, she cares about me.

Stephen clearly caught Ivens's anger, because he drew back and said, 'Before the war Alice and I both wanted those so-called normal things – home, family. But I don't. Not now. Truly, when I say I don't care, I don't.'

Ivens had not mistaken the gleam in Stephen's eyes as he'd talked of flying to France, of life in the forest. He'd

315

seen it in others, appalled by war but still hungering for it, fearful that the rest of their lives would be deathly dull in comparison. And meaningless.

Stephen rested his elbow on his knee and placed his forehead on the palm of his hand.

I've tried, thought Ivens. That's the truth. I could give up now because God knows I've really tried to persuade him to go back to her and his misery may only bring more misery to those around him. Yet a voice within him was saying, that's the truth, but only part of the truth.

'I think,' he said, 'the story for our generation is how we move on and for some of us – and I'd include you – peace is going to be as hard as war itself. All over the country people are wondering whether they did the right thing. What was it all for? Was it worth it?

'And,' continued Ivens, now with passion in his voice, 'all that loss *was* worth it because the bigger evil was defeated. We could be living under the Nazis now – and out here, where we live, in the middle of nowhere, would be the perfect place for their death camps for Jews and "defective" children and . . . Oh, it doesn't bear thinking of. And we don't have to think of it, thanks to men and women like you.

'God knows how my church would have acquitted itself if the Nazis had invaded. I'm fully aware of some of the choices the Church has made. But you've spared us those decisions which can show us at our very worst.'

'And best,' said Stephen.

Ivens caught Stephen's altered tone and said carefully: 'I asked you earlier whether you saw yourself as some paschal lamb sacrificed on behalf of us all.'

'I don't,' said Stephen, 'believe in your creed of someone being sacrificed to save the rest of us.'

'But I do. And you – and many others – have been sacrificed.'

Ivens looked away from Stephen to the altar and saw, not the wooden cross, but Alice as she knelt before him, saying it was our duty to be happy because Christ had suffered for us.

He persevered. 'But the sacrifice is not the whole story. It's only part one, so to speak. Part two is to rise again, to move on.'

Ivens got to his feet and walked slowly round to Stephen to sit in the pew beside him.

'Did your father,' he asked, 'ever talk about what he did in the Great War?' Stephen gave a hollow laugh. 'I assumed not,' said Ivens. 'But you have. You've trusted me with your story and now, I beg of you, trust me again when I tell you to talk to your wife. Allow yourself to be loved.'

'She doesn't love me anymore. And who could blame her? She's frightened of me now – I can tell. I've failed her.'

Ivens didn't let himself pause for breath. 'Isn't it too early to talk of failing? When you've still a lifetime ahead of you? Children, possibly.'

'I don't want children.'

'But she does?'

Stephen nodded. 'Very much.'

'Well then.'

'I'm afraid.'

'Not of her? Surely? I can see her.' Ivens closed his eyes. 'I can see her,' he repeated, 'welcoming you with open arms.'

'I'm frightened of the future.'

317

'You've been frightened before.'

'For me, yes. But how can I bring a child into this world where we just get better and better at destroying each other?'

'For all the horror, would you rather not have lived?' Ivens forced himself to hold Stephen's gaze as he said, 'Your wife once told me she tries to believe war doesn't – shouldn't – negate the good things. You saw yourself as a poet, a diplomat, a man of words and you gave all that up to be a soldier – what you least wanted to be. And thank God you did. You said yourself, how close Hitler was to winning. But he didn't win so we've another chance to be what we were born to be. Decent human beings. You're needed here. You've work to do.'

'Pretty words,' said Stephen once again, but more softly now.

'Words are what you understand. When I pray, and I need to pray,' Ivens said as much to himself as Stephen, 'my problems can be wordlessly solved and I find peace. But you're a poet. You must know what it's like when nothing makes sense but, by some miracle, it all comes together in a sort of order. You've begun searching for that order by talking to me. Now it's your wife you need to speak to.'

Ivens was aware of Stephen struggling beside him. But he was listening. And Ivens felt the weight on his shoulders grow heavier. This was Christian love and the burden felt overwhelming.

'Once,' he said, not allowing himself to give up, 'your wife kindly gave me a bottle of brandy. Go home, have a drink with her.'

'I promised myself I wouldn't drink, to do nothing to numb the pain.'

'All I'm saying is have a glass of brandy together. Not down a whole bottle. And tell her you've been speaking to me. Begin with that.'

Ivens watched Stephen hesitate and braced himself for countering more resistance. But, instead of objecting, Stephen said, 'Sometimes I wonder whether I should go back to France and confess to Agnes's parents that I was the one who shot her.'

'Why give them more grief?' Ivens kept his voice neutral. 'Sometimes,' he said, 'I hear of affairs, and people ask me whether they should confess to their husband or wife. And I always, always counsel not to. That it only spreads the pain, that there are some agonies we have to bear in secret. Before the war – forgive me – I don't think you'd ever fully lived. Because you'd not known defeat, what it is to make a mistake that can't be remedied, the anguish of hurting someone and being powerless to make amends.

'Many of us,' he persevered, 'go through life failing. Again and again. And every time we have to pick ourselves up with all our shame and sorrows, which can feel intolerable. Yet that doesn't make us worthless. If God relied on saints,' he said, putting a smile on his face, 'we'd be in a pretty poor place. You and I have both seen men and women consumed with guilt for surviving, for what they've done, unable to cope with civilian life again, retreating into nostalgia or raging at everything or—'

'Or,' said Stephen, 'acting like my father. Running his family as if we were his private army. My poor mother. She'd tell me he used to be so sweet-natured and we had to make allowances. Not that I did. I couldn't stand him. What about,' he went on hesitantly, 'your father?'

'He was killed – 1918 – 8th November,' said Ivens.

'Just days before the end!'

'Seventy-two hours. More like sixty to be exact.'

'Hours!'

'Hours? Minutes? Seconds? What's it matter? The tragedy's the same.' Ivens brought his hand to his temples in a gesture of futility. 'But the point about your father is that he chose to let the war turn him into some sergeant-major at home – or general I'm guessing – making you all unhappy. He had a choice. Just as you do. Give up and shut yourself away in the Big House or decide you've a life to lead.'

With that, Ivens rested back as if he might find some comfort, but the wooden pew was unyielding. 'Please,' he said, his voice a whisper now, 'trust me.'

'Trust me,' echoed Stephen. 'That's what I said to Agnes.'

'And she was right to trust you. But now you must trust your wife. At least say you've spoken to me. Will you promise me that? Say you met me in the church tonight?'

After a long pause, Stephen replied, 'I promise. But whether I can tell her any more I don't know.'

Then he fell back into silence and Ivens felt desperate for the man to go, to be left in peace.

At last Stephen spoke again: 'But you? Reverend? You've been good enough to listen to me. Is there anything I can do? For you?'

'Nothing!'

'But medically there have been so many advances during the war. Ironic, I know. But is there nothing that might help you?'

'Nothing.'

'At least let me walk you home.'

Ivens could see why Alice had fallen in love with this man. He was tainted with despair, but there was also a kindness of spirit, extraordinary courage.

Then Stephen reached out an arm as if he might help Ivens rise to his feet. And this gentle gesture from Alice's husband was intolerable.

'I need to stay here,' Ivens said. 'I've told you what you can do for me – confide in your wife. Now go. And may God be with you.'

Ivens could speak no more. He bowed his head as if mourning at a grave, wanting only to grieve in solitude.

He heard Stephen's footsteps as he walked back down the aisle. Then the latch of the door.

Eventually he said, 'Thank you for the strength, dear Lord.'

But never had he felt so desolate. He'd done the right thing, yet he was filled with a great, wearying loss.

He dropped to his knees.

'Dear God! Please! Let her be happy!'

 46

THE SKY WAS STILL dark when a blackbird began to sing. Alice listened, unmoved, pacing round the walled garden, hunched into her old oilskin. What she'd glimpsed in the church defied explanation. The man she'd gone to meet behind her husband's back had been punched in the face. By Stephen, undoubtedly. But George had ushered her away.

None of it made sense. All she could be sure of was that there had been fighting. She peered into the shadows, frightened that at any minute Stephen might emerge. There was a clamour of ducks rising up from the lake, the awful shriek of a muntjac deer, and she feared Stephen, on his way to find her, had disturbed them. And then he might use his fists. Again. This time on her.

But his presence was not as terrifying as his absence. Because a pool of blood could be spreading over the church floor and George lying injured. Or worse. And only an immense effort of will stopped her racing straight back to them.

She needed to remain calm, just hide here, out of Stephen's way till daybreak, then head for the station, telephone George, go to her sister's and leave Oakbourne. This time for good. And what then?

All she could be sure of was that her world would change. But, once she'd divorced Stephen, she would find her way. She had a skill. She'd watched her father develop roses for the small gardens in the new housing estates. And now the war was over, people's minds could return to roses. Perhaps she really could run her own business, and the more she counted her assets, the more they multiplied. She was strong, knowledgeable, experienced.

Suddenly she felt sick.

She crushed a sprig of wild mint between her fingers and gulped in the freshness. Get a grip! she cried inwardly. This is just 4 a.m. hysteria. But, hysteria or not, she couldn't escape that insistent question. What if she was?

That night with George she had not been careful. Instead, she'd thrown all caution aside with no regard for the consequences. And what if the consequence was . . . ?

She clutched her stomach. She couldn't possibly know yet. But what if waiting only brought the confirmation she was pregnant? That she was having George's child? Then, how could she possibly support herself gardening? She imagined herself heaving a baby about in a wheelbarrow, pruning fruit trees with her bent shoulders dragged down by a papoose on her back, in the lonely struggle of bringing up a—?

She could barely bring herself to say the word. But that's what her baby would be – a bastard.

And that's what it would be called.

Unless George married her.

But she'd no idea if she wanted to marry him. Or he her. Wouldn't marrying a divorcee – because that's what she'd be – mean he could no longer be a vicar? Giving up his vocation would destroy him! She couldn't do that. But if she was pregnant she would have to act. And act soon. The war may have meant society and its attitudes were changing. But not that fast. This child would be at the mercy of a hostile world and she'd be powerless to protect it from scandal, the village's so-called neighbourliness poisoned by knowing looks and sneering glances.

She stared at the earth, the birdsong echoing now beyond the walled garden, the thrush, pitched higher than the others, scattering notes as sweet as the lilac petals dropping in the breeze.

And she felt a faint stirring of hope.

What if?

What if she really was having a child?

Even if she had to bring it up alone, would it be so terrible? To watch a new life unfold, to have something to love. Oh! Something to love! And she could imagine this baby with George's dark eyes, his mischievous smile, his gaze of love. Of course it wouldn't be easy. But she had a sister who'd be a wonderful aunt. A sister who was a doctor, so that would save on medical bills. She could move somewhere no one knew her, say she was a widow. God knew there were enough of them about. No one need know the truth.

She stepped forwards to the garden door and looked up at the sky, so vast she could almost feel the earth spinning. Day was breaking, a silvery light spreading over the garden as if glittering with a sense of purpose.

What if life didn't always get worse? What if, once again, she might be happy?

It was possible.

The war was over. Yes, there were refugees, destruction, prisoners, hunger, untold misery . . . If only she could be free of it all and live in peace, to embrace the new world opening up: leaving Stephen, divorce, new beginnings, whatever they might be.

She looked across the lawn glistening with dewy daisies, the lake sparkling in the early morning sunshine while all around her was the countryside, green with fertile fields, playful lambs and promise.

I can do this, she told herself. A baby might be a figment of her imagination but a new life was undeniable. She would face the future, courageous, unafraid. She would find joy again.

And, slightly lightheaded with her visions, she closed the door to the walled garden with a sense of putting old sorrows behind her.

'Alice!'

She heard Stephen's voice.

'Alice!'

Then he appeared, rounding the path at the far corner of the garden, and ran straight for her.

47

'ALICE! I'VE BEEN LOOKING everywhere for you.'

She was aghast. He was still in his cricket whites, streaked with mud and grass stains. And blood. One arm was in a sling. 'What the hell have you done?' she screamed.

To George? she cried inwardly. Oh! She should have gone to him! Not left him in the church. She'd seen Stephen kill. She knew just what he was capable of. She turned and ran. But Stephen was faster.

He grabbed her arm. 'Alice, stop!'

'Get off me!' she yelled, trying to twist free. She had to find George. But Stephen's grip was too strong.

'Alice! Please!'

'Let me go!'

'Sorry,' Stephen muttered, releasing her but standing far too close. She pressed herself up against the garden wall. She felt as if a belt was tightening around her ribs. But then Stephen began blinking rapidly and it occurred to her if she was scared, so too was he.

'I have to tell you,' he said.

'Tell me what?' she hissed. All she wanted to know was how he had hurt George. Why he had blood on his clothes.

'What I did – in France.'

She looked at him in shock. For so long, this was the conversation she'd been desperate for. And here he was, completely out of the blue, unable to get the words out quickly enough.

Why now? she wanted to ask but he was already explaining: 'I spoke to the vicar. I told him. And I know what you're thinking. That I've never had a good word for him. But I was wrong. About him. About so much. And he thought I should have told you ages ago.'

'*He* told you to tell me?'

'Yes, though I said I've taken out so much on you. And how you've stood it I don't know. But I need to tell you. Now! *Now!*' he cried. 'Can't you understand? If I don't speak now, I might never do so. Oh, let's sit. Please!' He held open the door to the walled garden and gestured for her to go in. But she didn't move. 'Alice! Part of me doesn't want to talk about it. Ever! I can't bear going back there. It was hell enough telling Ivens but if—'

'But why spill out everything to him? And after all this silence, just holing yourself away, not saying a word. To me, to anyone. Being cruel and . . . and . . .' She spread her hands.

'Yesterday – it was a strange, strange day. And I ended up in church and Mr Ivens, I realise now, is a good man. I see why you like him. And, I suppose, in his line of work he's pretty good at extracting confessions. And I did something dreadful. I hit him. But he's all right! Don't look like that! I promise you he's . . .'

'You might have killed him!' She stared up at him fiercely. Let him hit her too. Then it would all be over and she could walk away forever. Because, she realised, it was too late for his confession. She could take no more.

327

'I'm not making excuses,' he was saying, 'though Ivens told me after he'd been deliberately provoking me.'

'He'd never do that.'

He sighed. 'Have I ever lied to you?'

'How would I know?'

He leant against the wall for support. 'Ivens,' he said, 'told me he envied me. He envied me *you*. And he kept insisting I told you – that was really important to him. He said *you* were the one to turn to for help – that I'd find salvation in my marriage. Salvation,' he repeated, 'that was his very word.'

Of course George would say that, she thought. He's an Anglican priest. He'd have forced himself to do what he sees as the 'decent' thing. He couldn't tell Stephen his marriage is over. But I can.

Be quick, she urged herself. 'Stephen, you're right, we need to talk.'

She saw the relief on his face. 'Thank you,' he said.

'No, I'm the one who needs to talk.'

But he didn't hear. He'd already gone back inside the walled garden and was pressing the slats of rotten wood on an old bench, before sitting down cautiously. 'We're safe,' he said, with a weak smile.

Take control, she urged herself. The kindest thing is to end things quickly.

'Stephen,' she began.

But he grasped her hand and, clearly aware of how she shrank back, he let go at once, saying, 'I know this must be a shock. That you might not even want to know anymore. Or care. And I wouldn't blame you.'

He was looking at her with a desperation she'd never seen before. Then he put his hand to his mouth and his nervousness made her recall a photograph of him as a little boy. He was standing on the top diving board of a new swimming pool his father had just opened and the local papers were there to take pictures. Stephen's elder brother, James, was away at school, so seven-year-old Stephen was chosen to be the first to dive. He'd begged his father not to make him do it. James was the far better diver, loved courting danger. But Stephen hated it. He'd stood there, stick-thin and shivering with terror and cold, his father insisting. So he'd forced himself over the edge.

'Alice? I'm begging you. I can't do this on my own.' Every instinct in her screeched that listening to him now would make it impossible for her to leave. His life was being put in her hands and she didn't want the responsibility. Not anymore. She searched round in the vain hope that there was an escape.

Leave me in peace!

Before her a great golden bee hummed over the honeysuckle then tumbled into a crimson poppy. A peacock butterfly flitted above purple trumpets of wild convolvulus. A robin hopped amongst the forget-me-nots seeded along the path and her idea of forging a future in some new world already seemed childish nonsense. Because there was no escape from this war. If she deserted her husband what would happen to him? And as she asked the question she knew she'd already made her choice.

She bowed her head as he told her about the camp in the forest, about Agnes, about the SS. He told her what would have happened if they'd taken Agnes alive and the choice he'd faced. He told her everything and by the time he'd got to how he'd tried to die, deliberately placing himself in danger as he'd hunted down Nazis at the end of the war, in

329

place of the misanthropic brute she'd known for the last nine months was a man sobbing.

She sat silent, rocked with horror at the story he'd concealed.

In this garden, she'd once said to George: what did our generation do to deserve two wars like this?

Nothing! She could scream with rage. They'd done no more and no less than anyone else. But life had played this cruel joke on them all and she had the irrational feeling that she should have protected Stephen, that she should have done whatever it took to have spared him this pain.

Yet now she had to find a way to shield him in peace.

But how? She could feel in her own body how he'd steeled himself to destroy that innocent life; his awful sickening lurch as he'd pulled the trigger; his shock as he'd heard the fire of the Resistance guns; his gut-wrenching grief at what he need not have done.

When George had heard this appalling confession she imagined him praying. But she did not believe in any God who could help her. Or Stephen.

George had told Stephen he would find 'salvation' in his marriage. And with her compassion for her husband's tortured soul it seemed as if the walls of the garden were closing in. George was right. Love was Stephen's only hope. But her love had been corrupted by war. Love, which she had believed made life glorious, now ground her down, its ecstasies transfigured into burden and duty. When George urged Stephen to speak to her he'd have known exactly what he was doing: making it clear there could be nothing between them now and if there ever was, it was over. It had to be.

She put her hand on Stephen's back, stroking him as if he was an inconsolable child. Words failed. All she could murmur to the pathetic figure hunched up beside her was: 'I'm so very sorry, that it had to be you, in that place, at that time, faced with that choice.'

'Why *not* me?'

'If I was Agnes's mother, I'd have been glad it was you who was there to protect her. Someone with your courage, someone brave enough to do what you did – the right thing.'

He looked at her uncertainly.

'Don't give up on me. Please, Alice. I'd understand if you wanted to call it a day. But just give us a year, to try again. I told the vicar I'd failed you and he said it was too early to speak of failing, that we have time, a whole life ahead of us. He said he could see us having children. You'd like that, wouldn't you? We don't need to make any quick decisions. But we were happy once, weren't we? Very happy.'

'Yes . . . once.'

'I can't bring Agnes back. I can't stop the evil. But I can stop being evil to you. I can put the war behind me and forget.'

He could never forget, she was certain. And for the first time she fully grasped the harsh reality of the times they lived in. They may have won the war. But not the peace. Whatever their intentions the war was as much part of them as the air they breathed.

Her role now was to look after a wounded soldier. But she knew what she needed to do first. 'I'm here, for you,' she said, 'but I'd like to see Mr Ivens. To make sure he's all right.'

'I'll come with you. I've a lot to apologise for. Not just hitting him. I know that when he called round I was hardly gracious. And all that time he was so ill.'

331

'*So ill?*'

'He said he'd be lucky to see it through next winter.'

With an effort that wrenched her as if she was lifting granite, she got to her feet. *Next winter?* So that was why he was at the hospital.

How could she have been so blind?

This beautiful man, her lover, so full of life, was dying.

'He probably didn't want to trouble you,' Stephen was saying. 'I suspect he's a proud man.'

Oh, why didn't he tell her? She had to help him. Do something. 'I must see him.'

'I'll come with you,' Stephen said again. 'We could begin doing things together.'

'No, no . . .'

The smile appearing on her face disguised the fear gripping her as she said calmly: 'We can both go, but later. This has been a lot to take in. I'm here for you. You can depend on that. But now I need to think – on my own.'

And, trying not to break into a run, she hurried out of the garden.

How she reached Ivens's lodgings she wasn't sure.

'Lady Rayne!' Mrs Turner opened the door as if expecting her. 'Mr Ivens thought you might call. He's gone to London. He left a note, saying there was an emergency to do with some friends. He arranged for the curate at Milton to take the Whit services today and caught the early train. I didn't even hear him leave. But in his message he said to give you this.'

Alice looked at the slim Manila envelope as if it was a telegram, sure to contain bad news.

She walked back down the garden path, along the narrow rutted road dotted with decrepit cottages, past the field where foundations for the new estate had been laid, and when she reached the privacy of the woods she tore open the letter.

Dearest Alice,

I cannot see you – I know you'll understand. I'm going to ask to be transferred back to London.
    God bless you.

 48

STANDING UNDER AN UNCLOUDED sky, waiting for Leclerc, his old Resistance comrade, to arrive at Oakbourne Station, Stephen had the all too familiar symptoms of nerves. Yet this shortness of breath and pulsing in his temples were absurd. The station master in his black uniform, giving him a polite nod, was the son of a man who used to work on the estate, not the Gestapo.

All I'm required to do, Stephen told himself, striding back and forth along the platform, is keep up a front – to be *Le Lièvre*, the man Leclerc had known him to be – for the next twenty-four hours.

He lit another cigarette and looked across the single railway track to a scene as placid and pastoral as an eternal Constable. A lark was rising. If it flew directly, it was three hundred-odd miles to Paris, then another sixty further south on to the forest. Is that what he and Leclerc would talk about? Old times?

During the war there'd been an unspoken agreement – what was done, was done. There could be no looking back. But peace changed people. And what, wondered Stephen, might peace have done to Leclerc? Turned him into another de Gaulle, trumpeting on about glorious French victories? *Then God help us*, he muttered, drawing hard on his cigarette.

The last time he'd seen Leclerc was May 1945 when they didn't even know each other's real names. They had sat in Montmartre toasting the defeat of the Nazis and promising to stay in touch in a way neither of them for one second believed they would.

'Bloody marvellous!' he muttered, as if it was all some crazy joke that a man who'd seen him slit the throat of a young German sentry was now coming to stay and meet his wife. He'd never before had a proper meal with Leclerc, and only just found out what he did for a living. He restored art, with an expertise in the Middle Ages, and nothing could be more incongruous for a man with Leclerc's strategic mind and power in persuading people to risk their lives. And kill.

A week ago, he'd have put Leclerc off, concocted some excuse. But if he was going to keep his word to Alice and attempt some sort of 'normality', he could no longer hide himself away.

Yet he felt wretched. As, he was pretty sure, his wife did too.

Alice was clearly suffering. Since he'd confided in her, she'd been as compassionate as he'd predicted. But she'd always been kind. Even, he acknowledged, when I was deliberately unkind to her. But the urgent passion with which she used to look at him, as if willing him to love her as he once had, was no longer there. Beneath her courtesy and concern, the strain in her eyes suggested some spring of love had died.

He finished his cigarette and, on the still, hot air, caught the smell of wild garlic growing in hollows near the embankment and from nowhere came the recollection of arriving home with his brother at the start of school summer holidays

335

and seeing his mother on the platform, her arms outstretched, overjoyed at the mere sight of him.

All that love!

All gone.

He lit another cigarette so he might breathe in the smoke instead of that all too evocative garlic. He wanted no more reminders of the past, good or bad, and he wandered up to the other end of the platform where there were foxgloves heavy with bees and a hum of insects from the long grass and chamomile. Then he heard the train whistle and level-crossing gates clanking and closing. Smoke billowed in the distance, getting closer. He's here for just a day and a night, Stephen told himself. Take it hour by hour, like you used to.

And he steeled himself as the train pulled in. The doors swung open and out clambered farmers sweltering in tweeds, mothers clutching flushed children and picnic baskets, walkers with rucksacks sticking to their shirts. Then Leclerc, almost unrecognisable in an immaculate, expensively tailored suit.

Stephen made himself walk forwards. *'C'est si bon de te voir!'* he said. 'It's so good to see you!'

Leclerc grasped Stephen's outstretched hand, then appraised him critically. 'You've changed! You used to be a much better liar. You don't want to see me at all!'

With one look Leclerc, his old friend, knew exactly what he was thinking and Stephen burst out laughing.

Leclerc nodded at Stephen's sling. 'What happened? You survived the war with barely a scratch and now look at you!'

'I fell – it's nothing. But come along!' said Stephen, reaching for Leclerc's case. 'Let me take this.'

'Hold on,' said Leclerc, not moving, uncharacteristically uncertain.

'What is it?'

'I'd hoped,' began Leclerc, then trailed off. And Stephen realised just what Leclerc was going to say. 'I'd hoped seeing you would be good for me – for you too maybe. That it would help with . . .'

'With intolerable memories,' murmured Stephen.

'Exactly. Some old soldiers like reunions, I know. My father found them a comfort.'

'Mine too,' said Stephen.

'But I'm not my father, and as I sat on the train the closer I got the more I thought of us drinking in one of your dingy pubs turning the past into great adventure stories – when the truth . . . The truth, Capitaine Lièvre, is unspeakable. I've seen you – that's enough. And you look – I can't lie and say you look well. But . . . But I realise there's nothing I want to talk to you about. Can you understand? Yes, of course you do. I'm sorry, but I just want to head straight back to London. Forgive me.'

'There's nothing to forgive,' said Stephen, but his disappointment felt out of all proportion. Leclerc was echoing sentiments he'd held just five minutes ago yet now he realised this man, with whom he'd once worked so closely, was more familiar to him than people he'd known on the estate his entire life. More familiar than his wife.

Stephen sighed. 'The next London train's not for another couple of hours so, rather than wait here, let's go and sit by the sea.'

Without saying another word, Stephen drove, steering one-handed through the dazzling afternoon, until he reached

337

a track that coiled through the salt marsh out to the coast. They climbed out of the car and walked in single file.

Then Stephen turned back to Leclerc: 'We don't have to talk about – well – anything. But enjoy the view. My wife loves this place. All the curlews and those little birds.' He pointed at a flock flying up over a barley field. 'Don't ask me what they are. I can't remember their names, but she does. And the names of flowers. Sea aster, apparently. Samphire, and there are great yellow poppies near the shore.'

Leclerc paused, breathing deeply. 'Aniseed.'

Stephen nodded. 'When birds brush their wings against the fennel they spread the perfume through the air – or so my wife tells me.'

Leclerc gave a shadow of a smile and Stephen led the way along the path, then climbed up through the dunes.

The tide was far out and in the distance, all shimmering blues, lay the sea. But before them, on the vast plain of sand, were abandoned coils of barbed wire.

'I used to think this place was timeless,' said Stephen. 'But now there's no mistaking the twentieth century.'

'Do you still bring your wife here?'

'Not now.'

And that, thought Stephen, says it all. He was aware of Leclerc sizing him up, as if considering asking a question, but after a few moments Leclerc sat down on the sand, lay back and closed his eyes.

It was stunningly hot, the temperature probably hitting eighty and, thought Stephen, we could just silently soak up the sun until I drive him back to the station. Then I'll be out of his life for ever, and he out of mine. But that now grieved him terribly, and he just gazed out to sea until a

sudden burst of laughter made him turn as a group of youngsters, aged about sixteen, bounded out from the dunes.

Youth in summertime, thought Stephen, as they jostled
one other, one of the girls stealing a boy's cap and tossing it
in the air until he grabbed it back and they fell, panting with
laughter.

'I feel I could be their grandfather,' said Leclerc, propping
himself up on an elbow.

'Me too,' said Stephen. 'It seems strange seeing young
men in ordinary clothes – not khaki.'

One of the girls, with long, lean legs, turned and caught
Stephen's eye. She smiled breezily then, swinging her chestnut
hair, strolled on with a slight swagger.

Leclerc gave a weary laugh then looked at his watch,
seemingly anxious to go. But the train back to London was
still not for a good hour.

Stephen retreated to safe ground. 'Your work?' he
ventured. 'Can you tell me what it is?'

'I don't think I'm breaching any secrets in telling you
I spent yesterday at Lambeth Palace examining a twelfth-
century version of St Mark's Gospel.'

'That's wonderful! Isn't it? I always think those illuminated
manuscripts are like visual prayers.'

Leclerc shrugged and lit a cigarette. 'They're an escape,
certainly.' Then he sighed. 'Have you been to London since
you got back?'

'I saw it on the train, obviously, but . . .' Stephen ran his
finger down the sharp edge of the marram grass. 'But this –
this beach – is the furthest I've been since I got home.'

Leclerc murmured, 'Whatever saves you from the
madhouse.'

Leclerc had once said the same about Benoit, a man to whom Stephen owed his life. If Benoit hadn't rescued him from that stinking prison when he was half-dead who knows what he'd have revealed when they stuck his head once more under that running tap. Yet that selfless soul was now drinking himself to death.

Stephen made himself ask: 'Do you know how Benoit's doing?'

'Last I heard, he's the same. Here, have one of these,' said Leclerc, holding out a packet of Gitanes, as if to say he didn't want to discuss Benoit. 'They're better than that awful stuff you Brits smoke.'

They lit up and Stephen breathed in the dark tobacco, so distinctive that even here, on this East Anglian beach, he could taste the anxiety and adrenaline of that French forest.

'I hadn't expected,' Leclerc went on, 'London to be quite such a wasteland. I didn't think war could shock me anymore. Though the good news is that it's meant more work for me.' He slapped his thigh with fierce false heartiness. 'All that art left to go to rack and ruin. Keeps me more than solvent. And busy, I suppose. Passes the time.' Then Leclerc suddenly dropped his voice. 'I miss the war. The camaraderie. How we got on with one another. Now France feels on the brink of civil war. Frenchman against Frenchman. It's so toxic and I hate it so much, I might leave.'

Stephen looked at him in surprise.

'I've just been offered a job in America, at some new museum in Texas where they've bought up all these old Bibles and they need someone – me – to keep them going for another few centuries.

340

'Except I don't know if I can bear to watch the Yanks prop up the stinking Germans. Doling out millions of dollars after we risked our lives, our sanity, everything to defeat them. But to hell with all that. I think I'll do it. If there are hand-outs going I don't see why I shouldn't get them as much as some Kraut.'

'I don't blame you. Anyway, I've not got a problem with the Yanks. Let's face it, without them the Nazis would be here. We'd be dead, those kids over there slave labour. And they're only chucking money at the Germans because now it's the Russians they hate.'

'You know who I hate the most?'

Stephen stared straight ahead. If he half-closed his eyes he couldn't see the barbed wire, only a misty meeting of sea and air on the horizon, children splashing in the waves, the sun turning the water into streams of silver. 'No,' he said, 'who do you hate the most?'

'My own people. Look at that *putain* Paquet – mayor now!'

'If anyone knew how to play the game it was him.'

'Now he's always the first to denounce anyone with a hint of collaboration. But think of the deals *he* was up to!' Leclerc turned angrily to Stephen. 'Remember the blacksmith out at Arrvenne? His daughter took up with a German soldier. Stupid, stupid girl. But she was only sixteen. The boy not much older – children, both of them. And what they did to her afterwards ... Paquet sanctioned all that. Jesus! She should be living her life like those kids. But instead ... It's Paquet making a great song and dance about this memorial. Though everyone's at it – sticking up stone crosses to the great French liberating heroes.'

'Some were heroes.'

341

'Not enough.'

'You were,' said Stephen. 'You could have kept your head down like so many others.'

'I might have done if I'd had a wife and children.'

Aware he was echoing Alice, Stephen said, 'Stop punishing yourself.'

Leclerc looked at him directly. 'Can you tell me you're not doing the same? What about Agnes?'

For a moment Stephen didn't even blink.

Agnes.

A choked groan shook his body. Then, as if it was an act of deliverance, he made himself say: '*I* killed her, Leclerc. Not the Nazis. *Me.*'

Ivens's God may have absolved him – Alice too – but all that really mattered was the judgement of those men who'd been with him in that shepherd's hut where he'd pulled the trigger. Who'd fought by his side. Who'd have died to protect him.

He felt Leclerc's hand on his shoulder as the shame of lying to those men bore down upon him.

He was aware of Leclerc's grip tightening. There was nowhere to run now. And Stephen, his body rigid, braced himself for retribution.

But Leclerc was looking at him with pity.

Again, Stephen forced himself to spell it out: 'I shot Agnes.'

Leclerc's expression turned to bewilderment as at last he spoke. 'I know. My poor friend, I've always known. We all did. Surely you realised?'

Blackness swirled before him. 'No – how could I?' He stumbled to his feet. 'You never said!'

342

'Of course we didn't. You know what it was like! Some things are too terrible—'

'But I . . .' Every moment since, he'd tortured himself for his lies and mistakes. 'But how . . . ?'

Leclerc was up now, taking him by the arm, away from all the picnickers and bathers turning to see what the raised voices were about.

'Hush!' Leclerc was saying.

'How . . . How did you know?'

'The damage to her face,' Leclerc said in a rapid under-tone. 'It was clearly a close-up shot. And you! You were so . . . You weren't yourself! Normally, you'd be taking control but you'd slumped onto the floor. And your gun was just lying there. And I picked it up and saw there was just one bullet left in the barrel and the look on your face said it all. You'd intended to use it on yourself.'

'But her parents? How can they ever forgive me?'

'They light a candle for you every mass. They know you did your best for her.' Stephen dropped back onto the sand. 'My dear *Lièvre*,' continued Leclerc, kneeling beside him, 'they know what those bastards would have done to her, and you had the courage to act.'

'I didn't have the courage to admit what I did.'

'Because some things are too terrible to put into words. And anyone who judges you has no idea what it was like to be in your shoes. Listen to me! You're a *genuine* hero. And God knows we need them. Not the likes of Paquet and those other shits wallowing in a myth of their own making.'

'Maybe . . .' Stephen faltered. 'Maybe we all need to find new ways of living with ourselves.'

'Obviously, given the conspiracy of lies the official records are going to be.'

'But Agnes will be on this memorial?'

'Of course. But you realise the date for the ceremony? It's 25th August. The liberation of Paris by the great de Gaulle who'd have us all believe he did it alone. And to think he made the Resistance get behind him as he pranced along the Champs-Élysées in his damned victory parade.'

'Bugger de Gaulle, Paquet, the lot of them,' said Stephen. 'But Agnes matters. Her parents matter.' And Alice's words came back to him as he said, 'They need to think their sacrifice was worthwhile. And you, Leclerc, your sacrifice.'

'My sacrifice? I'm off to be paid a fortune by the Yanks!'

'You know what I mean. The sacrifice of who we used to be.'

Leclerc just lit another cigarette. I've said too much, Stephen realised as Leclerc got up, shaking the sand off his suit, muttering, 'We must get back, if I'm to catch that train.'

They returned to the car, again driving in silence, and at the station Leclerc said, 'Don't wait. Go on home.'

'I want to say goodbye,' said Stephen. 'And thank you. For coming. For understanding.' Not that it let him off the hook. 'It helps,' he said, and again he grasped Leclerc's hand.

Leclerc sighed. 'I'm glad my coming wasn't a mistake. You'll give my apologies to your wife for not staying.'

'Of course.'

'I'm glad you have a wife – a wife who was still there for you.'

Alice would be at the house, but whether she still wanted him there, he'd no idea.

'Goodbye, my friend,' said Leclerc, as the train appeared round the bend. '*Adieu.*'

Not *au revoir*, thought Stephen.

Then Leclerc was gone and Stephen felt desperately alone. He'd been alone before but he'd embraced the pain as his punishment. Now, he thought, I miss my friend. And I grieve for him. And my wife.

And he was afraid.

He was afraid for Alice and what sort of compromise their marriage was going to be. He was afraid he could no longer make her happy and she would spend the rest of her life pretending he did. He was afraid of failing to be worthy of having survived. And, most of all, he was afraid he would sink even deeper into the lassitude that can come after staring death in the face.

Then it occurred to him there was a job he ought to do. Something important, that he should have thought of sooner. But he would do it today. He returned to his car, started the engine and, slowly, he moved forwards.

 49

ALL THOSE YEARS BEHIND barbed wire Dr Downes had yearned for such an English summer's evening. As he drove home at the end of his rounds, the sight of a man mowing his lawn, a woman staking a magnificent magenta hollyhock, children playing hopscotch, even the ducks waddling along the pavement seemed to be saying this is the peace and beauty you went to war to protect. He heard laughter from the Queen's Head and was tempted to stop for a pint but no, he wanted to see his family.

'Hello!' he called cheerily, letting himself into the house, the hall lovely and cool. 'I'm back!'

But no one answered and he went into the kitchen, where his wife was sitting in front of a basket of unshelled peas, her chin resting on her hand.

'Oh, hello,' she said, 'I didn't hear you come in. How are you?'

'Glad to be home,' he said, planting a kiss on the top of her head. 'What's for dinner?'

'I queued up for some fish.'

He glanced in the pantry at an unidentifiable dead thing lying on an enamel platter and was about to say, this is how they got the expression 'green about the gills', then thought better of it and began to head upstairs to change out of his suit. But Jane had begun attacking the peas with such unspoken frustration he asked, 'What's wrong?'

'Nothing.'

'Come on, Jane. Something's up.'

'I don't know . . . it's Christopher.'

He sighed. 'What's he done now?'

'Nothing!'

'It can't be nothing. Or you wouldn't be in a state. What's he said?'

'*Nothing!* That's the point.'

'He's just turned sixteen! He's hardly going to bound in and kiss his mother telling you what he's been doing all day. I'll have a word with him.'

'No! Don't.'

'Because you think I'll make it worse?' The expression on her face told him that's exactly what she thought. 'All right,' he snapped. 'Have it your way.'

He stomped upstairs, collapsed onto the bed and removed his leg. In the sweltering heat it had been monstrously cumbersome and his skin now was chafed raw. He pulled on some shorts then shoved his leg under the bed. Thumping about with a crutch would be more comfortable than strapping that contraption back on.

From the bedroom window he could see Juliet playing with Rusty in the garden. She glanced up and waved, pleased to see him. He'd get himself a cold drink, then sit outside and chat with her.

He hobbled onto the landing and passed Christopher's bedroom. But a sudden impulse made him turn back. He was perfectly able to talk to his own son without starting another world war.

And he opened Christopher's door.

'Get out!' yelled Christopher, spinning round, grabbing his shirt off the bed and covering himself. 'Get out!'

During his working life Downes had seen all manner of injuries. But nothing had prepared him for what he now witnessed. Because these wounds were on his own son.

'Christopher! Oh my dear, dear . . .' And instinctively he held out his arms, forgetting he was leaning on the crutch, which clattered to the floor.

'Get out!' cried Christopher, backing into the corner. 'Get out!'

Downes didn't move. 'Jane!' he called weakly. But Christopher's shouting had already brought her running up the stairs.

'What is it?'

'Christopher,' he said, in the sympathetic tone he used with terrified patients. 'Turn round, show your mother.'

Christopher sank down into the chair at his desk and slowly, as if recognising he had no option, lent forwards. On his thin, exposed shoulder blades, protruding like cherubs' wings, were cigarette burns. One was, at most, hours old, others had blistered, some were scarring over.

Jane gave an anguished cry then flung her arms around him.

'Leave me alone!' cried Christopher, pushing her off.

'Who did this?' Jane was saying. 'Darling, please! Was it boys at school?'

'If it was,' roared Downes, 'I'll thrash the living daylights out of them!'

'Dad! What deluded world do you live in?'

'I can . . .'

'What, Dad? Show me how to beat the shit out of them?'
Yes, thought Downes. 'You don't understand, do you? I'm
not like you, always fighting. I'm a pacifist.'

'You mean you *let* these monsters do this to you?'

'Are you mad? Of course I don't "let them". But I can't
run as fast as them. They catch me.' Downes reached for
the wall for support because he could see so clearly: his
sweet, bookish son running, running till the bullies caught
him. 'I'm not going to fight back,' continued Christopher.
'And when there's the next war – as there will be –
I'll be a conscientious objector and they can put me
in prison.'

'They won't do that,' said Jane savagely.

'Because you'll stop them, will you, Mum?'

'How long,' said Downes, 'has this been going on?'

Christopher said nothing. But it was clear from the number
of scars it had been going on for months.

'Darling, please,' ventured Jane. 'Who does this?'
Christopher just looked away. 'Is it Jack Ledbury and Tom
Mayhew?' Still he said nothing. 'It is them, isn't it?' And
Downes saw his son fighting back tears.

Downes had never heard of these boys. But he would find
them and show them what brutality really was.

'Why didn't you tell us?' Jane was asking now.

'Because Dad would only march into school shouting and
making everything worse.' Christopher glared at his father.
'Why did you tell them at school that when you were a POW
you learned Greek?'

'What?'

'In class one day Mr Clarke said you'd told him the Red
Cross dropped in Greek textbooks and you'd read Herodotus.'

349

'I saw him in town ages ago – it was just a bit of conversation.' Then Downes saw the horror on Jane's face.

'Is this,' she asked, 'to do with Dad?'

Christopher just dropped his head.

'Will someone tell me what's going on?' cried Downes, aware he was yelling now, just as Christopher predicted.

'Both those boys,' said Jane, 'lost their fathers in the war. And they've this impression – utterly wrong, I know, and Christopher knows this too – that POWs like you, in the German camps, had it easy.'

Downes was speechless. Not once had he talked about how he was incarcerated in one stalag after another, packed into stinking cattle trucks and moved all over Germany; how in January 1945 he was marched through blizzards to his final camp, Stalag 357 at Fallingbostel – a hellhole, disease-ridden, overcrowded. He'd deliberately told them nothing. Not simply because he wanted to forget. But because it couldn't possibly be right to inflict upon them the fear, degradation, filth, violence, hunger . . . He could go on. And on. But he didn't.

This evening, when the children complained about the fish – as they no doubt would – he would stop himself saying: 'I've seen men eat rats. And, by the way, once I ate a dog. Don't worry, Rusty! Dogs taste vile.'

What he'd determined to do was not look back, but ahead. Except when he woke at night, hearing men's screams as he fixed broken limbs with no anaesthetic. Except however hard he scrubbed his skin he could still remember his body crawling with lice. Except he could never use the lavatory without thinking what a luxury it was to have toilet paper. Of course they shouldn't know any of this! But the Greek had given him an escape, stopped him losing his mind. Like the young Classics scholar whose leg he'd saved only to give the boy the means to run for the barbed wire. Another boy who could not run fast enough.

'Oh, Christopher!' he murmured. 'I'm so, so sorry.'

What had got him through his long imprisonment was the dream that once the war was over everything would be all right. But it wasn't. And his own son was the proof. The insanity he thought he could leave behind was right here in his own home. And all he had to show for those lost years was his shaking, useless body and his rage – rage that only cut him off even more from the family he loved.

As his fury seized him once more he felt his nervous system so out of control he was about to slip lurching to the floor but Christopher leapt up and took him by the arm.

'Dad! These guys are jerks. If it hadn't been the Greek, they'd have found some other reason to get at me because I'm a million times cleverer than them and they're going to spend their lives in this God-forsaken place. Please, Dad! Oh, God! Don't cry!'

Downes realised tears were falling down his cheeks and this collapse was appalling. He should be consoling his son, not the other way round. But Christopher was the one standing upright, speaking with an assurance Downes hadn't heard from him before. 'School's just an endurance test – that's how I see it. And I'll survive. Just like you did. I'm strong. Like you.'

Suddenly the door opened and Eleanor stood there.

'What's going on? Didn't you hear the doorbell? It's Sir Stephen wanting to see you, Dad.'

'I can't see him now,' he said, wiping his eyes.

351

'You can,' said Jane gently.

'But I need to . . .' He gestured to Christopher's back.

'I'll look after him,' said Jane.

'Dad,' Christopher was saying, 'go and see what Sir Stephen wants. I'll be all right. Really. I'm stronger than those shits at school.'

'But this is going to stop,' said Downes. 'I give you my word, I'm not letting them do this to you again. I'm not.'

For the first time since he'd returned home he was aware of his son looking at him with compassion. Love even. Then, Christopher handed him his crutch and, with none of his usual sarcasm, said, 'Yes, Dad, of course you won't. But you've got to let me deal with this on my own.'

 50

DOWNES STAGGERED DOWNSTAIRS, SHOOK Stephen's
hand and leading him into his consulting room said the
words with which he always greeted his patients: 'How can
I help?' But he could think of nothing but how he might
help his son.

Stephen was speaking briskly: 'I'll be brief. It's the vicar.
I know you can't discuss another patient, but he's told me
about his heart. And I thought the war might have thrown
up some new medical techniques. Because if there is something and it's a question of money, I'd like to help.'

Downes tried to focus. 'Have you mentioned this to
Mr Ivens?' he asked.

'I thought it would be wrong to give him false expectations – if nothing can be done. That's why I came to
you first.'

Downes heard footsteps in the room above him. Jane was
putting aloe vera on Christopher's burns.

'Dr Downes? Are you sure you don't want me to come
back another time?'

'No, no . . .'

Helping Ivens was something he was trained for. He could
at least look after his patients, even if he'd failed to protect
his son from the bullies of the world.

'I've looked into Mr Ivens's case,' he said. 'But you realise you could be talking a lot of money?'

'I've got money – well, not right away. But I could sell some land.'

Never could Downes have imagined this conversation. He'd hailed the decline of the Oakbourne estate as a morality tale about the come-uppance of the privileged rich. But, again, he felt ashamed of his prejudices.

'The research,' he muttered, 'is still in such early stages. And it's pretty much all in America. He'd have to go there.'

'Is it worth mentioning to him?'

'Yes, but don't get his hopes up.'

'So what's the best strategy?' continued Stephen. 'You speak to him first? Then, if he's interested in pursuing this, we take it from there?'

Downes had the sensation he was back in the presence of a commanding officer giving orders – lightly concealed, yet orders nonetheless.

'Yes,' he said.

Then Stephen leant over the desk and shook his hand. 'Thank you! This matters a great deal to me. But I won't take up anymore of your time. Though just one thing, the other night you mentioned your son likes Classics. And I wondered whether he'd enjoy this.' He reached into his pocket and handed Downes a small leather-bound book – Σφῆκες by Aristophanes.

'Thank you,' Downes murmured. 'I'd get him to thank you himself but he's—' Busy, he thought, having his cigarette burns treated. Downes bit his lip and clenched the book hard, fixing his eyes on a hole in the carpet, unable to complete the sentence.

Stephen was saying, 'I loved it. You might enjoy it too. I've an English translation – *The Wasps*. At least I think so. We've sold so many books.' He headed for the door, and Downes limped round to open it. Then Stephen smiled, as though he'd just remembered something. 'But you won't need a translation! Ivens told me about you learning Ancient Greek in the camps. What an extraordinary achievement!'

The book slipped from Downes's grasp. Suddenly his one good leg felt like water and he thought he might topple over as he yelled, 'Sodding Greek, again! Why does everyone keep going on about it? That camp was sheer bloody hell, five years of just rotting away – my life, my mind, my skill – not some idle . . .'

'Dr Downes!' Stephen had grabbed his arm to stop him falling. 'I'm so sorry if you thought that's what I was implying. I know how terrible those camps could be,' he said, helping the doctor back to his chair. 'I once met a chap who'd escaped . . .'

Downes's voice rose once more. 'Oh, yes? Those men who escaped – people see them as heroes but I hate them for not thinking about the repercussions . . . how the guards took it out on us weaker ones without the strength or nous to escape. I know, compared with the Japanese camps, it was easy, but sometimes . . .'

'Is this what people are saying? That you had it easy?'

'Not to me, no, at least not to my face.'

'To whom then?'

'My son. Some thugs at school are . . . are . . .' Downes couldn't bring himself to spell out the full horror. 'They're hurting him. Because of me. I could kill them, but he won't fight back because he says he's not going to be like me – fighting all the time.' Downes's face twisted in self-mockery. 'The irony is, I didn't kill anyone the entire war. At least not deliberately.'

'You were captured at Dunkirk, weren't you?' Downes nodded. 'I was there too. With the BEF. And I left behind wounded men – in a hotel kitchen turned into a makeshift hospital.'

'My operating theatre was a casino,' said Downes, expecting Stephen to make some comment on how apt to be in a casino, given what a bloody gamble it all was. Instead, Stephen was watching him in the way he observed a new patient when trying to make a diagnosis.

Stephen spoke quietly: 'I heard some medics turned down the chance of getting home and volunteered to stay. Even though that meant being taken prisoner – at best.'

Downes shifted uncomfortably. From the garden, he could hear Juliet calling for Rusty, his wife and Christopher moving around upstairs. Yet they felt worlds away.

He cracked his knuckles. In that casino, he'd had to work with bare hands, unwashed hands once the water ran out, using instruments stained with blood from the previous casualty, tying arteries, sewing up bowels, hour after hour, not stopping, taking Benzedrine to keep himself going, tending to grotesque bundles of wool and splints and bandages that had once been lively young men, putting limbs in a bucket, chucking used syringes and empty anaesthetic ampoules in the corner, barely able to think with exhaustion and the deafening racket of the German bombardment.

Downes took a deep breath. The window was open, framed by a tangle of pale pink roses, and that morning he'd been struck by the loveliness of their perfume in the pure air. All he could smell now was burnt flesh and urine and wet woollen blankets drenched with dead men's blood, and he was aware of a sheen forming over his eyes. To divert Stephen's attention from the tears in danger of falling he reached for his pen and began doodling but the wretched pen wouldn't work and he found himself blurting out: 'I used to have a beautiful fountain pen. My mother bought it for me when I got into medical school and I kept it with me always.' He patted his top pocket. 'Even at Dunkirk. But when I was captured, some stinking German shit nicked it.'

'Dr Downes?' Stephen's eyes, bloodshot but steady, held his. 'Were you one of those doctors who made that sacrifice? Did you deliberately choose to remain behind?'

For a while, Downes sat in silence. He accepted the cigarette Stephen offered him. Then he just said, 'I had to stay.'

He exhaled slowly and watched the smoke take shape in the evening sun pouring through the window. A domestic scene bathed in beautiful light. An English Vermeer before his very eyes, but, in his mind, all he could see was Guernica.

It had been early dawn and he'd just turned his attention to a young private, drifting in and out of consciousness. Downes was cutting off the boy's jacket when the commanding officer arrived: the Germans were just two hours away so they had to get out as fast as possible. But one doctor and ten orderlies per hundred wounded needed to remain. 'I'm asking for volunteers,' the commanding officer had said.

Downes heard the order, but didn't stop working. Peeling away the boy's shirt he saw his right shoulder was almost blown off, his arm only held on by a few shreds of skin and muscle. He was assessing what, if anything, could be done when the boy's unlined face broke open with silent tears.

At the time, the choice was black and white in its starkness. Either inject the boy with morphine and head for the beaches in the hope of making it home. Or stay behind and attempt to stop this boy dying.

'I had to stay,' Downes repeated. 'I was an experienced surgeon. If I volunteered at least a few more stood a chance.'

He looked across at Stephen and caught a hint of – what? Admiration? Pity? Whatever it was, he didn't want it.

With sudden vehemence, he said, 'Or maybe I didn't want to be thought a coward. By others. By myself. I don't know anymore. Only it seemed the right call. *At the time.*'

He began tapping his pen up and down on the desk. Jane would never forgive him if she found out the truth. 'No heroics,' she'd begged when he'd left for France.

'In the camps, I never questioned whether I'd made the right call. But now – now I'm home . . .

'I had my doubts the moment I got to England. Did you know that when POWs got back, compensation forms were shoved at us?' Stephen shook his head. 'I didn't know what to put in for. Five years of my life? My leg? Anyway, on this form – I can see it now, number WO1784 – I put in for my fountain pen. And the bloody civil servant asked me for the receipt! As if the Nazis would have given me one!'

Downes pulled at the hair at his temples. 'Something snapped in me and I swung my crutch at him. If I hadn't been so weak, I'd probably have killed him.'

Stephen's expression didn't change.

'Anyway, they arrested me. Stuck me in a cell. But there was so much going on and, to give this chap his due, he dropped the charges, and they let me go.'

358

He looked down at the cigarette he was trying to hold still. It was almost burnt-out and he stubbed it down into the ashtray, over and over, forcing it to fall apart.

'The family don't know about that either,' he said. 'Though losing my temper is what they'd expect. But you know what I really want to be compensated for? My patience. Believe it or not, I used to be known for it. The best doctors are. You have to be the calm in the storm. And I was. All the time in the camp I kept my cool, was the one who'd talk down the lads when it all got too much – the lethargy, the humiliation of doing nothing, of surrendering. The way people at home saw us. One chap had a letter asking what German beer was like. Another's girlfriend told him not to get fresh with the local girls. Jesus! These were young men but so hungry and exhausted if Rita Hayworth had walked in they wouldn't have got off their bunks.'

He hurled the pen in the bin. 'Ironic, isn't it? I was more of a father to some of those boys than to my own son.'

Suddenly Downes shut up. He ached desperately to justify his actions but was ashamed hearing himself bleat on and on, losing all dignity.

Then Stephen said, 'We're a country full of secrets now. And we all just want to forget.'

'No! We can't be so defeatist. What kept me going was thinking if I ever got out I'd do so much. My son complains all I do is fight. But I need to be active, to stop poverty and sickness and injustice . . .'

He was conscious of Stephen's glance at his hands, shaking so hard now he had to hold them tight.

'You are fighting,' said Stephen. 'Right now we both are – for Ivens. But your son? What about him?'

'He wants to deal with the bullies himself.'
'Will he tell you if he can't?'
'That's what worries me. That he'll keep it all to himself.'
Stephen only smiled: 'A chip off the old block.'

 51

NO SOONER HAD STEPHEN left than Jane stormed into Downes's consulting room.

'What were you shouting at Sir Stephen for?'

He was taken aback by her fury.

'I shouldn't have, but—'

'But what? The man who saved your daughter's life offended your precious sensibilities? Christopher's right! Shouting's your answer to everything. You never bother to consider the effect you have on *us*. And because your son couldn't trust you not to go into the school screaming your head off he had no one to help him fight off those bullies, those . . . those . . .'

Never in twenty years of marriage had she lost her temper. But now she was crying, struggling not to make any noise, her body heaving, and he hauled himself round the desk to put his arm round her.

'Jane, my—'

'Get off me!' The disgust on her face said it all. She hated him. 'I used to think you were the kindest, gentlest man I'd ever known. But now! I'm sick of endlessly worrying what's going to throw you into one of your rages.'

Tears were streaming down her face and the only true response seemed more tears. Hers were more wounds he couldn't heal. Fully conscious of the inadequacy of the gesture, he handed her his handkerchief.

For a moment he thought she was going to reject even that but she muttered, 'Thanks.'

He watched her wipe her eyes, then fold the handkerchief, over and over, and once she couldn't fold it any smaller she looked up at him, her eyes colder than he'd ever known them.

'Please, Jane! Don't leave me. I can't lose you all over again. I can't.'

'I'm not going to leave you.'

But you would, he thought, if it wasn't for the children.

He tried to explain: 'Sir Stephen didn't mind me being angry. Really! He understood.'

'Understood what? Why you're entitled to shout all the time?'

'No. But . . .'

'But what? Did you talk about the war? Two veterans together? Because if you did, you need to tell me what he "understood" if we're going to have the remotest chance of finding anything we once had together.'

'At Dunkirk . . .' His voice trailed into nothing. 'I'm frightened you'll hate me . . . even more.'

'Talk to me, Jonathan, or I swear—'

He blurted it out: 'He asked whether I volunteered to stay.'

'*Volunteered?*'

'Yes.' He took a breath. 'And I did. I chose to stay. With my men. My patients. They needed me.'

And to his horror, he found himself growing angry again. This was why Pandora's Box was best kept shut. Too much pain was unleashed and if he lost control again the effect on his marriage would be catastrophic. He gripped the arms of his chair because he would not – *he would not* – shout that she couldn't possibly understand. He gritted his teeth and waited.

But, instead of rousing herself into a rage, his wife stared abstractedly at the floor, her expression unintelligible, the room very still, a world of hidden thoughts between them. Then the clock on the mantelpiece chiming seven brought her back.

'You're not,' she said, 'the only one with confessions to make. I'm going to tell you something, but if you ever mention it again, use it in an argument against me, if you tell the children, I swear I will leave you.'

'Oh, Jane!'

'Just listen.' She dropped her hands into her lap and began stroking them over and over. At night he'd often wake in the early hours and see her standing at the window, performing this same gesture. But he'd never dared ask what was troubling her. 'That summer of 1940 – when we'd no idea if you were even alive. Everyone – from the government to my mother – was telling me to get out of London before the Blitz began.

'These days, you're always going on at me to stop worrying, but that autumn, I didn't worry enough. Even after the bombing began I carried on persuading myself we'd be all right in London.

'You never asked *why* I didn't just jump on a train, get us all to Oakbourne, to safety. Well, you know how when you left I got a job at the hospital?' He nodded. A friend of hers who was a matron had begged her to help out with new nursing recruits. 'I got the job,' she continued, 'because they didn't want someone who just knew about medicine. They wanted a good role model, someone who knew how to make frightened, sick people feel safe.'

'You were always the nurse patients asked for—'

'But what about my children's safety?' she interrupted. 'I had total disregard for that.'

'No!'

'Look at the facts, Jonathan.' Her voice had changed. She spoke with icy calm: 'They were almost killed. Because of my decision. It's a "miracle" we survived, the air wardens told me. But at what cost? If I'd kept Eleanor safe she might not be desperate to control every damned thing. And Christopher might . . .' She paused and Downes almost wished she would begin sobbing again, anything rather than this slow, calculated self-torture.

'We were at war!' he cried. 'Facing terrible choices. And the good you did staying, the lives you saved!'

'Such noble altruism may have been true for you.' She actually looked at him with kindness. 'I always knew you wouldn't be able to turn your back on someone you could help. But I stayed for *me*. Can't you see the difference? I loved the work. I stayed out of vanity! Selfishness! For my own fulfilment! I put my needs before my children's and as a result—'

'Jane, stop! Don't destroy yourself like this.'

She was talking over him: 'The truth is – and again, if you tell the children this I will never forgive you – I find being a nurse so much easier than being a mother. I love my children. Of course I do! But sometimes the drudgery . . . Oh, it's more than that. It's the constant fear of failing them, whereas in the hospital – in the company of some really clever people and having their respect – I was confident I was doing a really good job.'

Her face was disfigured with something approaching despair and he was at a loss. She might no longer be blaming him, but this agony of self-recrimination was appalling.

Years ago, before they'd had children, when one of them was dealing with a hopeless medical case, they could help each other, find a way of bringing perspective. But now? She looked uncharacteristically fragile, a fine mesh of lines around her lips and eyes. He'd not noticed them before. I've not, he realised shamefully, looked.

Her eyes angled towards him, as if she was turning to him for help, and speaking warily, terrified of having misread the signals, he said, 'I imagine you also loved working at the hospital because – unlike home – people did as you told them?'

To his relief, he saw a slight smile surface. He continued. 'When I'm doing my rounds here, people tell me how wonderful you were during the war, helping out when Dr Hughes couldn't. Actually I often think they'd still rather see you than me.'

She shrugged, but she looked a little more like her usual self as she said, 'You'd have hated Hughes. I connived in the idea he was too unwell to do his job, but the truth was he was always well enough to see the "old families". So I—'

'So you covered for him! I love you, Jane!'

He might not have spoken. She just began unfolding and refolding the handkerchief again.

'So that's my secret,' she said, 'the truth of why I stayed. So as you can see I do understand why you volunteered.'

'Oh, Jane! I'd have stayed in London too. I know I would. Why didn't you tell me? I might have stopped you torturing yourself—'

'What?' She'd turned on him again. 'You tell me nothing either. All I know about the camps is from those letters you sent – five scraps of nonsense about cricket and chess. How dreadful the reality was I can only guess but it turned you into a . . .' A brute, thought Downes, as again she left her sentence unfinished.

'I know I've been a brute,' he said, then, as carefully as possible, he continued: 'But . . . you've changed too.'

She didn't disagree. She just sat looking unbearably sad and he wished in vain he might give her back the years they'd lost. 'Why,' she asked, 'won't you tell me the truth of those five years?'

'I can't. I simply can't.'

'But some doctors now . . .'

'Think it's best to have everything out in the open,' he interrupted, feeling cornered by her appeal to medical science. 'But not me.' And he was seized by a fear she was going to press him, make it a condition of staying. 'I can't bear you to know. Or worse, the children. Please,' he begged, 'don't ask me again. I love you, Jane, that's all you need to know.'

She turned her wedding ring round her finger, then eventually she just sighed, 'As you wish.' She picked up Σφῆκες. 'At least you kept that brilliant brain of yours engaged.'

'Greek wasn't just about using my mind. I'd read about their endless wars: you stole my wife so I've the right to steal yours; you killed my son so I'll kill yours . . . The vengeance that's never ending. The Greek gave me a glimpse of a world where men had also killed and died in war after war. But the miracle is, amongst all that barbarity and pain – no different in essence from ours – they built the most extraordinary civilisation! Such beauty!'

And he was aware she'd taken his hand. 'In that hell, what those Greeks gave me was the most precious gift of all. They gave me hope.'

52

ALICE WATCHED NERVOUSLY FROM the library window of Oakbourne Hall, torrential rain pounding against the diamond panes, the outlines of the garden and long gravel drive indistinguishable in shades of darkening grey.

'You wouldn't think it was Midsummer's Day,' said Stephen, fanning the fire to a roaring blaze. 'I almost wish it was winter, then we could close the curtains and not watch this rain all evening.'

'Yes,' she replied, but she was lying.

She found the rain oddly comforting, soaking into the soil as if it was also seeping into her mind because the solid ground on which she had once stood was gone, her old principle of truthfulness redundant in the complexities of her life now.

She glanced at Stephen, conscious of the worry in his downcast frown. The kind thing to do would be to put her arms around him, if not with love, at least with reassurance. But instead she turned back to the rain as if, in all those dissolving forms, she might find new answers. And fast. Because this evening Stephen had invited the man who had been her lover for 'farewell drinks'.

At any minute, George Ivens, along with the Downes family, would arrive at Oakbourne Hall. After tonight she would never see him again because tomorrow he was leaving for London, then Liverpool, from where he'd set off for America. Stephen and Dr Downes had arranged it all: the liner to New York, his lodgings, appointments with heart specialists.

She'd not been alone with him since they'd exchanged those hurried words in the church porch. And now, thanks to her husband's generosity, he'd be crossing the Atlantic. Going three thousand miles away . . .

'I thought I'd open the last of that brandy,' said Stephen, as if looking to her for approval. 'It's a special occasion.'

'Lovely,' she murmured.

What she would say once they came face to face, she'd no idea. Or how she would wish him goodbye. The note he'd left at Mrs Turner's had said it all: *I cannot see you – I know you'll understand.*

And she did understand. But she could find no comfort. Because he was so ill. And he would die.

'You've gone very white,' said Stephen. 'Everything all right?'

'Of course!' she smiled, as the doctor's car, headlamps flickering in the wet gloom, appeared down the drive.

'You stay in the dry,' said Stephen, 'I'll let them in.'

Stony-faced, she watched her husband rushing out and holding an umbrella protectively over the man she'd lain naked with. And in seconds she heard footsteps, laughter, and he was walking into the room with the Downes family, and she was taking coats, effusively thanking everyone for coming out on this filthy night, asking Eleanor about her exams, telling Juliet a stray cat had taken up residence in the kitchen to have her kittens.

Then George was standing before her and she was saying something inane about how she hoped he'd finished packing and he was smiling as if she was just one of his many flock.

And it was done.

They'd met, they'd spoken. Stephen was pouring brandies and telling Christopher he'd found a few books he might like and to help himself. She was saying to Juliet and Eleanor they were welcome to explore the house but to be careful on the back stairs as the treads were loose. Then, chatting with Dr Downes and his wife, she got on to growing tomatoes – a subject on which she could bore for Britain and was certain she was.

George, under Stephen's instructions, stood warming himself by the fire, listening to Stephen and Christopher talk about some French novel. He appeared unusually well, his complexion less ashen than usual, as though he'd caught the sun, and the bronze glow suited him. He'd had his hair cut and she found herself thinking she preferred all those dark, springing curls and how she'd twisted them round her finger and, as she watched him from the corner of her eye, the atmosphere in the six yards between them seemed so charged with unexpressed emotions she felt something might shatter.

'Alice!' Stephen handed her a heavy, cut-glass balloon of brandy.

'How lovely,' she said, the smell alone making her stomach churn. She'd been sick again that morning.

'Delicious,' said Jane Downes. 'I can't remember the last time I had brandy.'

Alice knew exactly when she'd drunk brandy – when she'd spent the night with George.

But she found herself saying, 'Nor me.'

370

Another lie.

Conversation drifted. The doctor and his wife joined in the discussion between Stephen and their son. Earlier, Alice had noticed Mrs Downes discreetly offer her arm to her husband; saw them exchange a flicker of pride as Christopher told Stephen about how he was reading *The Three Musketeers* in French. They give no semblance of having been separated for five years, thought Alice. But who really knew?

George was standing looking out at the rain, his face in profile. It was impossible to know what he too might be hiding.

She put more logs on the fire, gave Christopher another drink.

The evening wore on. They'd be gone soon. It would end. But then George walked up to her, standing close so no one else could see the plea on his face, his feelings perfectly clear: he wanted to speak to her, alone.

But in a voice clear enough for everyone to hear, he said: 'Sir Stephen once mentioned a hiding place in the house for Catholic priests on the run and I wondered whether I might see it, please? I'm curious and I might not ever get another chance.'

'Of course!' Smiling over at Stephen she said, 'I'm taking Mr Ivens to the scullery to see the fake fireplace.' And before anyone could say they wanted to join them, they hurried from the room.

Out in the hallway, George spoke hastily: 'Alice! I wanted a moment alone with you. I . . . Oh, we can't talk here. Take me to wherever we're supposed to be looking at this awful thing.'

She almost ran across the hall and down to the scullery, dank and damp-smelling, with empty shelves, paint peeling from the ceiling and a tap dripping into a stained, cracked sink.

This was her chance to confess everything she was concealing.

'Please,' he said urgently, walking round a rickety table and placing himself on the opposite side, the message obvious: he was here to talk. Nothing more. 'Tell me how you are.'

His eyes did not leave hers. She had to decide. And quickly. Because she was no longer in any doubt she was carrying his child. All month, as the suspicion that she was pregnant became an undeniable fact she'd agonised over whether she should be honest, give him all the hope of new life and say, 'You're going to be a father.'

He would be overjoyed. But what then? Once practicalities kicked in? To speak the truth would present him with a terrible dilemma. And that would be cruel, tantamount to asking him to stay and turn his back on the chance for a cure.

And that meant he would certainly die.

'Alice, talk to me.'

She said, 'Do you regret . . . ? Us? That night? Do you think I led you on and now I've let you down?'

'No! Oh, Alice. I've thought so much about what might have been, under different circumstances. But it's not possible. You have a new life now. We all do. You, me, your husband.'

Your husband. He was emphasising the words: this is your place still, your role.

'But,' he continued, more gently, 'I know how unhappy you've been. For a long time.'

'I'm all right,' she said, looking away.

'You always try to give the impression nothing's wrong. And then you change the subject.' He pointed up at a colossal cobweb. 'Any minute now you'll start explaining the life cycle of the spider.' She attempted to smile. 'And then you'll ask how *I* am.'

'But I want to know!' she said, because what had also kept her awake was picturing him in a foreign country, with no friends, no one to love and hold him as he lay sick and afraid in a lonely bed. 'All I really know,' she said, 'is that you're going to New York. And that's so far. But if you don't go . . .'

He finished her sentence: 'If I don't go, I definitely won't have much longer.'

'But you look so well,' she said, a crazy idea crossing her mind that this man she'd made love to wasn't as ill as everyone said.

'I'm very ill,' he said, as if reading her thoughts, and every instinct in her made her want to walk round the table to take him in her arms. But he took a step back.

'Are you scared?' she asked. Because she was terrified. For him.

'Of being an invalid – yes. Of dying slowly. And I'm desperately worried that's what you'll do too, in your way, just endure in some eternal winter, stoically making the best of things, letting the days . . . decades drift by in a living death, going through the motions as you shut yourself down, more and more.'

He took a deep breath and she had the sense he'd spent long hours preparing what he was about to say: 'You've got a second chance now. As I have. As Sir Stephen has. What happened in France – I'm not saying he's come to terms with it, or he ever will. But he's begun to *care*. All that indifference to himself, to the world, he's trying to put it behind him. The effort and money he's spent on helping me – that's a man who's hoping to give his life some meaning again.'

For a split second he hesitated as if accepting aid from her husband, of all men, stung him to the quick.

'I'm unbelievably grateful to you both,' he hurried on. 'And he seems to have taken Christopher under his wing too. If saving people is his way of coping then that's a pretty good way. The doctor's the same, throwing himself into trying to rescue the whole world, God help him. He and your husband seem to be striking up a friendship – an unlikely alliance if ever there was. But they might, in fact, get on very well together. Each with their causes. Each with their secrets they're trying to forget.

'And you, Alice, are my secret.' He stepped forwards, and for a moment she thought he was going to take her in his arms. But he said: '*Your husband* – you loved him once. And I can't imagine you loving him with anything less than body and soul.' Then he raised his arms, as if in a desperate plea. 'Don't you see? If anyone's capable of resurrection, it's you. God has made you so strong and if you don't believe me, look at your walled garden. It's going to be beautiful, isn't it?' He stopped suddenly. She could hear voices. 'Quickly,' he said, 'before the others come. It'll be beautiful, because *you* brought it back to life. And you can do the same for your husband.'

The scullery door opened and Jane Downes was smiling at them both. And then Stephen was there too, striding in with Dr Downes and Christopher.

374

Colour had risen to George's face but Alice, amazed at the calm in her voice, said, 'I was just explaining that in the sixteenth century the bricks on the fireplace would have been blackened to make it look authentic.'

'That's right,' said Stephen, 'and this is how the poor devil would hide.'

He crouched down in the fireplace to explain the mechanism for opening the priest hole. A smile froze on Alice's face. She had the impression the doctor's wife was observing her. Paranoia, she insisted. She can't have heard anything, and then Juliet came rushing in, begging to have one of the kittens. And with that Jane Downes was simply looking as if a cat was the last thing she wanted but was unable to refuse her daughter.

Then Alice overheard the doctor saying to Stephen that it must have been hard to return to find his home so damaged by war. And Stephen said he wished the Canadians had smashed up the damned priest hole because it was so dreadful to think of people needing to hide like this, half-suffocated and starved, praying they wouldn't be discovered, not just in Tudor England, but in every century, every country.

George was saying the miracle was that despite all the horror and fear over hundreds of years, this house had seen joy and hope as well, that people rose again and again. Then Jane Downes nudged her on the arm, indicating that George was addressing her.

'I was saying, Lady Rayne, how you once told me about the snowdrops here and how, year after year, regardless of how hard and frosty the ground, they manage to break through and live again. Don't they?'

'They do,' she murmured.

'And so beautifully,' he added, looking at her directly. But then he laughed, 'Enough preaching! If you don't know my thoughts on resurrection by now, I've failed. I must go!'

And next thing they were all heading back upstairs and collecting coats and Stephen was offering to find a box for the kitten, but Juliet just wanted to hold it. Then George was giving her a brief shake of the hand and she and Stephen were standing at the front door waving everyone goodbye.

And he was gone.

'What a wild night,' said Stephen. 'Come on in. You'll catch cold.'

But she waited a moment, letting the wet darkness enfold her, watching the retreating lights of the car, conscious that for the rest of her life she was going to have to lie. No one could ever know whose baby this was. It would be an act of appalling cruelty to inflict yet more pain upon the crushed man who was her husband. He would have to believe this baby was his.

She had the strength to live with that secret. But George was wrong in thinking her strength God-given. It was born of necessity. Of the times, of circumstances. And through her mind swept the terror she'd felt as a child because she'd not been allowed to have the light on at night. 'You have to learn to deal with the dark,' her father had insisted. And I did learn, she thought, in the end. But she had been so scared. And she placed her hand on her stomach as if to promise this child of hers that she would never turn off the light. Never! She would always keep it safe from fear.

But Stephen? With his intolerable memories?

Again and again, she'd relived his agony. Working in the garden, she'd find herself in France, firing a bullet into a child's head. In the middle of the night she'd awaken with a corpse in her arms, Agnes's blood on her hands. And, in the translucent darkness of the June night, she could not fight back the tears any longer. She doubled over, felled by pity, for George, heading alone into the darkness; for Agnes; for everyone ravaged by this awful war. But, most of all, she cried for the gentle soul she'd married.

There seemed no end to her crying. It was as beyond her control as the rain. But despite her sobbing she could hear the garden alive with running water, the rain beating and drumming, pounding into the hungry earth and, as one element embraced another, she knew exactly what drama was being enacted.

Leaves were unfurling, buds swelling, long stamens rising, flowers flagrantly tilting back their heads. Her garden was bearing fruit and from that drive for life there was no holding back. Through the blur of her tears, she saw clearly now. Her pain – there was no denying it and, she feared, no escape – could be creative, the fierce agony of birth. Not death.

She walked out into the garden. She stretched out her arms and lifted up her eyes to the rain. She let it wash over her tear-stained face. Then she crossed the threshold, back into the old house.

She knew exactly what she needed to do.

Stephen was warming his hands by the library fire. 'Alice! You're soaked! Shall I leave the fire? So you can get warm?'

She shook her head. 'You know how I love this wild weather.'

'I do. But are you sure you're all right?'

'I'm sure,' she said, and she began rounding up the glasses.

'Here, let me help you.' He took the tray from her and carried it down to the kitchen.

Without saying a word, she filled the kettle and put it on the range.

'How long is it,' he asked, 'since the boiler worked?'

'Not since the Canadians were here. They had a genius of a plumber. But it's had it now.'

'Like everything in this house. Oh, let me wash up,' he said, once the water had heated. 'You dry. Your hands look . . .'

'As if they've had it too?'

'No!'

'Stephen!' she said gently. 'I was just joking.'

Then, as if he was at a loss to know what else to say, he washed the glasses while she dried them, biding her time.

Only once he'd finished did he speak again: 'Alice, I'm frightened.' He paused, his hands hanging helplessly in the tepid water. 'I'm frightened if I don't keep busy I'll lose momentum and then I'll just stop. Forever. Helping George – that's as much about me as him. But he's gone, God help him. So I need something else to keep my mind off things. And there's so much to do – if I want. The doctor's asked me to help with some projects of his and there's this house and what we decide to do with it and how we make a living. But I'm so tired. And the truth is part of me just wants to sleep. And sleep. But I can't give in to it. And I know you've ideas. About the house. What we could do. But I've never listened. But now . . . Perhaps we might talk about it?'

The words died in his mouth and she looked at him, his eyes cast down. And seeing that helpless gesture she reached for his hands. Holding each in turn, very slowly, she dried them.

'Stephen, we'll be all right. I promise you.'

His face contorted: 'How can you possibly make such a promise?'

'On so sweet a night, how can you and I not be all right?'

She could see his hesitation, as if unsure of what she was actually saying. 'Only you,' he said, 'would love all this rain.'

'Believe me. It's a beautiful night!'

Then, clasping his hands in hers, she led him out of the kitchen, through the large hall, up the great staircase. She drew him towards her and, instead of turning to the back stairs that took him up to his attic room, he walked with her along the landing to her bedroom.

She lifted his bowed head, then kissed him. And, in a gesture she had once known so well, she put her arms around her husband's neck and pressed her body into his.

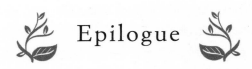

Epilogue

The Coronation: 2nd June, 1953

RED, WHITE AND BLUE banners flapped in the stiff breeze. Children dressed as kings and queens chased each other over the Oakbourne Hall terraces. An orb, decorated with silver and gold milk-bottle tops, now doubling as a football, landed at Jane Downes's feet and she kicked it back to the boys playing in the half-light.

It was the evening of the young queen's coronation and as soon as it was dark enough there would be fireworks on the lawn – the 'Grand Finale', proclaimed the printed programme. Jane, stepping back to let a little girl fly by in a crimson paper cape, didn't want the day to end.

She'd been gripped by the coronation, embarrassed at how fascinated she was by the significance of anointing a monarch with holy oil; ingredients for curried mayonnaise in Coronation Chicken; how Benjamin Britten hadn't completed his commission for a special anthem because he'd caught flu. When she'd made the mistake of telling her husband the coronation dress was embroidered with Tudor roses, shamrocks, thistles, leeks, protea, maple leaves ... he'd interrupted, 'They should get you to give the commentary, not Richard Dimbleby.' And he'd begun muttering about a carnival of costumes and mass hysteria.

That morning, with Jonathan and the children, she'd watched the entire ceremony up at the Big House. The Raynes had bought a television specially and invited those without one – most of the village – to come. By ten o'clock, a hundred or so were crammed into the library and for more than four hours she'd stood craning her neck, transfixed by the flickering black and white images.

She'd thought she knew exactly what to expect, but the final procession through London shocked her. As she'd watched the newly crowned queen leave Westminster Abbey in a golden coach, handsome prince by her side, she'd been overwhelmed. To see this culmination of centuries of ancient history and know what recent history had so narrowly escaped was too much.

Yet victory had cost them so dear. And the sight of such hope and joy on the faces of the thousands lining the London streets who'd endured and lost so much wrung her heart.

Eight years ago, they'd had their victory celebrations, their VE and VJ days. But the truth was, victory had, in the daily grind, felt as distant as the horizon. Years of austerity had followed as they'd just learned to accept endless queues and going without.

She'd hoped no one would notice her hurry from the room but Jonathan had followed her and, looking uncharacteristically moved himself, had said, 'It's all right, my love. It's all right.'

And that was the point. It *was* all right. It had taken the fairy tale of a princess being crowned for her to believe it: the dragged-out disaster of the war was over and the realisation that her children and their children might not have to experience what she had overwhelmed her with relief and gratitude.

She looked over the lawn towards the lake where she could see her husband chatting to Sir Stephen with his six-year-old son, James, on his shoulders. This community is my home, she thought. Our home. And that was because of the war.

If it hadn't been for the Blitz, she wouldn't be here now. Their old house in London was still nothing but a bombed pile of rubble – though she'd heard the entire street was going to be razed in preparation for building a block of flats.

This village was where even her husband belonged now.

Earlier in the day, when she'd huddled in the marquee out of the rain to watch the 'Entertainment by the Children', she'd pleaded inwardly: let all these untouched, eager children, singing with such blithe trust, know peace and prosperity for the rest of their lives.

Again, tears pricked her eyes because today she had a sense of the country coming together. Even, perhaps, the world. She thought of George Ivens in the Bronx in New York. Now he was chaplain and choir-master at a school for war orphans. It would be afternoon for him now, and he was putting on a Coronation Concert, beginning with four British folk songs – 'Westering Home', 'Danny Boy', 'Suo Gân' and Ivens himself performing 'Greensleeves'.

Ivens was still singing, still living. Years ago, she'd thought it would take a miracle for him to stand up on stage in 1953.

She had his latest letter in her bag to show Alice Rayne, who always asked after him.

And we're finishing the concert off, [he'd written], with 'Land of Hope and Glory'. Don't bridle, Jonathan. I know social changes haven't been fast enough for you. But when

I hear of all the good work you're doing at Oakbourne Hall I think that's where hope and glory lies – in the kindness of individuals like you.

'Evening,' interrupted a man marching past her as if he was still in the army. That this man had spoken at all though was a small miracle. He'd been amongst the troops liberating Belsen and, until recently, was locked in silence. Since Christmas, he'd been living at Oakbourne Hall and her husband had found a way to coax him to speak a little.

'Good evening, Jack,' she replied, but he'd gone, his eyes straight ahead, chin up.

Over the last few years, the Raynes had opened the house to more than twenty war veterans, some with quite obvious disabilities or sickness, others lost in a private agony of spirit.

It had begun with Leclerc, an old French friend of Stephen's – from the war, Jane assumed, though, like her husband and Stephen, he never talked about it. He'd been diagnosed with terminal cancer and, with no family of his own, Stephen and Alice had offered him a home.

Jane had helped nurse him. She'd warmed to his dry humour, and was grateful for the time he spent talking to her son, who now credited him, along with Stephen, for helping him get his place at Cambridge to read Modern Languages. While Leclerc was there, another 'friend' of Stephen's arrived from France. And word began to spread. Right now, eight men were staying up at the Big House, with another arriving at the end of the week – a former prisoner of the Japanese in a camp in Burma who'd not held down a job since.

'If some of those poor devils don't get help soon, the gutters and prisons will be overflowing,' Jonathan would say. He was right. But Jonathan benefited every bit as much as the men he helped. He could no longer practise as a GP – it was excruciating watching him hold a cup of tea as he tried not to let it spill over the sides – but he'd not needed steady hands to study psychiatry. With the traumatised souls in his care he was sensitive and skilful. More and more men were being referred to him.

She wished she might know what he actually did: how he encouraged them to talk, because he certainly wouldn't speak to her about anything more personal than 'What's for dinner?' During the last twelve months a few memoirs about the war had been published; time and distance enabled some to reveal what they'd once kept secret. But not her husband. When she'd mentioned buying a book by a man who'd escaped from Colditz he'd turned on her: that was the last bloody thing he'd ever read and went on, as usual, about forgetting the past and concentrating on the future.

So that's what he did.

He and Stephen spent ages discussing Oakbourne Hall: how they might expand their work, how to finance the staff and stop the dilapidated building from collapsing. 'A wing and a prayer should be our motto,' said Jonathan, forever complaining they didn't receive more state help, while Stephen argued he wasn't having civil servants tell him what to do and then got on with raising funds from wherever he could.

Now they were both walking slowly – for Jonathan's benefit – back to the house so they might best see the fireworks – a donation from the Lubbocks, thanks to profits from their ever-expanding beef farm. There was an energy about Stephen now – too frenetic at times, she thought privately. But, thank God, he was no longer laden with the despair that had felt downright dangerous when, all those years ago, she'd rushed to the house to stitch his cut wrist. (Slit wrist? she still wondered.)

But shortly afterwards, something in him had changed. Alice's pregnancy, she'd assumed, had given him heart. 'As thick as thieves' is how Stephen and his son were described in the village and Stephen had once said thank God times were changing because he wasn't going to send his son away to boarding school next year as had happened to him at just seven years old.

As Stephen came back to life, so had the Big House. Tonight, the doors and windows – albeit with rotten wood and peeling paint – stood wide open, lights shone, familiar faces milled about and the air was filled with the smell of sugar. After tea, the children had all been given candy floss and, standing under the newly planted oak, she breathed in its sweetness. She could hear leaves rustling, bursts of laughter, the first cry of the night from the tawny owl. Then a voice beside her saying: 'My goodness! How the heavens opened! So much for having the coronation in June for good weather!'

Jane turned to find Mrs Lubbock, resplendent as ever and smiling as though today the contrariness of an English summer was to be embraced rather than complained about.

The Lubbocks' son had asked Juliet to marry him. Jane and Jonathan kept protesting that at seventeen she was far too young. But, despite her objections, Jane could see Juliet blissfully content as a farmer's wife, apron on in a warm kitchen with rosy babies in her arms. Juliet was far more in tune with the times than Eleanor, who had just qualified as a doctor and, Jonathan worried, would have a lifetime fighting what he called the old boys' network of male chauvinistic idiots.

Jane agreed, but part of her envied Eleanor's battle. She'd think, I could have been a doctor too. But she had another mission now, a life-long task before her: nursing at Oakbourne Hall and persuading government bodies, charities, anyone who'd listen, about the importance of looking after men traumatised by the war.

She watched Alice Rayne join Stephen and Jonathan, and take Stephen's hand. As they ambled across the lawn Stephen and Jonathan kept stopping to chat with their neighbours. Alice said little. Stephen was the one known for his bonhomie. Alice could appear reserved as if, Jane sometimes thought, a confidence had been lost. Yet Alice had organised today's celebrations. She had been the driving force behind the planting of apple orchards at Oakbourne and in the last couple of years money had begun coming in from the cider they produced, so much so that next month they were installing a central heating system in the house.

'We can't expect these men to escape whatever hell they're in, if they're freezing,' Alice had once said to her. 'Only a saint can rise above being cold and hungry.'

Jane had become very fond of her. She'd too much experience of people blaring their compassion and Alice's quietness hid a tireless efficiency and common sense. Jane would see her up ladders painting ceilings, changing beds, cycling out in all weathers to inspect her apple trees. But her biggest achievement was the walled garden, whose sweet tomatoes, great, crunchy cucumbers and lettuces had filled the plates at today's celebratory tea. Roses and peonies, cut that morning, decorated the tables. But the miracle wasn't simply the garden's beauty and productivity.

A few years ago, Alice had ventured to Jonathan that the men in his care might find solace helping in the garden, that those whose bodies were perfectly robust but were struggling inside might calm their exhausted minds by working the land, feeling the earth in their hands. She'd spoken with such conviction that Jane had wondered whether she was talking about her own needs.

Jonathan had listened to her. And acted. Many of his patients tended to the fruits and flowers and vegetables, and some, not all – if only – truly did find comfort there.

But now Alice was striding across the lawn towards her, a broad grin on her face. 'I think we're going to be in for a treat,' she said. 'The Lubbocks have what looks like a ton of fireworks. James has never seen them before,' she went on, blowing a kiss to her son still on Stephen's shoulders, as he and Jonathan joined them.

'What a wonderful day it's been!' said Stephen.

'Hasn't it,' smiled her husband.

'Wonderful,' echoed Jane. And it was wonderful, she thought, to hear Stephen and Jonathan speaking without irony and cynicism, but straight from the heart. 'As was your singing,' she went on, looking up at James, who had sung 'Greensleeves', during the 'Entertainment by the Schoolchildren'. 'It was so beautiful!'

The notes of the familiar tune had soared through the warm, stuffy air and Jane had been astonished. From this little boy had emerged the most extraordinary, pure, pellucid song.

'Alas my love, you do me wrong
To cast me off discourteously
And I have loved you oh so long
Delighting in your company.'

'That reminds me,' continued Jane, 'I've George Ivens's latest letter for you to read if you want. Apparently he's also singing "Greensleeves" at a concert today.'

Stephen laughed. 'All over the world people are singing to welcome the New Elizabethan Age! Even the Americans! But you were a star, my boy,' he said, unable to hide his pride.

'His voice,' Jane murmured to Alice. 'What a gift!'

Alice gave her a polite half-smile.

'From whom . . . ?' began Jane. From whom, Jane was about to ask, does James get his lovely voice? But she stopped herself.

As if in a new light she saw James's dark curls, his head resting on Stephen's blond hair and Alice, just as fair.

Then, completely unbidden, came a recollection from the evening just before Ivens had departed for America. Alice and Ivens had left the library to look at the priest hole and Jane remembered opening the scullery door and being struck by an unusually charged atmosphere. She'd put it down to Ivens's anxiety about embarking on an arduous journey which might, ultimately, prove fruitless. But now . . . She wanted to push away the conclusion she was drawing.

She glanced at Alice, once more staring ahead with the distant expression that, not always kindly, she was known for.

It's none of my business, thought Jane. But . . . Oh poor thing! To carry such a secret!

And yet . . .

388

She saw Stephen slip his arm around his wife's waist and Alice rest her head against his shoulder.

And yet, from this secret, goodness had come.

Alice and Stephen had their beloved child. They'd found a sort of peace.

As have I, she thought. And my husband, my children. For now.

'Mummy!' James called out. 'When will the fireworks start?'

All the adults looked up and spoke in unison: 'Soon!'

In those dreadful years, the approach of night had brought gut-wrenching fear and doom, the inhuman blare of the sirens before the skies filled with fire and death. But tonight they all gazed up in hope, the sky a darkening indigo with fluffy, flamingo-pink clouds on the horizon like an eiderdown resting upon the curve of the earth.

Suddenly there was an explosion above her.

Emerald and turquoise stars filled the sky. Silver sparkles showered upon them. The faces around her – her family, her friends, her neighbours, the people she loved – glowed. A flash of brilliant yellow burst into a golden fountain and, as if defying all the darkness within and without, the night sky was alight with dazzling colour and beauty.

Acknowledgements

EVERY WRITER HAS A SPECIAL inspiration and for me that is the often over-looked pre-Second World War novelist and journalist Winifred Holtby. I came to her quite by chance. I was at my parents' home and looking for something to read. I found a book with a plain green cover – with no blurb, nothing to tell me what was inside, simply the author and title, *South Riding*. Published in 1936, it's an unfashionable read today – very long, a slow burn, taking its time to reveal its power. But to me it's a masterpiece. What I loved was how, to begin with, I had little sympathy with many of the characters but by the end I felt an incredible compassion for all these flawed human beings. For capturing that generation whose lives were soon to be over-turned by another world war, to me there is no one better than Holtby. She has been a major influence on me.

There are other authors upon whom I have leaned and learned from. Mollie Panter-Downes's *Letters from London* for *the New Yorker* give us a unique insight into daily life unfolding during the war years, along with her masterly novel, *One Fine Day*. For their stories of families struggling to reunite after years of separation I owe debts to Barry Turner and Tony Rennell's *When Daddy Came Home*, and Alan Allport's *Demobbed*; to Maureen Waller's *London 1945* and Lara Feigel's *The Love-charm of Bombs* for an under-standing of how London and Londoners were changed by war; to John Nichol and Tony Rennell's *Medic* for their accounts of being a doctor in the hell of Dunkirk; to Andrew Roberts' *Leadership in War* and his essay on Charles de Gaulle. There are many, invariably heart-breaking, tales of working with the French Resistance but the ones that stood out for me were: *Moondrop to Gascony* by Anne-Marie Walters, *The Secret War of Helene de Champlain, Hugh Dormer's Diaries* and *The White Rabbit* by Bruce Marshall. For a history of the collapse of the large estates in Britain, I turned to John Martin Robinson's *Felling the Ancient Oaks* and W.M. Roberts' *Lost Country Houses of Suffolk*.

As well as all these authors, I also want to thank the team at Manilla Press, especially Margaret Stead and Sophie Orme, for the speed and passion with which they committed to *The Walled Garden*. And lastly my agent, Clare Alexander, who encouraged me, calmed me and stood by me.

Hello!

Thank you for picking up *The Walled Garden*.

The story was very much inspired by where I live on the Suffolk coast. I love to walk, especially in winter, or very early in the morning when often I don't meet a soul. As a teenager, in school summer holidays, I steeped myself in the Brontës and Thomas Hardy, and that longing for wild open spaces has never left me. I set off at dawn down deserted paths, invariably heading towards the river as the austere contours of the fields reveal themselves, the moon frozen in a pale sky. I love the sound of the wind in the reeds, the buzzards circling high in the sky. And although I've walked here for years, every time it's a new experience: the river, sometimes rough and swollen like flowing pewter, at other times a mirror reflecting these vast East Anglian skies. But always, whatever the weather, this beautiful, bleak landscape moves me and saddens me and uplifts me, and engages my imagination.

Echoes of the Second World War are everywhere. Along the river wall I come across abandoned pill boxes, in the woods are derelict Nissen huts. Nearby is the site of a house where a local family were all killed outright when a German plane, about to return across the North Sea, offloaded its bombs. My own home is a converted out-building of what was once the 'Big House' – now demolished – where the army was billeted. And I wonder how people in that post-war era recovered from those terrible years.

Today we'd say they were suffering from PTSD. But in 1946, when *The Walled Garden* is set, there would have been nowhere to turn for help. The country was on its knees, bankrupt. But somehow you had to get by, try to reconstruct your broken life, your shattered relationships.

Yet this is a hopeful novel because although emotions were kept hidden, there is inspiration to be found. The story of my scarred characters is a story of how people who have seen the worst of human nature find a way to live again. And to love. In the resurrection of the walled garden, we see the beginnings of a resurrection of damaged souls and a damaged society.

If you would like to hear more about my books, you can visit **http://unbouncepages.com/the-walled-garden/** where you can become part of the Sarah Hardy reader's club. It only takes a few moments to sign up; there are no catches or costs.

Bonnier Zaffre will keep your data private and confidential, and it will never be passed on to a third party. We won't spam you with loads of emails, just get in touch now and again with news about my books, and you can unsubscribe any time you want.

And if you would like to get involved in a wider conversation about my books, please do review *The Walled Garden* on Amazon, on GoodReads, on any other e-store, on your own blog and social media accounts, or talk about it with friends, family or reader groups! Sharing your thoughts helps other readers, and I always enjoy hearing about what people experience from my writing.

Thank you again for reading *The Walled Garden*.

Best wishes,

Sarah
http://unbouncepages.com/the-walled-garden/